"The *Mystic River* author lives up to his reputation as a master plotter with this slow-burn thriller."
—O, *The Oprah Magazine*

"A psychological nail-biter. . . . I was thrilled to see him push the boundaries of human understanding for its own merits."
—NOAH HAWLEY, *New York Times Book Review*

"[Lehane's] work always combines pulp thrills with literary heart and sophistication."
—*Entertainment Weekly*

"A riveting exercise in psychological suspense."
—*Providence Journal*

"Lehane writes expert, compelling thrillers."
—TANA FRENCH, *Washington Post*

"Make no mistake, *Since We Fell* is crime fiction, filled with con men, murder, greed and revenge. But the love story gives this novel its heart."
—Associated Press

PRAISE FOR DENNIS LEHANE

"Endlessly surprising. . . . [A] twisty tale." —*Wall Street Journal*

"[Lehane] remains one of the great, diabolical thriller kings who seems intimately acquainted with darkness and can make it seep from the page." —*New York Times*

"A pleasantly twisted character study and a love story. . . . Lehane is, as ever, a graceful writer, observant of the world that shapes his characters' lives. . . . [He] is in command of what he's doing—unspooling plot twists and developing his character as Rachel descends into her own heart of darkness." —*Washington Post*

"A sleek thriller. . . . Its dialogue is crisp and often darkly funny, its characters vividly drawn, its plot a tightening wire of well-crafted suspense." —*Tampa Bay Times*

"[Lehane's] work always combines pulp thrills with literary heart and sophistication." —*Entertainment Weekly*

"The surfeit of plot twists and emotional baggage are buoyed by Lehane's hard-boiled lyricism and peerless feel for New England noir." —*USA Today*

"[*Since We Fell*] should have crime fiction fans busting out the bottle rockets and champagne. . . . The rare book that works seamlessly on the theme, the plot, and the sentence levels. It's impossible not to succumb." —LitHub

"With sharply acute characterization, this is classic Lehane." —*The Guardian*

"Another winner from the author of *Mystic River*. . . . A raucous mix of lust, greed, and betrayal."   —*AARP Magazine*

"A ride you won't want to miss."   —New York Journal of Books

"Lehane has written two books—one, an insightful examination of the search for identity and belonging, and two, a thriller that constantly leaves you guessing—and then smashed them together into one terrific read. Lehane is the master of complex human characters thrust into suspenseful, page-turning situations. In short, I hate him. But I'll read anything he writes."   —Gillian Flynn

"One doesn't 'read' *Since We Fell* so much as plunge and tumble through its pages like a raft in white water. It's a sweet bullet of a book, full of nuanced characterizations, a masterful evocation of time and place, and a seductive narrative voice. The publication of any Dennis Lehane novel calls for a celebration, but I think *Since We Fell* calls for the biggest party of them all."   —Richard Price

"The most thrilling novel I'll read all year. *Since We Fell* is simmering with emotion, menace, and humor. I loved it."   —Kate Atkinson

"Complex, tense, compelling, and an emotional and strategic hall of mirrors, where nothing is what it seems—but I would follow Dennis Lehane anywhere."   —Lee Child

"Once you pick up a Dennis Lehane novel, you're hooked. It's just that simple. *Since We Fell* is a complex, compelling page-turner of a novel from a master storyteller at the top of his game."

—Kristin Hannah

"Dennis Lehane's *Mystic River* is perhaps the best crime novel in the English language. In *Since We Fell* we see the same enormous talent and literary skill: this story is hard to put down; the mystery and intrigue never let go; the twists and turns are engaging and unexpected all the way down the track."   —James Lee Burke

SINCE WE FELL

SINCE WE FELL

DENNIS LEHANE

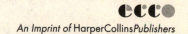
An Imprint of HarperCollinsPublishers

SINCE WE FELL. Copyright © 2017 by Dennis Lehane. All rights reserved. Printed in the United States of America. No part of this book may be used or reproduced in any manner whatsoever without written permission except in the case of brief quotations embodied in critical articles and reviews. For information address HarperCollins Publishers, 195 Broadway, New York, NY 10007.

HarperCollins books may be purchased for educational, business, or sales promotional use. For information please e-mail the Special Markets Department at SPsales@harpercollins.com.

A hardcover edition of this book was published in 2017 by Ecco, an imprint of HarperCollins Publishers.

FIRST ECCO PAPERBACK EDITION PUBLISHED 2018.

Designed by Suet Yee Chong

Library of Congress Cataloging-in-Publication Data has been applied for.

ISBN 978-0-06-212939-0

18 19 20 21 22   LSC   10 9 8 7 6 5 4 3 2 1

In memory of David Wickham,
a prince of Providence
and a real cool cat

When you just give love and never get love
you'd better let love depart
I know it's so, and yet I know
I can't get you out of my heart

—BUDDY JOHNSON, "SINCE I FELL FOR YOU"

Masked, I advance.

—RENÉ DESCARTES

AFTER THE STAIRCASE

On a Tuesday in May, in her thirty-seventh year, Rachel shot her husband dead. He stumbled backward with an odd look of confirmation on his face, as if some part of him had always known she'd do it.

He looked surprised too. She assumed she did as well.

Her mother wouldn't have been surprised.

Her mother, who never married, wrote a famous book on how to stay married. The chapters were named after stages Elizabeth Childs, Ph.D., had identified in any relationship that began in a state of mutual attraction. The book was entitled The Staircase *and became so successful that her mother was convinced (she'd say "coerced") into writing two sequels,* Reclimbing the Staircase *and* Steps of the Staircase: A Workbook, *each of which sold more poorly than the last.*

Privately, her mother thought all three books were "emotionally adolescent snake oil," but she reserved a wistful fondness for The Staircase *because she hadn't been aware, when she was writing it, how little she actually knew. She said this to Rachel when Rachel was ten. That same summer, late into her afternoon cocktails, she told her, "A man is the stories he tells about himself, and most of those stories are lies. Never look too closely. If you uncover his lies, it'll humiliate you both. Best to just live with the bullshit."*

Then her mother kissed her head. Patted her cheek. Told her she was safe.

Rachel was seven when The Staircase *was published. She remembered the endless phone calls, the flurry of trips, her mother's renewed dependence on smoking, and the desperate, chiseled glamour that overtook her. She remembered a feeling she could barely articulate, that her mother, never happy, grew even more bitter with success. Years later, she'd suspect the reason was because the fame and the money robbed her mother of excuses for her unhappiness. Her mother, brilliant at analyzing the problems of strangers, never had a clue how to diagnose herself. So she spent her life in search of solutions to problems that were born, raised, lived, and died within the boundaries of her own marrow. Rachel didn't know any of that at seven, of course, or even at seventeen. She only knew that her mother was an unhappy woman, so she was an unhappy child.*

When Rachel shot her husband, she was on a boat in Boston Harbor. Her husband remained on his feet for only the briefest of time—seven seconds? ten?—before he fell over the stern and into the water.

But in those final seconds, a catalogue of emotion found his eyes.

There was dismay. Self-pity. Terror. An abandonment so total it took thirty years off his life and turned him into a ten-year-old before her eyes.

Anger, of course. Outrage.

A sudden and fierce determination, as if, even as the blood spilled from his heart and over the hand he'd cupped below it, he'd be okay, he'd be fine, he'd get through this. He was strong, after all, he'd created everything of value in his life by force of will alone and he could will himself out of this.

Then the dawning realization: No, he couldn't.

He looked right at her as the most incomprehensible of emotions staked its claim and subsumed all others:

Love.

Which was impossible.

And yet . . .

There was no mistaking it. Wild, helpless, pure. Blooming and splattering in tandem with the blood on his shirt.

He mouthed it, as he often did from the other side of crowded rooms: I. Love. You.

And then he fell off the boat and vanished beneath the dark water.

Two days before, if someone had asked her if she loved her husband, she would have said, "Yes."

Actually, if someone had asked her the same question as she pulled the trigger, she would have said, "Yes."

Her mother had a chapter about that—Chapter 13: "Discordance."

Or was the next chapter—"The Death of the Old Narrative"—more applicable?

Rachel wasn't sure. She got them confused sometimes.

I / RACHEL IN THE MIRROR

1979–2010

1

SEVENTY-THREE JAMESES

Rachel was born in the Pioneer Valley of western Massachusetts. It was known as the Region of the Five Colleges—Amherst, Hampshire, Mount Holyoke, Smith, and the University of Massachusetts—and it employed two thousand faculty to teach twenty-five thousand students. She grew up in a world of coffee shops, B&Bs, wide town commons, and clapboard houses with wraparound porches and musky attics. In autumn, leaves fell by the tubful and choked the streets, spilled onto sidewalks, and clogged fence holes. Some winters, snow encased the valley in silence so dense it became its own sound. In July and August, the mail carrier rode a bicycle with a bell on the handlebar, and the tourists arrived for summer stock theater and antiquing.

Her father's name was James. She knew little else about him. She recollected that his hair had been dark and wavy and his smile sudden and unsure. At least twice he'd taken her to a playground with a dark green slide where the Berkshire clouds hung so low he'd needed to wipe the swing free of condensation before he could place her on it. On one of those trips he'd made her laugh but she couldn't recall how.

James had been an instructor at one of the colleges. She had no idea which one or if he'd been an adjunct, an assistant professor, or an associate on tenure track. She didn't even know if he taught at one of the Five Colleges. He could have been at Berkshire or Springfield Technical, Greenfield CC or Westfield State, or any of a dozen other colleges and junior colleges in the region.

Her mother was teaching at Mount Holyoke when James left them. Rachel was just short of three and could never say with certainty if she'd borne witness to the day her father walked out of the house or if she'd just imagined it to suture the wound his absence left behind. She heard her mother's voice coming through the wall of the small house they'd rented that year on Westbrook Road. *Do you hear me? If you go out that door, I will expunge you.* Shortly thereafter, the bump of a heavy suitcase on the stairs out back followed by the snap of a trunk closing. The rasp and whistle of a cold engine clamoring to life in a small car, then tires crunching winter leaves and frozen dirt followed by . . . silence.

Maybe her mother hadn't believed he'd actually leave. Maybe once he had, she'd assured herself he'd return. When he didn't, her dismay turned to hate and her hate grew depthless.

"He's gone," she said when Rachel was about five and had begun asking persistent questions about his whereabouts. "He wants nothing to do with us. And that's okay, sweetie, because we don't need him to define us." She got down on her knees in front of Rachel and tucked an errant hair behind her ear. "Now we won't speak of him again. Okay?"

But of course Rachel spoke of him and asked about him. At first it exasperated her mother; a wild panic would find her eyes and flare her nostrils. But eventually the panic was replaced with a strange, tiny smile. So tiny it was barely a smile at all, just a slight uptick of the right side of her mouth that managed to be smug, bitter, and victorious all at the same time.

It would be years before Rachel would see the onset of that smile as her mother's decision (whether conscious or unconscious, she'd never know) to make her father's identity the central battleground in a war that colored Rachel's entire youth.

Her mother promised to tell her James's last name on her sixteenth birthday, provided Rachel showed a level of maturity that would suggest she could handle it. But that summer, just before she turned sixteen, Rachel was arrested in a stolen car with Jarod Marshall, whom she'd promised her mother she was no longer seeing. The next target date was her high school graduation, but after an Ecstasy-related debacle at the semiformal that year, she was lucky to graduate at all. If she went to college then, a community college first to get her grades up, then a "real" one, her mother said, maybe then.

They fought continuously over it. Rachel would scream and break things and her mother's smile would grow colder and smaller. She would repeatedly ask Rachel, "Why?"

Why do you need to know? Why do you need to meet a stranger who's never been a part of your life or your financial security? Shouldn't you first take stock of the parts of you that are bringing you such unhappiness before you journey out into the world to find a man who can offer no answers and bring you no peace?

"Because he's my father!" Rachel screamed more than once.

"He's not your father," her mother said with an air of unctuous sympathy. "He's my sperm donor."

She said that at the tail end of one of their worst fights, the Chernobyl of mother-daughter spats. Rachel slid down the wall of the living room in defeat and whispered, "You're killing me."

"I'm protecting you," her mother said.

Rachel looked up and saw, to her horror, that her mother believed that. Far worse, she defined herself by that belief.

Rachel's junior year in college, while she was in Boston, sitting in Introduction to British Literary Studies Since 1550, her mother blew a red light in Northampton, and her Saab was T-boned by a fuel truck driving the speed limit. At first there was concern that the shell of the fuel truck had been pierced in the accident, but it turned out not to be the case. This was a relief for the fire and rescue crews who came from as far away as Pittsfield: The fuel truck had just topped off and the intersection was in a dense area by both a senior citizens home and a basement-level preschool.

The driver of the fuel truck suffered mild whiplash and tore a ligament in his right knee. Elizabeth Childs, once-famous author, died upon impact. If her national fame had long since subsided, however, her local celebrity still burned bright. Both the *Berkshire Eagle* and the *Daily Hampshire Gazette* ran her obituary on the front page, below the fold, and her funeral was well attended, though the gathering back at the house afterward was less so. Rachel would end up donating most of the food to a local homeless shelter. She spoke to several of her mother's friends, mostly women, and one man, Giles Ellison, who taught poli-sci at Amherst and who, Rachel had long suspected, had been her mother's occasional lover. She could tell her assumption was correct by the way the women paid special attention to him and by how little Giles spoke. A normally gregarious man, he kept parting his lips as if he wished to speak but then changed his mind. He looked around the house like he was drinking it in, as if its contents were familiar and had once brought him comfort. As if they were all he had left of Elizabeth and he was taking stock of the fact he'd never see them, or her, again. He was framed by the parlor window that looked down Old Mill Lane on a drizzly April day and Rachel felt a tremendous pity rise up in her for Giles Ellison, rapidly aging toward retirement and obsolescence. He'd expected to go through that rite of passage with an acerbic lioness by his side, but now he'd go through it alone. It was unlikely he'd find another partner as radiant with intelligence and rage as Elizabeth Childs.

And she had been radiant in her own officious, acerbic way. She didn't enter rooms, she swept into them. She didn't engage friends and colleagues, she gathered them to her. She never napped, rarely seemed tired, and no one could ever remember her falling ill. When Elizabeth Childs left a room, you felt it, even if you'd arrived after she'd gone. When Elizabeth Childs left the world, it felt the same way.

It surprised Rachel to realize just how little she was prepared for the loss of her mother. She had been a lot of things, most of them not positive in her daughter's opinion, but she had always been so utterly *there*. And now she was so utterly—and so violently—gone.

But still the old question persisted. And Rachel's clear access to the answer had died with her mother. Elizabeth may have been unwilling to provide that answer, but she had unquestionably been in possession of it. Now, possibly no one was.

However well Giles and her friends and agent and publisher and editor had known Elizabeth Childs—and they all seemed to know a version of her that differed slightly but crucially from the woman Rachel had known—none of them had known her longer than Rachel's lifespan.

"I wish I knew anything about James," Ann Marie McCarron, Elizabeth's oldest friend in the area, told Rachel once they were sufficiently lubricated for Rachel to broach the subject of her father, "but the first time I ever went out with your mother was months after they broke up. I remember he taught in Connecticut."

"Connecticut?" They sat on the three-season porch at the back of the house, just twenty-two miles due north of the Connecticut border, and somehow it had never occurred to Rachel that her father could just as easily have taught not at one of the Five Colleges or the fifteen other colleges on the Massachusetts side of the Berkshires but just half an hour south in Connecticut.

"University of Hartford?" she asked Ann Marie.

Ann Marie pooched her lips and nose at the same time. "I don't know. Could be." Ann Marie put her arm around her. "I wish I could help. And I wish you'd let it go too."

"Why?" Rachel said (the eternal *why*, as she'd come to think of it). "Was he that bad?"

"I never heard he was bad," Ann Marie said with a minor slur and a sad grimace. She looked out through the screen at the stone-colored mist in the gray hills and spoke with a firm finality. "Honey, I only heard that he'd moved on."

Her mother left everything to her in her will. It was less than Rachel would have imagined but more than she needed at twenty-one. If she lived frugally and invested wisely, she could conceivably live off her inheritance for ten years.

She found her mother's two yearbooks in a locked drawer in her office—North Adams High School and Smith College. She'd received her master's and Ph.D. from Johns Hopkins (at *twenty-nine*, Rachel realized, Jesus), but the only record of that was the framed diplomas on the wall by the fireplace. She went through the yearbooks three times, forcing a snail's pace upon herself each time. She found, in total, four pictures of her mother, two formal, two as part of a group. In the Smith yearbook she found no students named James because it was an all-girls school, but she did find two faculty members, neither of whom was the right age or had black hair. In the North Adams High School yearbook, she found six boys named James, two of whom could have been him—James McGuire and James Quinlan. It took her half an hour at the South Hadley Library computer to ascertain that James McGuire of North Adams had been paralyzed in a whitewater rafting accident while still in college; James Quinlan had majored in business administration at

Wake Forest University and rarely left North Carolina, where he'd built a successful chain of teak furniture stores.

The summer before she sold the house, she visited Berkshire Security Associates and met with Brian Delacroix, a private investigator. He was only a few years older than she was and carried himself with the rangy ease of a jogger. They met in his second-story office suite in an industrial park in Chicopee. It was a shoebox of an office, just Brian and a desk, two computers, and a row of file cabinets. When she asked where the "associates" in the firm name were, Brian explained that he was that associate. The main offices were in Worcester. His Chicopee satellite was a franchise opportunity and he was just starting out. He offered to refer her to a more seasoned operative, but she really didn't feel like climbing back in her car and schlepping all the way to Worcester, so she rolled the dice and told him why she'd come. Brian asked a few questions and wrote on a yellow legal pad and met her eyes often enough for her to feel a simple tenderness in his that seemed older than his years. He struck her as earnest and new enough at the business to still be honest, an opinion he validated two days later when he advised her not to hire him or anyone else for that matter. Brian told her he could take her case and probably bill her for at least forty hours of work before he came back with the same opinion he was offering now.

"You don't have enough information to find this guy."

"That's why I'm hiring you."

He shifted in his chair. "I did a little digging since our first meeting. Nothing big, nothing I'll charge you for—"

"I'll pay."

"—but enough. If he was named Trevor or even, heck, Zachary, we might have a chance of tracking down a guy who taught at one of over two dozen institutions of higher learning in Massachusetts or Connecticut twenty years ago. But, Miss Childs, I ran a quick computer analysis for you and in the last twenty years, at the twenty-seven schools I identified as possibles, there have been seventy-three"—he nodded at her shocked reaction—"adjunct, fill-in, assistant, associate, and full professors named James. Some have lasted a semester, some less, and some have gone the other way and attained tenure."

"Can you get employment records, pictures in the files?"

"I'm sure for some, maybe half. But if he's not in that half—and how would you even identify him?—then we'd have to track down the other thirty-five Jameses who, if demographic trends in this country are an indicator, are flung across all fifty states, and find a way to get their pictures from twenty years ago. Then I wouldn't be charging you for forty hours' work. I'd be charging for four hundred. And still no guarantee we'd find this guy."

She worked through her reactions—anxiety, rage, helplessness, which produced more rage, and finally stubborn anger at this prick for not wanting to do his job. Fine, she'd find someone who would.

He read that in her eyes and the way she gathered her purse to herself.

"If you go to someone else and they see you, a young woman who recently came into some money, they will milk you for that money and still come up empty. And that larceny, which is what it will be in my opinion, will be perfectly legal. Then you'll be poor and father-less." He leaned forward and spoke softly. "Where were you born?"

She tilted her head toward the south-facing window. "Spring-field."

"Is there a hospital record?"

She nodded. "Father is listed as UNK."

"But they were together then, Elizabeth and James."

Another nod. "Once when she'd had a few drinks, she told me that the night she went into labor they were fighting and he was out of town. She had me and, because he wasn't there, she refused to list him on the record out of spite."

They sat in silence until she said, "So you won't take my case?"

Brian Delacroix shook his head. "Let him go."

She stood, her forearms quaking, and thanked him for his time.

She found photographs stashed all around the house—the nightstand in her mother's bedroom, a box in the attic, filling a drawer in her mother's office. A good eighty-five percent of them were of the two of them. Rachel was struck by how clearly love for her shone in her mother's pale eyes, though, true to form, even in pictures, her mother's love looked complicated, as if she were in the process of reconsidering it. The other fifteen percent of the pictures were of friends and colleagues in academia and publishing, most taken at holiday cocktail parties and early summer cookouts, two at a bar with people Rachel didn't recognize but who were clearly academics.

None contained a man with dark wavy hair and an uncertain smile.

She found her mother's journals when she sold the house. She'd graduated from Emerson by that point and was leaving Massachusetts for graduate school in New York City. The old Victorian in South Hadley where she and her mother had lived since Rachel was in third grade contained few good memories and had always felt haunted. ("But they're faculty ghosts," her mother would say when the unexplained creak snaked out from the far end of a hallway or something thumped in the attic. "Probably up there reading Chaucer and sipping herbal tea.")

The journals weren't in the attic. They were in a trunk in the basement underneath carelessly packed foreign editions of *The Staircase*. They filled lined composition notebooks, the entries as haphazard as her mother had been ordered in her daily life. Half were undated, and her mother could go months, once even a year, without writing. She wrote most often about fear. Prior to *The Staircase*, the fear was financial—she'd never make enough as a professor of psychology to pay back her student loans, let alone send her daughter to a decent private high school and on to a decent college. After her book landed on the national bestseller lists, she feared she'd never write a worthwhile follow-up. She feared too that she would be called out for wearing the emperor's new clothes, for perpetrating a con job that would be discerned when she published again. It turned out to be a prophetic fear.

But mostly she feared for Rachel. Rachel watched herself grow in the pages from a rambunctious, joyful, occasionally irritating source of pride ("She has his appetite for play . . . Her heart's so lovely and generous that I'm terrified what the world will do to it . . .") to a despairing and self-destructive malcontent ("The cutting troubles me a bit less than the promiscuity; she's only thirteen for Christ's sake . . . She leaps into dark waters and then complains about the depth but blames *me* for the leaping").

Fifteen pages later, she came upon "I have to face the shame of it—I've been a subpar mother. I never had any patience for the underdeveloped frontal lobe. I snap too much, cut to the chase when I should model patience. She grew up with a brusque reductionist, I'm afraid. And no father. And it put a hole at the center of her."

A few pages later, her mother returned to the theme. "I worry she'll waste her life searching out things to fill the hole, transitory things, soul-baubles, new age therapies, self-medication. She thinks she's rebellious and resilient, but she's only one of those things. She needs *so much*."

A few pages later, in an undated entry, Elizabeth Childs wrote, "She is laid up right now, sick in a strange bed, and even needier than usual. The persistent question returns: *Who is he, Mother?* She looks so frail—brittle and mawkish and frail. She is a lot of wonderful things, my dearest Rachel, but she is not strong. If I tell her who James is, she'll search him out. He'll shatter her heart. And why should I give him that power? After all this time, why should he be allowed to hurt her again? To fuck with that beautiful, battered heart of hers? I saw him today."

Rachel, sitting on the second-to-last step of the basement staircase, held her breath. She squeezed the edges of the journal and her vision shimmied.

I saw him today.

"He never saw me. I parked up the street. He was on the lawn of the house he found after he abandoned us. And they were with him—the replacement wife, the replacement children. He's lost a lot of his hair and grown spongy above the belt line and below the chin. Small comfort. He's happy. God help me. He's happy. And isn't that the worst of all possible outcomes? I don't even believe in happiness—not as an ideal or as an authentic state of being; it's a child's goal—and yet, he is happy. He'd feel that happiness threatened by this daughter he never wanted and wanted even less once she was born. Because she reminded him of me. Of how much he grew to loathe me. And he would hurt her. I was the one person in his life who refused to adore him and he'd never forgive Rachel for that. He'd assume I told her unflattering things about him, and James, as we all know, could never abide criticism of his precious, earnest self."

Rachel had been bedridden only once in her life—freshman year of high school. She'd contracted mononucleosis just as she was heading into Christmas break. The timing turned out to be fortuitous. It took her thirteen days to get out of bed and five more to regain the strength to return to school. In the end, she missed only three days of classes.

But that would have been the window when her mother saw James. Which was also when her mother was a visiting professor at Wesleyan. She'd rented a house in Middletown, Connecticut, that year and that was the "strange bed" Rachel had been confined to. Her mother, she recalled now with a disconcerted pride, had never left her during the illness except one time, to get groceries and wine.

Rachel had just started watching *Pretty Woman* on VHS and was still watching it when her mother returned. Her mother checked her temperature and opined that she found Julia Roberts's toothy grin "cosmically grating," before she brought the grocery bags into the kitchen to unload them.

When she returned to the bedroom, glass of wine in one hand, warm, wet facecloth in the other, she gave Rachel a lonesome, hopeful look and said, "We did okay, didn't we?"

Rachel looked up at her as she laid the facecloth across her forehead. "Of course we did," she said because, in that moment, it felt like they had.

Her mother patted her cheek, looked at the TV. It was the end of the movie. Prince Charming, Richard Gere, showed up with flowers to rescue his Hooker Princess, Julia. He thrust the flowers forward, Julia laughed and teared up, the music boomed in the background.

Her mother said, "I mean, enough with the smiling already."

That put the entry of the diary at December 1992. Or early January 1993. Eight years later, sitting on the basement steps, Rachel realized her father had been living somewhere within a thirty-mile radius of Middletown. Couldn't be any more. Her mother had visited the street where he lived, observed him with his family, and then picked up groceries and stopped off at the liquor store for wine in under two hours. That meant James was teaching somewhere nearby, most likely at the University of Hartford.

"*If* he was still teaching by that point," Brian Delacroix said when she called him.

"True."

But Brian agreed that there was enough to go on now so that he could take her case and her money and still look himself in the mirror in the morning. So in the late summer of 2001, Brian Delacroix and Berkshire Security Associates launched an investigation into the identity of her father.

And came up with nothing.

No one by the name of James taught in higher education in northern Connecticut that year who wasn't already well accounted for. One had blond hair, one was African American, and the third was twenty-seven years old.

Once again, Rachel was told to let it go.

"I'm leaving," Brian said.

"Chicopee?"

"The business. So, yeah, Chicopee too, but I just don't want to be a private investigator. It's too grim, you know? All I seem to do is disappoint people, even when I deliver what they paid me to find. I'm sorry I couldn't help you, Rachel."

It hollowed out something in her. Another departure. Another person in her life, however minor of impact, who would leave whether she wanted it to happen or not. She had no say.

"What're you going to do?" she asked.

"I'm gonna go back to Canada, I think." His voice sounded strong, as if he'd arrived someplace he'd been meaning to arrive his whole life.

"You're Canadian?"

He chuckled softly. "Sure am."

"What's back there?"

"Family lumber business. How's things with you?"

"Grad school is great. New York right now," she said, "less so."

It was late September 2001, less than three weeks after the towers fell.

"Of course," he said gravely. "Of course. I hope things look up for you. I wish you good things, Rachel."

She was surprised how intimate her name sounded when it fell from his tongue. She pictured his eyes, the tenderness there, and was mildly annoyed to realize she'd been attracted to him and had failed to acknowledge it when it could have mattered.

"Canada," she said, "eh?"

That soft chuckle of his. "Canada."

They said their good-byes.

In her basement apartment on Waverly Place in Greenwich Village, easy walking distance to most of her classes at NYU, she sat in the soot and ash of lower Manhattan in the month after 9/11. The day of the attack, a thick dust grew woolen on her windowsills, the dust of hair and pieces of bone and cells piling up like a light snow. The air smelled burnt. In the afternoon, she wandered, ended up walking past St. Vincent's ER, where gurneys were lined up for patients who never arrived. In the days that followed, pictures began to appear on the walls and fences of the hospital, most often with a simple message—"Have You Seen This Person?"

No, she hadn't. They were gone.

She was surrounded by loss so much greater than any she'd experienced in her own life. Everywhere she turned she saw grief and unanswered prayers and a bedrock chaos that took so many forms— sexual, emotional, psychological, moral—that it quickly became the thread and thrum that united them all.

We are all lost, Rachel realized, and resolved to bandage her own wound as best she could and never pick at the scab again.

That autumn, she came across two sentences in one of her mother's journals that she repeated to herself as a mantra every night for weeks before going to bed.

James, her mother wrote, *was never meant for us.*

And we were never meant for him.

LIGHTNING

She suffered her first panic attack in the fall of 2001, just after Thanksgiving. She was walking along Christopher Street and passed a woman her own age who sat on a black iron stoop under the arched entrance to an apartment co-op. The woman was weeping into her hands, a not uncommon occurrence back then in New York City. People wept in parks and bathrooms and on the A train, some silently, some with vigor and volume. It was everywhere. But you still had to ask, you still had to check.

"Are you okay?" Rachel reached out to touch the woman.

The woman recoiled. "What are you doing?"

"I'm seeing if you're okay."

"I'm fine." The woman's face was dry. She smoked a cigarette that Rachel hadn't noticed before. "Are *you* okay?"

"Sure," Rachel said. "I was just—"

The woman was handing her several tissues. "It's all right. Let it out."

The woman's face was dry. Her eyes weren't red. She hadn't been covering her face. She'd been smoking a cigarette.

Rachel took the tissues. She dabbed her face, felt the stream there, felt the tears welling under her nose, dripping off the sides of her jaw and the point of her chin.

"It's all right," the woman repeated.

She looked at Rachel like it wasn't all right, it wasn't all right at all. She looked at Rachel and then past Rachel, as if hoping to be rescued.

Rachel mumbled several thank-yous and stumbled off. She reached the corner of Christopher and Weehawken. A red van idled at the light. The driver stared at Rachel with pale eyes. Smiled at her with teeth yellowed by nicotine. It wasn't just tears streaming out of her now, it was sweat. Her throat closed. She knew she was choking even though she hadn't eaten that morning. She couldn't breathe. She couldn't fucking breathe. Her throat would not open. Neither would her mouth. She needed to open her mouth.

The driver got out of the van. He approached her with his pale eyes and pale hawkish face and ginger hair cut tight to his scalp and when he reached her . . .

He was black. And a bit rotund. His teeth weren't yellow. They were copy-paper white. He knelt by her (how had she ended up sitting on the sidewalk?), his brown eyes large and fearful. "You okay? You need me to call someone, miss? Can you stand? Here, here. Take my hand."

She took his hand and he pulled her to her feet on the corner of Christopher and Weehawken. And it was no longer morning. The sun was dipping. The Hudson had turned a light amber.

The round kind man hugged her to him and she wept into his

shoulder. She wept and made him promise to stay with her, to never leave her.

"Tell me your name," she said. "Tell me your name."

His name was Kenneth Waterman, and of course she never saw him again. He drove her back to her apartment in his red van, which wasn't the big panel van that smelled of axle grease and soiled undergarments she'd imagined but was, instead, a minivan with child seats in the middle row and Cheerio crumbs on the floor mats. Kenneth Waterman had a wife and three children and lived in Fresh Meadows, Queens. He was a cabinetmaker. He dropped her home and offered to call someone on her behalf, but she assured him she was okay now, she was fine, it was just this city sometimes, you know?

He gave her a long, worried look, but cars were stacking up behind them and dusk was gathering. A horn blared. Then another. He handed her a business card—*Kenny's Cabinets*—and told her to call him anytime. She thanked him and got out of the minivan. As he drove away, she realized the van wasn't even red. It was bronze.

She deferred her next semester at NYU. Rarely left the apartment except to walk to her shrink in Tribeca. His name was Constantine Propkop and the only personal information he ever divulged was that his family and friends insisted on calling him Connie. Connie tried to convince her that the national tragedy she was using to shame herself out of recognizing the depths of her own trauma was doing her serious harm.

"There's nothing tragic about my life," Rachel said. "Was it sad sometimes? Sure. Whose wasn't? But I was well cared for and well fed and grew up in a nice house. I mean, boohoo, right?"

Connie looked across the small office at her. "Your mother withheld one of your most basic rights—your paternity—from you. She subjected you to emotional tyranny in order to keep you close."

"She was protecting me."

"From what?"

"Okay," Rachel corrected herself, "she *believed* she was protecting me from myself, from what I might do with the knowledge."

"Is that really why?"

"Why else?" Rachel suddenly wanted to dive out the window behind Connie.

"If someone has something you not only want but truly *need*, what will you never do to that person?"

"Don't say hate them because I hated her plenty."

"Leave them," he said. "You'll never leave that person."

"My mother was the most independent person I've ever met."

"As long as she had you clinging to her, she could appear to be. What happened once you were gone, though? Once she could feel you pulling away?"

She knew what he was driving at. She was the daughter of a psychologist, after all. "Fuck you, Connie. Don't go there."

"Go where?"

"It was an accident."

"A woman you've described as hyperalert, hyperaware, ubercompetent? Who had no drugs or alcohol in her system the day of her death? *That* woman drives through a stop sign on a dry road in broad daylight?"

"So now I killed my mother."

"That's the exact opposite of what I'm suggesting."

Rachel gathered her coat and bag. "The reason my mother never practiced was because she didn't want to be associated with half-assed quacks like you." She shot the degrees on his wall a look. "Rutgers," she scoffed and walked out.

Her next shrink, Tess Porter, had a softer touch, and the commute to her office was much shorter. She told Rachel they'd get to the truths of her relationship with her mother on Rachel's schedule, not her doctor's. Rachel felt safe with Tess. With Connie, she'd always felt he was poised to strike. So she, in turn, always felt poised to parry.

"What would you say to him, you think, if you found him?" Tess asked one afternoon.

"I don't know."

"Are you afraid?"

"Yes, yes."

"Of him?"

"What? No." She thought about it. "No. Not of him. Just of the situation. I mean, where do you start? 'Hey, Dad. Fuck you've been for my whole life?'"

Tess chuckled but then said, "There was some hesitation there. When I asked if you were afraid of him."

"Really?" Rachel gazed at the ceiling for a bit. "It's, like, she could contradict herself about him sometimes."

"How?"

"Most times, she described him in effeminate terms. 'Poor sweet James,' she'd say. Or 'Dear sensitive James.' Lots of eye rolls. She was too outwardly progressive to admit he wasn't masculine enough for her. I remember a couple of times she said, 'You've got your father's mean streak, Rachel.' And I'm thinking, 'I've got my *mother's* mean streak, bitch.'" She gazed up at the ceiling again. "'Look for yourself in his eyes.'"

"What's that?" Tess leaned forward in her chair.

"It's something she said to me a couple times. 'Look for yourself in his eyes. Tell me what you find.'"

"What was the context?"

"Alcohol."

Tess gave that a thin smile. "But what do you think she meant?"

"Both times she was pissed at me. I remember that much. I always took it to mean he . . . If he ever saw me, he'd . . ." She shook her head.

"What?" Tess's voice was soft. "If he ever saw you, he'd what?"

It took her a minute to compose herself. "He'd be disappointed."

"Disappointed?"

Rachel held her gaze for a bit. "Repulsed."

Outside, the streets grew enshrouded, as if something huge and otherworldly blotted out the sun and cast its shadow across the breadth of the city. The rain fell suddenly. The thunder sounded like the tire slaps of heavy trucks crossing an old bridge. The lightning was a distant crack.

"Why are you smiling?" Tess asked.

"Was I?"

She nodded.

"Something else my mother would say, particularly on days like today." Rachel tucked her legs under her. "She'd say she missed his smell. The first time I ever asked her what she meant, what he'd smelled like, she closed her eyes, sniffed the air, and said, 'Lightning.'"

Tess's eyes widened slightly. "Is that what you remember him smelling like?"

Rachel shook her head. "He smelled like coffee." Her gaze followed the splash of the raindrops out the window. "Coffee and corduroy."

She rebounded from that first bout of panic and low-grade agoraphobia in the late spring of 2002. She ran into a boy who'd been in her Advanced Research Techniques class the previous semester. His name was Patrick Mannion, and he was unfailingly considerate. He was kind of doughy and had the unfortunate habit of squinting when he couldn't hear properly, which was often because he'd lost fifty percent of the hearing in his right ear in a childhood sledding accident.

Pat Mannion couldn't believe Rachel kept talking to him after they'd exhausted the limits of discussing the one class they'd taken together. He couldn't believe she suggested they get a drink. And the look on his face when, back at his apartment a few hours later, she reached for his belt buckle was the look of a man who'd glanced up at the sky to check for clouds and witnessed angels passing overhead. It was a look that remained on his face, more or less, throughout their relationship, which lasted two years.

When she did eventually break up with him—ever so gently, almost to the point of convincing him that it was a mutual decision—he stared back at her with a strange, brutalized dignity and said, "I never used to understand why you were with me. I mean, you're gorgeous and I'm so . . . not."

"You're—"

He held up a hand to stop her. "Then one day, about six months ago, it hit me—love doesn't trump all for you, safety does. And I knew sooner or later you'd dump me before I'd dump you because—and this is the important part, Rach—*I would never dump you.*" He gave her a beautiful, broken smile. "And that's been my purpose all along."

After grad school, she spent a year in Wilkes-Barre, Pennsylvania, on the *Times Leader* and then returned to Massachusetts and quickly moved up to the features department at the *Patriot Ledger* in Quincy, where a story she wrote on racial profiling by the Hingham Police Department garnered some acclaim and enough attention that she received an e-mail from Brian Delacroix, of all people. He'd been traveling for business and had come across a copy of the *Ledger* in the waiting room of a lumber distributor in Brockton. He wanted to know if she was the same Rachel Childs and if she had ever found her father.

She wrote back that she was the same Rachel Childs and that, no, she hadn't found her father. Would he care to take another stab at the job?

> Can't. Slammed at work. Traveling traveling traveling. Take care,
> Rachel. You won't be at the Ledger long. Big things await. Love
> the way you write.

He was right—a year after that, she made it to the majors and the *Boston Globe*.

Which is where Dr. Felix Browner, her mother's OB/GYN, found her. The subject line of his e-mail was "Old Friend of Your Mom's," but once she responded to it, it became clear he was less a friend than someone Elizabeth Childs had utilized for medical purposes. Dr. Browner was also not the gynecologist her mother had been using by the time Rachel had knowledge of such things. When Rachel reached adolescence, Elizabeth had introduced her to Dr. Veena Rao, whom most of the women and young girls Rachel knew also used. She'd never heard of Felix Browner. But he assured her he had been her mother's doctor when Elizabeth first came to western Massachusetts and had, in fact, introduced Rachel herself to her first taste of oxygen. *You were a squirmy one,* he wrote.

In a subsequent e-mail he wrote that he possessed important information he'd like to share regarding her mother but he only felt comfortable sharing it face-to-face. They agreed to meet halfway between Boston and Springfield, where he lived, and settled on a diner in Millbury.

Before the meeting, she researched Dr. Browner and the picture was, as her instincts had been telling her since his first e-mail, not a flattering one. The year before, in 2006, he'd been barred from practicing medicine due to multiple allegations of sexual assault or sexual misconduct by female patients, the earliest dating back to 1976, when the good doctor was only a week out of med school.

Dr. Browner brought two rolling file cases to the diner with him. At sixty-two or so, he wore his thick silver hair in the almost mullet, almost shag style of someone who drove a sports car and patronized Jimmy Buffett concerts. He wore light blue jeans, penny loafers without socks, and a Hawaiian shirt under a black linen blazer. He carried an extra thirty pounds around his middle like a statement of success and had an easy way with the waitress and the busboys. He struck her as the kind of man who is well liked by strangers but baffled if someone doesn't laugh at his jokes.

After he'd expressed his sympathies for the death of Rachel's mother, he reminded her what a squirmy little newborn she'd been— "Like you were dipped in Palmolive." He then somewhat breathlessly revealed that his first accuser—"We'll call her Lianne and not just because it sounds like Lyin', okay?"—knew several of the other accusers. He ticked off their names and Rachel immediately wondered if he was using aliases or if he was violating the women's right to privacy with cavalier indifference: Tonya, Marie, Ursula, Jane, and Patty, he said, all *knew* one another.

"Well, it's a small region," Rachel said. "People know each other."

"Do they?" He shook a sugar packet before opening it and shot her a cold smile. "*Do* they?" He drizzled the sugar into his coffee, then reached into one of his file cases. "Lyin' Lianne, I've discovered, has had numerous lovers. She's been divorced twice *and*—"

"Doctor—"

He held up a hand to silence her. "*And* was named as the 'other woman' in a divorce. Patty drinks alone. Marie and Ursula have substance abuse issues, and Tonya—woo-hoo-hoo—Tonya sued *another* doctor for sexual assault." He bulged his eyeballs in mock outrage. "Apparently there's an epidemic of predatory doctors in the Berkshires. Heavens!"

Rachel had known a Tonya in the Berkshires. Tonya Fletcher. Managed the Minute Man Inn. Always seemed distracted and a bit perturbed.

Dr. Browner dropped a stack of paper the size of a cinder block on the table between them. Arched a triumphant eyebrow at her.

"What," Rachel said, "you don't believe in thumb drives?"

He didn't acknowledge that. "I have the goods on all of them, you see. You see?"

"I see," Rachel said. "And what would you like me to do with that?"

"Help me," he said, as if it were the only answer in the world.

"And why would I do that?"

"Because I'm innocent. Because I didn't do a single wrong thing." He turned his palms over and extended them across the table. "These hands bring life into the world. They brought you into the world, Rachel. These hands were the first that ever held you. These hands." He stared at them like they were his two great loves. "Those women took my name." He folded his hands together and looked down at them. "I lost my family over all the stress and discord. I lost my *practice*." Tears glistened in his lower eyelids. "And I didn't deserve it. I did not."

Rachel gave him what she hoped would be a sympathetic smile but suspected looked merely sickly. "I'm not sure what you're asking of me."

He leaned back from the table. "Write about these women. Show that they had an agenda, that they *chose* me to advance that agenda. That they set out to destroy me and now they have. They need to atone. They need to recant. They need to be exposed. Now they're suing me in civil court. Do you know, young lady, that the average civil case costs a quarter million to defend. Just to *defend*. Win or lose, you're out two hundred and fifty thousand dollars. Did you know that?"

Rachel was still stuck on "young lady," but she nodded.

"So, so, so, this *coven* has raped me. What other word could apply? They have wrecked my good name and destroyed my relationships with my family and my friends. But that's not enough, is it? No. Now they want to pick my bones. They want what little money I have left. So I can spend my remaining years destitute. So I can die on a cot in a shelter somewhere, a friendless nothing." He splayed his fingers over the stack of paper. "In these pages are all the dirty facts about these dirty women. Write about them. Show the world who they are. I'm handing you your Pulitzer, Rachel."

"I'm not here for a Pulitzer," Rachel said.

His eyes grew small. "Then why are you here?"

"You said you had information regarding my mother."

He nodded. "After."

"After what?"

"After you do the story."

"That's not how I work," Rachel said. "If you have information about my mother, just tell me and we'll see—"

"It's not about your mother. It's about your father." His eyes flashed. "As you yourself said, it's a small region. People talk. And the story about you, my dear, was that Elizabeth refused to tell you who your father was. We pitied you, you know, all the good towns-people. We wanted to tell you but none of us could. Well, *I* could have. I knew your father quite well. But doctor-patient confidential-ity laws being what they are, I couldn't reveal his identity against your mother's wishes. But now she's dead. And I'm no longer al-lowed to practice." He sipped his coffee. "So, Rachel, would you like to know who your daddy is?"

It took Rachel a moment to find her voice. "Yes."

"What's that?"

"Yes."

He acknowledged that with a downward flick of his eyelids. "Then write the fucking story, sweetheart."

3

JJ

The more Rachel dug—into the court records and the very files Browner provided—the worse it got. If Dr. Felix Browner was not a serial rapist he was giving the best impression of one Rachel had seen in some time. The only reason he wasn't in prison was because the one woman who had pressed charges within the statute of limitations, Lianne Fennigan, had overdosed on Oxycontin the final week of his trial, just before she was set to testify. Lianne survived the overdose but was in rehab the day she was supposed to deliver her testimony, and the DA accepted a plea that included revocation of the doctor's license, six years' probation, six months' time already served, and a gag order, but no prison time.

Rachel wrote up her story. She brought it with her to the diner in Millbury, pulled it out of her bag as she sat across from Dr. Felix Browner. He gazed at the small sheaf of pages but remained still.

"What," he said, "you don't believe in thumb drives?"

She gave that a tight smile of acknowledgment. "You look happy."

He did. He'd shit-canned the Jimmy Buffett look for a crisp white shirt under a dark brown suit. His hair was slicked back and heavily gelled. His caterpillar eyebrows were trimmed. His face had color and his eyes gleamed with possibility.

"I *feel* happy, Rachel. You look stupendous yourself."

"Thank you."

"That blouse brings out the green of your eyes."

"Thank you."

"Is your hair always so silky?"

"I just had a blowout."

"It becomes you."

She beamed her own bright smile his way. His eyes pulsed when it landed and he laughed a small private laugh. "Well, Lordy," he said.

She said nothing, just nodded in a knowing way and held his gaze.

"I think you *can smell* that Pulitzer."

"Well," she said, "let's not get ahead of ourselves." She handed the pages to him.

He settled into his chair. "We should order drinks," he said absently as he began to read. As he turned the first page, he looked across at her, and she smiled with encouragement. He read on and his brow knitted as anticipation transmogrified into consternation, then despair, and finally outrage.

"This," he said, waving off the waitress's approach, "says I'm a rapist."

"Kinda does, doesn't it?"

"This says the women's chemical dependency and alcohol abuse and sexual piggery are due to me."

"Because they are."

"This says I tried to *extort* you into wrecking these women's lives a second time."

"Because you did." She nodded pleasantly. "And you slandered them in my presence. And I bet if I did even a little digging at your local watering holes, I'd find evidence you slandered them to half the male population in western Mass. Which would be a violation of the terms of your probation. And that means, Felix, that when the *Globe* runs that story you are going straight to fucking D block."

She sat back, watched him go speechless. When he finally met her eyes, his swam with martyrdom and disbelief.

"These hands"—he raised them—"brought you into the world."

"Fuck your hands," she said. "We have a new deal. Okay? I *won't* file that story."

"Bless you." He sat up straight. "I knew the moment I—"

"Give me my father's name."

"I'll be happy to, but let's order a drink and discuss that idea."

She took the pages from his hand. "Give me my father's name right now or I file this story"—she pointed at the bar—"from that phone."

He slumped in the chair, considered the ceiling fan that rotated slowly above him with a rusty squeak. "She called him JJ."

Rachel placed the article back in her bag to hide the tremors that ran from her hands to her elbows. "Why JJ?"

He turned his hands up on the table, a beleaguered supplicant to fate. "What will I do now? How will I live?"

"Why did she call him JJ?" Her teeth, she realized, were gritted.

"You're all the same," he whispered. "You bleed men dry. Good men. You're a pestilence."

She stood.

"Sit." He said it loud enough that two diners looked their way. "Please. No, no. Just sit. I'll be good. I'll be a good boy."

She sat.

Dr. Felix Browner removed a single piece of paper from his suit jacket. It was old and folded in four. He opened it and handed it across the table to her. Her hand shook even worse as she took it, but she didn't care.

At the top of the page was the name of his clinic: Browner Women's Health Clinic. Below that: "Father's Medical History."

"He only came to my office twice. I got the impression they fought a lot. Pregnancies scare some men. Settle around them like a noose."

Under "Last Name," in neat block letters and blue ink, he'd printed "JAMES."

That's why they'd never found him. James was his surname.

His first name was Jeremy.

4

TYPE B

Jeremy James had been teaching full-time at Connecticut College, a small liberal-arts institution in New London, Connecticut, since September 1982. That same year, he bought a house in Durham, a town of seven thousand, sixty miles straight down I-91 from where Rachel grew up in South Hadley, and about a ten-minute drive from the house her mother had rented in Middletown, the year Rachel came down with mono.

He married Maureen Widerman in July 1983. Their first child, Theo, was born in September 1984. Their second, Charlotte, a Christmas baby, arrived at the end of 1986. *I have half siblings*, Rachel thought, *blood relations*. And she felt, for the first time since her mother had died, as if she were tethered somewhere in the universe.

With his full name in her possession, Rachel had Jeremy James's entire life laid out before her in under an hour, or at least the portion that was a matter of public record. He became an associate professor of art history in 1990 and a full professor with tenure in 1995. By the time Rachel tracked him down in the fall of 2007, he'd been teaching at Connecticut College for a quarter century and now chaired the department. His wife, Maureen Widerman-James, was the curator of European art at the Wadsworth Atheneum in Hartford. Rachel found several pictures of her online and liked her eyes enough to decide she was the way in. She'd looked up Jeremy James online and found his pictures as well. He was bald now and heavily bearded, and in all the photos he looked erudite and imposing.

When she introduced herself over the phone to Maureen Widerman-James, there was only the slightest of pauses before Maureen said, "For twenty-five years I've been wondering when you'd call. I can't tell you what a relief it is to finally hear your voice, Rachel."

When Rachel hung up, she stared out the window and tried not to cry. She bit her lip so hard it bled.

She drove out to Durham on a Saturday in early October. For most of its history, Durham had been a farming community, and the thin country roads she drove along were pocked by great old trees, faded red barns, and the occasional goat. The air smelled of woodsmoke and a nearby apple orchard.

Maureen Widerman-James answered the door to the modest house on Gorham Lane. She was a handsome woman with large round glasses that accentuated the calm but penetrating air of curiosity in her light brown eyes. Her chestnut hair was red at the roots and gray along the strands closest to her temples and forehead, and she had it in a messy ponytail. She wore a red-and-black work shirt untucked over black leggings and no shoes, and when she smiled, the smile took over her face in a flood of light.

"Rachel," she said with the same mixture of relief and familiarity she'd used on the phone. It cemented the unsettling realization that she'd said Rachel's name more than a few times over the decades. "Come in."

She stepped aside and Rachel entered a home that looked like the home of two academics—bookcases in the foyer, consuming the walls in the living room, under a window in the kitchen; walls painted in vibrant colors, the paint chipped in places and never touched up; figurines and masks from Third World countries in various states of display; Haitian art on the walls. Rachel had been in scores of homes like this during her mother's career. She knew what LPs would be on the built-in shelf in the living room, what magazines would dominate the basket in the bathroom, that the radio in the kitchen was tuned to NPR. She immediately felt at home here.

Maureen led her to a pair of pocket doors in the back of the house. She put her hands to the seam between them and looked over her shoulder. "Are you ready?"

"Who could be ready for this?" Rachel admitted with a desperate chuckle.

"You'll be fine," Maureen said warmly, but Rachel caught a sadness in her eyes as well. As much as they may have come to the beginning of one thing, they'd also reached the end of something else. Rachel wasn't sure if that's where the sadness stemmed from but she suspected it. Nothing would ever be the same in any of their lives.

He stood in the center of the room and turned as the doors opened. He was dressed not dissimilarly to his wife, though instead of leggings he wore gray jeans. His work shirt was also plaid and untucked, but his was blue and black, and worn unbuttoned over a white T-shirt. A few bohemian touches to him—a small silver loop in his left earlobe, three dark rope bracelets around his left wrist, a chunky watch with a fat black leather band on the other wrist. His bald head gleamed. His beard was trimmer than it was in the pictures she'd found online and he looked older, his eyes sunk a little farther back in their sockets, his face hanging a little lower. He was taller than she'd expected, but his shoulders were stooped at the points. He smiled as she reached him and it was the smile she remembered, the thing about him she'd remember not only to her grave but long after she was buried in it. That sudden, uncertain smile of a man who had, at some point in his life, been conditioned to ask for permission before he expressed joy.

He took her hands, his gaze searching her, drinking her, darting all over. "God," he said, "look at you. Just look at you," he whispered.

He pulled her to him with fumbling ferocity. Rachel returned the hug in kind. He was a heavy man now, around the middle and in the arms and back, but she hugged him so tight she could feel her bones make contact with his. She closed her eyes and heard the beat of his heart like a wave in the dark.

He still smells like coffee, she thought. No longer of corduroy. But coffee still. Coffee still.

"Daddy," she whispered.

And he pushed her, ever so gently, away from his chest.

"Sit." He waved Rachel vaguely toward a couch.

She shook her head, steeling herself for the latest shit sandwich. "I'll stand."

"Then we'll drink." He went to a bar cart and started fixing all three of them drinks. "She died when we were overseas, your mother. I did a sabbatical in France that year and didn't learn of her death for years. It wasn't as if we had any shared friends to tell me of her passing. I'm truly sorry for your loss."

He looked directly at her and the depth of his compassion hit her like a fist.

For some reason, the only thing she could think to ask was "How did you meet?"

He'd met her mother, he explained, on the train back from Baltimore, where he'd gone for his own mother's funeral in the spring of '79. Elizabeth was heading east with her Ph.D. from Johns Hopkins to her first teaching post at Mount Holyoke. Jeremy was in his third year as a part-time assistant professor at Buckley College, fifteen miles north. They were dating within a week, living together within a month.

He brought Rachel and Maureen a scotch and raised his own. They drank.

"It was your mother's first year on the job in an extremely liberal region of a liberal state at the end of a liberal decade, so cohabitation without marriage was acceptable. Pregnancy without marriage might have even been more so; some looked on it as admirable, spitting in the face of the dominant paradigm and all that. However, if she'd simply been knocked up by a person unknown? *That* would have made her seem tawdry and pathetic, a foolish victim unable to rise above her class. At least that's what she feared."

Rachel noticed Maureen watching her carefully, half her scotch already gone.

Jeremy started rushing through his sentences, his words spilling and stumbling. "But it was one thing to, to, to sell the idea to the general populace, the people she worked with, et cetera. It was quite another thing to try to sell it at home. I mean, I'm not a math professor but I can still do math. And your mother's was off by two months."

Here it is. He just said it, Rachel thought, and took a big pull on her scotch, but I'm not hearing it somehow. I know what he's saying but I don't. I can't. I just can't.

"I would have been willing, even happy, to be part of selling the fiction, but I wasn't willing to keep up the lie in our kitchen, in our bedroom, in the day to day of our lives. It was insidious."

Rachel could feel her lips moving ever so slightly but no words left her mouth. The air in the room was thin, the walls contracted.

"I took a blood test," Jeremy said.

"A blood test," Rachel repeated slowly.

He nodded. "The most basic kind. It would never conclusively prove paternity but it would conclusively *dis*prove it. You're type B, yes?"

A numbness spread through her like she'd mainlined Novocain into her spinal cavity. She nodded.

"Elizabeth's was A." He drained his scotch. Put the glass down on the edge of the desk. "Mine is also A."

Maureen placed a chair behind Rachel. Rachel sat in it.

Jeremy was still talking. "You understand? If your mother was A and I'm A but you're B? Then—"

Rachel waved at the room. "Then there's no way you can be my father." She finished her scotch. "I understand."

For the first time she noticed the pictures on his desk and scattered on the bookshelves and side tables in the office, all of the same two people—his and Maureen's children, Theo and Charlotte, through the years. As toddlers, at the beach, birthday parties, graduations. Landmark moments and others that could have been forgotten were it not for the camera. But full lives lived, from birth to college. For the past seventy-two hours, give or take, she'd thought they were her half siblings. Now they were just someone's kids. And she was back to being an only child.

She caught Maureen's eye and shot her a broken smile. "I guess this isn't something you could have told me over the phone, huh? No. I get it, I do."

She stood and Maureen came out of her own chair and Jeremy took two quick steps toward her. She realized they thought she might faint.

"I'm okay." She found herself looking at the ceiling, noting that it was copper, of all things. "I'm just really . . ." She searched for the right word. "Sad?" She answered her own question with a nod. "That's it. Sad. Tired too. You know? Been a long hunt. I'm going to go."

"No," Jeremy said. "No."

"Please," Maureen said. "Don't go. We made up the guest room. Be our guest tonight. Take a nap. Stay. Rachel, please."

She slept. She never would have thought it possible with all the shame. Shame in knowing how much they pitied her. That they'd avoided this conversation for as long as they had because they hadn't wanted to reduce her to what she was now: an orphan. She could hear a distant tractor as she closed her eyes and the sound chugged through dreams she couldn't remember. When she opened her eyes ninety minutes later she felt, if anything, even more exhausted. She went to the window and parted the heavy curtains and looked out on the Jameses' backyard and the backyard that abutted it, that one strewn with children's toys, a short slide of hard plastic, a pink-and-black buggy. Beyond the yard sat a small Cape with a pale slate roof, and beyond that farmland. The tractor she'd heard sat idle in a field.

She'd thought she'd known what it was to feel alone but she hadn't. She'd had an illusion to keep her company, a belief in a false god. A mythical father. When she saw him again, she'd been telling herself in one way or another since she was three years old, she'd feel whole, if nothing else. But now she had seen him again, and he was no more connected to her than the tractor.

She came down the stairs and they were waiting for her in the small parlor at the bottom. Rachel stopped in the doorway and noted the pity in their eyes again. She felt like an emotional beggar, going from door to door her whole life, asking perfect strangers to feed her. Fill her. Fill her again.

I'm a bottomless vessel. Fill me up.

She met Jeremy's gaze and it occurred to her that maybe it wasn't pity she saw there but his own shame.

"I get that we weren't blood," she said.

"Rachel," Maureen said, "come in."

"But that made it okay for you to leave me?"

"I didn't want to leave you." He held out his hands. "Not you. Not my Rachel."

She entered the room. She stood behind the chair they'd placed across from the sofa where they both sat.

He lowered his hands. "But once she'd decided I was the enemy— and she decided that the first day I showed any doubt about going along with her fantasy of who impregnated her—there was no quarter."

She took the seat.

"You know your mother better than anyone, Rachel. So I'm sure you were well acquainted with her rage. Once it found a target to focus on or a cause in which to channel itself? There was no stopping it. Certainly no speaking truth to it. And once I got a blood test, I transformed from an enemy to a cancer in the body of that house. And she went after me with single-minded"—he searched for the word—"madness. She was either going to bring me fully to heel or she was going to expel me."

"Expunge you."

He blinked. "What did you say?"

"She screamed it at you that last night—*I will expunge you.*"

Jeremy and Maureen exchanged startled looks.

"You remember that?"

Rachel nodded. She poured herself a glass of water from the pitcher on the coffee table between them. "And that's what she did. If she'd expelled you, Jeremy, that would have worked out okay for both of us, I think. But when she expunged you, you were erased. The dead have names and grave markers. The expunged never existed."

She sipped her water and looked around the parlor at its books and pictures and the record player and LPs just where she'd predicted they would be. She noted the hand-knitted throws and the place where the love seat buckled on the ridgeline and the various scrapes in the hardwood floor and the scuff marks in the wainscoting and the slightly cluttered nature of it all. She thought how nice it must have been to grow up here, to have been the children of Jeremy and Maureen. She lowered her head and closed her eyes and in the darkness she saw her mother and the playground with the low clouds and the wet swings where Jeremy had taken her as a small child. She saw the house on Westbrook Road with its piles of sodden leaves the morning after he'd left. Then she saw an alt-life in which he hadn't left and Jeremy James was her father in all but blood and he raised her and counseled her and coached her middle-school soccer team. And in that alt-life, her mother wasn't a woman consumed by a thirst to bend all the people in her life to fit her own fucked-up narrative of that life but was instead the person she was in her writing and her teaching—objective, rational, self-deprecating, capable of a love that was simple and direct and mature.

But that's not what she and Jeremy got. They got a conflicted, aggressive, toxic mess of outsize intelligence, outsize anxiety, and outsize rage. And all of it bound up in an outwardly competent, cool, and calm Nordic exterior.

"*I will expunge you.*"

You expunged him, Mother. And in the process you expunged me and yourself out of the family we could have been, we so easily and joyfully could have been. *If you'd just gotten out of your own fucking way, you horrible demon bitch.*

She raised her head and pushed the hair out of her eyes. Maureen was there with a box of tissues as Rachel had somehow known she would be. What was that kind of attentiveness called? Oh, right. Mothering. So that's what it looked like.

Jeremy had moved to the floor in front of her, sat looking up with his hands clasped around his knees and his face lit with kindness and regret.

"Maureen," he said, "could I speak to Rachel alone for a minute?"

"Of course, of course." Maureen returned the box of tissues to a credenza, then changed her mind, brought it back and placed it on the coffee table. She refilled Rachel's glass of water. She fussed with the corner of a throw rug. Then she gave them both a smile that was supposed to be comforting but curdled into something terrified. She left the room.

"When you were two," Jeremy said, "your mother and I fought pretty much every minute we were in each other's presence. Do you know what it's like to fight with someone every day? Someone who claims to dislike conflict but who in fact lives for it?"

Rachel cocked her head at him. "You're really asking me this?"

He smiled. And then the smile went away. "It scours the soul, damages the heart. You can feel yourself dying. Living with your mother—from the time she'd decided I was the enemy onward, anyway—was to live in a state of perpetual war. I was walking up the driveway after work once, and I threw up. Just puked into the snow covering our lawn. And there was nothing specifically wrong at that particular moment, but I knew that the second I walked into the house, she'd come at me about something. Could be anything—my tone of voice, the tie I chose that day, something I'd said three weeks earlier, something someone else had said about me, a feeling she had, an intuition she'd received as if by divine providence that something was not right about me, a dream that suggested the same . . ." He shook his head and let out a small gasp, as if surprised how fresh the memories could be even now, almost thirty years later.

"So why did you hang in there as long as you did?"

He knelt before her. He took her hands and pressed them to his upper lip and breathed in the smell of them. "You," he said. "I would have stayed because of you and puked in the driveway every night and gotten an ulcer and early heart disease and every other possible malady if it meant I could have raised you."

He let go of her hands and sat on the coffee table in front of her.

"But," she managed.

"But," he said, "your mother knew that. She knew I had no legal footing but she knew I'd stay in your life, whether she liked it or not. So one night, the last night we ever made love, I remember that well, I woke up and she was gone. I ran to your room and you were there, sleeping away. I walked around the house. There was no note, no Elizabeth. No cell phones back then and we hadn't made any friends I could call."

"You'd been there two years by that point. You had no friends?"

He nodded. "Two and a half." He leaned forward on the edge of the coffee table. "Your mother torpedoed any attempts at a social life. I couldn't see it at the time—we were so overwhelmed with work and having a baby and then a newborn and all the labor-intensive stages of, well, having a child. So I'm not even sure I noticed how cut off we were until that night. I taught in Worcester back then, at Holy Cross. My commute was a bear, and your mother sure wasn't going to socialize in Worcester. But when I'd suggest going out with her coworkers, fellow faculty and such, she'd say, 'So-and-so secretly hates women,' or 'So-and-so is just so pretentious,' or, the nuclear option, 'So-and-so looks at Rachel funny.'"

"Me?"

He nodded. "How was I going to respond to that?"

"She used to do the same thing with my friends," Rachel said. "All these backhanded slights, you know? 'Jennifer seems nice . . . for someone with her insecurities.' Or 'Chloe could be so pretty but why does she dress that way? Does she know the message she's sending?'" Rachel rolled her eyes at it now, but she could feel the stab of it just below her rib cage to realize how many friendships her mother had shamed her out of.

Jeremy said, "Sometimes she'd actually make plans with another couple or a group of coworkers and we'd be all set to go. And then, right at the last minute, it would fall through. The sitter's car broke down, Elizabeth felt ill, you looked like you were coming down with something—'Doesn't she feel hot, JJ?'—the other couple called to cancel, even though I couldn't recall hearing the phone ring. The excuses always seemed perfectly reasonable in the moment. It was only over time, in the rearview, that I saw how they piled up. Either way, we had no friends."

"So this night she disappeared?"

"She came back at dawn," he said. "She'd been beaten." He looked at the floor. "And worse. All the visible injuries were to her body, not her face. But she'd been raped and battered."

"By who?"

He met her eyes. "There's the question. She'd been to the police, though. Had pictures taken. She consented to a rape kit." He sucked a wet breath to the back of his throat. "She told the police she wouldn't identify her attacker. Not then anyway. But once she came home and told me, she assured me that if I didn't come to my senses and admit the truth, she—"

"Wait a minute," Rachel said, "what truth?"

"That I'd impregnated her."

"But you hadn't."

"Right."

"So . . ."

"So she insisted I say I had. She said the only way we could be together was if I was wholly honest with her and stopped lying about fathering you. I said, 'Elizabeth, I'll tell the world I'm Rachel's father. I'll sign all documents to that effect. If we divorce, I'll pay child support until she's eighteen. But what I won't do, what I can't do, what it is categorically *insane* to ask me to do is to claim to you, her mother, that I planted the seed. That's too much to ask of anyone.'"

"And what did she say to that?" Rachel asked, even though she had a pretty good idea.

"She asked me why I insisted on lying. She asked me what sickness was in me that I would try to make her seem as if *she* were being unreasonable about something so crucial. She asked me to admit that I was trying to make her look as if she were insane." He pressed his palms together, as if in prayer, and his voice grew very soft, almost a whisper. "The game, as I understood it, was that she could never believe I loved her unless I agreed to abide by an unreasonable contract. The unreasonable aspect of the demand was the point. That was her deal breaker—meet me there in the cave of my own insanity or meet me nowhere."

"And you chose nowhere."

"I chose the truth." He leaned back on the table. "And my sanity."

Rachel felt a bitter smile tug the corners of her mouth. "She didn't like that, did she?"

"She told me if I was determined to live a life of cowardice and lies, then I could never see you again. If I left that house, I was leaving your life forever."

"And you left."

"And I left."

"And never attempted contact?"

He shook his head. "That was her checkmate, in the end." He leaned forward. Placed his palms softly on her kneecaps. "If I ever tried to make contact, your mother told me, she'd tell the police that I was the man who'd raped her."

Rachel tried to get her head around it. Would her mother have gone to those lengths to drive Jeremy James—or anyone for that matter—from her life? That would be beyond the pale even for Elizabeth, wouldn't it? But then Rachel recalled the fates of others who'd run afoul of Elizabeth Childs during her childhood. There'd been a dean whom Elizabeth had ever so gradually poisoned the faculty against; a fellow psych professor whose contract was not renewed; a janitor who was fired; an employee at the town bakery who was let go. All these people and a couple more had crossed Elizabeth Childs—or she believed they had—and her retaliation was heartless and calculated. Her mother, she knew all too well, had thought at all times in tactical terms.

"Do you think she was raped?" she asked Jeremy.

He shook his head. "I think she had sex with me and then she either paid or coerced someone into beating her up. I've had years to think about it and that's the scenario I find likeliest."

"Because you wouldn't live a lie within your own home?"

He nodded. "And because I'd seen the depths of her own insanity. And that she could never forgive."

Rachel kept twirling it in her head, over and over. Eventually she admitted to the man who should have been her father, "When I think of her—and I think of her too much—I sometimes wonder if she was evil."

Jeremy shook his head. "No. She wasn't. She was just the most profoundly damaged human being I've ever met. And she was relentlessly hostile if crossed, I'll give you that. But there was great love in her heart."

Rachel laughed. "For who?"

He gave her a look of dark befuddlement. "For you, Rachel. For you."

5

ON LUMINISM

After she met the man she'd mistakenly believed to be her father, a surprising thing happened—she and Jeremy James became friends. There wasn't much tentative about it; they dove in, more like long-lost siblings than a sixty-three-year-old man and a twenty-eight-year-old woman who turned out not to be related.

When Elizabeth Childs died, Jeremy and his family had been in Normandy, where Jeremy had used his sabbatical to research a subject that had long fascinated him—the possible link between luminism and expressionism. Now, as his academic career was winding down and retirement loomed, Jeremy was trying to write his book on luminism, an American style of landscape painting often confused with impressionism. As Jeremy explained it to Rachel, who knew less than zero about art, luminism grew out of the Hudson River School. It was Jeremy's belief that the two schools shared a link, even if prevailing theory—dogma actually, Jeremy would scoff—held that the two schools had developed independently of each other in the late 1800s on opposite sides of the Atlantic.

A man named Colum Jasper Whitstone, Jeremy told her, had worked as an apprentice to two of the most famous luminists— George Caleb Bingham and Albert Bierstadt—but vanished in 1863 along with a large sum of money from the Western Union office where he was employed. Neither the money nor Colum Jasper Whitstone was ever heard of again in the Americas. But the diary of Madame de Fontaine, a wealthy widow and arts patron in Normandy, twice made mention of a Callum Whitestone in the summer of 1865, referring to him as a gentleman from America with good manners, refined tastes, and a cloudy heritage. When Jeremy first told Rachel this his eyes were lit like a birthday child's and his baritone voice grew several octaves lighter. "Monet and Boudin painted the Normandy coast the same year. They would set up every day, just down the street from Madame de Fontaine's summer cottage."

Jeremy believed these two giants of impressionism had crossed paths with Colum Jasper Whitstone, that Whitstone was, in fact, the missing link between American luminism and French impressionism. All he had to do was prove it. Rachel pitched in with research, aware of the irony that she and her not-father were searching for a man who'd vanished into the dust and void of a hundred and fifty years when together they couldn't identify the man who'd fathered Rachel a little over thirty years before.

Jeremy often visited her apartment during research trips to the MFA, the Boston Athenaeum, and the Boston Public Library. She'd departed the *Globe* for TV by then and had moved in with Sebastian, a producer at Channel 6. Sometimes Sebastian was there and would join them for dinner or drinks, but mostly he was working or on his boat.

"You're such an attractive couple," Jeremy said one night at her apartment, and the word *attractive* left his mouth sounding unattractive. He had developed an ability to say all the right things about Sebastian—taking note of his intelligence, his dry wit, his good looks, his air of competency—without sounding like he meant any of them.

He examined a picture of the two of them on Sebastian's beloved boat. He placed it back on the mantel and gave Rachel a pleasant, distracted smile, as if he were trying to come up with one more positive thing to say about the two of them but had drawn a blank. "He sure works a lot."

"He does," she agreed.

"He wants to run the whole station one day, I bet."

"He wants to run the network," she said.

He chuckled and carried his glass of wine to the bookshelves, where he zeroed in on a photograph of Rachel and her mother that Rachel had almost forgotten was there. Sebastian, not a fan of the photo or its frame, had crammed it at the end of a row of books, backed into a shadow cast by a copy of *History of America in 101 Objects*. Jeremy removed it gently and tilted the book so it remained standing. She watched his face turn both dreamy and desolate.

"How old were you in this?"

"Seven," she said.

"Hence the missing teeth."

"Mmm-hmm. Sebastian thinks I look like a hobbit in that picture."

"He said that?"

"He was joking."

"That's what we're calling it?" He carried the photograph back to the couch and sat beside her.

Seven-year-old Rachel, missing both upper front teeth and one lower, had stopped smiling for cameras at the time. Her mother wouldn't hear of it. Elizabeth found a set of rubber fangs somewhere and used a Sharpie to black out one of the upper teeth and two of the lower. She'd had Ann Marie take a series of pictures of her and

Rachel vamping for the camera one drizzly afternoon at the house in South Hadley. In this, the only photograph to survive from that day, Rachel was wrapped in her mother's arms, both of them beaming their hideous smiles as broadly as possible.

"I'd forgotten just how pretty she was too. My goodness." Jeremy gave Rachel an ironic smile. "She looks like your boyfriend."

"Shut up," Rachel said, but it was unfortunately true. How had she never noticed before? Both Sebastian and her mother looked like Aryan ideals—hair several shades whiter than vanilla, cheekbones as sharp as their jawlines, Arctic eyes, and lips so small and thin they couldn't help but appear secretive.

"I know men marry their mothers," Jeremy said, "but this is—"

She nudged an elbow into his paunch. "Enough."

He laughed and kissed her head and put the photograph back where it belonged. "Do you have more?"

"Pictures?"

He nodded. "I never got to see you grow up."

She found the shoebox of them in her closet. She dumped them out onto the small kitchen table so that her life took the shape of a messy collage, which seemed all too fitting. Her fifth birthday party; a day at the beach when she was a teenager; semiformal during junior year of high school; in her soccer uniform sometime during middle school; hanging in the basement with Caroline Ford, which would have been when she was eleven because Caroline Ford's father had been visiting faculty for that one year only; Elizabeth and Ann Marie and Don Klay at a cocktail party by the looks of it; Rachel and Elizabeth the day Rachel graduated from middle school; Elizabeth, Ann Marie, Ann Marie's first husband, Richard, and Giles Ellison at the Williamstown Theatre Festival and again at a cookout, everyone's hair a little thinner and a little grayer in the latter; Rachel, the day her braces were removed; two of Elizabeth and half a dozen unidentified friends at a bar. Her mother was quite young, possibly still in her twenties, and Rachel didn't recognize any of the other people or the bar where they were gathered.

"Who are those people?" she asked Jeremy.

He glanced at it. "No idea."

"They look like academics." She picked up the photograph and the one below it, which appeared to have been taken within a minute of the first. "She looks so young, I figured it was taken when she first got to the Berkshires."

He considered the photo in her right hand, the one in which her mother was caught unaware, her eyes on the bottles behind the bar. "No, I don't know any of those people. I don't even know that bar. That's not in the Berkshires. At least not any place I've ever been." He adjusted his glasses and leaned in. "The Colts."

"Huh?"

"Look."

She followed his finger. In the corner of the frame of both photographs, just past the bar, at the entrance to the kind of paneled hallway that usually leads to restrooms, a pennant hung on the wall. Only half of it had made it into the frame, the half with the team logo: a white helmet with a dark blue horseshoe in the center. The Indianapolis Colts logo.

"What was she doing in Indianapolis?" Rachel said.

"The Colts didn't move to Indy until 1984. Before that, they were in Baltimore. This would have been taken when she was at Johns Hopkins, before you were born."

She laid the picture in which her mother wasn't looking at the camera back down on top of the collage and they both peered at the one where the principals looked into the lens.

"Why are we staring at this?" Rachel eventually asked.

"You ever know your mother to be sentimental or nostalgic?"

"No."

"So why did she keep these two pictures?"

"Good point."

There were three men and three women, including her mother, in the center of the frame. They'd gathered at one corner of the bar and pulled their stools close together. Big smiles and glassy eyes. The oldest of them was a heavyset man farthest to the left. He looked to be about forty, with muttonchop sideburns, a plaid sport coat, bright blue shirt, and wide knit tie loosened below an unbuttoned collar. Beside him was a woman in a purple turtleneck with her dark hair pulled back in a bun, a nose so small you had to look for it, and barely any chin. Next to her was a thin black woman with a Jheri-curl perm; she wore a white blazer with the collar turned up over a black halter top, a long white cigarette held up by her ear but not yet lit. Her left hand rested on the arm of a trim black man in a tan three-piece suit with thick square glasses and an earnest, forthright gaze. Beside him was a man wearing a white shirt and black tie under a velour zip-front pullover. His brown hair was parted in the middle, blown dry, and feathered along the temples. His green eyes were playful, maybe a bit lascivious. He had his arm around Rachel's mother, but they all had their arms around each other, huddling close together. Elizabeth Childs sat on the end; she wore a billowy pinstriped blouse with the top three buttons undone, publicly revealing more cleavage than she ever had in Rachel's lifetime. Her hair, which had always been cut short during her years in the Berkshires, fell almost to her shoulders and was, true to the times, feathered on the sides. But even with the fashion fails common to the era, her mother's sheer force of self pulled one to her. She stared back from a remove of more than three decades as if she'd known as the picture was being taken that circumstances would one day put her daughter and a man she'd almost married in the exact position where they now found themselves—searching her face, yet again, for clues to her soul. But in pictures, as in life, those clues were opaque and fruitless. Her smile was both the most brilliant of the six and the only one that didn't quite reach her eyes. She was smiling because it was expected of her, not because she felt it, an impression underscored in the other photo, which looked to have been taken seconds before or seconds after the posed shot.

Seconds after, Rachel realized, because the tip of the black woman's cigarette glowed a fresh red in the second photo. Her mother's smile was gone and she was turning back to the bar, her eyes on the bottles to the right of the cash register. Whiskey bottles, Rachel was mildly surprised to note, not the vodka bottles she would have expected her mother to show an interest in. Her mother was no longer smiling but she looked happier because of it. Her face bore an intensity that Rachel would have characterized as erotically charged had its focus been anything but the bottles of whiskey. It appeared as if her mother had been caught in a reverie, in anticipation of an encounter with whomever she was leaving that bar with or meeting up with afterward.

Or she was just glancing at whiskey bottles and wondering what she'd have for breakfast tomorrow. Rachel realized with no small amount of shame that she was projecting at a nearly unforgivable level because she wanted to find value in photos that had none.

"This is silly." She went to get the bottle of wine they'd left on the counter.

"What about it is silly?" Jeremy placed both photos side by side.

"I feel like we're looking for him here."

"We are looking for him here."

"It's two photographs from a night at a bar when she was in grad school." She refilled their glasses and left the bottle on the table between them. "Nothing more."

"I lived with your mother for three years. Except for pictures of you, there were no pictures. Not one. I now discover the existence of these two, tucked away somewhere the whole time I lived with her but never to be shared with me. Why? What's in these pictures on this night that matters? I say it's your father."

"Could just be a night she was fond of."

He raised an eyebrow.

"Could just be two pictures she forgot she had."

The eyebrow stayed up.

"Fine," she said. "Make your pitch."

He pointed at the man closest to her mother, Velour Man with the feathered brown hair. "He has the same color eyes as you."

Fair enough. Like Rachel, he *did* have green eyes, though his were a much brighter shade; hers were so light they were almost gray. And like Rachel, he did have brown hair. The shape of his head wasn't far off from Rachel's own; the size of the nose was about right. His chin was quite pointed, whereas Rachel's was more squared off, but then her mother's had been squared off too, so one could argue she'd simply gotten her mother's chin but her father's eyes and hair. He was a handsome man, porn 'stache notwithstanding, but there was something lightweight about him. And her mother did not have a known affinity for the lightweight. Jeremy and Giles might not have been the most overtly masculine men Rachel had ever come across but there was steel at the core of both of them and their intelligence was prodigious and immediately identifiable. Velour Man, on the other hand, looked like he was on his way to emcee a Junior Miss pageant.

"Does he seem like her type?" Rachel said.

"Did I?" Jeremy asked.

"You have gravitas," Rachel said. "My mother dug gravitas."

"Well, it's not *this* guy." Jeremy put his finger on the heavyset guy with the eyesore of a sport coat. "And it's not this guy." He put his finger on the black guy. "Maybe the cameraman?"

"Camerawoman." Rachel showed him the reflection in the bar mirror of a woman with a mane of brown hair spilling from underneath a multicolored knit cap, the camera held in two hands.

"Ah."

She looked at the other people who'd been inadvertently captured on film. Two old men and a middle-aged couple sat midway down the bar. The bartender made change at the cash register. And a youngish guy in a black leather jacket was frozen in midstride after coming through the front doors.

"What about him?" she asked.

Jeremy adjusted his glasses and hunched in close to the photo. "Can't get a good enough look. Wait, wait, wait." He got up and went to the canvas backpack he took everywhere on his research trips. He removed a magnifying glass paperweight and brought it to the table. He held it over the face of the guy in the leather jacket. The guy had the surprised look of a man who'd almost stepped into a photographer's shot and ruined it. He was also darker skinned than he'd appeared from a remove. Latin American or Native American possibly. But not in line with Rachel's own ethnic makeup, in either case.

Jeremy moved the magnifying glass back over to Velour Man. He definitely had the same color eyes as Rachel. What had her mother said? *Look for yourself in his eyes.* Rachel stared at Velour Man's magnified eyes until they blurred. She looked away to readjust her vision and then back again.

"Are those my eyes?" she asked Jeremy.

"They're your color," he said. "Different shape, but you got your bone structure from Elizabeth anyway. Do you want me to make a couple calls?"

"To whom?"

He placed the paperweight down on the table. "Let's take another leap and consider that these were her fellow students in the Ph.D. program at JHU that year. If that presumption is correct, everyone in this picture is probably identifiable. If it's incorrect, I'm only out a few phone calls to friends who work there."

"Okay."

He took pictures of both photographs with his phone, checked the images to make sure they were captured correctly, and put the phone in his pocket.

At her door, he turned back and said, "Are you all right?"

"Fine. Why?"

"You seem kinda hollowed out suddenly."

It took her a minute to find the words. "You're not my father."

"No."

"But I wish you were. Then this would be over. And I'd have a cool guy like you for a dad."

He adjusted his glasses, something she learned he did whenever he felt uncomfortable. "I've never in my life been called a cool guy."

"That's why you're cool," she said and kissed his cheek.

She received her first e-mail from Brian Delacroix in two years. It was brief—three lines—and complimented her on a series of stories she'd done two weeks before on allegations of kickbacks and patronage in the Massachusetts probation department. The head of the department, Douglas "Dougie" O'Halloran, had run the department like his personal fiefdom, but now, based on work done by Rachel and some of her old colleagues at the *Globe*, the DA was prepping indictments.

When Dougie saw you coming toward him, Brian wrote, he looked fit to shit a collie.

She caught herself beaming.

It's good to know you're out there, Miss Childs.

You too, she considered writing back.

But then she saw his PS:

Crossing back across the southern border. Returning to New England. Any 'hoods you'd recommend?

She immediately Googled him, something she'd consciously refrained from doing until now. There was only one picture of him in Google Images, slightly grainy, which had first appeared in the *Toronto Sun* coverage of a charity gala in 2000. But there he was, in an incongruous tux, head turned to the side, identified in the caption as "Lumber scion Brian Delacroix III." In the accompanying article, he was described as "low-key" and "notoriously private," a graduate of Brown with an MBA from Wharton. Who'd then taken those degrees and become . . .

A private investigator in Chicopee, Massachusetts, for a year?

She smiled to remember him in that shoebox office, a golden boy trying to reject the path his family had laid out for him but clearly conflicted about this choice he'd made. So earnest, so honest. If she'd walked through any other door, handed any other private investigator her case, he or she would have done exactly what Brian had warned her they would—bled her dry.

Brian, on the other hand, had refused to do so.

She stared at his photograph and imagined him living a neighborhood or two over. Or maybe a block or two over.

"I am with Sebastian," she said aloud.

"I love Sebastian."

She closed her laptop.

She told herself she'd respond to Brian's e-mail tomorrow, but she never got around to it.

Two weeks later, Jeremy James called and asked if she was sitting down. She wasn't but she leaned against a wall and told him she was.

"I've identified pretty much everyone. The black couple are still together and both work in private practice in St. Louis. The other woman died in 1990. The big guy was faculty; he passed too a few years back. And the guy in the velour pullover is Charles Osaris, a clinical psychologist who practices on Oahu."

"Hawaii," she said.

"If he turns out to be your dad," Jeremy said, "you'll have a great place to visit. I'll expect an invitation."

"But of course."

It took her three days to call Charles Osaris. It wasn't a case of nerves or trepidation of any kind. It was rooted instead in despair. She knew he wasn't her father, knew it in the pit of her stomach and in every electromagnetic strand of her lizard brain.

Yet some part of her hoped for the opposite.

Charles Osaris confirmed that he had been in the Johns Hopkins Ph.D. program in clinical psychology with Elizabeth Childs. He could recall several nights when they went to a bar called Milo's in East Baltimore, where, indeed, a Baltimore Colts pennant had hung on the wall to the right of the bar. He was sorry to hear Elizabeth had passed away; he'd found her an intriguing woman.

"I was told you two dated," Rachel said.

"Who on earth would tell you something like that?" Charles Osaris let out a sound that was half bark, half laugh. "I've been out of the closet since the seventies, Miss Childs. I never had any illusions about my sexuality, either—confusion, yes, but illusions, no. Never dated a woman, never even kissed one."

"Clearly I was misinformed," Rachel said.

"Clearly. Why would you ask if I dated your mother?"

Rachel came clean, told him she was looking for her father.

"She never told you who he was?"

"No."

"*Why?*"

And Rachel responded with the explanation that, with every passing year, seemed more ludicrous. "For some reason she thought she was protecting me. She confused keeping something secret with keeping me safe."

"The Elizabeth I knew was never confused about anything in her life."

"Why else keep something so big a secret?" Rachel asked.

When he responded, his voice was newly tinged with sadness. "I knew your mother for two years. I was the only man within a ten-mile radius who wasn't trying to separate her from her clothing, so I probably knew her as well as anyone. She felt safe with me. And, Miss Childs, I didn't know her at all. She didn't let people in. She liked having a secret life because she liked secrets. Secrets were power. Secrets were better than sex. Secrets, I firmly believe, were your mother's drug of choice."

After her conversation with Charles Osaris, Rachel had three panic attacks in one week. She had one in the employee bathroom at Channel 6, another on a bench along the Charles River during what was supposed to be her morning jog, and the third in the shower one night after Sebastian fell asleep. She hid them all from Sebastian and her coworkers. As much as one could feel in control during a panic attack, she felt in control of herself; she was able to continually remind herself that she wasn't having a heart attack, that her throat wasn't permanently constricting, that she could in fact breathe.

Her desire to remain indoors intensified. For a few weeks, only conscious effort and internal howls of defiance pushed her out the door every morning. Weekends, she stayed in completely. For the first three weekends, Sebastian assumed it was part of the nesting instinct. By the fourth, he'd grown irritable. Back then, they were on the guest list to just about every party in the city—any gala, any charity function, any see-or-be-seen excuse to imbibe. They'd become a power couple, fixtures of gossip items in the *Inside Track* and *Names & Faces*. Rachel, try as she might, couldn't deny how much she enjoyed the position. If she had no parents, she'd realize in retrospect, at least the city welcomed her into the tribal fold.

So she got back out there. She shook hands and kissed cheeks and drank in the attention of the mayor, the governor, judges, billionaires, comedians, writers, senators, bankers, Red Sox, Patriots,

Bruins, and Celtics players and coaches, and college presidents. At Channel 6, she rocketed through the ranks, racing from freelance to the education beat to crime to general assignment in sixteen months flat. They put her face on a billboard with Shelby and Grant, the evening anchors, and prominently featured her in a commercial to introduce their revamped logo. When she and Sebastian decided to marry, it felt like they'd elected themselves homecoming king and queen, and the city applauded the decision and gave its full blessing.

It was a week after the invitations went out that she ran into Brian Delacroix. She'd just interviewed two reps at the statehouse over a projected budget shortfall. Her crew went to the van but she decided to walk back to the station. She'd just crossed to the other side of Beacon when Brian walked out of the Athenaeum accompanied by a shorter, older man with ginger hair and a matching beard. She experienced that electric bolt of confusion and recognition that usually only occurred when she passed someone famous in the street. It was a feeling of *I know you. But I really don't.* Both men were ten or twelve feet from Rachel when Brian's eyes found hers. A flash of recognition was followed immediately by a flash of something she couldn't identify—was it annoyance? fear? neither?—and then that flash vanished and was replaced with what, in retrospect, she could only describe as manic joy.

"Rachel Childs!" He crossed the distance to her in one long stride. "What's it been—nine years?"

His handshake was firmer than she expected, too firm.

"Eight," she said. "When did you—?"

"This is Jack," Brian said. He stepped aside so the smaller man could step into the space he'd made and now they were a threesome standing on the sidewalk at the peak of Beacon Hill as lunchtime crowds streamed around them.

"Jack Ahern." The man shook her hand. His handshake was much lighter.

There was a strong whiff of Old World to Jack Ahern. His shirt had French cuffs with silver cuff links that peeked out from under the sleeves of his bespoke suit. He wore a bow tie and his beard was precisely trimmed. His hand was dry and uncallused. She imagined he owned a pipe and knew more than most about classical music and cognac.

He said, "Are you old friends with—?"

Brian cut in. "Friends would be a bit strong. We knew each other a decade ago, Jack. Rachel's a reporter on Channel 6 here. She's excellent."

Jack gave her a polite nod approximating respect. "Do you like the work?"

"Most days," she said. "What kind of work are you in?"

"Jack's in antiquities," Brian said in a rush. "He's up here from Manhattan."

Jack Ahern smiled. "By way of Geneva."

"I'm not sure what that means," Rachel said.

"Well, I live in Manhattan and Geneva, but I consider Geneva home."

"Isn't that something?" Brian said, even though it wasn't. He glanced at his watch. "Gotta go, Jack. Reservations for twelve-fifteen. Rachel, a pleasure." He leaned in and kissed the air to the side of her cheek. "I heard you're getting married. Very happy for you."

"Congratulations." Jack Ahern took her hand again with a courtly bow. "I hope you and the groom will be very happy."

"Take care of yourself, Rachel." Brian was already moving away with a distant smile and too-bright eyes. "Great seeing you."

They walked down to Park Street and took a left and passed from view.

She stood on the sidewalk and took stock of the encounter. Brian Delacroix had filled out some since 2001. It became him. The Brian she had met had been too skinny, his neck too slim for his head. His cheekbones and chin had been a little too soft. Now his features were clearly defined. He'd reached the age—thirty-five, she was guessing—where he'd probably begun to resemble his father and had stopped looking like someone's son. He dressed far better and was easily twice as handsome as he'd been in 2001, and he'd been plenty handsome then. So in regards to personal appearance, all changes to the good.

But the energy that had come off him, cloaked in pleasantries though it may have been, struck her as mildly unhinged and anxious. It was the energy of someone trying to sell you a timeshare. She knew from her research that he ran International Sales and Acquisition for Delacroix Lumber, and it saddened her to think that nearly a decade in sales had turned him into a glad-handing, air-kissing showman.

She pictured Sebastian, working away at 6 right now, probably leaning back in a chair, chewing a pencil as he cut tape, Sebastian the king of the crisp edit. Actually, everything about Sebastian was crisp. Crisp and clean and squared away. She could no more picture him in sales than she could picture him tilling the land. Sebastian was attractive to her, she realized in that moment, because there was nothing desperate or needy in his DNA.

Brian Delacroix, she thought. Such a shame life turned you into just another salesman.

Jeremy walked her down the aisle at the Church of the Covenant, and his eyes were wet when he lifted her veil. Jeremy, Maureen, Theo, and Charlotte all came to the reception at the Four Seasons. She only saw them a couple of times, but it was as comfortable with Jeremy and as awkward with Maureen and the children as it had always been.

After their first meeting, when Maureen had seemed genuinely pleased Rachel had found them, she grew more distant with each subsequent encounter, as if she'd only been welcoming of Rachel because she'd never expected her to hang around. She wasn't rude by any means, or cold; she was simply not present in any substantive way. She smiled at Rachel and complimented her looks or clothing choice, asked about her job and Sebastian, and never failed to mention how happy Jeremy was to have her back in his life. But her eyes refused to lock onto Rachel's and her voice carried a tone of strained brightness, like an actress trying so hard to remember her lines she forgot their meaning.

Theo and Charlotte, the almost half siblings she never had, treated Rachel with a mixture of deference and furtive panic. They hurried through all conversations, bobbing their heads at the floor, and never once asked her a question about herself, as if to do so would confer upon her the stature of the factual. Instead, it seemed imperative for them to continue to see her as something out of the mythic mist, inexorably moving toward their front door, but never actually arriving.

When Maureen, Theo, and Charlotte said their good-byes, about an hour into the reception, the relief at standing five steps from the exit door was so total it infused their limbs. Only Jeremy was shocked by the abruptness of their departure (both Maureen and Charlotte feared they were coming down with summer colds, and the drive back was long). Jeremy took Rachel's hands in his and told her not to forget about the luminists or Colum Jasper Whitstone on her honeymoon; there'd be work to do when she returned.

"Of course I'll forget," she said, and he laughed.

The rest of the family drifted out to the valet stand to wait for the car.

Jeremy adjusted his glasses. He fiddled with his shirt where it bunched up around his belly, always self-conscious around her about his excess weight. He shot her his uncertain smile. "I know you would've wanted your real father to walk you down the aisle, but—"

She gripped his shoulders. "No, no. I was honored."

"—but, but . . ." He shot his wavering smile at the wall behind her but then looked at her again. His voice grew deeper, stronger. "It meant the whole wide world to me to be able to do it."

"Me too," she whispered.

She placed her forehead on his shoulder. He placed his palm on the back of her neck. And in that moment, she felt as close to whole as she imagined she ever would.

After the honeymoon, she and Jeremy found it difficult to get together. Maureen wasn't feeling well, nothing serious, just age, he supposed. But she needed him around, not gallivanting off to Boston to while away the summer in the reading rooms of the BPL or the Athenaeum. They managed to squeeze in lunch once in New London, and he looked weary, the flesh on his face too gray and tight to the bone. Maureen, he confided, was not well. She'd survived breast cancer two years ago. She had endured a double mastectomy, but her latest scans had come back inconclusive.

"Meaning?" She reached across the table and covered his hand with her own.

"Meaning," he said, "her cancer could have recurred. They're going to run more tests next week." He adjusted and readjusted his glasses, then looked over them at her with a smile that said he was changing the subject. "How are the newlyweds?"

"Buying a house," she said brightly.

"In the city?"

She shook her head, still coming to terms with it. "About thirty miles south, give or take. It needs updates and renovations so we won't move in right away, but it's a good town, good school system if we have kids. It's not far from where Sebastian grew up. It's also where he keeps his boat."

"He loves that boat."

"Hey, he loves me too."

"I didn't say he didn't." Jeremy shot her a wry smile. "I just said he loves that boat."

Four days later, Jeremy suffered a stroke in his office at the college. He suspected it was a stroke but he wasn't a hundred percent sure, so he drove himself to the nearest hospital. He drove his car halfway up onto a curb and staggered to the entrance. He made it to the ER on his own two feet but promptly suffered a second stroke in the waiting room. The first orderly to reach him was surprised by the strength in Jeremy's soft professor's hands when he grabbed the lapels of the orderly's lab coat.

The last words Jeremy would speak for some time made little sense to the orderly or to anyone else, for that matter. He yanked the orderly's face down to his own and his eyes bulged in their sockets.

"Rachel," he slurred, "is in the mirror."

6

DETACHMENTS

Maureen shared the orderly's claim with Rachel during Jeremy's third night in the hospital.

"'Rachel is in the mirror'?" Rachel repeated.

"That's what Amir said." Maureen nodded. "You look tired. You should get your rest."

Rachel had to be back at work in an hour. She'd be late. Again. "I'm fine."

In the bed, Jeremy stared up at the ceiling, his mouth agape, his eyes wiped clean of awareness.

"The drive must be terrible," Charlotte said.

"It's not bad." Rachel sat on the windowsill because there were only three chairs in the room and they were all occupied by family.

"The doctors said he could be like this for months," Theo said. "Or longer."

Both Charlotte and Maureen began weeping. Theo went to

them. The three of them huddled in their grief. For a few minutes all Rachel could see of them was their heaving backs.

A week later Jeremy was moved to a neuro-treatment facility and gradually recovered some motor ability and the most rudimentary kernels of speech—*yes, no, bathroom*. He looked at his wife as if she were his mother, at his son and daughter as if they were his grandparents, at Rachel as if he were trying to place her. They tried reading to him, scrolled through his favorite paintings on an iPad, played his beloved Schubert. And none of it connected. He wanted food, he wanted comfort, he wanted relief from the pains in his head and body. He engaged the world with the terrified narcissism of an infant.

The family made it clear to Rachel that she could visit as much as she wanted—they were far too polite to say otherwise—but they failed to include her in most conversations and were always visibly relieved when she had to go.

At home, Sebastian grew resentful. She'd barely known the man, he'd argue. She was sentimentalizing an attachment that didn't really exist.

"You need to let it go," he said.

"No," she replied, "you do."

He held up an apologetic hand and closed his eyes for a moment to let her know he had no interest in a big fight. He opened his eyes and his voice was softer and conciliatory. "You know they're considering you for Big Six?"

Big Six was what they called the national network in New York.

"I didn't know that." She tried to keep the excitement from her voice.

"You're being groomed. Now isn't the time to ease up on the throttle."

"I'm not."

"Because they'll test you on something big. Something national-scale."

"Such as?"

"A hurricane, a mass murder, I dunno, a celebrity death."

"How will we soldier on," she wondered aloud, "after Whoopi has passed?"

"It'll be hard," he agreed, "but she would have wanted us to show courage."

She chuckled and he nestled into her on the couch.

Sebastian kissed the side of her neck. "This is us, babe, me and you. Joined at the hip. Where I go, you go. Where you go, I go."

"I know. I do."

"I think it'd be cool to live in Manhattan."

"Which neighborhood?" she asked.

"Upper West Side," he said.

"Harlem," she said at the same time.

They both laughed it off because it felt like what one did when crucial differences in a marriage revealed themselves in strictly theoretical terms.

Jeremy James improved significantly through the fall. He remembered who Rachel was, though not what he'd said to the orderly, and he seemed to tolerate her presence more than rely on it. He had retained most of his knowledge of the luminist movement and of Colum Jasper Whitstone, but it was disjointed, his general sense of chronology off, so that Whitstone's vanishing in 1863 was placed on a timeline just prior to Jeremy's first trip to Normandy in 1977, when he was a graduate fellow. He thought Rachel was younger than Charlotte and couldn't understand some days why Theo could take so much time off from high school to visit him.

"He doesn't apply himself in the first place," he told Rachel. "I don't want him using my sickness to apply himself even less."

He moved back into the house on Gorham Lane in November and was attended to by a hospice nurse. He grew physically stronger. His speech grew clear. But his mind remained elusive to him. "I can't quite *grasp* it," he said once. Both Maureen and Rachel were in the room and he gave them his hesitant smile. "It's like I'm in a beautiful library but none of the books have titles."

In late December of 2009, Rachel twice caught him checking his watch in the first ten minutes of her visit. She couldn't blame him. Without their shared detective stories to discuss—he to find evidence of Colum Jasper Whitstone crossing paths with Claude Monet, she to find her father, and the both of them to understand Elizabeth Childs—they had little to talk about. No shared ambition, no shared history.

She promised to stay in touch.

Leaving his house, she walked down the flagstone path to her car, and she felt the loss of him anew. Felt too the old suspicion that life, as she had thus far experienced it, was a series of detachments. Characters crossed the stage, and some hung around longer than others, but all ultimately exited.

She looked back at his house as she reached her car. *You were my friend*, she thought. *You were my friend.*

Two weeks later, on January 12, a magnitude 7.0 earthquake hit Haiti at five o'clock in the afternoon.

As Sebastian had predicted, Rachel was assigned to cover it for Big Six. She spent her first few days in Port-au-Prince. She and her crew covered the airdrops of food and supplies, which most days ended in riots. They covered the corpses stacked up in the parking lot of General Hospital. They covered the makeshift crematoriums that sprang up on street corners all over the city, the bodies burning like sacrificial appeasements, gray sulfur roiling amid the oily black smoke, the body within already an abstraction, the smoke as unremarkable as all the other smoke—from the buildings that continued to smolder, from the gas lines that had yet to burn out. She reported from tent cities and medical relief posts. Down in what had once been the shopping district, she and her camera operator, Greta

Kilborne, shot footage of the police firing on looters, of a young man with protruding teeth and ribs, lying in ash and rubble with his foot blown off at the ankle, a few cans of the food he'd been stealing lying just out of his reach.

In the days after the earthquake, the only thing that teemed in Port-au-Prince more than disease and hunger was the press corps. Soon she and Greta decided to follow the story to the epicenter of the quake, in the coastal town of Léogâne. Léogâne was only forty kilometers south of Port-au-Prince, but the journey took them two days. They could smell the dead three hours before they arrived. There was no infrastructure left, no aid, no government relief, no police to shoot looters because there were no police.

When Rachel compared it to Hell, Greta disagreed.

"In Hell," she said, "someone's in charge."

Their second night, at a squatters camp cobbled together from sheets—sheets for roofs and sheets for walls—she, Greta, one ex-nun, and one almost-nurse moved four young girls from tent to tent. The six wannabe rapists who moved through the camp looking for the girls were armed with knives and *serpettes*, the machetes with hooked blades common among farmers. Before the earthquake, half these men, Rachel was assured, had held good jobs. Their leader, Josué Dacelus, had come from the countryside just east of the quake zone. Ninth in line for a small sorghum farm in Croix-des-Bouquets, he soured on the world when it sank in that he would never inherit the farm. Josué Dacelus looked like a movie star and moved like a rock star. He usually wore a green-and-white soccer polo over tan cargo pants with the cuffs rolled up. On his left hip he wore a Desert Eagle .45 automatic, and on his right, he wore a *serpette* in a battered leather scabbard. He assured everyone that the *serpette* was for his protection. The .45, he said with a wink, was for theirs. Lot of bad men around, lot of horror, lot of evildoers. He'd bless himself and raise his eyes to the heavens.

Eighty percent of Léogâne had been cratered by the quake. Leveled. Law and order was a memory. There were rumors that British and Icelandic search-and-rescue teams had been sighted in the area. Rachel had confirmed earlier in the day that the Canadians had docked a destroyer in the harbor, and Japanese and Argentinian doctors were trickling into what remained of downtown. But so far, no one had reached them.

That morning and afternoon had been spent helping Ronald Revolus, the man who'd been on his way to becoming a nurse before the quake. They'd transported the three mortally wounded members of the camp to a med tent run by Sri Lankan peacekeepers three miles east. It was there she'd spoken to a translator who'd assured her they'd get help to them as soon as they were capable. Hopefully by the following night, two days at the most.

Rachel and Greta returned to the camp and the four girls had arrived. The itchy, hungry men in Josué's gang noticed them immediately, and their awful intentions spread from the mind of one to the mind of all in the time it took to get the girls water and check them for injury.

Rachel and Greta, who failed as reporters that night by getting involved in a story they should have covered if anyone would have put it on the air, worked with the ex-nun and Ronald Revolus to move the girls all over the camp, rarely staying in one hiding spot for more than an hour.

The light of day wouldn't stop the men—rape was nothing to be ashamed of in their minds or the minds of most of their peers. Death, so the norm in recent days, was only to be lamented for natives and even then, only if they were close family. They'd continued drinking through the night's search and into the dawn, and the hope was they'd have to sleep at some point. In the end, two of the four girls were saved when a UN truck trundled into the camp that morning accompanied by a bulldozer to pick up the corpses in the ruined church at the bottom of the hill.

The other two girls, however, were never seen again. They'd arrived in camp just hours before, both freshly orphaned and freshly homeless. Esther wore a faded red T-shirt and jean shorts. The one in the pale yellow dress was Widelene, but everyone called her Widdy. It made sense that Esther was sullen, nearly mute, and rarely met one's eyes. What made no sense was that Widdy was sunny and had the kind of smile that blew canyons through the chests of its recipients. Rachel knew the girls only for that one night, but she'd spent most of it with Widdy. Widdy and her yellow dress and her boundless heart and her habit of humming songs no one could recognize.

It was remarkable how completely they disappeared. Not just their bodies and the clothes they'd been wearing but their very existence. An hour after sunup, their two companions went mute when asked about them. Within three hours, no one in the camp besides Rachel, Greta, the ex-nun Veronique, and Ronald Revolus claimed to have seen them. By nightfall of the second day, Veronique had changed her story and Ronald was questioning his memory.

At nine that night, Rachel accidentally caught the eye of one of the rapists, Paul, a high school science teacher, who was always unceasingly polite. Paul sat outside his tent and clipped his nails with rusty nail clippers. By that point, rumors had spread that if the girls ever had been in the camp—and they hadn't, that was crazy talk—three of the six men who had roamed the camp drinking heavily that night had gone to sleep by the time the girls who never existed may or may not have disappeared. So if those girls had been raped (and they hadn't been; they couldn't have been; they didn't exist), Paul was involved. But if they'd been murdered (and they hadn't been; they couldn't have been; they didn't exist), Paul had been sleeping by that point. Just a rapist, Teacher Paul, just a rapist. If the fates of the girls haunted him in any way, however, he hid it well. He looked in Rachel's eyes. He used his thumb and index finger to make a gun. He pointed it at her crotch and then slipped the finger into his mouth and sucked on it. He laughed without making a sound.

Then he rose to his feet and crossed to Rachel. He stood in front of her and searched her eyes.

Very politely, almost obsequiously, he asked her to leave the camp.

"You lie," he explained gently, "and it makes people anxious. They do not tell you this because we are a polite people. But your lies make everyone very upset. Tonight"—he held up one finger—"no one will show how upset they are. Tonight"—again with the finger—"no harm will likely come to you and your friend."

She and Greta left the camp twenty minutes later, hitching the only ride out with the Sri Lankans. At their relief center, she pleaded with them and the Canadian peacekeepers who'd worked their way inland from their ship.

No one got her sense of urgency. No one got within a zip code of it. A couple of girls disappeared? Here? There were *thousands* of disappeared at last count and the number would only grow.

"They're not disappeared," one of the Canadians said to her. "They're dead. You know that. I'm sorry but so it is. And no one's got the time or resources to search for the bodies." He looked around the tent at his companions and a few of the Sri Lankans. Everyone nodded in agreement. "None of us anyway."

The next day Rachel and Greta moved on to Jacmel. Three weeks later they were back in Port-au-Prince. By this point, Rachel was starting her day with four black-market Ativans and a shot of rum. Greta, she suspected, had relapsed into the predilection for heroin chipping she'd told Rachel about their first night in Léogâne.

Eventually, they received word that it was time to head home. When Rachel protested, her assignment editor confided via Skype that her stories had grown too strident, too monotonous, and had taken on an unfortunate air of despair.

"Our viewers need hope," the assignment editor said.

"Haitians need water," Rachel said.

"There she goes again," the editor said to someone offscreen.

"Give us a few more weeks."

"Rachel," he said, "Rachel. You look like shit. And I'm not just talking about your hair. You're skeletal. We're pulling the plug."

"No one cares," Rachel said.

"We cared," the assignment editor said sharply. "The United States is sending over a billion and a half fucking dollars to that island. And this network covered the shit out of it. What more do you want?"

And Rachel, in her Ativan-addled brain, thought, *God.*

I want the capital-G God the televangelists claim moves tornadoes out of their paths. The one who cures cancer and arthritis in the faithful, the God professional athletes thank for taking an interest in the outcome of the Super Bowl or the World Cup or a home run hit in the eighty-seventh game of the hundred sixty-two played by the Red Sox this year. She wanted the active God who inserted Himself in human affairs to reach down from Heaven and cleanse the Haitian water supply and cure the Haitian sick and uncrumble the crumbled schools and hospitals and homes.

"The fuck are you babbling about?" The assignment editor peered into the screen at her.

She hadn't realized she'd spoken.

"Get on a plane while we're still paying for it," the assignment editor said, "and get back to your little station."

And that's how she learned any ambitions she'd had to make the national network scene were dead. No New York for her. No career track to Big Six and beyond.

Back to Boston.

Back to Little Six.

Back to Sebastian.

She weaned herself off Ativan. (It took four attempts but she got there.) She cut her drinking back to pre-Haiti levels (or in the neighborhood anyway). But the bosses at Little Six never gave her a lead story again. A new girl, Jenny Gonzalez, had arrived during the time she'd been gone.

Sebastian said, "She's smart, accessible, and she doesn't look at the camera sometimes like she might head-butt it."

The ugly truth was that Sebastian was right. Rachel would have loved to hate Jenny Gonzalez (Lord knows she tried), to believe her looks and sex appeal had gotten her where she was. And while those things certainly didn't hurt, Jenny had an MA in journalism from Columbia, could improv on the fly, always hit her marks fully prepared, and treated everyone from the receptionist to the GM with the same respect.

Jenny Gonzalez didn't replace Rachel because she was younger, prettier, and more well endowed (though she was all those things, goddammit)—she replaced Rachel because she was better at her job, had a more easygoing nature, and people loved talking to her.

There had still been a chance for Rachel, though. If, through clean living, she reversed the aging process she'd accelerated in Haiti, if she removed the chip on her shoulder that had first appeared and then kept growing there, if she kissed ass and played ball and transformed herself back into that slightly sexy, slightly tomboyish, slightly nerdy (they gave her red horn-rimmed glasses in place of her contacts), wholly knowledgeable ace reporter they'd hired away from the *Globe* for big bucks in the first place . . . *then* she still had a home at Little Six.

She tried. She covered a cat that barked like a dog and the annual "breaking of the ice" by the L Street Brownies, a group of mostly naked men who were the first to brave the waters of Boston Harbor every year. She reported on the baby koala born at Franklin Park Zoo and the running of the brides at Filene's Basement.

She and Sebastian rehabbed the house they'd bought south of the city. Their schedules were such that when he was at the house, she was at work, and vice versa. To rarely see each other was such a pleasant arrangement that she would, in hindsight, come to believe it added a year to their marriage.

She received a couple of e-mails from Brian Delacroix. And

even though one of them—You did magnificent work in Haiti. People in this city care now because you cared—carried her through an otherwise shitty day, she reminded herself that Brian Delacroix was a salesman, one with a weird energy that probably stemmed from his soul being at odds with the career decisions he'd made. She couldn't trust there was a *real* Brian left anymore, so her responses to his e-mails were limited and polite: Thanks. Glad you enjoyed it. Take care.

She told herself she was happy. She told herself she was trying to get back to the reporter and wife and person she'd been before. But she couldn't sleep and she couldn't stop watching the feeds from Haiti, following the country as it scrabbled for rebirth but mostly just continued to die. Cholera broke out along the Artibonite River. This was followed by rumors that UN soldiers were the source of it. She begged Klay Bohn, her assignment editor, to let her go back for a week. Even at her own expense. He didn't even dignify the request with a response, just told her she was expected in the parking lot behind the station, where she'd hop a van to cover a six-year-old in Lawrence who claimed God had given him the numbers his mother used to win the lottery.

When cameras secretly filmed UN soldiers removing a leaking pipe from the ground along the banks of the Artibonite and the footage went viral, Rachel was interviewing a hundred-year-old Red Sox fan attending his first game at Fenway.

As the cholera continued to spread, Rachel covered back-to-back house fires, a hot-dog-eating contest, a weekend of gang-related shootings in Dorchester, two elderly sisters who created end tables out of bottle caps, a BC party that got out of control in Cleveland Circle, and a former Wall Street broker who turned his back on high finance to do outreach work with the homeless on the North Shore.

The stories weren't all tripe, they weren't all inconsequential. Rachel had almost convinced herself that she occasionally per-

formed a valid public service when Hurricane Tomas hit Haiti.
Only a few people died, but the shelters were wiped out, sewers
and septic tanks overflowed, and the cholera outbreak metastasized
across the island.

She'd been up all night, following the available footage and reading the reports as they came across the wires, when Brian Delacroix's name popped up in her in-box. She opened his e-mail and all
it said was:

Why aren't you in Haiti? We need you there.

It was as if someone had placed a warm hand to the side of her
neck and tilted her face to his shoulder and let her close her eyes.
Maybe, since that off-kilter encounter outside the Athenaeum,
she'd been judging Brian too harshly. Maybe she'd just caught him
on a bad day, as he was trying to close a deal with Jack Ahern, an
antiquities dealer from Geneva. Rachel had no idea where lumber
and antiquities could cross paths, but she didn't really understand
finance—maybe Jack Ahern was an investor of some kind. In either case, so Brian had acted a little odd, a little nervous. What was
wrong with being a little odd and a little nervous?

Why aren't you in Haiti? We need you there.

He understood. Somehow from a remove of years and through
the scantest of cyber-contact, he grasped that it was crucial she get
back there.

And as if she'd ordered it up like a pizza, half an hour later Sebastian came home and said, "They're sending you back."

"Back where?"

He pulled a plastic bottle of water from the fridge and placed it to
the side of his head. He closed his eyes. "You have the contacts, you
know the customs, I guess."

"Haiti. They're sending me back to Haiti?"

He opened his eyes as he continued to massage his temple with the bottle. "Haiti, yeah." Though he'd never spoken the words, Rachel knew he blamed Haiti for her career decline. And he blamed her career decline for his own career stagnation. So when he said "Haiti," it sounded like an obscenity.

"When?" Her blood was tingling. She'd been up all night but now she was wide awake.

"Klay said no later than tomorrow. Do I have to remind you that you can't fuck this up?"

She felt her face drop. "That's your pep talk?"

"It is what it is," he said wearily.

She could think of a lot of things to say, but they all would have led to a fight and she didn't want to fight right now. So she tried, "I'll miss you."

She couldn't wait to get on the plane.

"Miss you too," he said as he stared into the refrigerator.

7

HAVE YOU SEEN ME?

Back in Haiti, the same heat and crumpled buildings and exhausted despair. The same bewildered looks on most of the faces. Where there was no bewilderment, there was rage. Where there wasn't rage, there was hunger and fear. But mostly bewilderment: After all this suffering, the faces seemed to ask, are we to accept that suffering is the point?

On her way to do her first story, meeting the crew out in front of Choscal Hospital in the dense slum of Cité Soleil, Rachel walked streets so poor a newcomer would have been unable to discern the difference in the neighborhood before the quake and after it. Photos were pasted to broken lamp poles and impotent power-line poles and the low walls that lined the streets—pictures, in some cases, of the dead, but primarily of the missing. Under most of the photos a question or plea was written:

Èske ou te wè m?

Have you seen me?

She hadn't. Or maybe she had. Maybe the face of the middle-aged man she passed as she turned a corner was one of the bodies she'd seen in the collapsed church or the hospital parking lot. In either case, he was gone. And not coming back, she was fairly sure.

Rachel crested a small hill and the breadth of the ghetto spread out before her, a spillage of steel and cinder-block shacks sun-blasted to monochrome. A boy rode past her on a muddy bicycle. The boy looked to be about eleven, twelve at most, and had an automatic rifle strapped to his back. As he looked over his shoulder at her, Rachel reminded herself that this was gang territory. Mini war gods ran the show and fought for turf from one end to the other. Food didn't flow into here, but guns sure as shit did. She shouldn't have been walking around there alone. She shouldn't have been walking around there without a tank and air support.

But she didn't feel fear. She just felt numb. She felt overwhelmed with numbness.

At least she thought that's what it was.

Have you seen me?

No, I haven't. No one has. No one did. No one will. Even if you'd lived a full life. Didn't matter—you vanished the moment you were born.

That was the mood she carried into the little plaza in front of the hospital. The sole good news about what followed was that it only went live to the local market, in this case, Boston. Big Six was going to decide later if they'd use it. Little Six, though, believed a live feed would stoke a sense of urgency in a story everyone suspected was losing viewer interest because of tragedy fatigue.

So she went live standing in front of Choscal Hospital. The sun slipped out from a black brick of clouds directly above her head and set itself to sear. Grant, the anchor at Little Six, somehow managed to sound twice as stupid coming through an international feed.

Rachel rattled off the statistics—thirty-two confirmed chol-era cases lay bedridden in the hospital behind her; post-hurricane flooding was contributing to the spread on a national scale and complicating relief efforts; the situation was expected to grow more dire by the day. Behind the camera crew, Cité Soleil spread out like a sacrifice to the sun god, and Rachel could feel something sever within her. It was a spiritual piece and untouched by this world up until this moment, a sliver of soul perhaps, and the heat and loss hunted it down as soon as it detached and ate it. In its place, a sparrow flapped its wings in the center of her chest. No warning, no buildup. It suddenly hovered in the center of her chest, flapping as hard as it could.

"And excuse me, Rachel," Grant was saying in her ear, "but Rachel . . ."

Why did he keep saying her name?

"Yes, Grant?"

"Rachel?"

She consciously avoided gritting her teeth. "Yes?"

"Do you have any estimates on how many people have contracted this deadly disease? How many people are sick?"

The question struck her as absurd.

How many people are sick?

"We're all sick."

"I'm sorry?" Grant said.

"We're all sick," Rachel said. Was it her imagination, or did the words come out a tad slurry?

"Rachel, are you saying that you and other members of our Channel Six crew have contracted cholera?"

"What? No."

Danny Marotta removed his eye from the lens and gave her a "You okay?" look. Widdy walked behind him with a graceful stride that didn't fit with her youth or the blood on her dress, or the second smile carved into her throat.

"Rachel," Grant was saying. "Rachel? I'm afraid I don't understand."

And Rachel, sweating profusely by this point, shaking so hard the mic jumped in her hand, replied, "I said we're all sick. We're all, we're all, what, I mean, we're just sick. You know?" The words sluiced out of her like blood from a puncture wound. "We're lost and sick and we all pretend otherwise, but then we all go away. We all just fucking go away."

By the time the sun went down footage of Rachel repeating "We're all sick" to a baffled anchorman as her hands and shoulders shook and her eyelids batted at the sweat that drizzled from her forehead had gone viral.

It was the consensus of upper management during a postmortem meeting that while it was commendable that the feed was cut four seconds before Rachel said "fucking," it should have been cut ten seconds earlier. As soon as it became clear that Rachel was unhinged—and most agreed that moment occurred the very first time she said "We're all sick"—they should have cut to commercial.

Rachel was fired over cell phone, as she walked across the tarmac at Toussaint Louverture Airport toward the plane home.

Her first night back, she went to a bar in Marshfield, a few blocks away from their house. Sebastian was working through the night and had made it clear he had no desire to see her right now. He said he'd stay on his boat until he could "process what she'd done to them."

She couldn't blame him really. It would be a few weeks before the reality of what had become of her career would sink in, but when she caught her reflection in the bar mirror as she drained her vodka, she was startled by how frightened she looked. She didn't feel frightened, she felt numb. Yet she stared over the scotch and whiskey bottles to the right of the cash register at a woman who looked a bit like her mother, a bit like herself, and every bit terrified.

The bartender clearly hadn't seen the video of her meltdown. He

treated her the way bored bartenders the world over treated customers they couldn't give a shit about. It was a slow night, so he wasn't
making his nut in tips no matter how hard he shucked and smiled.
So he did neither. He read a newspaper at the other end of the bar
and texted with someone on his phone. She checked her own texts
but she didn't have any—everyone she knew was ducking and hiding
until the gods decided how fiercely they wanted to continue their assault or whether they could relent and spit her back out. She did have
one e-mail, though, and even before she tapped the mail icon, she
knew who it was from and smiled when she saw Brian Delacroix's
name.

> Rachel,
>
> You didn't deserve to be punished for being human while
> surrounded by inhumanity. You didn't deserve to be fired or
> condemned. You deserved a fucking medal. Just one man's
> opinion. Hang in there.
>
> BD

Who are you? she thought. *You strange man with (mostly) perfect
timing? One of these days, Brian Delacroix, I would like to . . .*
What?
*I would like to give you a chance to explain that weird encounter outside
the Athenaeum. Because I can't connect that guy with the guy who just sent
me this note.*
The bartender brought her another vodka, and she decided she'd
head back to her apartment, maybe compose an e-mail to Brian
Delacroix that articulated some of the thoughts that had just passed
through her head. She handed the bartender her credit card and told
him he could cash her out. As he rang up the sale, she felt beset by
déjà vu stronger than any she could remember. No, it wasn't simply
déjà vu: She'd experienced this precise moment before, she was sure

of it. She caught the bartender's eyes in the mirror, and he gave her a curious look in return as if unsure why she stared so intently at him.

I don't know you, she thought. *But I know this moment. I've lived it.*

And then she realized she hadn't. Her mother had. It was a restaging of the photograph of her mother in roughly the same place at a similarly shaped bar, in similar lighting, thirty-one years before. Like her mother, she stared absently at the bottles. Like the bartender in the picture, the bartender tonight had his back to her as he rang up the sale. His eyes hung in the mirror. Her eyes hung in the mirror.

Look for yourself in his eyes, her mother had said.

Rachel is in the mirror, Jeremy had said.

The bartender brought her the check. She added a tip and signed it.

She left her drink unfinished on the bar and hurried back to the house. She went to her bedroom and opened the shoebox full of photos. The photographs from the bar in East Baltimore were on the top of the pile where she and Jeremy had left them two summers ago. Rachel followed her mother's gaze over the whiskey bottles to the mirror behind them, to what Elizabeth had really been looking at, to what had put the charged look, the *eroticized* look, on her face.

The bartender's face loomed above the cash register, his eyes locked on Elizabeth's. The green in his eyes was so pale it was almost gray.

Rachel took the photograph to her bathroom mirror. She held it up beside her head. His eyes were her eyes—same color, same shape.

"Well, shit," she said. "Hi, Dad."

8

GRANITE

She'd assumed the bar was long gone, but when she Googled Milo's East Baltimore, it popped right up on her screen, replete with pictures. It had changed some—three large windows had been hung in the brick wall facing the street, the lighting was softer, the cash register was computerized, and the stools now had backs and ornate arms—but the same mirror hung behind the bar and the bottles were placed in the same hierarchy. The Baltimore Colts pennant on the wall had been replaced with one for the Baltimore Ravens.

She called and asked for the owner.

When he got on the phone, he said, "This is Ronnie."

She explained that she was a reporter for Channel 6. She didn't say which Channel 6 and she didn't say she was working on any particular story. Usually, identifying herself as a reporter immediately opened a door or immediately slammed it shut; either scenario tended to avoid time wasted on further explanations.

"Ronnie, I'm trying to track down a bartender who worked at Milo's in 1979. And I wondered if you'd have employment records from that era you'd be willing to share."

"Bartender back in seventy-nine?" he said. "Well, that was probably Lee, but let me check with my father."

"Lee?" she said, but he'd put the phone down. For a few minutes she heard very little, maybe a conversation being held somewhere far away from the receiver, hard to tell, but then she heard footsteps approach the phone and the scrape of it being lifted off the bar.

"This is Milo." A scratchy voice, followed by the huff of breath being expelled through the nostrils.

"*The* Milo?"

"Yeah, yeah. What's this you need?"

"I was looking to get in touch with a man who tended bar there almost thirty-two years ago. Your son mentioned a Lee?"

"He worked for us back then."

"And you remember him?"

"Well, yeah, he worked here at least twenty-five years. Left about eight years ago."

"And he was the only bartender who worked there back then?"

"No, but he was the main one. I worked the bar some, my late wife, and old Harold, who was going senile right around then. That clear it up for you?"

"Do you know where I could find Lee?"

"Why don't you tell me why you're asking, Miss . . . ?"

"Childs."

"Miss Childs. Why don't you tell me why you're asking about Lee?"

She couldn't think of a single reason to lie, so she told him. "It's possible he knew my mother."

"Lee knew a lot of women."

She took the plunge. "It's possible he was my father."

There was nothing but the sound of him breathing through his nostrils for so long she almost spoke again out of sheer anxiousness.

"How old are you?" he said eventually.

"Thirty-one."

"Well," Milo said slowly, "he was a good-looking son of a bitch back then. Dated a few—ten—women, I seem to remember. Even a penny can shine, I guess, when it's newly minted." More breathing.

She thought he was going to say more but after a while realized he wouldn't be doing so. "I'd like to reach out to him. If you'd feel okay helping me, that would—"

"He's dead."

Two small hands grasped the sides of her heart and pushed inward. Ice water surged up the back of her neck and flooded her skull.

"He's dead?" It came out louder than she'd intended.

"'Bout six years now, yeah. He left us, went to work for another bar in Elkton. A couple years after that, he died."

"How?"

"Heart attack."

"He would've been young."

"Fifty-three?" Milo said. "Maybe fifty-four. Yeah, he was young."

"What was his full name?"

"Well, miss, I don't know you. I don't know if you could lodge some paternity thing against the people he left behind. I don't know enough about such things. But again, I don't know you, that's the problem."

"Would it help if you did know me?"

"Absolutely."

She took the train to Baltimore the next morning from Back Bay station. She innocently met the eyes of a college-age girl she passed on the platform, and the girl's eyes bulged with sudden recognition. Rachel walked to the end of the platform with her head down. She took a spot near an older gentleman in a gray suit. He flashed her a sad smile and went back to reading *Bloomberg Markets*. She couldn't tell if the sadness in his smile stemmed from pity for her or if he just possessed a sad smile.

She got on the train without further incident and found a seat near the rear of a half-empty car. With every mile the train covered, she felt she escaped her newfound identity as a public basket case just a bit more; by the time she passed through Rhode Island, she felt nearly relaxed. She wondered if some of her ease stemmed from the knowledge that she was returning, if not home, at least to her genesis. She also took strange comfort that she was following in reverse part of the journey her mother and Jeremy James had taken to western Massachusetts in the spring of 1979. Now it was mid-November, more than three decades later. The cities and towns she passed were caught between late fall and early winter. Some municipal parking lots had already shored up road salt and sand. Most trees were bare, and the sky was sunless, as bare as the trees.

"This is him here." Milo placed a framed photograph on the bar in front of her, his stubby index finger positioned beside the face of a lean man of advancing hairline and advancing age. He had a high forehead, sunken cheeks, and her eyes.

Milo was about eighty and breathed with the aid of a liquid-oxygen canister perched in a hip pack nestled at the small of his back. The clear silicone tubing ran up his back and then hooked over his ears before draping down his cheekbones to where the nasal cannulas entered his nostrils. He'd been living with emphysema since his early seventies, he told Rachel. Lately the hypoxia had been progressing but not so fast it kept him from sneaking eight or ten cigarettes a day.

"Good genes," Milo said as he placed an unframed photo down in front of her. "I got 'em. Lee didn't."

The unframed shot was a bit more candid than the first, which was a staff photo in which everyone was posing. This unframed photograph was from decades back. Lee had a full head of lanky dark brown hair, and his eyes were set farther up in his face. He was smiling at something a customer had said. While several of the other patrons laughed with their heads thrown back, Lee's was a small smile, a withholding one; it wasn't an invitation, it was a moat. He looked to be no more than twenty-seven or twenty-eight, and she could immediately see what her mother had been drawn to. That small smile was all coiled vitality and inflamed reticence. It promised too much and too little at the same time. Lee looked like the worst boyfriend and greatest fuck of all time.

She could see why her mother had described him as smelling like "lightning." And she suspected that if she herself had walked into this bar in 1979 and this man had been standing behind it, she would have stayed for more than one drink. He fit the look of the profligate poet, the drug-addled painter-genius, the musician who'd die in a car crash the day after he signed his big record contract.

The tour of Lee's life she received from Milo in photos, however, was of a journey confined mostly to the very bar where she now sat. She could feel his world and his options and his opportunities for casual sex with vibrant women decrease with every photo. Soon the world beyond the bar wasn't something to dream of, it was something to hide from. The women who once pursued him turned into women who had to be pursued. They then became women who had to be lubricated with the proper amounts of humor and alcohol. Finally, one day, they'd be repulsed or amused to discover he thought of them sexually.

But as Lee's sexual voltage decreased, year by year, his smiles grew wider. By the time he'd reached her middle-school years and still wore the black vest over a white shirt that Milo required of his bartenders, his skin had mottled, his face had sunk, and his smile had yellowed and picked up two gaps in the back rows. But with every photo, he looked looser, less burdened by the weight of whatever had been behind that fuck-you smile, that fuck-you sexual charisma. The soul seemed to flower as the body declined.

Milo next produced a stack of photographs from the annual Independence Day friends-'n'-family softball game and picnic. There were two women who appeared and reappeared in the photos alongside Lee. One woman was thin and brunette and possessed a face tight with strain and anxiety; the other was blowsy and blond and usually had a drink in one hand and a cigarette in the other.

"That was Ellen," Milo said of the dark-haired woman. "She was angry. No one ever knew why. Kinda woman could suck the life out of a birthday party, a wedding, a Thanksgiving—and I seen her kill all three. She left Lee around eighty-six, I want to say. Eighty-seven? No later. Other one was his second wife. That's Maddy. Last I heard she was still alive. Living in Elkton. She and Lee had a few good years and then sort of drifted apart."

"Did he have any kids?" Rachel asked.

"Not with these women." Milo watched her carefully across the bar for a moment as he reached behind his back to adjust something on his oxygen dispenser. "You think you're his, huh?"

"I'm pretty sure of it," Rachel said.

"You got his eyes," Milo said, "that's for sure. Pretend I said something funny."

"What?"

"Laugh," he said.

"Ha ha," she said.

"No, for real."

She looked around the bar. It was empty. She chuckled out a version of her laugh. She was surprised how authentic it sounded.

"That's his laugh," Milo said.

"Then it's settled," she said.

He smiled. "When I was young, people said I looked like Warren Oates. You know who that is?"

She shook her head.

"Movie actor. Was in a lot of westerns. Was in *The Wild Bunch*."
She gave him an embarrassed shrug.

"Anyway, I did look like Warren Oates. Now people say I look like Wilford Brimley. Know who *that* is?"

She nodded. "The Quaker Oats guy."

He said, "That's him."

"You *do* look like him."

"I do." He held up a finger. "And yet, best of my knowledge, I'm not related to him. Or to Warren Oates." He held his thumb and index a hairbreadth apart. "Not even a little bit."

She acknowledged his point with a slight tip of her head. Arrayed across the bar top was a man's life in photographs, just as her life had been arrayed before her and Jeremy James two summers back. A collage, yet again, that said everything and said nothing. A person could be photographed every day of his life, she suspected, and still hide the truth of himself—the essence—from all who came along in pursuit of it. Her mother had stood in front of her every day for twenty years and she knew her only as much as Elizabeth had deemed fit to show. And now here was her father, staring back out at her from 4 × 6s and 5 × 7s and 8 × 10s, in focus, out of focus, oversaturated, and underlit. But in all cases, he was ultimately unknowable. She could see his face, but not behind it.

"He had a couple of stepkids," Milo told her. "Ellen had a son when he met her, Maddy had a daughter. Don't know that he formally adopted either of them. Never got a feeling one way or the other whether he liked them or they liked him back or if it went the other way. Or somewhere in between." He shrugged, looked down at the collage. "He knew a lot about whiskey, had a couple motorcycles over the years he was fond of, had a dog for a while that got cancer so he never got another."

"And he worked here for twenty-five years?"

"'Bout that."

"Did he have any ambitions beyond being a bartender?"

Milo looked off for a bit, trying to remember. "When he was really into motorcycles, he talked with another guy for a while about opening a garage together where they'd fix 'em, maybe customize 'em. When the dog died, he read up a lot on veterinary schools. But nothing ever came of any of it." He shrugged. "If he had any other dreams, he kept 'em tucked on a high shelf."

"Why did he stop working here?"

"Didn't like taking orders from Ronnie, probably. Hard to take orders from a man you watched grow up. Got tired of the commute maybe too. He lived in Elkton. Traffic between here and there gets worse every year."

He looked at her in such a way that she knew he was sizing her up, making a decision. "You wear nice clothes, look like you got a good life."

She nodded.

"He didn't have no money. You know that? What little he had the exes took."

Again she nodded.

"Grayson."

The small hands caressed her heart this time, coldly, but lighter than a whisper.

"Leeland David Grayson," Milo said. "That was the man's full name."

She met his second wife, Maddy, at a small park in Elkton, Maryland, a town that felt tossed aside, its hills dotted with the shells of factories and foundries no one living could probably remember in their heyday.

Maddy Grayson was teetering between overweight and corpulent, the rowdy smile she'd worn in most of the pictures replaced with one that seemed to drain a second after it appeared.

"It was Steph, my daughter, who found him. He was on his knees in front of the couch, but his right elbow was still on the couch. Like he'd got up for a drink or a piss and that's when it took him. He'd been there at least a day, maybe two. Steph had gone around to borrow some money because, well, Lee could be a soft touch on his drinking days. But outside of that, he wanted to be left alone. What he liked to do on his days off was drink decent whiskey, smoke cigarettes, and watch old TV shows. Never new ones. He liked stuff from the seventies and the eighties—*Mannix* and *The A-Team. Miami Vice.*" She turned on the bench slightly, excited. "Oh, he loved *Miami Vice.* But the early ones, you know? He always said the show went to hell when Crockett married the singer. Said it got hard to believe after that." She fumbled in her purse and came back with a cigarette. She lit it and exhaled and followed the smoke with her gaze. "He liked those shows because things made sense back then, you know? World made sense. Those were good days, sensible days." She looked around the empty park. "Not like now."

Rachel was hard pressed to imagine two decades in her lifetime that made less sense to her than the seventies and the eighties or two that seemed less stable or compassionate in general. But she didn't think there was much point in mentioning that to Maddy Grayson.

"Did he ever want anything?" she asked.

"How do you mean?" Maddy coughed into her fist.

"Like to become, I dunno, something?" Rachel regretted her choice of words as soon as they left her mouth.

"Mean like a doctor?" Maddy's eyes grew hard fast. She looked angry and confused and angry about the confusion.

"Well, I mean"—Rachel stuttered and tried for a friendly smile—"something besides a bartender."

"What's wrong with being a bartender?" Maddy tossed her cigarette to the pavement in front of her and turned her knees toward Rachel. She matched Rachel's desperate smile with an iron one. "No, I'm asking. For more'n twenty years, people went to Milo's because they knew Lee was behind the bar. They could tell him anything and he wouldn't judge. They could come to him when their marriages went tits-up, they lost their jobs, their kids turned into assholes or druggies, fucking world went to shit all around them. But they could sit in front of Lee and he'd serve them a drink and hear them when they talked."

Rachel said, "Sounds like an amazing guy."

Maddy pursed her lips and reared back, as if she'd seen a cockroach climb out of her pasta bowl. "He wasn't an *amazing guy*. He was an asshole a lot of days. I couldn't live with him in the end. But he was a great bartender and a lot of people were better off for knowing him."

"I didn't mean to suggest otherwise."

"But you did."

"I'm sorry."

Maddy pushed a breath through her lips that managed to be both derisive and melancholy at the same time. "The only people who ask questions like 'Did he want to be something besides a bartender?' are people who can become whatever they want. The rest of us are just Americans."

The rest of us are just Americans.

Rachel recognized the grubby self-aggrandizement of the line as well as the faux modesty. She could already hear herself quoting it at cocktail parties, could hear too the laughs it would garner. But even as she heard the laughs, they shamed her. She was guilty, after all, of success, a success that stemmed from birthright and privilege. She took hope for granted, saw opportunity as her due, and had never really had to worry about vanishing into a sea of unseen faces and unseen voices.

But that was the country her father had inhabited. The country of the unseen and the unheard. And, upon their deaths, the unremembered.

"I'm sorry if I offended you," she said to Maddy.

Maddy waved it off with a freshly lit cigarette. "Honey, your shit don't mean shit to me." She gave Rachel's knee a friendly squeeze. "If Lee was your flesh and blood, then good. I hope it brings you peace. Woulda been nice for you, I guess, if you'd known him." She tapped the ash of her cigarette. "But we don't get what we want, just what we can handle."

She visited his grave. It was marked by a common granite headstone, black sprinkled with specks of white. She'd seen the same granite in the kitchen countertops of at least two colleagues. They'd used a lot less granite on Lee Grayson, though. It was a small stone, no more than a foot and a half tall and twenty inches wide. Maddy had told her Lee had purchased it on layaway around the time his own folks passed away, paid it off about three years before he died.

LEELAND D. GRAYSON
NOVEMBER 20, 1950
DECEMBER 9, 2004

There had to be more to it. There had to be.

But if there was, she couldn't find it.

She'd cobbled together the thumbnail of a biography from what Milo had said about him, what Maddy had said about him, and stray bits both had recalled others had said about him.

Leeland David Grayson had been born and raised in Elkton, Maryland. He'd passed through a kindergarten, a grade school, and a high school. He'd worked for a paving company, a trucking company, a shoe store, and as a driver for a florist before finding work at Milo's in East Baltimore. He'd spread his seed at least once (or so it seemed), married, divorced, remarried, and divorced again. Owned a house that he'd lost in Divorce #1. Rented a smaller place from then on. Over the course of his life, he'd owned nine cars, three motorcycles, and one dog. Died in the same town where he was born. Fifty-four years on this earth and, to the best of anyone's recollection, he'd expected little of others and gave about the same in return. Wasn't an angry man, though most got the sense it would be foolish to push him. Wasn't a happy man, though he liked a good joke when he heard it.

Someday all who had reason to remember him would pass from the earth. Judging by what Rachel had seen of the ways people looked after their health in Lee's circle of friends and acquaintances, that someday would come sooner rather than later. Then the only person who would know his name would be whoever mowed the grass near his headstone.

He didn't live his life, her mother would have said, it lived him.

And in that moment, Rachel realized why her mother had probably never told Lee about her or her about Lee. Elizabeth had seen how his life would play out. She had known his wants were small, his imagination limited, his ambitions nebulous. Elizabeth Childs, who'd grown up in a small town and chosen to live in a small town, had despised small-town thinking.

Her mother had never told Rachel who her father was because to admit she'd given her body to him in the first place would have been to admit that some part of her had never wanted to escape where she'd come from.

So instead, Rachel thought, you robbed us of each other.

Rachel sat at his grave for the better part of an hour. She waited to hear his voice in the wind or the trees.

And it came, it actually came. But it wasn't pretty.

You want someone to tell you why.

Yes.

Why there's pain and loss. Why earthquakes and hunger.

But mostly:

Why no one gives a shit about you, Rachel.

"Stop," she was pretty sure she said aloud.

You know what the answer is?

"Just stop."

Because.

"Because what?" she said to the quiet of the cemetery.

Because nothing. Just because.

She lowered her head and didn't weep. Didn't make a sound. But for a very long time, she couldn't stop shaking.

You've come a long way to get this answer.

And here it is. At long last. Right in front of your face.

She raised her head. Opened her eyes. Stared at it. A foot and a half tall, twenty inches wide.

It's granite and dirt.

And there's no more to it.

She didn't leave the cemetery until the sun fell halfway down its black trees. It was close to four in the afternoon. She'd arrived at ten in the morning.

She never heard his voice again. Not once.

On the train back north, she looked out the window, but it was night and all she could see of the cities and towns was the blur of lights and the dark in between.

Most of the time, she couldn't see anything at all out there. Just her own reflection. Just Rachel. Still alone.

Still on the wrong side of the mirror.

II / BRIAN
2011–2014

9

THE SPARROW

Rachel and Brian Delacroix crossed paths again six months after their last e-mail contact, in the spring, at a bar in the South End.

He ended up there because it was a few blocks from his apartment and that night, the first of the year to hint of summer, the streets smelled damp and hopeful. She went to the bar because she'd gotten divorced that afternoon and needed to feel brave. She worried her fear of people was metastasizing and she wanted to get on top of it, to prove to herself she was in command of her own neuroses. It was May, and she'd barely left the house since early winter.

She'd go out for groceries but only when the supermarket was at its emptiest. Seven o'clock on a Tuesday morning was ideal, the pallets of shrink-wrapped stock still waiting in the middle of the aisles, the dairy guys talking smack to the deli guys, the cashiers putting their purses away and yawning into cardboard cups of Dunkin's, bitching about the commute, the weather, their impossible kids, their impossible husbands.

When she needed her hair cut, she always scheduled the last appointment of the day. Same for the rare manicure or pedicure. Most other wants could be satisfied online. Soon, what started as a choice—staying out of the public eye to avoid scrutiny or its bedfellow, judgment—grew into a habit that bordered on addiction. Before Sebastian officially left her, he'd been sleeping in the guest room for months; prior to that, he'd slept on his boat in the South River, a tidal flat that emptied into Massachusetts Bay. It was fitting—Sebastian had probably never loved her, probably never loved any human being, but, man, he loved that boat. Once he was gone, though, her primary motivation for leaving the house—to escape him and all his toxic disregard—was neutralized.

But spring hit, and she could hear voices, unhurried and pleasant, return to the street along with the shouts of children, the clack of stroller wheels along the sidewalk, the squeak and snap of screen doors. The house she'd purchased with Sebastian was thirty miles south of Boston in Marshfield. It was a seaside town, though their house sat a full mile inland, which was fine because Rachel wasn't a fan of the ocean. Sebastian, of course, loved the sea, had even taught her to scuba dive back in the early days of their courtship. When she finally admitted to him that she hated being submerged in liquid as potential predators watched her from the depths, instead of being flattered she'd temporarily conquered her fear to make him happy, he accused her of pretending to love the things he loved in order to "trap" him. She'd retorted that one only trapped things one wanted to eat and she'd lost her appetite for him a long time ago. It was a nasty thing to say, but when a relationship collapsed with the speed and severity of hers and Sebastian's, nasty became the norm. Once the divorce was final, they would put the house on the market and split any profit to be had, and she'd need to find another place.

Which was fine. She missed the city, had never taken to having to drive everywhere. And if her notoriety was difficult to escape in the city, it was impossible in a small town, where gazes came steeped in gradations of provincialism. Just a couple of weeks back, she'd been caught out in the open while pumping gas; she hadn't realized until she pulled in with a bone-dry tank that the station was self-serve only. Three high school girls, reality-TV-ready in their push-up bras, yoga pants, satiny blowouts, and diamond-cut cheekbones, exited the Food Mart on their way to a boy in a skintight thermal sweatshirt and distressed jeans, who pumped gas into a pristine Lexus SUV. As soon as they noticed Rachel, the trio started whispering and shoving each other. When she looked over, one of them reddened and dropped her gaze but the other two doubled down. The dark-haired one with the peach highlights mimed someone guzzling from a bottle and her honey-blond partner-in-bitch screwed up her features into a pantomime of helpless weeping, then wrung her hands in the air as if freeing them of seaweed.

The third one said, "Guys, stop," but it came out half lament, half giggle, and then the laughter broke from all their pretty-ugly mouths like Friday-night Kahlúa vomit.

Rachel hadn't left the house since. She almost ran out of food. She did run out of wine. Then vodka. She ran out of sites to surf and shows to watch. Then Sebastian called to remind her the divorce hearing was scheduled for that Tuesday, May 17, at three-thirty.

She made herself presentable and drove into the city. She realized only after she'd gotten on Route 3 heading north that it had been six months since she'd driven on a highway. The other cars raced and revved and swarmed. Their bodies gleamed like knives in the harsh sunlight. They engulfed her, stabbing at the air, surging and stabbing and braking, red taillights flashing like furious eyes. *Great*, Rachel thought as the anxiety found her throat and her skin and the roots of her hair, *now I'm afraid of driving*.

She managed to make it into the city, and it felt like she was getting away with something because she shouldn't have been on the road, not feeling this vulnerable, this hysterical. But she made it. And no one was the wiser. She left the garage and walked across the street and appeared at the appointed time at Suffolk Probate and Family Court on New Chardon Street.

The proceedings were a lot like the marriage and a lot like Sebastian—perfunctory and bloodless. After it was over and their union was, as far as the Commonwealth was concerned, legally dissolved, she turned to share a look with her newly minted ex-husband, a look if not of two soldiers who'd found a modicum of victory in walking off the battlefield with their limbs intact at least one of common decency. But Sebastian wasn't across the aisle any longer. He was already halfway out of the courtroom, his back to her, head up, strides long and purposeful. And once he was through the doors, the rest of the people in the courtroom were looking at her with pity or revulsion.

That's who I've become, she thought, *a creature below contempt*.

Her car was parked in the garage across the street, and from there it was two right turns and a merge onto 93 South to head home. But she thought of all those cars merging and speeding, tapping their brakes and switching lanes with violent jerks of the wheel, and she turned west into the city instead and drove over Beacon Hill, through Back Bay and farther on until she reached the South End. She felt okay during the drive. Only once, when she thought a Nissan was going to pass her on the right as she approached an intersection, did her palms sweat. After a few minutes of driving around, she found the rarest of all things for this neighborhood, a parking spot, and pulled into it. She sat there and reminded herself to breathe. She waved on two cars that mistook her for someone who was about to depart, not someone who'd just arrived.

"Turn off your fucking engine, then," the driver of the second car yelled, and left a burnt-rubber vapor in his wake that smelled like a smoker's burp.

She left her car and wandered the neighborhood, not entirely aimless but close, remembering that somewhere around here was a bar where she'd once spent a happy night. That was when she was still in print journalism with the *Globe*. Rumors had circulated that the series she'd written on the Mary Ellen McCormack housing project might be nominated for a Pulitzer. It wasn't (though she did win the Horace Greeley Award and the PEN/Winship for excellence in investigative journalism), but she didn't care in the end; she knew she'd done good work, and back then, that was enough. It was an old-man bar with a red door called Kenneally's Tap, tucked on one of the last ungentrified blocks in the neighborhood, if she remembered correctly, the name itself a throwback to a time before all Irish bars had to sound vaguely literary, like St. James's Gate, Elysian Fields, the Isle of Statues.

She eventually found the red door on a block she hadn't initially recognized because its Toyotas and Volvos had been replaced with Benzes and Range Rover Sports, and the functional bars on the windows had been replaced by filigreed ones with more substantial aesthetic appeal. Kenneally's was still there, but its menu was posted out front now, and they'd gotten rid of the mozzarella sticks and the deep-fried chicken poppers and replaced them with pork cheeks and braised kale.

She walked straight to a free chair in the far corner near the waitstaff station, and when the bartender found her, she ordered a vodka-rocks and asked if he had the day's paper lying around. She wore a gray hoodie over a white V-neck T-shirt and dark blue jeans. The flats on her feet were black, scuffed, and as forgettable as the rest of her ensemble. It didn't matter. For all the talk of progress, of equal footing, of a post-sexist generation, a woman still couldn't sit alone at a bar and have a drink without drawing stares. She kept her head down and read the *Globe* and sipped her vodka and tried to keep the addled sparrow in her chest from flapping its wings.

The bar wasn't more than a quarter full, which was good, but the clientele was a lot younger than she'd counted on, which wasn't. The old-timers she'd expected to find had been reduced to a quartet of geezers who sat at a scarred table near the back room and slipped out for frequent smoke breaks. It had been naïve to think that here, in the trendiest of all Boston neighborhoods, the shot-'n'-a-beer crowd could have held the line against the single-malt cohort.

Old-timers who embraced day drinking and swilled PBRs and 'Gansett tall boys without an irony chaser rarely watched the six o'clock news. The younger crowd didn't watch it either, at least not in real time, but they might DVR it or stream it through their laptops later. And they certainly accessed YouTube on a regular basis. When the clip of Rachel's meltdown went viral last fall, there were eighty thousand hits in the first twelve hours. Within twenty-four, there were seven memes and a video mash-up of Rachel blinking, sweating, stuttering, and hyperventilating, backed by a remix of Beyoncé's "Drunk in Love." That's how it had played out—a drunk reporter loses control during a live report from a Port-au-Prince ghetto. Within thirty-six hours of the incident, the video had two hundred and seventy thousand hits.

Her few friends told Rachel she likely overestimated the number of people who recognized her in public. They assured her that the very nature of the viral age, its need for constant replenishment of content, ensured that the video, while watched by many, was remembered by few.

It was fair to assume, however, that half the people in the bar under thirty-five had seen it. They may have been stoned or drunk at the time, which raised the possibility they'd see the single woman at the bar in the baseball cap reading the newspaper and make no connection. But then again, maybe a few of them had been sober and possessed strong memories.

With a few swift upticks of her gaze, she got a sense of the other people at the bar itself: two office women sipping martinis with an added splash of something pink; five male brokers who pounded beers and fist-bumped over whatever game was on the TV above them; a mixed-sex group of techies in their late twenties who managed to keep their shoulders hunched even when they drank; and a well-dressed and well-groomed couple in their early thirties, the male clearly drunk, the woman clearly disgusted and a little afraid. Those two were the nearest to Rachel—four seats to her right— and at one point one of those seats half toppled into another two, the front pair of legs rising off the floor. The woman said, "Jesus, *enough*," and it was in her voice as it had been in her eyes, the fear and disgust. When the guy said, "Fuckin' calm yourself, you spoiled fuckin'—" Rachel accidentally caught his eye, then his girlfriend's, and they all pretended it didn't happen as he righted the chair.

She neared the end of her drink and decided this had been a bad idea. Her fear of particular people—i.e., people who'd seen her have an unrestrained panic attack on the six o'clock news—had blinded her to her terror of people in general, an ever-burgeoning phobia she was only now beginning to suspect the breadth of. She should have run back to the house after court. She never should have sat at a bar. Jesus. The sparrow flapped its wings. Not too spastically, not frantically, not yet. But the tempo was increasing. She was aware of her heart dangling in her chest, suspended from cords of blood. The eyes of the bar were on her, and in the garble of a group of voices behind her, she was nearly positive she heard someone whisper, "*That* reporter."

She put a ten-dollar bill on the bar, relieved she had one, because she couldn't imagine waiting for change. Couldn't sit in this seat a second longer. Her throat closed. Her vision blurred at the edges. The air looked as if it had been smelted. She went to stand, but the bartender placed a drink in front of her.

"A gentleman sent this over with his 'respect.'"

The group of suit-clad guys across the bar watched the game. They gave off a former-frat-boy-rapist vibe. Early to mid-thirties, the five of them, two going fleshy, all with eyes that were too small and too bright at the same time. The tallest of them gave her a chin tilt of recognition and raised his glass.

She said to the bartender, "Him?"

The bartender looked over his shoulder. "No. Not the group. Another guy." He scanned the bar. "He must have hit the head."

"Well, tell him thank you, but—"

Shit. Now the drunken boyfriend who'd knocked over the chair was approaching, pointing at her like he was a game-show host and she'd just won a dinette set. His disgusted and frightened girlfriend was nowhere to be seen. The closer he got, the less good-looking he was. It wasn't that he wasn't fit or didn't have a luxurious tousle of dark hair and full lips draped over a white, wholesome smile, or that he didn't move with a certain style, because all of that was part of the package. *As are the eyes, as rich and brown as English toffee, but, oh my, Rachel, what lies behind them—what lies* in *them—is cruelty.* Self-impressed, unreflective cruelty.

You have seen this look before. In Felix Browner. In Josué Dacelus. In projects and high-rises. In self-satisfied predators.

"Hey, sorry about that."

"About what?"

"My girlfriend. My now *ex*-girlfriend, and that's been a long time coming. She's got a thing for drama. Everything's drama."

"I think she was just worried you'd had too much to drink."

Why are you even talking, Rachel? Walk away.

He opened his arms wide. "Some people when they have an extra one or two, they get mean, ya know? That's a problem drunk. Me? I get happy. I'm just a happy guy looking to make friends and have a fun night. I don't see how that can be a problem."

"Well, good luck. I gotta—"

He pointed at her drink. "You gotta finish that. Be a crime to let it go to waste." He held out his hand. "I'm Lander."

"Actually, I'm good."

He dropped his hand and turned his head to the bartender. "A Patrón Silver, my good man." He turned back to her. "Why were you watching us?"

"I wasn't watching you."

The bartender brought his drink.

He took a sip. "But you were. I caught your eye."

"You guys were getting a little loud and I looked up."

"We were loud?" He smirked.

"Yes."

"Offended your sense of proprietary, did it?"

"No." She didn't correct his malapropism, but she did fail to stifle a sigh.

"Am I boring you?"

"No, you seem like a nice guy, but I've got to go."

He gave her a big friendly smile. "No, you don't. Have that drink."

The bird was starting to flap hard now, its head and beak rising to the base of her throat.

"I'm going to go. Thank you." She slung her bag over her shoulder.

He said, "You're the woman on the news."

She didn't feel like living through the five or ten minutes it would take to deny it and then redeny it and then ultimately give him his due, and yet she still played dumb. "What woman?"

"The one who flipped out." He glanced at the drink in front of her that she still hadn't touched. "Were you drunk? Or high? Which was it? Come on. You can tell me."

She gave him a tight smile and went to move past him.

Lander said, "Hey, hey, hey," and put his chest between her and the door. "I just want to know . . ." He took one step back and squinted at her. "Just want to know what you were thinking. I mean, I want to be friends."

"I'd like to go." She gestured with her right hand for him to step aside.

He reared his head back, curled his lower lip, and mimicked her

gesture. "I'm just asking a question. People put their trust in you."
He tapped a single finger off her shoulder. "I know, I know, I know,
you think I'm drunk and maybe, you know, maybe I am. But what
I'm saying is important. I'm a fun guy, I'm a nice guy, my friends
think I'm hilarious. I got three sisters. Thing is, point is here, that
you think like it's okay to start throwing back the sauce on the
job because you probably got a net to land in if it backfires. Am I
right? Some doctor or venture capitalist hubby who . . ." He lost the
thought, then caught it again, splayed his pink fingers against the
base of his pink throat. "*I can't* do that. I gotta go make the money.
I bet you got some sugar daddy pays for your Pilates and your Lex
and the lunches where you hang with your homegirls and shit all
over everything he does for you. Have that drink, bitch. Somebody
bought it for you. Show some respect."

He wavered in front of her. She wondered what she'd do if he
touched her shoulder again. Nobody was moving in the bar. No
one was saying anything. No one was trying to help. They were all
just watching the show.

"I'd like to go," she repeated and took a step toward the door.

He put that single finger on her shoulder again. "One more
minute. Have a drink with me. With us." He waved at the bar.
"Don't make us feel like you think bad of me. You don't think bad
of me, right? I'm just a guy in the street. I'm just a regular dude.
I'm just—"

"Rachel!" Brian Delacroix materialized by Lander's left shoulder, slid past his hip, and was suddenly standing beside her. "I'm so
sorry. I got hung up." He gave Lander a distant smile before turning back to her. "Look, we're late, I'm sorry. Doors were at eight.
We gotta go." He took her vodka off the bar and downed it in one
easy swallow.

Brian wore a navy blue suit, white shirt with the top button
undone, black tie loosened and slightly askew. He remained quite

handsome but not in the way that made you think he'd hold up the bathroom every morning. His look was more rugged, his face just on the right side of craggy, his smile a bit crooked, his wavy black hair not fully tamed. Weathered skin, crow's-feet around the eyes, strong chin and nose. His blue eyes were open and amused, as if he were perpetually surprised to find himself in situations such as these.

"You look spectacular, by the way," he said. "Again, sorry I got held up. No excuse."

"Whoa, whoa." Lander squinted at his own drink for a moment. "Okay?"

This could easily be a scam perpetuated by the both of them. Lander played the wolf, she was the unwitting sheep, and the part of the shepherd was played by Brian Delacroix. She hadn't forgotten that weird vibe he'd given off that day at the Athenaeum and found their just happening to find each other on the day of her divorce a bit too coincidental.

She decided not to play along. She held up her hands. "Guys, I think I'm just gonna—"

But Lander didn't hear her because he pushed Brian. "Yo, bro, you need to step off."

Brian gave her an amused cock of the eyebrow when Lander called him "bro." She had to work at it to keep her own smile from breaking out.

He turned to Lander. "Dude, I would, but I can't. I know, I know, you're disappointed, but, hey, you didn't know she was waiting on me. You're a fun guy, though, I can tell. And the night's young." He indicated the bartender. "Tom knows me. Right, Tom?"

Tom said, "I do indeed."

"So—what's your name?"

"Lander."

"Cool name."

"Thanks."

"Honey," he said to Rachel, "why don't you pull the car around?"

Rachel heard herself say, "Sure."

"Lander," he said, but he met Rachel's eyes and flicked his own toward the door, "your money's no good here tonight. Whatever you imbibe, Tom will put it on my tab." He flicked his eyes at her again, a little bit more insistently, and this time she moved. "You want to buy a round for those girls over there by the pool table? That's on me too. The one in the green flannel and the black jeans has been looking at you since I came through the door . . ."

She made the door and didn't glance back, though she wanted to. But the last look she'd caught on Lander's face was of a dog waiting, head cocked, for either a treat or a command. In under a minute, Brian Delacroix had taken ownership of him.

She couldn't find her car. She walked block after block. She cut east, then west, turned north, retraced her steps south. Somewhere in this collection of wrought-iron fences and railings and chocolate or redbrick townhouses was a light gray 2010 Prius.

It was Brian's voice, she decided as she headed up a side street toward the lights of Copley Square. It was warm, confident, and smooth, but not huckster-smooth. It was the voice of a friend you'd been hoping to meet your whole life or a caring uncle who'd left your life too soon but had now returned. It was the voice of home, but not home the reality, home as a construct, home as an ideal.

A few minutes later, that voice entered the air behind her: "I won't take it personally if you think I'm a stalker and pick up your pace. I won't. I'll stay planted to this spot and never see you again."

She stopped. Turned. Saw him standing back at the mouth of the alley she'd crossed thirty seconds before. He stood under the street-light with his hands clasped in front of him, and he didn't move. He'd added a raincoat over the suit.

"But if you're open to a little more of the evening, I'll stay ten paces back and follow you wherever you'll let me buy you a drink."

She looked at him for a long time, long enough for her to notice that the sparrow had stopped flapping in her chest and the base of her throat had come unblocked. She felt as calm as she'd felt since she was last safe behind closed doors in her own home.

"Make it five paces," she said.

10

LIGHTS UP

They walked through the South End, and soon she realized why he wore the raincoat. There was a mist in the air so thin she didn't notice it until her hair was damp and her forehead was wet. She raised her hood above her head, but of course it was damp now too.

"Did you send over the vodka?"

"I did."

"Why?"

"Honestly?"

"No, inauthentically."

He chuckled. "Because I had to use the bathroom and I wanted to make sure you'd still be there when I got out."

"Why not just walk up to me?"

"Nerves. It's not like you've seemed elated the times I've initiated contact over the years."

She slowed then and he caught up.

"I did like getting your e-mails," she said.

"Odd. You didn't respond like it."

"It's been a complicated decade for me." She gave him a smile that felt hesitant but hopeful.

He removed his raincoat and draped it over her shoulders.

"I'm not taking your coat," she said.

"I know you're not. I'm lending it to you."

"I don't need it."

He stepped back, got a look at her. "Fine. Give it back."

She smiled, rolled her eyes. "Well, if you insist."

They walked on, their footsteps the only sound for a full block.

"Where are you taking us?" he said.

"I was hoping the RR still exists."

"It does. One block up, two over."

She nodded. "Why do they call it that? There are no tracks near it."

"The underground railroad. They used to run most of the slaves out through that block. This building here"—he pointed at a red-brick mansion tucked between a row house and what had once been a church—"was where Edgar Ross set up the first black-run printing press in the early 1800s."

She shot him a sidelong glance. "Aren't we a font?"

"I like history." He gave her a shrug that was somehow cute on a big man.

"Left here."

They turned left. The street was older and quieter. A lot of the garages or garage apartments had been livery stables at one time. The windows were thick and leaded. The trees looked as old as the Constitution.

"I liked your hard news stories better than the soft ones, by the way."

She chuckled. "You didn't feel sufficiently informed when I did that story on the cat that barked?"

He snapped his fingers. "Promise me it's archived."

They heard a metallic pop and the street turned black. Every light—in the houses, in the streetlamps, in the small office building at the end of the street—snapped off.

They could see each other, if barely, in the pewter gloaming cast by the tall buildings that fringed the neighborhood, but this near-dark was alien and carried with it the arrival of the postponable truth that all urban dwellers kept tucked on high shelves—we are unprepared for most forms of survival. At least those that don't come with amenities.

They continued up the street with a bit of wonder. The hairs on her skin were alive in a way they hadn't been five minutes ago. Her hearing was sharper. All her pores were wide open. Her scalp was cold, damp, adrenalized.

Haiti had felt like this. Port-au-Prince, Léogâne, Jacmel. In some neighborhoods they were still waiting for the lights to come back on.

A woman stepped out of a building on the corner. She held a candle in one hand and a flashlight in the other, and as she swept the flashlight across their torsos, Rachel made out the sign above her head and realized they were at the RR bar.

"Oh, hey!" The woman waved the flashlight up and down and the light anointed them before rejoining their bodies at the knees. "What're you two doing out in this?"

"Looking for her car," he said. "Then we just decided to look for your bar, then this happened."

He raised his hands to the dark, and there was another metallic groan, and the lights came back on.

They blinked into the soft shafts of neon cast by the beer sign in the window and the bar sign above the door.

"Nice trick," the bartender said. "You do birthday parties?"

She opened the door for them and they went inside. It was as Rachel remembered, maybe even better, the lights a little lower, the smell of old beer soaked into black rubber replaced with the faintest hint of hickory. Tom Waits on the jukebox when they came through the door, fading as they ordered their drinks, and replaced by Radiohead from the *Pablo Honey* era. Tom Waits she could place in his proper context because most of his best music pre-dated her. But it was often a shock, however predictable, however mild, to realize there were people legally drinking in bars who'd been in diapers when Radiohead was part of her college-years soundtrack. *We age as the rest of the world watches*, she thought, *but somehow we're the last to know.*

There was no one else in the bar but them and Gail, the bartender.

Halfway through their first drinks, Rachel said to Brian, "Tell me about the last time I saw you."

His eyes narrowed in confusion.

"You were with an antiquities dealer."

He snapped his fingers. "Jack Ahern, right? Was that Jack?"

"It was."

"We were heading to lunch, ran into you up at the top of Beacon Hill."

"Yes, yes," she said, "those are the facts. But I'm after the vibe. You were off that day, m' man, couldn't get rid of me quick enough."

He was nodding. "Yeah, sorry about that."

"You admit it?"

"Hell, yeah." He turned on his seat, choosing his words. "Jack was an investor in a small subsidiary I was creating at the time. Nothing big, just a company that makes high-end wood floors and shutters. Jack's also a self-appointed moralist, very fifteenth century in that regard, Lutheran fundamentalist or Calvinist fundamentalist, I can't remember which."

"I get them confused too."

He shot her a wry grin. "Anyway, I was married then."

She took a long pull on her drink. "Married?"

"Yeah. Heading for divorce but married in that moment. And I'm a salesman, I was selling that marriage to my moralistic client."

"I'm with you so far."

"Then I see you crossing the street toward me and I know if I don't get ahead of it, he's gonna see it, so I got all hyper like I do when I'm really nervous and I bungled the whole fucking thing."

"You said 'get ahead of it.' What's 'it'?"

He cocked his head and then his eyebrow at her. "Do I really have to say the words?"

"It's your explanation, my friend."

"'It' would be my attraction to you, Rachel. My ex used to get on me about it—'Are you watching your *girlfriend* on the news again?' My friends could see it. I'm damn sure Jack Ahern would have picked up on it if my tongue was hanging out in the middle of Beacon Street. I mean, Jesus, ever since Chicopee. Come on."

"You come on. I didn't know about this."

"Oh, well, yeah. I guess, why would you?"

"You could've mentioned it."

"In an e-mail? That you'd be reading with that picture-perfect husband of yours?"

"He was anything but."

"I didn't know that at the time. Plus, I was married."

"What happened to her?"

"She left. Went back to Canada."

"So we're both divorced."

He nodded and raised his glass. "To that."

She clinked his glass, drained her own, and they ordered two more.

She said, "Tell me something you don't like about yourself."

"I *don't* like? I thought the point was to show off your best self in the early going."

"The early going of what?"

"Meeting someone."

"Dating? Are we calling this a date?"

"I hadn't thought of it that way yet."

"You've got your drink, I've got mine, we're turned toward each other, trying to ascertain if we enjoy each other's company enough to do it again."

"That does sound like a date." He held up a finger. "Unless it's like an NFL preseason game to a date."

"MLB spring training to a date," she said. "Wait, what do they call the preseason in the NBA?"

"The preseason."

"I know, but what do they call it?"

"That's what they call it."

"You sure? Seems unoriginal."

"And yet there it is."

"And how about the NHL?"

"Fuck if I know."

"But you're Canadian."

"Yes," he admitted, "but I'm not very good at it."

They both laughed for no other reason but that her mother's first stage—the spark—had been reached. Somewhere from the walk along cobblestones on a block so quiet the only sounds were the echoes of their footsteps to the smell of his damp raincoat collar under her chin to the two-minute blackout to the birthing of them as a duo as they crossed the threshold into the bar and Tom Waits growled softly through a fading chorus to right now, bantering over a vodka and a scotch respectively, they'd crossed a second threshold—leaving behind who they'd been before their attraction had been certified mutual and moving forward with that attraction taken as a given.

"What don't I like about *myself*?"

She nodded.

He lifted his drink and rattled the cubes softly from one side of the glass to the other. The playfulness left his face and was replaced by something sad and bewildered though not bitter. She liked that lack of bitterness immediately. She'd grown up in a house of bitterness and then, when she was sure it would never touch her again, she married it. She'd had her fill.

Brian said, "You know when you're a kid and you don't get picked for the team, or someone you like doesn't like you back, or your parents reject or marginalize you not because of something you did but because they were fucked up and toxic?"

"Yes and yes and yes. I can't wait to see where you're going with this."

Now he took a drink. "I think of those times—and there are lots of them in a childhood; they accrue—and I realize that I always believed to my core that they were right. I *wasn't* worthy of the team, I wasn't fit to be liked back, my family rejected me because I deserved to be rejected." He put his glass on the bar. "What I don't like about myself is that sometimes I don't really like myself."

"And no matter how much good you do," she said, "no matter how great a friend you are, how great a wife or husband, how great a humanitarian, nothing, I mean, nothing—"

"Nothing," he said.

"—will ever make up for what a piece of shit you really are."

He gave her a broad and beautiful smile. "I see you've spent time in my head."

"Ha." She shook her head. "Just mine."

They said nothing for a minute. They finished their drinks, ordered two more.

"And yet," she said, "you project confidence amazingly well. You handled that d-bag in the bar like you were his hypnotist."

"He was an idiot. Idiots are easy to outwit. That's why they're idiots."

"How do I know you weren't in on it together?"

"In on what?"

"You know," she said, "he makes me feel scared, you come to my rescue."

"But I got you out of there and I stayed behind."

"If he was in on it with you, you could have been out that door five seconds after me and followed me."

He opened his mouth and then closed it. He nodded. "That's a good point. Are you often approached this elaborately?"

"Not that I know of."

"It would take an awful lot of work on my part. Wasn't that guy with a girlfriend at one point? They were fighting?"

She nodded.

"So I would have had to—let me order this correctly—known you were coming to the bar tonight, hired a friend to pretend he was there with a girlfriend, start a fight with her, get her to leave, then approach you and be belligerent, all so I could step in and buy you the time you needed to leave so I could then—"

"Okay, okay."

"—*run* across the bar the moment you left it, slip out the door behind you, and follow you through the city on empty, quiet streets in hard-heeled shoes."

"Okay, I said. Okay." She gestured at his suit, his white shirt, his handsome raincoat. "You're just very put together so I'm trying to wrap my head around the part where you don't really like yourself. Because you, my friend, exude confidence."

"In a dickish way?"

"Actually, no." She shook her head.

"Most times I am confident," he said. "The rational adult me? He's got his shit squared away. There's just this tiny splinter-me that can be accessed at midnight in a dark bar by a woman who asks what I don't like about myself." He turned fully toward her again and waited. "Speaking of which . . ."

She cleared her throat because for a moment she feared she'd tear up. She could feel it threatening, and it was embarrassing. She'd covered a 7.0 magnitude earthquake on an island already racked by poverty beyond most humans' ability to imagine. She'd spent a month in a housing project walking solely on her knees in order to duplicate the perspective of a child in the same circumstances. She once climbed to the canopy of a tree, two hundred feet above the ground in the Brazilian rain forest, and slept there overnight. And today, she'd barely managed to drive thirty miles from the suburbs to the city without cracking up.

"I got divorced today," she said. "I lost my job—no, correct that, my *career*—six months ago, as you well know, because I had a panic attack on the air. I've grown terrified of people, not particular people, but in general, which is worse. I've spent the last few months a virtual shut-in. And honestly? I can't wait to get back to it. Brian, there's nothing I like about myself."

He said nothing for a minute. Just looked at her. It wasn't an intense stare, didn't feel like a come-on or a challenge. It was an open look, forgiving, uncolored by judgment. It was impossible for her to characterize until she realized it was the look of a friend.

She noticed the song then. It had been playing for maybe half a minute. Lenny Welch, one of the earliest but most enduring one-hit wonders, singing "Since I Fell for You."

Brian's head was cocked to it, his gaze gone to another place. "This played on the radio once when I was a kid at this lake we'd go to. All the adults were funny that day, a blast to be around. Took me years to realize they were all high. I couldn't understand why they kept sharing the same cigarette. Anyway, they danced by the lake to this, a bunch of stoned Canucks in nylon bathing suits."

Where did it come from, what she said next? Could that impulse be traced? Or was it simply chemical? Neurons firing away, biology trumping intellect.

"Wanna dance?"

"Love to." He took her hand and they found the small dance floor just past the bar itself in a dark room lit only by the glow of the jukebox.

Their first dance then. The first time their palms and chests touched. The first time she was close enough to smell what she would always identify as Brian's essential smell—a hint of smoke entwined with the smell of his unscented shampoo and a vaguely woodsy musk to his flesh.

"I sent you the drink because I didn't want you to leave the bar."

"Because you had to go to the bathroom, I know."

"No, I went to the bathroom because right after I sent the drink, I freaked out. I just, I dunno, whew, I just didn't want to see you look at me like some fucking stalker. So I went to the bathroom to, I dunno, cringe? I just went in there and stood with my back against the wall and called myself stupid about ten times."

"You did not."

"I did. I swear. When I used to watch you on the news, you were honest. You didn't editorialize, you didn't wink at the camera or wear your biases on your sleeve. I trusted what you said. You did your job with integrity. And that came through."

"Even with the cat that barked?"

His face grew serious though his tone remained light. "Don't minimize what I'm saying about you. I go through a day, sometimes a week, where everyone lies to me, everyone's trying to play me. From the car salesman, to the vendors, from my doctor trying to upsell me drugs because he's trying to fuck the pharmaceutical rep, to the airlines and the hotels and the women in the hotel bars. I would get back from a trip, and I would turn on Channel 6 and you—you—wouldn't lie to me. That meant something. Some days, particularly after my marriage blew up and I was alone all the time, that meant everything."

She didn't know what to say. She was unaccustomed to compliments lately and unfamiliar with trust.

"Thanks," she managed and looked at the floor.

"This is one sad song," he said after a bit.

"It is."

"You want to stop?"

"No." She loved the press of his palm at the small of her back. It made her feel like she'd never fall. Never be hurt. Never lose. Never be abandoned again. "No, let's keep going."

11

APPETITES

The beginning of their love affair injected her with a false sense of calm. She almost convinced herself the panic attacks were a thing of the past, even though their most recent onset had been the most acute.

Her and Brian's first official date was a cup of coffee the morning after they met. Too buzzed to drive the night before, Rachel had splurged on a river-view room at the Westin Copley Square. It had been over a year since she'd stayed in a hotel; in the elevator, she'd imagined ordering a snack from room service and watching a movie on-demand, but she fell asleep somewhere between kicking off her shoes and pulling back the bedspread. At ten the next morning, she met Brian at Stephanie's on Newbury. Tendrils of vodka still shivered in her blood and in the mild gumminess of her brain. Brian, on the other hand, looked great. He was actually better looking in daylight than in bar light. She asked him about his job and he told her it paid the bills and let him indulge his love of travel.

"There's gotta be more to it than that."

"Not actually." He chuckled. "Here's what I do, day in, day out—I negotiate terms with lumber suppliers based on whether there's a lot of lumber this month or a little. Was there a drought in Australia or did the rainy season last too long in the Philippines? Those factors change the price of lumber, which changes the price of—where do we start?—that napkin, this tablecloth, that sugar packet. I'm falling asleep talking about it." He took a sip of coffee. "What about you?"

"Me?"

"Yeah. Will you ever go back to journalism?"

"I doubt anyone would hire me."

"If they would? Say someone who never saw that video?"

"And where would I find them?"

"I hear Chad has terrible Internet service."

"Chad?"

"Chad."

She said, "Well, if I can ever get on a plane again, I'll take a run at the news stations in . . ."

"N'Djamena."

"Capital of Chad, yes."

"On the tip of your tongue, I'm sure."

"It *was*."

"No, I know."

"I would've gotten it."

"I'm not arguing."

"Not with your mouth maybe," she said, "but with your eyes."

"Yours are remarkable, by the way."

"My eyes."

"And your mouth."

"You can hang with me anytime."

"That's the plan." His face grew a bit somber. "Did you ever think you might not have to go as far as Chad?"

"What do you mean?"

"I wonder if you're as recognizable as you think."

She cocked an eyebrow at him. "I was on the news five nights a week in this city for almost three years."

"You were," he said. "But what's the viewership? About five percent of a city of two million? So that's a hundred thousand people. Spread out over however many square miles make up the greater metro area. I bet if you polled everyone in this restaurant, only one or two would recognize you and maybe only because we asked and made them take a second look."

She said, "I can't decide if you're trying to make me feel better or worse."

"Better," he said. "Always better. I'm trying to get you to see, Rachel, that, yeah, a few people remember that video and a smaller percentage of those connect it to you when they see you out in public, but it's a shrinking demographic and it shrinks further every day. We live in a world of disposable memory. Nothing's built to last, not even shame."

She crinkled her nose at him. "You talk pretty."

"You are pretty."

"Awwwww."

Second date was a dinner on the South Shore near her place. Third date was back in Boston, another dinner, and afterward they made out like high school kids, her back against a lamp pole. It started to rain, not the soft mist of the night they'd met but a pelting that coincided with a plummet into raw cold, as if winter was taking one last desperate bite out of them.

"Let's get you to your car." He tucked her under his raincoat. She could hear the drops hitting the outside of the coat like small stones, but everything remained dry except her ankles.

They passed a small park where a homeless man lay on a bench.

He stared out at the street as if he were trying to spot something he'd lost there. He'd covered himself in newspaper, but his head shook persistently in the wet. His lips quivered.

"It's a mean spring," the man said.

"And almost June too," Brian said.

"Supposed to clear by midnight." Rachel felt anxious and guilty about owning a bed, a car, a roof.

The man gave that news a hopeful pursing of his lips and closed his eyes.

In her car, she got the heat turned on and rubbed her hands together. Brian leaned into the open window for a short kiss that turned into a long one and the rain battered her roof.

"Let me drive you home," she said.

"It's ten blocks in the wrong direction. The coat'll keep me dry."

"You don't have a hat."

"Ye of little faith." He stepped back from the car and produced a Blue Jays ball cap from his coat pocket. When he put it on, he curved the bill with a snap of his fingers and saluted her with a cocked grin. "Drive careful. Call me when you get home."

"One more." She crooked a finger at him.

He leaned into the car one more time, kissed her, and she could smell the faintest hint of sweat from the underside of his cap brim and taste scotch on his tongue and she pulled hard on the lapels of his coat and deepened the kiss.

He walked back the way they'd come. She turned on her wipers and went to pull away from the curb, but her windows had fogged up. She turned on the defrost and sat watching the glass clear before she pulled onto the street. At the next corner, she was about to turn right when she looked to her left and saw Brian. He stood in the small park. He'd removed his coat to lay it over the homeless man.

He stepped out of the park, turning his shirt collar up against the rain, and ran up the street toward his home.

Her mother, of course, had a whole chapter devoted to what Rachel had just witnessed: "The Act That Causes the Leap."

Their fourth date, he made dinner at his apartment. While he was loading the dishwasher, she removed her T-shirt and bra and came to him in the kitchen wearing nothing but a pair of tattered boyfriend jeans. He turned just as she reached him and his eyes widened and he said, "Oh."

She felt in complete control, which of course she wasn't, and free enough to dictate the terms of their bodies' first engagement. That night they started in the kitchen but finished in his bed. Started round two in the bathtub and finished on the counter between the his-and-her sinks. Then went for the trifecta in the bedroom again and did surprisingly well, although there was nothing left to come out of Brian at the end but a shudder.

Throughout that summer, the giving of the body went spectacularly well. The giving of everything else, however, was a slower process. Particularly once the panic attacks returned. For the most part, they descended when Brian was out of town. Unfortunately, the first rule of accepting him as her boyfriend was accepting that he was out of town a lot. Most of his trips were quick two-nighters to Canada, Washington State and Oregon, twice a year to Maine. But others—to Russia, Germany, Brazil, Nigeria, and India—took much longer.

Sometimes when he was first gone, it felt good to return to herself. She didn't need to see herself in terms of being half of a couple. She'd wake up the morning after he'd left and feel ninety percent Rachel Childs. Then she'd look out the window and fear the world and remember that ninety percent of herself was still at least forty percent more than she liked.

By the second afternoon, the thought of going outside came laden with barely suppressed hysteria swaddled in more manageable everyday dread.

What she saw when she pictured the outside world was what she felt when she dared enter it—that it came at her like a storm cloud. Encircled her. Took bites of her. Inserted itself into her body like a straw and sucked her dry. In return, it gave her nothing. It thwarted all her attempts to engage it in kind, to be rewarded for her attempts to be a part of it. It sucked her up into its swirl, spun her, and then spit her out of its maelstrom before moving on to its next victim.

While Brian was in Toronto, she froze in a Dunkin' Donuts on Boylston. For two hours she couldn't move from the small counter that looked out onto the street.

While Brian was legging back from Hamburg one morning, she got into a cab on Beacon Street. They'd driven four blocks when she realized she'd entrusted a complete stranger with carrying her safely across the city for money. She had him pull over, overtipped him, and got out of the cab. She stood on the sidewalk, and everything was too bright, too sharp. Her hearing was too acute, as if the ear canals had been cored; she could hear three people on the far side of Mass Ave talking about their dogs. A woman, ten feet below on the river path, berated her child in Arabic. A plane landed at Logan. Another took off. And she could hear it. Could hear the cars honking on Mass Ave, and cars idling on Beacon and revving their engines on Storrow Drive.

Luckily there was a trash barrel nearby. She took four steps and threw up in it.

As she walked back toward the apartment she shared with Brian, the people she passed stared brazenly at her with contempt and disgust and something that she could only identify as appetite. They contemplated nipping her as she passed.

A Scientologist accosted her at the next block, shoved a pamphlet in her hand, and asked if she'd like to take a personality test, she sure looked like she could use some good news, ma'am, might learn things about herself that would—

She wasn't ever positive but suspected she might have thrown up on him. Back at the apartment she found specks of vomit on her shoes, but when she'd puked into the big barrel she'd been certain it had been all net.

She removed her clothes and took a twenty-minute shower. When Brian came home that night she was still in her robe and almost to the bottom of a bottle of pinot grigio. He made his own drink, single malt with a single cube of ice, and sat with her in the window seat overlooking the Charles and let her talk it out. When she finished, the disgust she'd expected to see in his face—the disgust that surely would have lived in Sebastian's—wasn't there. Instead, she saw only . . . What was that?

Good Lord.

Empathy.

Is that what it looks like? she thought.

He used the tips of his fingers to brush her wet bangs back and kissed her forehead. He poured her more wine.

He chuckled. "You really puked on a Scientologist?"

"It's not funny."

"But, babe, it is. It really is." He clinked his glass off hers and drank.

She laughed, but then the laugh died and she thought of who she'd once been—in the housing projects, in the prowl cars on ride-alongs, in the halls of power, in the streets of Port-au-Prince, and that endless night in the squatters camp in Léogâne—and she couldn't connect that Rachel with this one.

"I'm so ashamed." She looked at this man who was better than any she'd ever known, certainly kinder, certainly more patient, and the tears came, which only deepened her shame.

"Ashamed of what?" he said. "You are not weak. You hear me?"

"I can't even walk out the fucking door," she whispered. "I can't even get in a fucking cab."

"You'll see someone," he said. "You'll figure it out. You'll heal. In the meantime, where would you want to go?" His arm swept the apartment. "What's better than here? We've got books, a full fridge, an Xbox."

She dropped her forehead against his chest. "I love you."

"I love you too. We can even do the wedding here."

She took her head off his chest, looked in his eyes. He nodded.

They got married in a church. It was a few blocks away. Only their closest friends attended—on her side, Melissa, Eugenie, and Danny Marotta, her cameraman in Haiti; on his side, his business partner, Caleb, Caleb's wife, Haya, a stunning Japanese immigrant who was still struggling to learn English, and Tom, the bartender from the bar where they'd met. No Jeremy James this time to walk her down the aisle; she hadn't heard from him in two years. As for Brian, when she'd asked if he wanted his family there, he shook his head and a darkness settled on him like an overcoat.

"I do business with them," he said. "I do not love them. I do not share the beautiful things in my life with them."

When he spoke of his family Brian didn't use contractions. He spoke slowly and precisely.

She said, "But they're your family."

He shook his head. "You're my family."

After the wedding, they all went for drinks at the Bristol Lounge. Later, she and Brian walked home through the Common and the Public Garden, and she'd never felt better in her life.

As they waited out a light to cross Beacon Street, however, Rachel saw two dead girls standing in the middle of the overpass that led to the Esplanade. The one in the faded red T-shirt and the jean shorts was Esther. The one in the pale yellow dress was Widdy. The two girls stepped up onto the overpass guardrail. Traffic streamed off Storrow Drive and flowed below them as they dove headfirst from the rail and vanished before they hit the pavement.

She didn't tell Brian. She made it back to the apartment without another hitch and they drank some champagne. They made love and had some more champagne and lay in bed and watched a harvest moon rise over the city.

She saw the two girls fall from the overpass and vanish. She catalogued all the people who had vanished from her life, not just the big ones, but the small, everyday ones, and she experienced a sudden grasp of what she feared most out in the world—that they'd all vanish on her one day, everyone. She'd turn a corner and the wide avenues would be empty, the cars abandoned. Everyone would have snuck out some galactic back door while she paused to blink, and she would be the only person alive.

It was an absurd thought, something a child with a martyr complex would marinate in. Yet it felt elemental to understanding the core of her fears. She looked at her newly minted husband. His blinking lids had grown heavy with sex and champagne and the gravity of the day. She knew in that moment that she'd married him for entirely different reasons than she'd married Sebastian. She'd married Sebastian because subconsciously she'd known that if he ever left her, she wouldn't give much of a shit. But she married Brian because although he left her in small ways—enough that she could trust the imperfection of that model—he'd never leave her in the big ones.

"What're you thinking about?" Brian asked. "You seem sad."

"I'm not," she lied. "I'm happy," she said, because it was also true.

It was eighteen months before she left the apartment again.

12

THE NECKLACE

The weekend before he left for London, fast approaching their second wedding anniversary, Brian and Rachel rode the elevator down from the fifteenth floor and left their building. It was raining—it had done nothing but rain that week—but the rain wasn't heavy, more like a mist she'd barely notice until the wet found her bones, similar to the weather the night they'd met. Brian took her hand and led her up to Mass Ave. He wouldn't tell her where they were going, only that she was ready for it. She could handle it.

Rachel had left the condo a dozen times over the last six months, but she had done so when the environment was at its most controllable—early mornings and weekday evenings, often in the coldest weather. She went to the supermarket but, as before, only in the early morning hours of a weekday, and she always stayed in on weekends.

But here she was, out and about in Back Bay late on a Satur-

day morning. Despite the weather, Mass Ave was crowded. So were
the cross streets, Newbury in particular. The Masshole fans of Red
Sox Nation were out in force, the team trying to squeeze in at least
one home game in a week when the rest had been rained out. So
Mass Ave was teeming with red or blue T-shirts and red or blue ball
caps and the people who wore them: studly young frat-boy types in
jeans and flip-flops already hitting the bars; middle-aged men and
women with competing beer guts; kids darting in and out of the fray
along the sidewalks, a quartet of them sword fighting with toy bats.
Cars sat in traffic so long the drivers turned off the engines. Horns
beeped and horns bayed and jaywalkers weaved through it all, one
guy shouting, "Ti-tle town, ti-tle town!" every time he slapped a
trunk. Beyond the sports fans—obnoxious or otherwise—were the
yuppies and buppies and the urban hipsters so recently graduated
from Berklee College of Music or BU to a daunting lack of pros-
pects. Farther down Newbury would be the trophy wives with their
duck lips and their purse dogs, sighing at every slip in customer service before demanding to see someone's manager. It had been so
long since Rachel had risked entering a crowd that she'd somehow
forgotten how overwhelming it could be.

"Breathe," Brian said. "Just breathe."

"Exhaust fumes?" she said as they crossed Mass Ave.

"Sure. Builds character."

It was when they reached the far sidewalk that she realized what
he had in mind. He turned them toward the Hynes Convention
Center subway stop.

"Whoa." She clamped her free hand over his wrist.

He turned with the tug, looked into her face. Smiled. "You can
do this."

"No, I can not."

"You can," he said softly. "Look at me, honey. Look at me."

She looked into his eyes. There was a part of Brian that could inspire or grate, depending on her mood, a can-do attitude that bordered on evangelical. He preferred music and movies and books that, in one way or another, reaffirmed the status quo or at least the idea that good things come to good people. But he was no naïf, either. He held enough empathy and wisdom in those blue eyes for a man twice his age. Brian saw the bad in the world, he just chose to believe he could dodge it through force of will.

"You win," he'd said more times than she could count, "by refusing to lose."

To which she'd replied, more than once, "You lose by refusing to lose too."

But she needed that part of him now, that mix of Vince Lombardi and self-help guru, that relentlessly upbeat (sometimes just relentless) attitude that her cynical self would have deemed far too predictably American were her husband not Canadian. She needed Brian to out-Brian himself now, and he did.

He held up their entwined hands. "I will not let go."

"Shit." She heard the suppressed hysteria in her voice even as she smiled, even as she knew she was going to do it.

"I will not," he repeated, "let go."

And the next thing she knew, she was on the escalator. No modern wide escalator, this. The escalator at Hynes was narrow, black, and steep. Definitely not up to current code. She feared that if she leaned forward for any reason, she'd bring herself, Brian, and everyone in front of them tumbling to the bottom. She kept her chin and head up, spine straight, as they descended. The lights dimmed until the descent felt like part of some primitive ritual, one of fertility perhaps or birth. Behind her were strangers. In front of her were strangers. Faces and motives shrouded in the dim light. Hearts beating like the tick of a bomb.

"How you doing?" Brian asked.

She squeezed his hand. "Hanging in there."

A single drop of sweat left her hair by the temple and slid behind her left ear. It found the back of her neck and rode the line of it into her blouse where it dissolved against her spine.

She'd last suffered a panic attack on the same elevator she and Brian had taken down from their condo this morning. That had been seven months ago. No, eight, she realized with some pride. Eight, she thought, and squeezed her husband's hand again.

They reached the platform. The crowd wasn't too thick once it cleared the narrow escalator. She and Brian walked a quarter way down the inbound side of the platform and she was surprised to discover her hands were dry. Through most of her twenties and early thirties she'd traveled extensively. Descending into a dark tunnel with hordes of strangers to board a tube packed with even more strangers hadn't even registered on the threat scale back then. Same thing with going to concerts and sporting events and movie theaters. Even in the tent cities and refugee camps of Haiti, she'd had no issues with panic. She'd had plenty of other issues over there and immediately upon her return—alcohol, Oxycontin, and Ativan sprang immediately to mind—but not panic.

"Hey," Brian said, "you with me?"

She chuckled. "I think that's my question for you."

"Oh, I'm here," he said. "I am right here."

They found a bench built into a wall that sported a map of the MBTA routes—green line, red line, blue line, orange, and silver, crisscrossing like veins before branching out on their own.

She kept both her hands in his now and their knees touched. People would look and see an attractive couple, clearly connected.

"You're always here," she said to him. "Except—"

"When I'm not," he finished for her, and they both chuckled.

"When you're not," she agreed.

"That's just travel, though, babe. You can come with me anytime."

She gave that a roll of her eyes. "I'm not certain I can get on this train. I'm sure not getting on a plane."

"You'll get on this train."

"Yeah? Makes you so sure?"

"Because you're stronger now. And you're safe."

"Safe, uh?" She looked out at the platform and then back at his hands, his knees.

"Yes. Safe."

She looked at him as the train blew into the station hard enough for the air to muss Brian's unruly hair even further.

"You ready?"

"I don't know."

They stood.

"You are."

"You keep saying that."

They waited for the exiting passengers and then stepped to the threshold where the car met the platform.

"We go on together," he said.

"Shit, shit, shit."

"Want to wait for the next one?"

The platform was empty. Everyone was on.

"We can wait for it," he said.

The doors started to close with a *whoosh* and she jumped on, pulling Brian with her. The doors snapped back as they passed between them, but then they were in the car, a pair of old white ladies giving them annoyed looks, a young Hispanic boy with a violin case on his lap giving them a curious one.

The car lurched. The train headed into the tunnel.

"You did it," Brian said.

"I did it." She kissed him. "Wow."

The car lurched again, this time as it maneuvered into a turn, the wheels screech-clacking. They were fifty feet underground traveling twenty-five miles an hour in a metal can along tracks that were over a hundred years old.

I am down here in the deep dark, she thought.

She looked at her husband. He was looking up at one of the ads above the doors, his strong chin tilted up with his gaze.

And I am less afraid than I would have imagined.

They rode the train to Lechmere, the last stop. They walked in the mist into East Cambridge and had lunch at a chain restaurant on the ground floor of the Galleria Mall. She hadn't been in a mall for as long as she hadn't been on the subway, and as they waited for the check, she realized the mall wasn't an accident.

"You want me to stroll through this mall?" she said.

He was all innocent surprise. "Why, I hadn't thought of that."

"Uh-huh. This mall of all malls? It'll be filled with teenagers and noise."

"Yup." He handed the waiter his credit card on the small black tray.

"Oh dear," she said.

He raised his eyebrows.

"And if I said the subway was enough daredevil shit for one day?" she asked.

"Then I would respect that."

And he would, she knew. He would. If asked what she loved most about her husband, she might have to say his patience. It appeared, at least when it came to her affliction, bottomless. For the first couple of months after her last attack, the one on the elevator, she took the stairs up to their apartment on the fifteenth floor. And when he was in town, Brian wouldn't hear of her doing it alone. He'd huff and puff up those stairs with her.

"On the bright side," he said once, when they paused to rest between ten and eleven, their faces sheened with perspiration, "we almost bought that unit on the twenty-second floor in that place on Huntington." He lowered his head, took a deep breath. "I don't know if it would have led to divorce, but we'd definitely be in mediation."

She could still hear the echoes of their laughter in the stairwell—light and weary, threads of it rising toward the roof. He'd taken her hand and led her up the final five flights. They'd taken a shower together and then lay on the bed naked and let the ceiling fan dry what the towels hadn't. They didn't make love right away, just lay there holding hands and chuckling at the absurdity of their situation. And that's how Brian looked at it—as a situation, an act of God foisted upon them, so beyond their power to change it that to try would be like trying to change the weather. Unlike Sebastian, as well as some of her friends, Brian never presumed that the panic attacks were within Rachel's control. She didn't have them because she was weak or self-indulgent or prone to drama; she had them because they afflicted her, like any malady of the body—the flu, a cold, meningitis.

When they did make love, it was as the last of the day bled out into the dusk beyond the bedroom window. The river turned purple and then black, and making love with Brian felt, as it sometimes did when they were connecting on every level, like they were drifting over thresholds of bone and slipping through walls of blood, like they were fusing.

That day became a standout that she would string together with other standouts, one after the other, for eight months, until she could look back on the state of her marriage and realize there had been far more superior days than inferior ones. She began to feel safer, sure enough of herself that one day three months ago, without warning anyone—Brian, her friends Melissa and Eugenie, her shrink, Jane—she took the elevator again.

And now here she was in a mall, riding down an escalator into a maelstrom of bodies. Teenagers mostly, as she'd predicted, on a Saturday of all days, and a rainy one, the kind of day mall managers prayed for. She could feel eyes on them—real or imagined, she had no idea—and the press of bodies as they passed and she could hear so many disparate voices, so many snatches of conversation—

". . . said you 'fronting now, Poot . . ."

". . . pick up, pick *up* . . ."

". . . and, like, I'm expected to just drop everything? Because he happens . . ."

". . . not if you don't like it, of course not . . ."

". . . Olivia has one and she's not even eleven yet."

She was surprised at how calmly she took in all these souls hurtling toward her, past her, and streaming on tiers above and below her with their aggressive need for goods and services, for the itchy satisfactions to be found in acquisition for its own sake, for human connection and disconnection in equal measure (before she quit counting, she noted twenty couples where one was ignoring the other to talk on a cell phone), for someone, anyone, to tell them why they did it, why they were here, what separated them from insects moving underground right now in colonies that bore a remarkable resemblance to the three-tiered mall in which they found themselves wandering, roving, stalking on a Saturday afternoon.

Normally, it was just this type of thinking that preceded a panic attack. It started with a tickle in the center of her chest. The tickle quickly became a piston. Her mouth would turn Saharan. The piston would transform into the sparrow, imprisoned and panicked. It would flap its wings—*whomph, whomph, whomph, whomph*—in the hollowed-out core of her, and sweat would sluice down the sides of her neck and pop on her forehead. Breathing would feel like a luxury with an expiration date.

But not today. Not even close.

Soon she even gave into the pleasures of a mall, bought herself a couple of blouses, a candle, some overly expensive conditioner. A necklace in the window of a jewelry store caught both their eyes. They didn't even speak about it for the first minute, just exchanged glances. It was two necklaces, actually, a smaller one within a larger, strings of black onyx bead balls, the chains white gold. Not expensive, not even close, probably not even something she'd pass on to a daughter, should she and Brian ever have one, and yet . . .

"What's the pull?" she asked Brian. "What do we like about this?"

Brian looked at her for a long time, trying to sort through it himself. "Maybe because it's a pair?"

He slipped it around her neck in the store. Had a little trouble with the clasp—it was too tight but the salesman assured them that was normal; it would loosen with use—but then the beads draped themselves over her blouse, just below her throat.

Outside the jeweler, he ran his palms along hers.

"Dry as a bone," he said.

She nodded, her eyes wide.

"Come on." He led her to a photo booth under the escalators. He inserted the required coins and pulled her into the booth with him, made her laugh by feeling her breasts up as she was pulling the curtain closed behind them. When the flashbulb flashed within the booth, she pressed her cheek to his and they made goofy faces, sticking out their tongues or blowing kisses at the lens.

When they were done, they looked at the strip of four panels and the photos were as silly as she'd expected, their heads half out of frame in the first two.

"I want you to sit for another strip," he said. "Just you."

"What?"

"Please," he said, suddenly somber.

"Okay . . ."

"I want to mark this day. I want you to look in that lens with pride."

She felt silly in the booth alone, could hear him out there inserting the coins. But she felt a sense of accomplishment too; he was right on that. A year ago, she couldn't imagine walking out the front door. And now she was in a jam-packed mall.

She stared at the lens.

I am still afraid. But I am not terrified. And I am not alone.

When she came out of the booth, he showed her the strip and she liked what she saw. She looked a little tough actually, not the kind of woman you'd fuck with.

"Every time you see these pictures or you wear that necklace," Brian said, "remember how strong you are."

She looked around the mall. "This was all you, babe."

He took her hand and kissed the knuckles. "I just nudged."

She felt like weeping. She didn't know why at first, but then it hit her.

He knew her.

He knew her, this man she'd married, this man she'd committed herself to walking through this life with. He knew her.

And—wonder of wonders—he was still here.

13

REFRACTION

Monday morning, a few hours after Brian left for the airport, Rachel tried to return to work on the book. She'd been writing it for the better part of a year but still wasn't even certain what genre it fell into. It had started as straight journalism, an account of her experiences in Haiti, but once she realized it was impossible to write the account without inserting herself into the narrative, the book morphed into something resembling memoir. While she hadn't yet attempted a chapter that detailed her on-camera breakdown, she knew she'd have to give it context once she did. Which led to a chapter about her mother, which led to another chapter about the seventy-three Jameses, which led to an overhaul of the entire first part of the book. At this point, she had no idea where the book was going and no idea how she'd get there even if she did, but most days she loved writing it. Other days, it fought her to a draw before her second cup of coffee. Today was one of those days.

There seemed to be little rhyme or reason as to why one day snatching the correct words from the ether was like opening a faucet and other days it was like opening a vein, but she began to suspect both the good and the bad parts of the process were connected to the fact that she was writing without a map. No plan at all, really. She fell quite naturally, it seemed, into a more free-flowing approach than she ever would have allowed herself as a journalist and gave herself over to something she didn't quite understand, something that, at the moment, spoke in cadence more than structure.

She wouldn't show the book to Brian, but she did discuss it with him. He was, as always, unfailingly supportive, though she wondered if, once or twice, she caught a patronizing glint in his eyes, as if he didn't quite believe the book was more than a dalliance, a hobby that would never turn into something whole and finite.

"What are you going to call it?" he asked her one night.

"*Transience*," she told him.

That's as close as she could get, thus far, to a unifying theme. Her life and the lives of those she'd most memorably encountered seemed marked by a state of never quite taking root. Of floating. Of spiraling helplessly toward the void.

That morning, she wrote a few pages about her days with the *Globe*, but it felt dry and, worse, rote, so she cashed in early and took a long shower and got dressed for her lunch date with Melissa.

She crossed the Back Bay in the steady rain—the endless rain, the omnipresent rain, "Biblical rain," Brian had said last night, "Noah rain." It wasn't quite that bad, but it had been wet for eight days now. Lakes and ponds upstate were overflowing into roadways, turning some streets into tributaries. In two cases, cars had been carried off. Over the weekend, a commercial jet had slid off a runway. No injuries reported. Those in a ten-car pileup on 95 hadn't been so lucky.

She needn't worry as much as some—she didn't fly, she rarely drove (it had been two years since the last time), and she and Brian lived high above street level. Brian flew, though, all the time. Brian drove.

She met Melissa at the Oak Room in the Copley Plaza Hotel. The Oak Room wasn't called the Oak Room anymore. Since Rachel's meltdown, it'd had a facelift and, after decades as the Oak Room, became OAK Long Bar + Kitchen, but Rachel, Melissa, and pretty much everyone they knew still called it the Oak Room.

She hadn't been to Copley Square by herself in a couple of years. At the onset of her last prolonged spate of panic attacks, the buildings that surrounded the square—the Old South Church, the Boston Public Library Main Branch, Trinity Church, the Fairmont, the Westin, and the towering Hancock with its mirrored blue windows reflecting the square back on itself—had one day given her the impression they were leaning in, not buildings anymore so much as walls, great walls built to pen her in. This was doubly unfortunate because she'd always admired Copley for its role as a representative hybrid of old and new Boston, the old represented by the beaux-arts classicism and lustrous limestone of the BPL and the Fairmont and, of course, Trinity Church, with its clay roof and heavy arches, the new by the icy functionality and hard, sleek lines of the Westin and the Hancock Tower, structures that gave the impression of aggressive indifference to both history and its sob sister, nostalgia. But for almost two years, she'd walked around it, not through it.

Walking into the square for the first time since her wedding day, Rachel had expected palpitations, accelerant in the blood. Yet as she walked up the burgundy carpet under the Fairmont awning, she felt only the slightest uptick in her heart rate before it reset itself almost immediately to normal. Maybe it was the rain that calmed her. With an umbrella over her head, she was just another near-spectral being in dark clothes hidden beneath a cowl of plastic moving through a city of near-spectral beings in dark clothes hidden beneath cowls of plastic. In this kind of rain and murk, she imagined murders were likelier to go unsolved and affairs unpunished.

"Mmmm," Melissa said when she mentioned this to her. "Thinking of an affair, are we?"

"God no. I can barely get out of the house."

"Bullshit. You're here. You took the T around town this weekend, gallivanted through a mall." She reached out and pinched Rachel's cheek. "Such a big girl now, aren't we?"

Rachel swatted her hand and Melissa sat back and laughed a hair too loud. Rachel had eaten a large salad and slow-sipped a glass of white wine, but Melissa, on her day off, barely touched her meal and was downing Bellinis as if prosecco would be outlawed at the stroke of midnight. It made her sharper, funnier, but louder too, and Rachel knew from past experience how quick the humor could turn into self-loathing, the sharpness could dim, but the loud would just get louder. A couple of times, Rachel had noticed other patrons looking their way, though that could have nothing to do with Melissa's volume and everything to do with Rachel.

Melissa took a sip of her drink, Rachel noting with some relief that the sips were smaller now. Melissa had been Rachel's producer on dozens of stories at 6 but not, as luck would have it, on any of the Haiti stories. When Rachel suffered her meltdown in Cité Soleil, Melissa was on her honeymoon on Maui. The marriage had lasted less than two years, but Melissa still had her job, which she'd always loved far more than Ted. So, as she'd say with a bright, bitter smile and two thumbs-up, win-win.

"So if you were to have an affair with someone in this room, who would it be?"

Rachel gave the room a quick sweep. "No one."

Melissa craned her head, staring openly at the room. "It is pretty grim pickings. But, wait, not even that guy in the corner?"

Rachel said, "With the half-fedora and the soul patch?"

"Yeah. He's all right."

"I don't want to have an affair with 'all right.' I don't want to have an affair at all. But if I did, it would be with the be-all and end-all."

"And what would he look like?"

"Beats me. I'm not the one looking for a man."

"Well, it wouldn't be the tall dark stranger. You're already married to him."

Rachel cocked her head at that.

Melissa mimicked the gesture. "*I* don't know the guy." She splayed her fingers against her chest. "Whenever I talk to your admittedly handsome, admittedly charming, admittedly funny and intelligent groom there, I always get the feeling after he walks away that he said absolutely nothing."

"I've seen you guys talk for half an hour."

"And yet . . . I know nothing about him."

"He's from British Columbia. He's—"

"I know his bio," Melissa said. "I just don't know Brian. All that charm and eye contact and questions about me and my hopes and dreams is so beautifully packaged, I'm continually surprised to wake up the next day and realize he made sure all I did was talk about myself."

"But you like talking about yourself."

"I *love* talking about myself, but that's not the point."

"Oh, you have one?"

"Bitch, I do."

"Bitch, spit it out."

They smiled across the table at each other. It was like working together again.

"I just wonder if anyone knows Brian."

"Me included?" Rachel laughed.

"Forget it."

"That's your implication."

"I said forget it."

"And I asked if you're including me in the list of people who don't *know* my husband."

Melissa shook her head and asked Rachel about the book she was writing.

"I'm having trouble giving it shape."

"What shape?" Melissa asked with a breezy dismissiveness. "There was an earthquake in Haiti, then a cholera outbreak, *then* a hurricane. And you were there for all of it."

"When you put it that way," Rachel said, "it sounds exactly like disaster porn. Which is what I fear most."

Melissa waved that off, which was usually what she did when Rachel ventured into a topic Melissa didn't understand or didn't want to.

Times like these, Rachel wondered why she continued to hang out with Melissa. She embraced the shallow the way others searched for the profound and she could reduce any attempt at complexity to a target of casual scorn. But the last few years had stripped Rachel of almost all her friends, and it scared her to think she'd one day wake up with none at all. So she half listened to Melissa prattle on about her own work, about the latest round of who's-fucking-whom at WCJR, both figuratively and literally.

Rachel interjected "Wow" and "No way" and "That's hilarious" where expected, but part of her remained back at the comments Melissa had made about Brian, and her irritation continued to rise. She'd woken this morning in a great mood. All she'd wanted since was to keep that mood alive. She just wanted to stay happy for a day. And not the bullshit, shiny happy of a beauty pageant contestant or a religious fanatic, just the hard-earned happiness of a self-aware human being who'd worked on her fears over the weekend with her loving, if often preoccupied, husband.

Tomorrow she'd allow all the doubts back in. Tomorrow she'd open herself up to the spiritual termites of minor despair and ennui. But today, on this miserable, soupy day, she wanted to remain not miserable. But it seemed like Melissa was determined to hurl ice water on her glow.

When Melissa went to order another round, Rachel begged off with claims of a hair appointment on Newbury Street. She could tell Melissa didn't believe her, but she didn't much care. The rain had softened outside to a light drizzle and she wanted to walk in it through the Public Garden to the Charles and then follow the river until she crossed the footbridge to Clarendon and walked back to her building. She wanted to smell the soaked soil and wet asphalt in equal measure. In Back Bay, in this kind of weather, it was easy to imagine Paris or London or Madrid, to feel part of a larger continuum.

Melissa stayed behind for "one last drink" and they exchanged kisses on the cheek before Rachel left. She turned right and headed down St. James. Walking the length of the hotel, she could see it reflected in the Hancock Tower, could see herself there as well, to the far left of the left pane of glass, part of a mirrored triptych. The left pane was dominated by the sidewalk and Rachel walking along the edge of it, a short line of cabs to her left just peeking into frame. The middle pane reflected a canted version of the grand old hotel, and the third pane showed the tiny street in between the hotel and the Hancock. It was such a small street that most would assume it was an alley if they noticed it all. It was used primarily, if not exclusively, by delivery trucks. A laundry truck was backed up to a pair of double doors at the rear of the hotel, a black Suburban idled at the back of the Hancock, its exhaust mingling with the exhaust of a sewer grate, the rain turning silver as it fell through the smoke.

Brian walked out of the Hancock and opened the back door of the SUV. It looked like Brian anyway, but it couldn't be. Brian was in the air, over the middle of the Atlantic by now, legging toward London.

But it was Brian—same jawline, just beginning to widen slightly as he approached forty, same lock of black hair falling over his fore-

head, same soft copper trench coat over black pullover that he'd left
the house in this morning.

She went to call his name but something in the set of his face
stopped her. He wore a look she'd never seen before; it was somehow heartless and hunted at the same time. This couldn't, she told
herself, be the same face that watches me sleep at night. He climbed
into the SUV—this watery, refracted reflection of her husband. Rachel reached the corner just as the reflected SUV transformed into
the actual one. It passed her, its windows black, and turned onto St.
James. She pivoted in place, her mouth open but no words leaving
it, and watched it cross into the middle lane, pass through the traffic light at Dartmouth, and descend the on-ramp for the Mass Pike.
She lost it there to the dark tunnel and the traffic merging behind it.

She stood on the sidewalk for a long time. The rain grew heavy
again. It pelted her umbrella and rebounded off the sidewalk into her
ankles and calves.

"Brian," she finally said.

She repeated his name, though this time it was no longer a statement but a question.

14

SCOTT PFEIFFER OF GRAFTON, VERMONT

She took the direct route back to the condo. She reminded herself that the world was filled with people who looked near identical to others. She didn't even know how precise the resemblance was; she'd seen a reflection. A reflection that was refracted off mirrored glass in the rain. If she'd had a moment to get a clear view, if he'd paused at the car door and she'd come around the corner in time to look directly at him, she probably would have seen him for the stranger he was. He wouldn't have had the barely perceptible bump halfway up the bridge of his nose. Or his lips would have been thinner, his eyes brown, not blue. He wouldn't have had Brian's smattering of pockmarks below the cheekbones, pockmarks so faded you could only see them if you were close enough to kiss them. This stranger might have smiled with hesitation at the woman staring so blatantly at him in the rain, wondered if perhaps there was something wrong with her. Maybe recognition would have dawned on his not-quite-

Brian's face and he'd have thought, "It's that woman from Channel 6 who had the freak-out on-air a while back." Or maybe he wouldn't have noticed her at all. He'd simply have gotten into the car and been driven off. Which ultimately is what happened.

The fact was, Brian did have a double. They'd been talking about him for years: Scott Pfeiffer of Grafton, Vermont.

When he was a freshman at Brown, people would tell Brian there was another kid his age, a pizza delivery guy, who looked just like him. It got to the point where Brian had to see for himself. One day he stood on the sidewalk outside the pizza parlor until he saw his twin step out from behind the counter carrying a stack of pizza boxes in a red leather thermal bag. Brian stepped aside as Scott walked out of the shop and got into a white van with DOM'S PIZZA stenciled on the door and drove off into Federal Hill to deliver his pies. Brian couldn't explain why, but he never introduced himself to Scott. Instead, by his own admission, he "kinda" began stalking him.

"Kinda," she said when he told her.

"I know. I know. But if you could have seen the resemblance you would have understood how fucking *eerie* it was. The idea of introducing myself to myself? It was just too weird."

"But he wasn't yourself. He was Scott—"

"—Pfeiffer of Grafton, Vermont, yes." Brian would often refer to him that way, as if somehow the full description made Scott a little less real, a bit more like a character in a comedy sketch. Scott Pfeiffer of Grafton, Vermont.

"I took a bunch of pictures of him."

"You *what*?"

"Right?" he said. "I told you it was definitely stalking."

"You said it was kinda stalking."

"Used a zoom lens. I used to stand in front of my bathroom mirror in Providence and hold the pictures up beside my face—full-on, left profile, right profile, chin down, chin up. And, I swear, the only difference was that his forehead was maybe a tenth of an inch taller and he didn't have this bump."

The bump on the bridge of Brian's nose was the result of a fifth-grade hockey injury that relocated some of the cartilage there. It was only visible in profile, never head-on, and even then one had to be looking for it.

Christmas, his sophomore year, Brian followed Scott Pfeiffer home to Grafton, Vermont.

"Your family didn't miss you on Christmas?" she asked.

"Not that I ever heard." He spoke in that flat tone—dead tone, would be the less charitable description—he used whenever he discussed his family.

Scott Pfeiffer of Grafton, Vermont, had the kind of life Brian probably never would have coveted if he hadn't seen it up close. Scott was working full-time at Dom's Pizza to put himself through Johnson & Wales, where he was majoring in restaurant management, while Brian majored in international finance at Brown, lived off a trust annuity from his grandparents, and had no idea what his tuition was, only that his parents must have paid it on time because he never heard otherwise.

Scott's father, Bob Pfeiffer, was the butcher at the local supermarket, and his mother, Sally, was the town crossing guard. They also served as the treasurer and vice-president, respectively, of the Windham County Rotary Club. And once a year they drove two hours to Saratoga Springs, New York, and stayed in the same motel where they'd spent their honeymoon.

"How much do you know about these people?" Rachel asked.

"You learn a lot when you stalk someone."

He used to watch the family and pray for a scandal. "Incest," he admitted, "or for Bob to get caught grabbing some undercover cop's Johnson in a public restroom. I would have taken embezzlement, though I don't know what you'd embezzle from a supermarket meat locker. Steaks, I guess."

"Why would you pray for that?"

"They were too perfect. I mean, they lived in this cute fucking colonial right on the town common. White, of course, picket fence, wraparound porch with, yes, an actual porch swing. They sat out there on Christmas Eve in their sweaters, brought out little space heaters, and sat drinking hot chocolates. Told each other stories. Laughed. At one point the daughter, she was like ten, sang a Christmas carol and they all applauded. I've never seen anything like it."

"Sounds sweet."

"It was hideous. Because if someone can be that happy? That *perfect*? What's that say about the rest of us?"

"But there are people out there like that," she said.

"Where?" he said. "I never met them. You?"

She opened her mouth and then closed it. Of course she hadn't, but why did she think she had? She'd always thought of herself as a fairly skeptical, if not downright cynical, person. And after Haiti, she would have sworn she'd been stripped of the last vestiges of sentimentality or romanticism. But buried somewhere deep in her brain lay the belief that perfect, happy—and perfectly happy—people walked this earth.

No such beast, her mother had often reminded her. Happiness, her mother used to say, was an hourglass with a crack in it.

"But you said yourself," she said to Brian, "they were happy."

"They certainly seemed to be."

"But then . . ."

He smiled. Triumphantly but with a whiff of despair. "Bob always stopped off at this little Scottish pub on the way home. One day I sat beside him. He gave me this huge double take, of course, and told me how much I resembled his son. I acted surprised. Acted surprised again when the bartender said the same thing. Bob bought me a drink, I bought Bob a drink, and so on. He asked me who I was, so I told him. Told him I went to school at Fordham, not Brown, but otherwise I stuck pretty close to the truth. Bob told me he wasn't a big fan of New York City. Too much crime, too many immigrants. By the third drink, 'immigrants' became 'wetbacks' and 'towel heads.' By the fifth drink, he was on about the 'niggers' and the 'fags.' Oh, and the dykes. Hated lesbians, our Bob did. Said if his daughter ever turned into one he'd, lemme see if I get this quote right, superglue her cunt. Turned out Bob had fascinating ideas on corporal punishment that he'd been employing for years, first on Scott and then on Nannette, that was the daughter's name. Once ol' Bob got talking, he couldn't stop. At one point, I realized that everything that had left his mouth for fifteen minutes was repulsive. Bob was a scared-shitless coward of a monster hiding behind his impeccable blandness."

"Whatever happened to Scott?"

Brian shrugged. "He never went back to school. Probably lack of finances. Last I checked, and this was fifteen years ago, he was working at one of the Grafton B&Bs."

"And you never introduced yourself?"

"God no."

"Why not?"

He shrugged. "Once I was sure his life was no better than mine, I lost all interest."

So, coincidence of coincidences, Rachel had just come across Scott Pfeiffer of Grafton, Vermont. Maybe he was in town for a food and beverage services conference. Maybe he'd made something of himself, owned a small chain of quality inns across New England. She wished the best for Scott, after all. Even though she'd never met him, he'd become part of the fabric of her memory and she hoped his life worked out.

But how could they both be wearing the same clothes?

That was the detail she couldn't dismiss no matter how hard she tried. Accepting that Brian's double or near double had happened to be in the same city of two million was easy enough, she supposed, but to swallow that both men wore a thin copper-colored rain-coat over a black cotton pullover with the collar turned up, a white T-shirt, and midnight blue jeans, that required the kind of faith re-ligions were founded on.

Wait, she asked herself as she turned up Commonwealth toward her building, *how did you see the blue jeans? There was an SUV between you and his legs.*

The same way she'd seen the rest of him, she realized—reflected in the glass. She'd first seen his face, the coat and pullover. Then, as the confusion set in, she'd caught the back of him as he stepped into the car, ducking his head under the doorframe, pulling the flap of the coat in after him. In the moment, she hadn't realized she'd seen all that, but on the walk home, it reassembled for her. So, yes, the Refracted Man (or Scott Pfeiffer of Grafton, Vermont) had been wearing the same color jeans Brian had left the house in. Same jeans, same coat, same sweater, same color T-shirt.

In the apartment, she half talked herself out of it again. Coinci-dences *did* happen in this life. She dried her hair and went into the spare bedroom he often used as his home office. She called his cell. It went directly to voice mail. Made sense. He was either still in the air or had just landed. Made perfect sense.

An ash-blond desk sat before a window that looked out across the river at MIT and Cambridge. They were high enough that on a clear day they could make out Arlington and parts of Medford if they put in the effort. Now, though, behind the sheets of rain, it was an impressionist painting, the buildings retaining their shapes but stripped of all specificity. Normally Brian's laptop sat here, but of course he'd taken it on his trip with him. She put her own laptop there and considered her options. She tried his cell a second time. Voice mail.

His primary credit cards, an Amex and a mileage-plus Visa, were business cards. The records were at his offices, which were through the soup and across the river in Cambridge, just on the edge of Harvard Square.

The statements on their personal credit cards, however, were easily accessible. She brought the one for the Mastercard up on her screen. She went back three months and found nothing out of the ordinary, so she went back six. All ordinary purchases. What had she been expecting to find? If she did find some irregularity, the inexplicable purchase, the mystery website, would it turn out to be clear evidence he was in Copley Square early this afternoon when he was supposed to be in London? Or would it just turn out to be proof he surfed porn sites or that her last birthday present hadn't been tucked away a month early as he'd claimed but had actually been purchased in a mad scramble that morning?

She didn't even find that.

She went to the British Airways site and checked arrival information on Flight 422, Logan to Heathrow.

Delayed departure due to weather.
Expected arrival: 8:25 pm (GMT +1).

That was fifteen minutes from now.

She checked their ATM statements and found no large cash withdrawals. With some guilt she realized the last time he'd used the card had been as a point-of-sale purchase—the necklace he'd bought her at the mall.

She looked at her cell, willing it to vibrate, for "Brian" to show up in the caller ID. Somehow he'd clear this whole thing up. She'd finish the phone call laughing at her own paranoia.

Wait. Cell phone records. Of course. She didn't have his—his cell phone was provided by his company and therefore a business expense—but she had her own. She spun in the chair once and set to tapping away on the keyboard. In a little over a minute, she had her cell records dating back a year. She called up the iCal and matched dates he'd been out of town against her records.

And there they all were—incoming calls from his cell phone when he'd been in Nome, Seattle, Portland. But they didn't tell her anything. He could have made those calls from anywhere. So she scrolled to another week—God, that black icy week in January— incoming calls from Brian when he'd been in (or claimed to have been in) Moscow, Belgrade, Minsk. And there in the fifth column of the bill were the international long-distance charges she'd accrued for answering those calls. Not small charges either (Why was she getting charged for answering her phone? She needed a new pro- vider), but sizable ones. Ones that correlated with calls made from the other side of the world.

As she clicked back over to the British Airways site, her phone vibrated. Brian.

"Hey," she said.

An elongated hiss followed by two soft pops.

And then his voice. "Hey, babe."

"Hey," she said again.

"I'm—"

"Where are—?"

"What?"

"—you?"

"I'm in the customs line. And my phone's about to die."

Her relief at hearing his voice was immediately replaced with irritation. "They didn't have an outlet in first class? On British Airways?"

"They did but mine didn't work. You okay?"

"Uh-huh."

"Sure?"

"Why wouldn't I be?"

"I dunno. You just sound . . . tight."

"Must be the connection."

He didn't say anything for a bit. And then: "Okay."

"How's the customs line?"

"Massive. I'm taking a guess but I'm pretty sure a Swiss Air flight and an Emirates flight arrived the same time as us."

Another bit of dead air.

"So," she said, "I met with Melissa today."

"Yeah?"

"And after? I was walking on—"

She heard a series of *beep-clicks*.

"Phone's dying, babe. I'm really sorry. Call you from the ho—"

The line went dead.

Had it sounded like customs in the background? What did customs sound like? It had been a while since she'd been out of the country. She tried to picture it. She was pretty sure a *ding* went off when a checkpoint became open. But she couldn't remember if it was a soft *ding* or a loud one. Either way, she hadn't heard any *dings* during their conversation. But if the line was long enough, and Brian was still at the back of it, maybe he wasn't close enough to the checkpoints for the *dings* to be heard.

What else had she heard? Just a general hubbub. No distinct conversations. Plenty of people didn't talk in lines, particularly after a long flight. They were too tired. Too knackered, as Brian sometimes said with a faux British accent.

She stared out the window through the rain at the Monet version of the Charles and Cambridge beyond. Not all its shapes were foreign to her. Downriver she could discern the spiky amorphous sprawl of the Stata Center, a complex of brightly colored aluminum and titanium buildings that called to mind an implosion. Usually she abhorred modern architecture, but she had an inexplicable fondness for the Stata. Something about its haphazard lunacy seemed inspired. Back upriver, she could identify the dome of the main building at MIT, and farther still, the spire of the Memorial Church at Harvard Yard.

She'd had lunch in the Yard a few times with Brian. It was just a few blocks from his office and he'd met her there their first summer together, sometimes with burgers from Charlie's Kitchen or pizza from Pinocchio's. His office was about as unassuming as they came, six rooms on the third floor of a nondescript three-story brick building on Winthrop Street that looked as if it belonged in an old mill town like Brockton or Waltham far more than in the backyard of one of the most elite universities in the world. A small gold plate outside the main door identified it as Delacroix Timber Ltd. She'd been there three times, maybe four, and outside of Brian and his junior partner, Caleb, she couldn't name the other employees or recall much about them except that they were young and cute, males and females, with the avid eyes of the ambitious. Interns mostly, Brian had told her, hoping to prove their mettle and get promoted to a paying position on the mother ship in Vancouver.

Brian Delacroix's break from his family had always been a personal one, he explained to Rachel, never a professional one. He liked the lumber business. He was good at it. When his uncle, who'd run the U.S. operation from offices on Fifth Avenue in Manhattan, dropped dead of a stroke while walking his dog through Central Park one night, Brian—never a source of disappointment to his family, just one of confusion—stepped into the role. After a year, he found Manhattan to be too much—"You can't turn it off," he'd say—and moved the operation to Cambridge.

She looked at the clock in the upper right corner of her laptop: 4:02 P.M. There'd still be someone at the office. Caleb, at the very least, who worked like a madman. Rachel could pop over, tell Caleb Brian had left something behind in his office and asked her to retrieve it. Once there, she could hop on his computer or take a peek through the credit card statements in his files. Make sure everything added up.

Was it a crime to suddenly and wholly mistrust your husband? She wondered this as she tried to hail a cab on Commonwealth.

It wasn't a crime or even a sin, but it didn't speak to a rock-solid foundation in their marriage, either. How could she mistrust him this fast, after she'd been singing his praises just this afternoon to Melissa? Their marriage, unlike those of so many of their friends, was strong.

Wasn't it?

What was a strong marriage? What was a good marriage? She knew terrible people who had wonderful marriages, glued together somehow in their terribleness. And she knew fine, fine people who'd stood before God and all their friends to profess their undying love to each other only to toss that love on a slag heap a few years later. In the end, no matter how good they were—or thought they were— usually all that remained of the love they'd so publicly professed was vitriol, regret, and a kind of awed dismay at how dark the roads they'd ventured down became by the end.

A marriage, her mother often said, was only as strong as your next fight.

Rachel didn't believe that. Or didn't want to. Not when it came to her and Brian. When it came to her and Sebastian, that had definitely been true, but she and Sebastian were a disaster from the start. She and Brian were anything but.

Yet in the absence of a logical reason why she would stumble across a man who looked like her husband and was dressed identically slipping out of the back of a building in Boston when her husband was supposed to be on a flight to London, she had to go with the only rational answer—that the man exiting the Hancock early this afternoon had been Brian. Which meant he wasn't in London. Which meant he was lying.

She flagged down a cab.

15

WET

I don't want him to be lying, she thought as the cab crossed the BU bridge and rounded the rotary to turn onto Memorial Drive. *I don't want to believe any of this. I want to feel exactly as I did this weekend—in love and in trust.*

But what is my alternative? Pretend I didn't see him?

This wouldn't be the first time you saw something that wasn't there.

Those times were different.

How?

They just were.

The cabdriver never said a word during the drive. She glanced at his hack license. Sanjay Seth. He looked sullen in the photo, one step short of scowling. She didn't know this man and yet she allowed him to transport her, just as she allowed strangers to prepare her food and go through her trash and give her a body scan and fly a plane. And she hoped they didn't fly that plane into a mountain or poison her food just because they were having a bad day. Or, in the case of this cab, she hoped he wouldn't accelerate and drive her to a remote spot at the back of a failed industrial park and climb in the backseat, telling her just what he thought of women who didn't say "Please." The last time she'd taken a cab, this line of thinking had compelled her to abort the ride, but this time she pressed her fists into the sides of her thighs and kept them there. She maintained a steady inhale and exhale that was neither too deep nor too shallow and looked out the window at the rain and told herself she'd get through this just like she got through the subway ride and the mall.

When they neared Harvard Square, she asked Sanjay Seth to pull over at the corner of JFK and Winthrop because Winthrop was a one-way heading in the wrong direction. She didn't feel like waiting while the cab slogged through 4:50 traffic for another five or ten minutes to come around the block just so he could get her a hundred feet closer.

As she approached the building, Caleb Perloff exited it. He tugged on the door to make sure it had locked behind him, his rain-coat and Sox ball cap as wet as everyone else's in the city, and then turned to see her standing on the sidewalk below him.

She could tell by the look on his face that he couldn't put the two together—Rachel here on the other side of the river in Cambridge, outside their offices, when Brian was overseas.

She felt ridiculous. What possible explanation could she have for standing here? She'd had the cab ride over to think about it and she hadn't managed to come up with one viable reason she'd need access to her husband's office.

"So this is where it all happens," she tried.

Caleb shot her that wry smile of his. "This is the spot." He craned his head to look up at the building and then back at her. "Did you know that the price of timber went down one-tenth of one cent yesterday in Andhra Pradesh?"

"I did not, no."

"But on the other side of the world, in Mato Grosso—"

"That's where again?"

"Brazil." He rolled the *r* as he came down the steps toward her. "In Mato Grosso, the price *rose* half a cent. And all signs point to it continuing to rise over the next month."

"But in India?"

"We get that tenth of a cent discount." He shrugged. "But it's also kinda volatile right now. And shipping costs are higher. So who do we make a deal with?"

"That's a dilemma," she admitted.

"And what about all the timber we export?"

"Another wrinkle."

"Can't just let it rot."

"Couldn't do that."

"Let the bugs get to it. The rain."

"Heavens. The rain."

He held his hand up to it, a soft drizzle at the moment. "Actually, it's been dry in BC this past month. Odd. Dry there, wet here. Usually works the other way." He cocked his head at her.

She cocked hers at him.

"Brings you by, Rachel?"

She never knew how much Brian had told anyone about her condition. He'd said he didn't mention it, but she figured he had to tell someone, if only after a few drinks. They had to wonder at some point why Rachel hadn't been able to join them at this party or that, why she'd skipped out on the Fourth of July fireworks with everyone last year at the Esplanade, why they rarely saw her out at the bars. Someone as bright as Caleb would have realized at some point that the only time he saw Rachel was in controlled environments (usually the condo) with small groups. But did Caleb know she hadn't driven a car in two years? Hadn't taken the subway in almost as long prior to this past Saturday? Did he know she once froze in the food court of the Prudential Center Mall, that she'd had to sit, surrounded by

well-meaning security personnel, short of breath and certain she'd
pass out, until Brian arrived to take her home?

"I was shopping in the 'hood." She gestured toward the square.

He looked at her empty hands.

"Couldn't find a thing," she said. "Turned into a browse day." She
squinted through the mist at the building behind him. "Thought I'd
take a look at the competition for my husband's attentions."

He smiled. "Want to come up?"

"*I'll just pop into his office to . . .*"

"*He left something in his drawer that he . . .*"

"*So this is his command center. Mind if I just hang out here for a bit?
You can close the door behind you.*"

"Did you remodel?" she said.

"Nope."

"Then there's nothing I need to see. Just thought I'd stroll by
before I headed home."

He nodded as if it all made perfect sense. "Want to share a cab?"

"That'd be great."

They walked back up Winthrop and crossed JFK. It was close
to five and the traffic heading into Harvard Square had clotted. To
catch a cab heading out of the square, their best chance was to walk
a block to the Charles Hotel. But what had been a flat pewter sky just
a minute before had turned swollen and black.

"That's not good," Caleb said.

"I wouldn't think so, no."

They came to the end of Winthrop and could see from there that
the cab stand in front of the Charles was empty. The traffic snaking
toward the river was as bad as, if not worse than, the traffic heading
into the square.

The black above rumbled. A few miles to the west, a bolt of lightning split the sky.

"A drink?" Caleb said.

"Or two," she said as the sky opened. "Jesus."

The umbrellas were poor protection once the wind kicked in. The rain fell with weight and clatter, the drops exploding off the pavement as they ran back up Winthrop. It sliced in from the right and the left, the front and the back.

"Grendel's or Shay's?" Caleb said.

She could see Shay's on the other side of JFK. Close, but still another fifty yards in the rain. And if traffic moved, they'd have to work their way to a crosswalk. Grendel's, on the other hand, was just to their left.

"Grendel's."

"Good choice. We're too old for Shay's anyway."

In the vestibule, they added their umbrellas to the dozen or so already leaning against the wall. They removed their coats and Caleb took off his Sox cap, which had soaked through. His brown hair was cut so tight to his scalp he freed it of moisture by swiping his palm across it. They found a place to hang their coats by the hostess stand and were led to a table. Grendel's Den was a basement-level place and they ordered their first round as shoes of every variety ran past on the cobblestones outside. Soon the rain had grown so heavy no one ran past.

Grendel's had been around so long that not only could Rachel recall being turned away from the door with a fake ID in the nineties, but her mother had recalled frequenting the place in the early seventies. It catered mostly to Harvard students and faculty. Out-of-towners tended to wander in only on summer days when management placed tables out front by the green.

The waitress brought a wine for Rachel and a bourbon for Caleb and left menus. Caleb used his napkin to blot his face and neck dry.

They both chuckled a few times without saying anything. It could be years before they saw rain like this again.

"How's the baby?" she asked.

He beamed. "She's magical. I mean, for the first ninety days, their eyes don't really lock onto anything besides the breast and the mother's face, so I was starting to feel left out. But on that ninety-first day? AB looked right at me and I was a goner."

Caleb and Haya had named their six-month-old Annabelle but Caleb had been referring to her as AB since the second week of her life.

"Well"—Caleb raised his glass—"cheers."

She met his glass with her own. "To dodging pneumonia."

"We hope," he said.

They drank.

"How's Haya?"

"She's good." Caleb nodded. "Real good. Loves being a mom."

"How's her English coming?"

"She watches a ton of TV. It really helps. You can have a solid conversation with her now if you have a little patience. She's very . . . deliberate about choosing her words."

Caleb had returned from a trip to Japan with Haya. He spoke halting Japanese; she spoke barely any English. They were married within three months. Brian didn't like it. Caleb wasn't the settling-down type, he'd say. And what were they going to talk about over the dinner table?

Rachel had to admit that it colored her opinion of Caleb when he introduced her to the luminous, mostly mute, subservient woman with the kind of face and body that could launch a thousand wet dreams. What else had bound him to her, if not that and that alone? And was the master-servant vibe she got when she saw them together an outgrowth of some hidden he-man fantasy he'd always secretly pursued? Or was Rachel just being bitchy because it hadn't escaped her notice that while Caleb had married a woman who didn't speak English, his partner Brian had married a shut-in?

When she brought that up to Brian, he said, "It's different with us."

"How?"

"You're not a shut-in."

"I beg to differ."

"You're just going through a phase. You'll rebound. But him? Having a kid? The fuck's that all about? He *is* a kid."

"Why's it bother you so much?"

"It doesn't bother me 'so much,'" he said. "It's just not the right time in his life."

"How did they meet?" she said.

"You know the story. He went to Japan on a deal and came back with her. Didn't come back with the deal, by the way. He got under-cut by some—"

"But how does he just 'come back' with a Japanese citizen? I mean, there are immigration laws designed to keep people from just popping into our country and deciding to stay."

"Not if she's here on a legal visa and he marries her."

"But it doesn't strike you as odd? She meets him over there and just decides to chuck her life aside and join him in America, a country she's never seen where people speak a language she doesn't know?"

He gave it some thought. "You've got a point. What's your theory then?"

"Internet-order bride?"

"Don't they all come from the Philippines and Vietnam?"

"Not all."

"Huh," Brian said. "Internet-order bride. The more I think of it, I wouldn't put it past him. We're back to my point—Caleb's not mature enough for marriage. So he picks someone he barely knows who can barely communicate."

"Love's love," she said, throwing one of his own preferred bromides back at him.

He grimaced. "Love's love until you toss kids into the mix. Then it becomes a business partnership with guaranteed economic instability."

It wasn't that he didn't have a point, but she did wonder if he was talking about himself in those moments, about his fears regarding the fragility of their own relationship and the potential calamity that could be wrought by bringing a child into it.

An icy thought slid through her before she could stop it: *Oh, Brian, have I ever really known you?*

Caleb was giving her a curious smile from the other side of the table, as if to ask, *Where did you go?*

Her phone vibrated on the table. Brian. She resisted the childish impulse to ignore it.

"Hey."

"Hey," he said warmly. "Sorry about earlier. Friggin' thing just died. Then I was worried I'd forgotten my adapters. But I did not, my wife. And here we are."

She got out of the booth, moved a few feet away. "Here we are."

"Where you at?"

"Grendel's."

"Where?"

"That college bar by your office."

"I know it, I just can't figure out how you turned up there."

"I'm with Caleb."

"Uh, okay. Help me out here. What's going on?"

"Nothing's going on. Why would something be going on? It's raining like holy hell but otherwise just grabbing a drink with your partner."

"Well, that's great. What brought you over to Harvard Square?"

"A wild hair. It had been a while. I got an urge to visit some bookstores. I went with it. Where you staying this time? I forgot."

"Covent Garden. You said it looked like a place Graham Greene would have liked."

"When did I say that?"

"When I sent you a picture last time. No, two times ago."

"Send me one now." As soon as the words left her mouth, adrenaline flooded her blood as if poured from a bucket.

"What?"

"A picture."

"It's ten o'clock at night."

"A selfie from the lobby then."

"Hmm?"

"Just send me a picture of you." Another sunburst of adrenaline exploded at the center of her. "I miss you."

"Okay."

"You'll do that?"

"Yeah, sure." A pause and then: "Everything okay?"

She laughed and it sounded shrill to her own ears. "Everything is fine. Perfectly fine. Why do you keep asking?"

"You just sound funny."

"Tired, I guess," she said. "All this rain."

"So we'll talk in the morning, then."

"Sounds great."

"Love you."

"Love you too."

She hung up and went back to the booth. Caleb looked up as she sat, his thumb working his cell phone keypad as he gave her a smile. She was a little amazed at people who could do the talk-with-one-person-text-with-another trick. It was usually computer geeks and tech nerds like, well, Caleb.

"How's he doing?"

"He sounded good. Tired but good. Do you ever go on any of these trips?"

Caleb shook his head and continued tapping away on his phone.

"He's the voice of the company. Him and his old man. He also has the business acumen. I just keep the trains running on time."

"Are you demurring?"

"Hell, no." After a few more distracted seconds, he pocketed his phone. He folded his hands on the table, looked at her to let her know she had his full attention again. "Without me and people like me in the here and now, that two-hundred-year-old lumber firm wouldn't last six more months. Sometimes—not every day but sometimes—the speed of a transaction can save a couple, three million dollars. It's that fluid out there." He waved his fingers at the global "there."

The waitress returned and they ordered another round.

Caleb opened the menu. "Do you mind if I eat? I walked in the office at ten this morning and didn't get up from my desk again until I walked out at five."

"Sure."

"You?"

"I could eat."

The waitress returned with their drinks and took their orders. As she left, Rachel noticed a man around the same age as Brian, forty or so, sitting with an older woman who gave off a stylish professorial air. She could have been sixty, yet it was a sexy-as-hell sixty. Normally Rachel would have studied her to see what about her gave off that impression so forcefully—was it her clothes, the way she sat, the cut of her hair, the intelligence in her face?—but instead Rachel focused on the man. He had sandy blond hair going gray over the ears and hadn't shaved in a couple of days. He drank a beer and sported a gold wedding band. He also wore exactly what her husband had worn this morning, sans the raincoat—blue jeans, white T-shirt, black pullover sweater with an upturned collar.

Was this what she'd missed being holed up so much of her time? It wasn't like she didn't get out, but she certainly didn't get out much. Maybe she'd overlooked the prevalence of some styles. When had all men decided, for example, to stop shaving until every third or fourth day? When had half-fedoras and porkpie hats come back into style? Where did the brightly colored tennis shoe spring from? When was the moment all casual bicyclists decided they should dress in skintight spandex, replete with brand names all over the shirts and leggings, as if they required corporate sponsorship to pedal to Starbucks?

Back when Rachel had been in college, hadn't every third boy worn a plaid shirt, V-neck tee, and ripped jeans? If she went to the hotel bars frequented by middle-aged Republican salesmen right now, how many would be dressed in light blue oxford shirts and tan pants? So, by that metric, wasn't it entirely possible that the combination of dark pullover, white T-shirt, and blue jeans—which had probably never gone fully in or out of style, basic as it was—could be worn by three men in Boston-Cambridge on the same day? If she walked through a mall right now, she'd probably see it on a couple more, not to mention on the mannequins fronting the J. Crew and Vince stores.

Their food arrived. Caleb made short work of his burger, and she devoured her salad. She hadn't realized how hungry she was.

When they'd both cleaned their plates, they sat in the warmth of the low lights and gathering dusk. The rain had let up and a steady stream of footsteps returned to the cobblestones just above their heads as people ventured back out into the evening.

His smile wrapped around his bourbon as he raised the glass to his lips.

She could feel the wine when she smiled back.

They'd shared a moment—no more than that—when she'd first been dating Brian. In a pantry at the apartment of a friend of Brian's in the Fenway. Rachel had gone into the pantry for olives, Caleb had been coming out with Stoned Wheat Thins, if she remembered correctly, and they'd paused as their bodies passed. Their eyes met and neither dropped their gaze. Then it became something of a challenge—who literally would blink first?

"Hi," she'd said.

"Hi." The word stumbled out of the back of his throat.

Vasoconstriction, she remembered thinking. The process by which skin capillaries constrict in order to elevate core body temperature. Corresponding increase in respiratory rate and heartbeat. A flush to the skin.

She'd leaned toward him at the same moment he'd leaned toward her and their heads touched, her breasts pressed against his chest, the edge of his right hand brushed the edge of her left on its way to her hip. Of all the places their bodies met in that second or two, it was most intimate when his hand grazed hers. When that hand found her hip, she turned away and sidestepped deeper into the pantry. He let out a small sound—some hybrid hiccup-laugh of amazement and exasperation and embarrassment—and was gone from the pantry in the time it took for her to look back.

Vasodilation: When the core body temperature is too high, blood vessels below the skin dilate so heat can escape the body and core temperature can be restored.

It took her almost five minutes to figure out where the fucking olives were.

She sipped her wine and Caleb sipped his bourbon and the bar filled up around them. Soon they couldn't see the door. In the past, that could have easily shot bolts of anxiety into her bloodstream, but tonight it only made things seem warmer, more intimate.

"How's Brian been handling all this rain?" Caleb asked.

"You know him—positive mental attitude. He's the only person in the city who hasn't bitched about it yet."

Caleb shook his head. "Same at the office. We're all drowning, he's like, 'It creates a mood.'"

She finished the sentence with him. "He says the same thing at home. I'm like, 'What mood? Abject depression?' He says, 'No. It's fun. It's sexy.' I said, 'Honey, it was fun and sexy on day one, and that was ten days ago.'"

Caleb chuckled into his glass, took a drink. "Man would find a silver lining in a concentration camp. 'You don't see barbed wire of that quality in other death camps. Plus the showerheads are top-notch.'"

Rachel drank some more wine. "It's awesome."

"It is awesome."

"But it can be exhausting."

"Wipe you the fuck out. I never met someone who needs positivity like that guy. And it's weird 'cause it's not like Hallmark positivity, it's just a can-do thing. You know?"

"Oh, I know. Do I ever know." She smiled at the thought of her husband. Couldn't stand movies with bummer endings, books where the hero lost, songs about alienation.

"I get it," he'd said to her once. "I read Sartre in college, I had friends who dragged me to a Nine Inch Nails concert. The world's a pointless, chaotic mess where nothing means nothing. I do understand. I just choose not to engage that philosophy because it doesn't help me."

Brian, she'd long ago realized with both admiration and irritation, didn't do depressing. He didn't do hopeless or bleak chic or whining. Brian did objectives and strategies and remedies. Brian did hope.

Once, during an irritable mood, when Brian said, "Anything's possible," she said, "No, Brian, it's not. Curing world hunger is not possible, flapping our arms to take flight is not possible."

A small, strange fire grew in his eyes. "No one's got long game anymore. Everyone wants it now."

"What are you even talking about?"

"That if you believe, really believe, and if your strategy is sound, and if you're willing to leave everything you've got on the field of battle to win the day"—he held his arms wide—"you can do *any-thing*."

She'd smiled at him and left the room before she'd be forced to decide if the man she'd married was just a tiny bit crazy.

On the other hand, she never had to worry about him whining or bitching or kvetching in any way. Sebastian, no surprise, had been a whiner. A glass-half-empty negativist who showed in a thousand ways, both large and small, that he believed the world awoke every morning thinking about ways to urinate in his food. Brian, on the other hand, seemed to approach each day as if there was a present hidden somewhere within it. And if he didn't find it, there'd be no point bitching about it.

Another Brianism: "A complaint that's not looking for a solution is a disease that's not looking for a cure."

Caleb said, "He loves quoting that one at the office. I keep ex-pecting to see it on a plaque someday, hanging in the waiting room."

"You gotta admit, though, it really works for him. You ever known Brian to stay in a bad mood more than a few minutes?"

He nodded. "I'll give you that. Why, some people would follow him into a burning cave—they just feel he'd get them out the other side somehow."

She liked that. It made her see her husband as heroic for a mo-ment, a leader, an inspiration.

She sat back in her chair and Caleb sat back in his and for a min-ute or so neither of them said a word.

"You look good," Caleb said eventually. "I mean, you always look good, but you look . . ."

She watched him search for the word.

He found it. "Secure."

Had anyone ever said that about her? Her mother used to say she rushed around so much she would've forgotten her head most days if it wasn't already attached. Two ex-boyfriends and her ex-husband had all told her she was "anxious." In her twenties, alcohol, cigarettes, and books, always books, could anchor her in place. When she quit smoking, a treadmill replaced the window seat until her doctor, noting a rash of shin splints and a pretty significant weight drop in a body that was never in danger of being overweight, convinced her to complement the running with yoga. Worked well for a while, but the yoga eventually led to the "visions" and the visions, post-Haiti, led to the panic attacks.

Secure. No one had ever accused her of that. What could make Rachel Childs-Delacroix appear secure?

Her phone vibrated by her elbow. A text from Brian. She opened it. She smiled.

There stood Brian, still in the clothes he'd worn today, smiling big, if a bit blearily, his hair mussed from travel. Behind him, a facade of brown wainscoting, wide double doors, large yellow lanterns hanging from either side of the entrance, and above it all the name of the establishment, COVENT GARDEN HOTEL. He'd sent her a few pictures of the street over the years—a curved tidy London street of retail shops and restaurants, red brick and white trim. The doorman, or whoever took the photo, would have had to step off the sidewalk to get the full facade of the hotel into the frame.

Brian was waving, a shit-eating grin dominating his handsome, weary face, as if letting her know he understood this wasn't just an ordinary selfie, she didn't just "miss him." This had been a test of sorts.

And damn, she thought as she slid the phone into her pocket, did you ever pass.

She and Caleb did end up sharing a cab. He had the farther trip; he lived in the Seaport District. On the short ride back to her place they kept the conversation on the rain and the effect on the local economy. The Red Sox, for example, were approaching a Major League Baseball record for rainouts.

At her place, Caleb leaned in for the kiss to the cheek and she was already turning away when his lips landed.

In the condo, she took a shower and the hot water hitting skin pickled throughout the day by cold rain was so exquisite it felt sinful. She closed her eyes and could see Caleb in the bar and then in the pantry, and she flashed on Brian the last time they'd been in this shower together, just a few days ago, and he'd slipped up behind her and run the bar of soap over each nipple, then up one side of her neck and down the other and caressed her abdomen with it in an ever-shrinking circle.

She duplicated his efforts now, could feel him hardening between her legs. She could hear her own breathing mingle with the shower spray as Brian became Caleb and Caleb became Brian and she dropped the soap to the tile and placed one hand to the wall. She thought of Brian in the shower the other day and Brian in front of the Covent Garden Hotel, that shit-eating grin of his, those blue eyes filled with boyish glee. Caleb vanished. She used a single finger to bring herself to a climax that moved through her body as if the hot water had entered her and flushed her capillaries.

After, she lay in bed and was drifting to sleep when an odd thought occurred to her:

When he'd decided to order dinner, Caleb had said he'd spent the entire day—10 A.M. to 5 P.M.—behind his desk. Said he never got up. Never went out. But when she'd shown up outside the building, he'd just been exiting. He still hadn't stepped out from under the overhang above the door.

Yet his coat and his hat had been soaking wet.

16

REENTRY

Friday. The return.

She thought about picking him up at the airport, but she didn't own a car anymore. She'd sold it when she moved in with Brian; the condo came with only one parking spot. After that, she'd driven Zipcars if she needed to get somewhere. She couldn't believe how convenient they were actually—one lot was within a block of the condo—but then came the Dunkin' Donuts and the food court and the vomiting on the Scientologist. After that, Brian asked her not to drive for a bit.

When it came time to renew her license, they had one of their fiercer fights. She couldn't imagine not renewing, but he countered that he was owed—*owed*—peace of mind. "It's not about you," she recalled shouting across the kitchen bar. "Why do you think everything's about you? Even this?"

Mr. Unflappable slapped the kitchen bar top. "Who did they

call when you couldn't leave the food court? And who did they call when—?"

"So this is about intrusions on your time?" She twisted a dish towel around one hand, tightening it until the blood bloomed under her skin.

"No, no, no. I'm not going to play that."

"No, no, no," she mimicked, feeling like an asshole, but feeling good too because the fight had been building for a week by that point.

For a microsecond, she thought she caught a rage bordering on hatred slip through his eyes before he took a long, slow breath. "An elevator doesn't go sixty miles an hour."

She was still back at that flash of rage. *Was that the real Brian I just saw?*

Eventually she realized it wouldn't return. Not today anyway. She dropped the dish towel to the counter. "What?"

"You can't get mortally wounded if you have a panic attack in an elevator or a mall or, I dunno, in a park or walking down the street. But in a car?"

"It doesn't work that way. I don't have panic attacks when I'm driving."

"You only started having these things a few years ago. How do you know how the next one will manifest? I don't want to get the call that you're wrapped around a pole somewhere."

"Jesus."

He said, "Is it an unreasonable fear?"

"No," she admitted.

"Out of the realm of possibility?"

"No, it's not."

"What if you started having trouble breathing, you're sweating so hard you can't see through it, and you hit somebody in a crosswalk?"

"Now you're bullying."

"No, I'm just asking."

In the end, they reached a compromise. She renewed her license but promised not to use it.

But now that she'd strolled through a mall and ridden the subway, walked past old South Church into Copley Square, taken a cab through the rain, and sat in a crowded basement bar and all of it without a single uptick in her heart rate, not a single twitch in a throat vein, wouldn't it be cool to show up outside baggage claim at Logan? He'd freak, of course, but would his apprehension be overwhelmed by his pride?

She went so far as to update her Zipcar account info—the credit card she'd first used had expired—but then remembered he'd driven himself to the airport and left the Infiniti in long-term parking.

So that was that. Her gratitude at being able to pass the cup induced some guilt—she felt gutless, weak—but maybe it was better she not drive if even the scantest trepidation remained.

When he came through the door, he wore the mildly surprised look of a man trying to reacquaint himself with the part of his life that didn't include airports and hotels and room service and constant change but the opposite—routine. He glanced at the magazine basket she'd placed by the sofa as if he couldn't place it, because he couldn't; she'd purchased it while he was gone. He wheeled his suitcase to a corner and took off his copper raincoat and said, "Hey," with an uncertain smile.

"Hey." She hesitated before she crossed the apartment to him.

If he'd been away for more than twenty-four hours, there was always a hiccup or two upon reentry. An awkward stumble toward reassembly. He'd left their lives, after all, the things that defined them as "we," which meant they each had spent the week becoming "I." And just when that had become the new normal, he stepped back into the frame. And they tried to figure out where "I" ended and "we" began again.

They kissed and it was dry, almost chaste.

"You tired?" she asked because he looked it.

"Yeah. Yeah, I am." He looked at his watch. "It's, what, midnight over there."

"I made you some dinner."

He smiled broadly and easily, the first real Brian smile since he'd come through the door. "No way. Going all domestic on me and whatnot? Thanks, babe."

He kissed her a second time and this one had a little heat to it. She felt something loosen in her and returned the kiss in kind.

They sat and ate salmon cooked in foil with brown rice and a salad. He asked her about her week and she asked him about London and the conference, which apparently hadn't gone well.

"They set up these boards so they can convince the world they give a shit about the environment and the ethics of timber acquisition. Then they stack the board with industry assholes whose only ambition besides sampling the local hookers is to make sure nothing gets done." He rubbed his eyes with the heels of his palms and sighed. "It's, um, frustrating." He looked down at his empty plate. "You?"

"What about me?"

"You seemed off whenever we talked on the phone."

"No, I'm fine."

"Sure?"

"Uh-huh."

As he yawned into his fist and gave her a weary smile, it was clear he didn't believe her. "I'm gonna shower."

"Okay."

He cleared their plates and put them in the dishwasher. As he headed for the bedroom, she said, "All right. You want to know?"

He turned just short of the doorway and let loose a soft sigh of relief. Held out his hands. "That would be lovely."

"I saw your double."

"My double?"

She nodded. "Getting into a black Suburban behind the Hancock on Monday afternoon."

"When I was in the air?" He stared back at her, confused. "So, give me a sec here because I'm wiped . . . uh, you saw a guy who looked like me and—"

"No, I saw your double."

"So maybe you saw Scott—"

"—Pfeiffer of Grafton, Vermont? I considered that. Problem was, this guy was also dressed in the exact same clothes you left the house in."

He took that in with a slow nod. "You didn't think you saw my double. You thought you saw me."

She poured them both a little more wine and brought his glass to him. She leaned against the back of the couch. He leaned against the doorjamb.

"Yes."

"Ah." He closed his eyes and smiled and a weight seem to rise from his body and leave through the vent above him. "So the weird tone and the selfie you wanted me to send that was all because you thought . . ." He opened his eyes. "You thought *what*?"

"I didn't know what I thought."

"Well, you either thought Scott Pfeiffer made a trip into Boston or that I was lying about being out of the country."

"Something like that." It sounded so ridiculous now.

He grimaced and drank some wine.

"What?" she asked. "No, what?"

"You think that little of us?"

"No."

"You thought I was living some kind of double life."

"I definitely didn't say that."

"Well, what else would it be? You claim you saw me on a street in Boston when I was on a 767 over probably, I dunno, Greenland by that point. So you grill me about where I am when I call from Heathrow and you grill me about not charging my phone and—"

"I didn't grill you."

"No? And then you ask me to take a picture of myself so I can prove I'm, you know, exactly where I'd fucking said I'd be, and then you go out with my partner and, what, grill him too?"

"I'm not going to listen to this."

"Why would you? You might actually have to take responsibility for acting like an asshole." He lowered his head and held up a weary hand. "You know what? I'm tired. I'm not going to say anything helpful right now. And I need to, I dunno, process this. Okay?"

She tried to decide how angry she wanted to stay and if she was mad at him or just herself. "You called me an asshole."

"No, I said you were acting like one." A thin smile. "It's a small distinction but a meaningful one."

She gave him back her own thin smile, placed a hand to his chest. "Go take your shower."

He closed the bedroom door behind him and she could hear the water run.

She found herself standing over his raincoat. She put her wine on a side table and wondered why she didn't feel guilt right now. She should; he was right—she'd walked down an insulting road thinking her husband of two years was so untrustworthy that he'd lie about which city he was in. But she didn't feel guilt. All week she'd told herself that what she'd seen had been an optical illusion. The selfie proved it. Their own history together, one in which she'd never known him to lie about anything, proved it.

So why didn't she *feel* mistaken? Why didn't she feel guilty about mistrusting him? Not wholeheartedly, of course, not with full certitude. But just a little bit, just a niggling sense that all was not as it should be.

She took his raincoat off the back of the chair where he'd left it, a pet peeve of hers. He couldn't just reach into the hall closet and hang it on a hanger?

She reached into the left pocket and came back with an airline ticket—Heathrow to Logan, dated today—and some loose change. His passport was there too. She opened it and rifled through the visa pages, which were cramped with stamps from all the countries he'd visited. Problem was, the stamps weren't in any kind of order. They seemed to show up on whichever page the immigration officer had decided to flip to that day. She listened to the muffled sound of the water running in the bathroom and continued to rifle the pages—Croatia, Greece, Russia, Germany, and then there it was: Heathrow on May 9, this year. She returned the passport to his coat and reached into the other pocket: a swipe card for the Covent Garden Hotel, 10 Monmouth Street, and a tiny receipt the size of her thumb for a news and magazine shop just up the street at 17 Monmouth. It was dated today, 05/09/14, 11:12 in the morning, and gave evidence that Brian bought a newspaper, a pack of gum, and a bottle of Orangina, and paid with a 10-pound note and received 4.53 pounds sterling as change.

The shower turned off. She put the swipe card back in the pocket of the coat and returned the coat to the back of the chair. But she slipped the receipt into the back pocket of her jeans. She had no idea why. Instinct.

17

GATTIS

Every year, on the anniversary of the night they met, Brian and Rachel returned to the RR and danced to "Since I Fell for You." If it could be found on a jukebox these days, it was usually the Johnny Mathis version, but the RR's jukebox had the original version, the granddaddy of them all by one-hit wonder Lenny Welch.

It wasn't a love song so much as it was a loss song, the lament of someone trapped in a hopeless addiction to a heartless lover who will, there is no doubt, ultimately destroy him. Or her, depending on which version you listened to. Since their first dance to the song, they'd heard most of them—Nina Simone's, Dinah Washington's, Charlie Rich's, George Benson's, Gladys Knight's, Aaron Neville's, and Mavis Staples's. And those were just the headliners. Rachel had once looked it up on iTunes and found two hundred and sixty-four versions, performed by everyone from Louis Armstrong to Captain & Tennille.

This year, Brian rented out the whole back room and invited some friends. Melissa showed up. So did Danny Marotta, Rachel's former cameraman at 6; Danny brought his wife, Sandra, and Sandra brought a coworker, Liz; Annie, Darla, and Rodney, who'd all accepted buyouts from the *Globe* in the years since she'd left, dropped by. Caleb showed up with Haya, somehow dressed to lay waste in a simple black cotton sheath dress and black flats, black hair swept back off the curve of her elegant neck in an updo, and all of her made somehow earthier and even sexier by the baby on her hip. The perfect baby, by the way, the dark good looks of both parents fused into a child with the most symmetrical face, eyes of warm black oil, skin the color of desert sand just after sundown. Rachel caught Brian, usually circumspect in such matters, pushing his eyeballs back into his head a few times when Haya and AB passed by, like some fantastical ur-humans who'd stepped from a creation myth. Haya got some of the youngest guys—Brian and Caleb's latest interns, no point in learning their names, they'd be replaced with new ones the next time she looked—to take long looks, even though all their female counterparts were blindingly pretty and flush with firm, unblemished early-twenties flesh.

On another night, Rachel might have felt a twinge of jealousy or at least competitive edge—the woman had just given fucking birth, for Christ's sake, and she looked ready for the center spread in a lingerie catalogue—but tonight she knew how good she looked. Not in an advertising-of-the-wares way. But in an elegant, understated way that told everyone in the room she didn't feel any need to trumpet what God had placed in good proportion in the first place and which genetics—and Pilates—were leaving, thus far, in place.

She and Haya caught up by the bar at one point as AB slept in the car seat at her mother's feet. Because of the language barrier, they'd rarely spoken other than a few passing hellos and had hardly seen each other in a year, but Caleb had said Haya's grasp of English was vastly improved. Rachel decided to brave the waters and found that he hadn't been exaggerating: Haya now spoke well, if deliberately.

"How are you?"

"I am . . . happy. How are you?"

"Great. How's Annabelle?"

"She is . . . fussy."

Rachel glanced down at the child sleeping in her seat in the middle of a party. Earlier, while she'd been on Haya's hip, she'd never once squawked or even squirmed.

Haya stared back at Rachel, her beautiful face a blank, her lips set.

"Thank you so much for coming," Rachel said eventually.

"Yes. He . . . is my husband."

"That's why you came?" Rachel felt a small smile tug her lips. "Because he's your husband?"

"Yes." Haya's eyes narrowed in confusion. It made Rachel feel guilty, as if she were bullying the woman over language and cultural barriers. "You look . . . very beautiful, Rachel."

"Thank you. So do you."

Haya looked at the baby at her feet. "She is . . . waking."

Rachel had no idea how she predicted it, but about five seconds later, Annabelle's eyes popped open.

Rachel squatted by her. She never knew what to say to babies. She'd watched people over the years interact with them in a way she found unnatural—jabbering in that infantile tone of voice no one ever adopted unless they were talking to babies, animals, or the very old and infirm.

"Hello," she said to Annabelle.

The child stared back at her with her mother's eyes—so clear and untainted by skepticism or irony that Rachel couldn't help but feel judged by them.

She placed one finger on Annabelle's chest and the child closed her hand around it and tugged.

"You've got a strong grip," Rachel said.

Annabelle let go of her finger and looked up at the cowl of her car seat with a hint of distress, as if she were surprised to find it there. Her face crumpled and Rachel only had time to say, "No, no," before Annabelle wailed.

Haya's shoulder brushed Rachel's as she reached for the handle of the car seat. She lifted the seat up onto the bar. She rocked the seat back and forth and the baby immediately stopped crying and Rachel felt embarrassed and incompetent.

"You have a gift with her," she said.

"I am . . . her mother." Again Haya looked a bit confused. "She is tired. Hungry."

"Of course," Rachel said because it seemed to be the kind of thing one said.

"We must go. Thank you for . . . asking us to your . . . party."

Haya lifted her daughter from the seat and held her to her shoulder, the baby's cheek pressed to the side of her neck. Both mother and daughter looked of a piece, as if they shared the same lungs, saw through the same eyes. It made Rachel and her party seem frivolous. And a little sad.

Caleb came over to gather the car seat and pink baby bag and white muslin blanket, then he walked his wife and daughter out to the car and kissed them both good night. Rachel watched them through the window and knew she didn't want what they had. On the other hand, she knew that she did.

"Look at you," Brian said when someone—Rachel suspected Melissa—put a dollar in the jukebox and pressed B17, "Since I Fell for You," and they were compelled to dance to it a second time that night. He raised his eyebrows at their reflection in the full-length mirror on the back wall, and she saw herself head-on. She was surprised, as she always was in the very first millisecond of seeing herself, that she was no longer twenty-three. Someone had once told

her that everyone had a fixed age in their mind's-eye image of themselves. For some it was fifteen or fifty, but everyone had one. Rachel's
was twenty-three. Her face had, of course, grown longer and more
lined in the ensuing fourteen years. Her eyes had changed—not the
gray-green of them—but they were less sure and less adrenalized.
Her hair, so dark a shade of cherry it looked black in most lights, was
cut short with a side bang, a look that softened the harder curves of
her heart-shaped face.

Or so a producer had once told her when he convinced her to
not only cut her hair but straighten it. Before that conversation, it
had always been a long tangle that fell to her shoulders. But the
producer, after prefacing his critique with "No offense," words that
always preceded something offensive, told her, "You're a few steps
short of beautiful but the camera doesn't know that. The camera
loves you. And that's making our bosses love you."

That producer was, of course, Sebastian. She thought so much of
herself that she married him.

As she and Brian swayed on the dance floor, she acknowledged
what a huge improvement he was over Sebastian. A step up in every
way—better-looking, kinder, better conversationalist, funnier, and
smarter, even though he tried to downplay that part of his makeup,
whereas Sebastian always played it up.

But there was the issue of trust again. Say what you would about
Sebastian being an asshole, but he was a genuine asshole. Such an
asshole that he didn't think he had to hide the fact. Sebastian didn't
hide anything.

On the other hand, with Brian, she didn't know what she had
lately. Things had been unnervingly polite between them since he'd
returned from his trip. She had nothing to support her mistrust,
so she didn't press the issue. And he seemed fine with that. And
yet they moved around each other in the apartment like they were
circling a jar of anthrax. They pulled up short in conversations lest
they say something that could lead to conflict—his habit of leaving

yesterday's clothes hanging over the bedpost, her predilection for not changing the toilet paper roll if there was still one square left stuck to the cardboard—and chose their words with ultimate care. Soon they'd stop discussing potential spots of tension altogether, which would only lead to resentment. They smiled distantly at each other in the morning, smiled distantly at each other in the evening. Spent more time on their laptops or their cells. In the past week, they'd made love once and it was the carnal version of their distant smiles—as binding as water, as intimate as junk mail.

When the song ended, the group clapped and a few whistled and Melissa tapped a fork into her wineglass and shouted, "Kiss! Kiss!" until they finally obliged.

"How self-conscious do you feel right now?" she asked Brian as she leaned back in his arms.

Brian didn't reply. He was trying to make sense of something behind her.

She turned as his fingers parted and she stepped out of his grip.

A man had entered the room. He was in his early fifties, with long gray hair tied back in a ponytail. Quite skinny. He wore a gray unstructured sport coat over a blue-and-white Hawaiian shirt and dark jeans. His skin was leathery and tan. His blue eyes were so bright they looked aflame.

"Brian!" He opened his arms.

Brian exchanged a quick glance with Caleb—it was so fast that if Rachel hadn't been standing three inches from his face she would have missed it—and then a smile flooded his face and he approached the man.

"Andrew." He grasped the man behind his elbow with one hand while shaking his hand with the other. "What brings you to Boston?"

"A show at the Lyric." Andrew raised his eyebrows.

"That's great."

"It is?"

"Isn't it?"

Andrew shrugged. "It's a job."

Caleb walked a pair of drinks over. "Andrew Gattis, back in da house. Stoli still your poison?"

Andrew drained the drink in one swallow and handed the glass back to Caleb. He took the second drink from him, nodded his thanks, and took a moderate sip. "Good to see you."

"You too."

Andrew chuckled. "It is?"

Caleb laughed and clapped him on the shoulder. "That seems to be your line tonight."

"Andrew, my wife, Rachel."

Rachel shook Andrew Gattis's hand. It was surprisingly smooth, even delicate.

"A pleasure, Rachel." He gave her a knowing, reckless smile. "You're smart."

She laughed. "I'm sorry?"

"You're smart." He was still shaking her hand. "I can see that. Shit, anyone can. The beauty, I get. Brian always liked beauty, but the—"

"Play nice," Brian said.

"—brains, that's a new one."

"Hey, Andrew." Brian's voice was very light.

"Hey, Brian." He let go of her hand but kept his eyes on hers.

"Still smoke?"

"I vape."

"Me too."

"No shit?"

"Care to join me for one on the sidewalk?"

Andrew Gattis cocked his head at Rachel. "Think I should?"

"What?"

"Join your husband for a vape?"

"Why not?" she said. "For old times. You can catch up."

"Mmm." He looked around the room, then back at her. "What were you dancing to?"

"'Since I Fell for You.'"

"Who would dance to that?" Andrew gave them both a big, baffled smile. "It's a hopeless song. It's all about emotional imprisonment."

Rachel nodded. "We're trying to be post-ironic, I think. Or meta-romantic. I can never decide which. Enjoy your vape, Andrew."

He tipped an imaginary hat to her and turned toward Brian and Caleb.

The three of them headed for the door, but Andrew Gattis suddenly turned back. He said to Rachel, "Google it."

"What?"

Brian and Caleb, almost at the door, noticed he wasn't with them.

"'Since I Fell for You.' Google it."

"There's about two hundred covers of it, I know."

"I'm not talking about the song."

Brian headed back toward them and Andrew sensed it. He pivoted and met Brian halfway across the floor and they went outside to smoke.

She watched them on the street, all three of them exhaling their vapor. They laughed a lot, like the dearest of old friends, and there was a lot of bro-fection—fist bumping, shoulder slapping, pushing. At one point Brian grabbed Andrew by the back of the neck and pulled him in so their foreheads were touching. They were both smiling, laughing actually, Brian's lips going a mile a minute and the two of them nodding with their heads adhered like Siamese twins.

When they broke the clinch, the smiles died for a moment, and then Brian looked in the window and caught Rachel's eyes and gave her a thumbs-up, as if to say, *It's all okay, it's all okay.*

This is a man, she reminded herself, who would literally give you the coat off his back.

When they returned, Andrew seemed interested in everyone in the room but Rachel. He flirted with one of Delacroix Lumber's employees for a while, chatted up Melissa, spent a fair amount of time talking to Caleb, both of them wearing very somber expressions, and he got drunk with exceptional speed. Within an hour of arriving, he took one step sideways for every five steps forward.

"He never could handle his liquor," Brian said after Andrew knocked one of the intern's bags off the back of a chair and then toppled the chair trying to remedy the situation.

When the chair fell everyone laughed, though few seemed to find it funny.

"A buzzkill, this guy," Brian said. "Always has been."

"How do you know him?" Rachel asked.

Brian didn't hear her. "Let me deal with this."

He walked on over and helped Andrew right the chair. He put a hand on his arm and Andrew yanked the arm back, knocking a half-full glass of beer off the bar in the process. "You fucking roofie me, Bri?"

"All right," Caleb said. "All right."

The bartender, Gail's CrossFit-addict nephew, Jarod, came down the bar, his face tight. "We okay down here?"

"Andrew?" Brian said. "The gentleman's asking us if we're okay. Are we okay?"

"Tip fucking top." Andrew saluted the bartender.

Which pissed Jarod off. "Because I can arrange a ride home for you, sir. You follow what I'm saying?"

Andrew slipped into a rich British accent. "I do, my good publican. And I'd much prefer not to cross paths with the local constabulary tonight."

Jarod told Brian, "Get your friend in a cab."

"You got it."

Jarod picked up the glass that had fallen behind the bar. Remarkably, it hadn't shattered. "He's still here."

"I'm on it," Brian said.

By this point Andrew had the scowling, inward look of the petulant drunk. In her youth, Rachel had seen her mother and two of her mother's boyfriends sport similar looks as a regretful day crossed the plane into a regrettable night.

Andrew grabbed his sport coat off the back of a chair, almost toppling it as well. "You still keep the place in Baker Lake?"

Rachel had no idea who he was talking to. His eyes were on the floor.

"Let's go," Brian said.

"Don't fucking touch me."

Brian held his hands high, like a stagecoach driver in the Old West during a stickup.

"That's some pure fucking wilderness there," Andrew said. "But then you always liked the wild, Bri."

He stumbled toward the door, Brian walking behind him, arms still half raised.

On the sidewalk two things happened almost simultaneously: The cab arrived and Andrew took a swing at Brian.

Brian easily ducked the punch and then caught a reeling Andrew in his arms like he was catching a woman in an old movie on her way to the fainting couch. He stood him up straight and slapped him in the face.

Everyone saw it. They'd been watching the drama unfold since the two of them had exited the bar. A few of the young interns gasped. A few others laughed. One young guy said, "Shit. Don't fuck with the boss man, huh?"

There was something about both the speed and the casual ease of the slap that made it seem twice as brutal. It wasn't the way someone slapped a man who was a threat, but the way someone slapped a child who was an annoyance. There was contempt in it. Andrew's shoulders heaved and his head bobbed and it became clear he was weeping.

Rachel watched her husband saying something to the cabdriver, who was out of his cab and trying to wave off the fare, keep a potentially violent drunk out of his taxi.

But Brian handed him some bills and the cabbie took them. Then they both poured Andrew into the back of the cab, and the cab headed up Tremont.

When Brian came back in the bar, he seemed surprised that anyone had been paying attention. He took Rachel's hand and kissed her and said, "Sorry about that."

Half of her was still back at the slap, the effortless cruelty of it. "Who is he?"

They went to the bar and Brian ordered a scotch, slipped Jarod fifty bucks for his trouble, and turned to her. "He's an old friend. An embarrassing, pain-in-the-ass, never-adapted-to-growing-up old friend. You got any of those?"

"Well, sure." She took a sip of his scotch. "Well, I used to."

"How'd you get rid of them?"

"They got rid of me," she admitted.

That pierced something in him. She could see the pain find him, and she loved him very much at that moment.

He reached out with the same hand that had slapped his friend and caressed her cheek.

"Fools," he whispered. "They were all fools."

18

CULTURE SHOCK

She spent the morning after the party Googling with a hangover while Brian went for a run along the river.

First she looked up "Since I Fell for You." As she'd expected, the first page contained nothing but links to versions of the song. On the second page she found a reference to an episode of a TV show, *L.A. Law,* that had been on when she was in grade school. She remembered her mother watching the show religiously and once putting her hands to her mouth as one of the characters—a woman with tall hair and wide lapels—fell down an elevator shaft. Rachel looked up the "Since I Fell for You" episode on IMDb and nothing about the description struck any chords.

On the third page, she found a link to a movie from 2002 starring Robert Hays, Vivica A. Fox, Kristy Gale, and Brett Alden, with special appearances by Stephen Dorff and Gary Busey. She clicked on the link and got a 401 message that the site no longer existed. So she opened a fresh window and Googled "Since I Fell for You 2002 movie."

Even with the added specificity, most of the links that appeared were to the song. Finally, though, one to "Since I Fell for You/May-December (2002) VHS eBay." When she clicked the link, it brought her to eBay and a screenshot of a VHS tape. The enlargement function was for shit, but she did get close enough to make out the two main actors' faces. It took her a minute to recognize the male as the guy who'd starred in *Airplane*. The female, she was pretty sure, was in *Independence Day;* she'd played the twit who'd risked everybody's life at one point to save her dog. To the right of the photo was a description, probably pulled from the back of the VHS:

> Widower Tom (Hays) finds himself falling for lovely housekeeper LaToya (Fox), who's half his age. Meanwhile, Tom's son (Alden) and LaToya's handicapped roommate (Gale) are also falling for each other in this heartfelt dramedy that asks if love can ever be wrong.

Rachel hopped back on IMDb and cross-referenced Robert Hays's and Vivica A. Fox's credits for other links or information. She found none. She did further due diligence and checked for the title in the credits of Stephen Dorff, Gary Busey, and the two actors she'd never heard of, Kristy Gale and Brett Alden.

Messrs. Dorff and Busey didn't even list the film in their credits.

Kristy Gale seemed to have had a blink-and-you'll-miss-it career in straight-to-video and had appeared in only one major theatrical release, *Scary Movie 3*, as "Girl on Unicycle." Her page hadn't been updated since 2007, which was also the date of her last credit, something called *Lethal Kill*. (Was there another kind? Rachel wondered.)

No page existed for Brett Alden. He must have had his one acrid taste of the off-off-off Hollywood Boulevard life and run back home to Iowa or Wisconsin. Rachel clicked back on the open eBay window and purchased the tape for $4.87 and chose second-day air for delivery.

She got another cup of coffee and came back to her laptop, still in her pajamas, and looked out at the river. Sometime last night, it had stopped raining. And sometime this morning, the sun—yes, the sun—rose. Everything appeared not just clean but polished, the sky looking like a frozen tidal wave, the trees along the river as sharp as jade. And here she sat indoors, with a hangover that thumped in her head and throbbed in her chest and made every synapse hiccup at least once before it fired. She clicked on her music folder and chose a playlist she'd compiled to chill herself out on days when the nerves were too close to the skin—The National, Lord Huron, Atoms for Peace, My Morning Jacket, and others of that ilk—and started looking into Baker Lake.

There were three of them—the biggest in Washington State, another in the Canadian Arctic, and a third in Maine. The one in Washington looked touristy, the one in Canada was populated mostly by Inuit, and the one in Maine was wilderness, the nearest town, by the looks of it, forty miles away. As for proximity to a major city, it was actually closer to Quebec City than Bangor.

"Camping trip?"

She spun with the chair to face him: Brian, covered in sweat from his run, standing eight feet behind her, drinking from a water bottle.

"Reading over my shoulder?" She smiled.

He matched her smile. "Just walked in, happened to see the back of my wife's head and 'Baker Lake' beyond it."

She dug her toe into the rug and swiveled the chair again, back and forth this time. "Your friend mentioned it last night."

"Which friend?"

She gave him an arched eyebrow.

"I had several there last night."

"Any others that you bitch-slapped?"

"Ah." He took a small step back and another sip of water.

"Yes. Ah. What *was* that about?"

"He got drunk, nearly got us tossed from our favorite bar, and then took a swing at me on the sidewalk."

"Yes, but why?"

"*Why?*" He peered at her in a way she found vaguely reptilian. "He's a violent drunk. He always was."

"So why did Caleb bring him two drinks at the same time?"

"Because he's Caleb. I dunno. Ask him."

"It just seems an odd thing to do—give a violent drunk a plethora of liquor as soon as he walks through the door."

"Plethora?"

She nodded. "Plethora."

He shrugged. "Again, you'd have to ask Caleb. Maybe next time you guys hang out while I'm away."

She mock-pouted, something she knew irritated him to no end. "That threatens you?"

"Didn't say it did." A blithe shrug from his broad shoulders, trying to play it cool while the temperature in the room ticked up five degrees.

"That you can't trust your partner?" she said. "Or you can't trust your wife?"

"I can trust both of you. I just find it odd that you, virtually a shut-in for the last two years, hopped a cab to Cambridge and stumbled across my business partner."

"I didn't stumble across him. I went to your building."

He squatted on the rug and rolled the bottle between his palms. "And why would you do that?"

"Because I thought you were lying to me."

"This again?" His laugh was unpleasant.

"I guess so."

"You understand how nuts you sound?"

"No. Illuminate it for me."

He rose up and down on his haunches several times, as if preparing his calves for the blast of a starter's pistol. "You thought you saw me in Boston when I was actually thirty thousand feet in the air."

"Unless"—she crinkled her nose at him—"you weren't."

He batted his eyelashes at her. "Then you put me through a series of hoops to prove I was actually in London. Hoops that I successfully jumped through. But that wasn't enough. You"—he coughed out a laugh of sudden disbelief—"you walk around for the last week giving me looks like I'm the . . . the leader of a fucking sleeper cell."

"Or," she said, "you could be like that guy who pretended to be a Rockefeller."

"I could." He nodded as if that made absolute sense. Drained his water. "He killed people, didn't he?"

She stared back at him. "I believe that he did, yes."

"Left the wife alive," he said.

"That was sporting of him." She felt an inexplicable smirk tugging at the corners of her mouth.

"Stole their kid but left behind the silverware."

"Place settings are important."

"Hey."

"What?"

"Why are you smiling?"

"Why are you?"

"Because this is so ridiculous."

"Beyond the pale," she agreed.

"So do we keep circling it?"

"I don't know."

He knelt at her feet, took her hands in his, looked in her eyes. "I flew out of Boston last Monday on British Airways."

"You don't have to—"

"The flight was delayed because of weather for seventy-five minutes. I spent the time wandering E Terminal, read an *Us Weekly* someone left behind at an empty gate. A janitor caught me doing it. You ever gotten a disapproving look from an airport janitor? Shrivels the testes, it does."

She grinned and shook her head. "Really, I believe you."

"Then I grabbed a cup of Dunkin's, and by that point we were boarding. I got on, found out the outlet in my seat wasn't working. Fell asleep for an hour or so. Woke up, read my board meeting materials even though I knew it was pointless, and watched a movie where Denzel refused to take any shit."

"That was the name of it?"

"In several foreign territories, yes."

She met his eyes again. There was always something in that act; you either ceded power, took it, or shared it. They came to a mutual decision to share it.

She put a hand lightly to the side of his head. "I believe you."

"You haven't been acting like it."

"And I wish I could tell you why. It's probably just all this fucking rain."

"Rain's gone."

She acknowledged that with a nod. "But, hey, I did a lot these two weeks—the subway, the mall, the cab, I even walked into Copley Square."

"I know you did." The empathy in his face—the love—was so genuine it hurt. "And I couldn't be prouder."

"I know you went to London."

"Say it one more time."

She kicked his inner thigh softly with her bare foot. "I know you went to London."

"Trust is back in the house?"

"Trust is back in the house."

He kissed her forehead. "I'm going to take a shower." He touched her hips with both hands as he rose from his knees.

She sat in the chair with her back to her laptop, her back to the river, her back to the perfect day, and she wondered if they'd been off all week because she'd been off. If Brian was acting weird because she was acting weird.

As she'd just pointed out to him, in the last fourteen days she'd ridden a subway, entered a mall, walked into Copley Square, and trusted a stranger to drive her—all for the first time in two years. For most, these were tiny accomplishments, but for her they were monumental. But maybe those accomplishments had also scared the shit out of her. Every step she took out of her comfort zone was either one step closer to better mental health or one step closer to another breakdown. But another breakdown now, after so much progress, would feel ten times as debilitating.

For the last two years, one refrain had raced back and forth through her brain pan—*I can't go back there. I can't go back there*—every fucking minute of every fucking day.

So it made sense that when she engaged in acts that promised liberation at the same moment they threatened imprisonment she might start to deflect the totality of it by obsessing over something else, something that began with a credible basis—she'd seen an awfully realistic replica of her husband in a place he wasn't supposed to be—but had clearly evolved past a rational place.

He was a good man. The best she'd ever known. Didn't make him the best in the world, just the best for her. With the exception of The Sighting, as she'd come to think of it, he'd never given her reason not to trust him. When she was unreasonable, he was understanding. When she was frightened, he soothed. Irrational, he could translate. Frantic, he was patient. And when it had been time for her to venture back into the world, he recognized it, and he led her there. Held her hand, told her she was safe. He was there. They could stay or they could go, he had her back.

And *this man*, she thought as she swiveled back to the window and caught her own ghostly reflection hovering over the river and the green banks beyond, is the man you've chosen to mistrust?

When he came out of the shower, she was waiting on the bathroom counter, her pajamas pooled on the floor. He grew hard in the time it took to reach her. There was some awkwardness after he entered her—the countertop was narrow, the condensation was thick, her flesh squeaked against the mirror behind her, he slipped out twice—but she knew from the look in his eyes, a kind of shocked wonder, that he loved her like no one ever had. It seemed to do battle within him sometimes, this love, which made its reappearances so exhilarating.

We won, she thought. *We won again.*

She banged her hip on the faucet one time too many and suggested they move to the floor. They finished on top of her pooled pajamas, with her heels digging into the hollows behind his knees—a ridiculous sight, she imagined, to God, if He was looking, to their dead, if their dead could see through time, through galaxies—but she didn't care. She loved him.

The next morning, he left for work while she was still sleeping. When she went into their walk-in closet to pick out her outfit for the day, his suitcase was open on the wooden rack he otherwise kept folded and stowed beside his shoes. He was mostly packed, one empty square of the suitcase awaiting his shaving kit. A garment bag hung from a hook nearby, three suits inside.

The next trip was tomorrow. And it was one of the big ones he took every six weeks or so. This time it was to Moscow, he'd told her, as well as Kraków and Prague. She lifted a few of his shirts, noticed he'd packed only one sweater and one coat, the thin raincoat he'd worn on his last trip. Seemed light for Eastern Europe in May. Wouldn't the average temperature there be in the high forties or low fifties?

She checked it on her phone.

Actually, temperatures in all three cities were expected to be mostly in the high sixties.

She went back to their bedroom and flopped on the bed and asked herself what the fuck was wrong with her. He'd passed every test she'd put before him. All yesterday, after they'd made love, he'd been attentive and funny and a joy to be around. A dream husband.

And she rewarded that by checking the weather report to see if he'd packed appropriately for the places he was claiming to go to.

Claiming. There it was again. Jesus. Maybe she needed to double up on sessions with Jane for a while, get this paranoia under control. Maybe she just needed to do something with her time besides lying around imagining ways in which her marriage could be a sham. She needed to get back to writing the book. She needed to sit in the chair and not get up until she fixed whatever was causing her blockage in the Jacmel sections.

She got off the bed and took the laundry basket into the alcove where they'd stacked a washer and dryer. She went through his pants because he always left coins in his pockets and retrieved a total of seventy-seven cents and a couple of balled-up ATM receipts. She checked the receipts—of course she did—and found two cash withdrawals for Brian's standard "fast cash" amount of $200, a week apart. She tossed the receipts into the small wicker trash basket and added the change to the cracked coffee cup she kept up on a shelf for just that purpose.

She went through her own pockets, found nothing in any of them until she came across the receipt she'd stolen from his raincoat over a week ago. Well, *stolen* was a harsh word. Appropriated. That seemed better. She sat on the floor with her back to the washer and smoothed it against her knee and wondered yet again why it bothered her. It was just a receipt from a shop in London where he'd purchased a pack of gum, a *Daily Sun*, and a bottle of Orangina at 11:12 A.M. on 05/09/14 for a grand total of 5.47 pounds sterling. The address of the shop was 17 Monmouth Street, which put it just down the street from the Covent Garden Hotel.

Here she went again. It was *just* a receipt. She tossed it in the trash basket. She added detergent to the washer and turned it on. She walked out of the alcove.

She came back. She pulled the receipt out of the trash and looked at it again. It was the date that bothered her. 05/09/14. May 9, 2014. Which, yes, was the date Brian was in London. Month, day, year. But in Britain, they didn't record their dates that way. Instead of month, day, year, they would write day, month, year. If this receipt were truly from a shop in London, it wouldn't read 05/09/14. It would read 09/05/14.

She put it in the pocket of her pajama pants and made it to the bathroom before she threw up.

She survived dinner with him, though she barely spoke. When he asked if anything was wrong, she said her allergies were acting up and the manuscript was turning into far more work than she'd anticipated. When he pressed, she said, "I'm just tired. Can we leave it there?"

He nodded, a resigned and deflated look on his face, a martyr forced to bear the hostile caprices of an unreasonable wife.

She slept in the same bed as him. She hadn't believed she'd be able to fall asleep, and for the first hour or so she just lay there, one side of her face pressed to the pillow, and watched him sleep.

Who are you? she wanted to ask. She wanted to straddle him and pound his chest and scream it.

What have you done to me?

What did I do to myself when I committed to you? When I locked myself to you?

Where do your lies lead?

If you're a fraud, what does that make my life?

Somehow she fell asleep, a restless sleep, and woke the next morning with a startled "Oh" escaping her lips.

While he took his shower, she went into the living room and looked out the window at the small red Ford Focus she'd rented yesterday from the Zipcar lot around the corner. Even from this height, she could make out the orange parking ticket a meter maid had slipped under the right windshield wiper. She'd expected that; she'd parked in a resident-only parking zone yesterday because it was the only way she could place the car where she needed it to be today—with a view of their garage exit.

She dressed in workout clothes and a hoodie. When the shower shut off, she knocked softly on the bathroom door.

"Yeah?"

She opened the door, leaned into the frame. He had a towel around his waist and his neck and jaw were covered in shaving gel. He'd been about to cover his cheeks but now he looked at her, a small swirl of purple gel in his right palm.

"I'm gonna go work out."

"Now?"

She nodded. "That instructor I like? On Tuesdays she's only there at this time."

"Okay." He crossed to her. "See you in a week."

"Fly safe."

They stood there, faces a few inches apart, his eyes searching hers, her eyes not moving at all.

"Bye."

"Love you," he said.

"Bye," she said again and closed the door behind her.

19

ALDEN MINERALS LTD.

Yesterday, when she'd driven the Zipcar from the lot around the corner to the parking spot by their building, she'd covered a distance of two blocks, and even that had been a little nerve-racking. Now, as she watched Brian pull out of the garage and drive up the ramp to street level, all the oxygen in her body pushed into her heart. Brian turned onto Commonwealth and immediately got into the left lane. She pulled out with a jerk. A cab hurtled up on her left. A horn blared. The cab veered around her, the driver throwing his hand in the air at this idiot who couldn't balance driving and paying attention at the same time.

She sat, half in the parking spot, half in the lane, and heat flushed through her head and throat.

Quit.

The next time he goes on a trip, try it again.

But she knew if she listened to that voice she'd never do it at all.

She'd spend the next year (or years) indoors, in fear, in mistrust and resentment until those very things became a balm, an ironic salve, the worry stone she caressed until that caress replaced every caress she'd ever give or receive again. And the worst of it was that by that point, she'd have convinced herself it was more than enough.

She pulled out onto Commonwealth and could hear her own breathing, never a good sign. If she didn't get it back in tempo, she'd hyperventilate, maybe black out and crash, as Brian had once predicted. She exhaled slowly through pursed lips. Brian took a left on Exeter. She dropped in behind the cab that had almost hit her as it made the same turn. She exhaled again, just as slowly, and her breathing resumed a manageable rhythm. Her heart, on the other hand, continued to scamper like a penned animal watching the farmer approach with an ax. She gripped the steering wheel like an old lady or a driving instructor, her neck tight, palms wet, shoulder blades scrunched.

Brian took a left past the Westin and she lost him for a moment, which was not the place to lose him. He had too many options there—he could loop around onto the Mass Pike, head straight down Stuart, or turn right onto Dartmouth and head into the South End. She caught his brake lights as he did just that and passed the mall on his right. She lost the cover of the cab, though, as it continued straight and she turned right. Brian was half a block ahead but there were no cars in between them. If she got any closer he'd be able to see her face in his rearview.

She'd considered a disguise yesterday but it seemed so ridiculous— what was she supposed to do, wear a Groucho face? A hockey mask? As it was, she wore a newsboy cap, something she rarely did, and sunglasses with wide round rims that he'd never seen before, so she'd pass the test if he looked at her from a reasonable distance but definitely not close up.

He turned left on Columbus, and another car slid into the mix, a black station wagon with New York plates. Rachel dropped in behind it and they continued in unison for a couple of miles. All three of them left Columbus for Arlington together and Arlington for Albany and headed toward I-93. When she realized they might be getting on the expressway, she feared she might projectile-vomit onto the dashboard. The surface streets were hard enough, the noise, the bumps, the jackhammers breaking open pavement at a construction site, the pedestrians who dashed across the crosswalks, the other cars pressing in, cutting in front, riding up hard on her tail. But that was at twenty-five miles an hour.

There wasn't much time to think about it because there was Brian pulling onto 93 South. Rachel followed, feeling as if the on-ramp sucked her forward. Brian punched the gas and bolted across three lanes of traffic into the left lane, his Infiniti rocking on its wheels. She stepped on her own gas pedal and the immediate result wasn't much different than if she'd stepped on a boulder and expected it to gallop. The small Ford inched forward and then inched forward a tiny bit faster and then a little bit faster again. By the time it reached the seventy-five miles an hour or so that Brian had reached near instantaneously, his Infiniti was a quarter mile ahead. She kept pressing on the pedal, staying one lane to his right, and soon she made up enough of the distance that by the time they'd passed through Dorchester into Milton she had a perfect bead on him from five cars back.

She'd concentrated so hard on the task at hand that she'd forgotten all her terror at being on the expressway in the first place. Now it returned, but it wasn't quite terror, just a persistent fluttering at the base of her throat accompanied by the certainty that her skeleton might burst through her skin.

And a sense of betrayal and rage as toxic as Drano. Because what was abundantly clear, though there had never been much doubt, was that Brian was not headed to the airport. Logan was fifteen miles in their rearview.

When they left 93 for 95 South and the signs for Providence, she considered the possibility that he could have chosen to fly out of TF Green Airport, the only major airport in Rhode Island. She'd known people to prefer it to the crowds at Logan, but she also knew for certain they wouldn't have a direct flight to Moscow.

"He's not going to any fucking Moscow," she said aloud.

A few miles later she was proved correct when he engaged his turn signal at least ten miles short of the airport and began to glide smoothly across the lanes. He got off in Providence, at the Brown University exit, where the neighborhoods of College Hill and Federal Hill met. Several other cars chose the same exit, including Rachel's, three back of his. At the top of the exit ramp, Brian went right but the two cars between them took a left.

She slowed as she neared the intersection, let him get as far ahead as possible, but there wasn't much stalling to be done. A Porsche swung wide on her left, engine revving, and shot out in front of her. She'd never been happier for a small penis driving a small penis car to act like a small penis because she again had cover between her and Brian.

It didn't last, though. At the first light, the Porsche drifted into the left-turn-only lane, then floored it, zipping around Brian as they crossed the intersection, and roaring up the road ahead of him.

Little dicks, Rachel thought again, and their little dick cars. Shit.

Now there was no buffer between her and her husband, no way to control whether he looked into his rearview and recognized her. She passed through the intersection. She kept four car lengths between them, but the driver of the car behind her was already craning his head to see past her, as if to discern why she'd commit the unforgivable sin of not keeping pace with the car in front of her.

They drove into a neighborhood of Federalist clapboard homes, Armenian bakeries, and limestone churches. Once, Brian's head tilted up and to the right—he was clearly checking his rearview—and she damn near stomped her brake pedal in panic. But, no, no, he looked back at the road. In two more blocks, she saw what she'd been looking for—the shoulder widened by a doughnut shop and a gas station. She put on her turn signal. She pulled over by the doughnut shop and prepared to pull right back out again as the green Chrysler pulled past her.

But behind the green Chrysler was a brown Prius and behind the Prius was a tan Jaguar and right behind the Jaguar was a Toyota 4Runner with monster wheels and, Jesus, behind the 4Runner was a minivan. By the time she pulled back out, not only was she five cars back, but the minivan was too tall to see past. And even if she could, she'd then find herself staring at the back of the 4Runner, which was even taller than the minivan.

The traffic stopped at the next signal and she had no way of knowing if Brian had actually passed through the signal before the light turned red.

The traffic moved again. She followed as they continued along in a straight line, no curves in this road. Just give me one curve, she prayed, just one fucking curve and maybe, just maybe, I'll be able to catch a glimpse of him.

A mile up, the road forked. The Prius, the minivan, and the 4Runner all went right onto Bell Street, while the Chrysler and the Jaguar stayed the course on Broadway.

Only one problem—Brian's Infiniti was no longer in front of the Chrysler. It was nowhere at all.

She screamed through gritted teeth and gripped the steering wheel so hard it felt like she might rip it out of the drive shaft.

She banged a U-turn. She did it without thought or warning, meriting angry beeps from both the car behind her and the oncoming one in the opposite lane that she cut off. She didn't care. She didn't feel fear, she felt rage and frustration. But mostly rage.

She drove back up Broadway, drove all the way to the gas station and the doughnut shop where she'd lost sight of him. She U-turned again—this time with warning and a bit more finesse—and drove back down the way she'd just come. She looked at every side street as best she could at thirty miles an hour.

She reached the fork again. Resisted the urge to indulge in another scream. Resisted the urge to cry. She took a left into a tiny lot outside a VFW Post and turned back again.

If she hadn't hit a red light, she never would have found him. But she did. And as she sat at it, with another gas station and a drab insurance agency to her right, she looked down the cross street and saw a large Victorian with a tall white sign on its front lawn that listed the businesses housed within. And there, in the parking lot that branched off the side of the building under a wrought-iron fire escape, was Brian's Infiniti.

She found a parking space six houses past the Victorian. Walked back up the sidewalk. The street was lined with old oaks and maples, the shaded parts of the sidewalk still a bit damp from the dew the trees had shed this morning, the May air filled with the scents of decay and rebirth in equal measure. Even now, approaching a building in which her husband hid the truth of himself—or certainly *a* truth of himself—she could feel the street and its odors calm her.

The sign on the front lawn listed three psychiatrists, a family practitioner, a mineral company, a title company, and two attorneys. Rachel stayed in the shade of the great trees until she reached the alley along the side. A large sign at the entrance to the alley warned that the parking spaces were for occupants of 232 Seaver Street only, while a series of smaller signs bolted to the siding identified whose spot was whose. Brian's Infiniti was parked in the spot reserved for Alden Minerals Ltd.

She'd never heard of Alden Minerals Ltd., and yet it seemed vaguely familiar, as if she *had* heard of it. But she was certain she hadn't. Yet one more paradox in a week full of them.

Alden Minerals Ltd. was on the second floor, suite 210. Seemed like now would be as good a time as any to storm up the stairs and burst into the suite and see exactly what her lying husband was up to. Yet she hesitated. She found a spot under the fire escape and leaned against the building and tried to ferret out if there could be any logical explanation for any of this. Men sometimes engaged in elaborate hoaxes on their wives if they were, say, planning a surprise party.

No. They didn't. At least not to the point where they claimed to be in London when they were in Boston or claimed to be flying to Moscow when they were driving to Providence. No, there was no acceptable explanation for this.

Unless . . .

What?

Unless he's a spy, she thought. *Don't spies do this kind of thing?*

Well, yes, Rachel, a sarcastic voice that sounded like her mother's agreed, *they surely do. So do cheating husbands and sociopaths.*

She leaned against the building and wished she still smoked.

If she confronted him right this second, what would she gain? The truth? Probably not, not if he'd been lying to her this successfully for this long. And whatever he told her, she wouldn't believe it anyway. He could show her his CIA credentials and she'd think of the selfie he'd "sent" from London (how *did* he fake that, by the way?) and tell him to take his fake CIA credentials and find a way to go fuck himself with them.

If she confronted him, she'd get nowhere.

Harder to admit, of course, was that if she confronted him, whether he lied to her in the moment or not, the relationship—or whatever she'd call it from here on—would leak out on the floor. And she wasn't ready for that yet. It was a humiliating realization, but at this moment she couldn't stomach the loss of him from her life. She pictured their condo emptied of his clothes, his books, his toothbrush and titanium razor, the food he liked gone from the fridge, the scotch he preferred removed from the liquor cabinet or, worse, forgotten and left behind as a reminder until Rachel poured it down the sink. She pictured the magazines he subscribed to still showing up months

after he left and her long empty days bleeding into long endless evenings. Since her on-air meltdown, she'd lost most of her friends. She
had Melissa, yes, but Melissa was the type of friend who expected her
to "buck up" and "think positive" and—*Excuse me, waiter, could I have
one more of these with less ice this time?*—"shake it off." Beyond that, her
friends weren't friends at all but casual acquaintances; it was hard,
after all, to maintain social contact with a virtual shut-in.

These last few years, her one true and constant friend had been
Brian. She relied on him the way trees relied on their roots. He
was her world in full. And the rational part of her knew that, of
course—*of course*—she would have to divest herself of him. He was a
fraud. And theirs was a house of sand. And yet she—

He walked out of the back of the building and crossed directly
in front of her. He was texting someone as he walked to his car and
she stood less than six feet away from him under the fire escape.
She waited for him to see her. Tried to think of what she'd say. He'd
changed into a dark blue suit with a white shirt, silver-and-black-
checked tie, and dark brown shoes. He wore a brown leather laptop
bag over his right shoulder. He climbed in the Infiniti and shrugged
the bag off onto the passenger seat, still texting with one hand as
he shut the door with the other. He pulled the seat belt strap across
his chest. He started the engine, still texting, and then must have
hit "send" because he flipped the phone onto the passenger seat and
backed out of the space, his eyes on his rearview. All he had to do
was move his gaze down six inches and he'd be staring at her. She
imagined the shock would be so great he'd forget he was in reverse
and back straight into the light pole across the alley. But it never
happened. He backed up, turning the wheel as he did, and then he
was facing forward, looking out at Seaver Street. He drove out of the
alley and turned left on Seaver.

She ran to her car, thankful she'd dressed in sneakers as part of
her "workout" ruse. She got in the car and turned around, drove up
the street and went careening through the intersection as the yellow

turned red. A minute later, she spotted him on Broadway, three cars ahead.

She followed him back into College Hill. On a block caught somewhere between decay and refurbishment, he pulled to the curb. She pulled over fifty yards back in front of a boarded-up travel agency and a defunct record store. Past that was a furniture rental store that seemed to have cornered the market on black lacquer dressers. Next was a liquor store and then a camera store, Little Louie's. Camera stores, she suspected, would all go the way of record stores and travel agencies (liquor stores, she suspected, would hold the line the world over), but Little Louie's was, as yet, hanging on. Brian entered it. She thought of walking up the sidewalk and getting a glimpse of what he might be doing in there, but she quickly deemed that idea too unpredictable to risk. This was confirmed when Brian walked back out within two minutes of entering. If she'd given in to her impulse, she would have been caught flatfooted in the middle of the sidewalk. He drove off and she pulled away from the curb. As she passed the camera shop, she could see that it was fairly dark inside; the windows displayed only photographs of cameras and newspaper ads taped to the glass. She had no idea what went on in that store, but she suspected selling cameras wasn't the main priority.

Brian led them out of Providence, through a series of smaller and smaller towns, where the clapboard homes grew more and more distressed, and farms sprouted up here and there, until he pulled into a strip mall that appeared to be reasonably new. He drove past the Panera Bread on the edge of the mall to a small freestanding bank, pulled into a parking space, and got out of the car. He walked to the bank, the laptop bag over his right shoulder again.

She idled in the strip mall lot, in front of a CVS and a Payless ShoeSource. While she waited, she took her phone out of the cup holder and saw that she'd received a text.

She opened it. It was from Brian and it had been sent twenty minutes ago as he'd walked out of the Seaver Street building and crossed directly in front of her.

Babe, on the runway. Taking off soon. Land in about 10 hours. Hope you're still up when I call. Love you so much.

Ten minutes later, he came out of the bank but no longer carried the laptop bag.

He got in the Infiniti and drove out of the lot.

She followed him back into Providence. He stopped at a florist and purchased a bouquet of white and pink flowers, and her stomach turned. She wasn't sure she was ready for where this was headed. He stopped one more time and purchased a bottle of champagne from a liquor store. Now she *knew* she wasn't ready. He turned off the main road at Federal Hill, long an Italian-American stronghold and the seat of power for the New England mafia but by now just another handsome, gentrified neighborhood of chic restaurants and redbrick row houses.

He pulled the Infiniti into a slot in front of one of those row houses, its windows open to the fine day, white curtains wafting in white-trimmed windows. She parked across the street and a few houses down from where he stood on the sidewalk with the bouquet in his hand. He put two fingers into his mouth and let loose a loud, sharp whistle, something she'd never seen him do in all their time together. It wasn't just the whistle that was new, she realized. He moved differently, his shoulders higher, his hips looser, springing off the balls of his feet with a dancer's confidence.

He walked up the steps and the front door opened.

"Oh, Jesus," Rachel whispered. "Jesus, Jesus, Jesus."

It was a woman who answered the door, about thirty-five or so. She had curly blond hair and a long, pretty face. But none of that held Rachel's attention when Brian handed her the flowers and the champagne, then knelt on the landing to kiss her pregnant belly.

20

VHS

She couldn't remember driving back to the highway. The rest of her life she'd wonder how a completely sober person could operate a motor vehicle for several miles through a medium-size city and not remember it.

She'd picked Brian as her spouse because he seemed safe. Because he was can-do. Earnest bordering on grating. A man who would never cheat. Never lie. Certainly never live a double life.

Yet she'd watched her husband enter the row house with his arm around the waist of his pregnant wife(?), girlfriend(?), and shut the door behind them. Rachel had no idea how long she sat in her car, staring at the house, enough time to note that the paint was peeling a bit from a windowsill on the second floor; the cable from a rusted satellite dish dangled off the roof down the front of the building. The window trim was white; the brick facade, recently washed by the look of it, was red. The front door was black and looked to have been painted many times over the course of a century or more. The knocker was pewter.

And then she was on the highway with no idea how she got there.

She thought she'd cry. She didn't cry. She thought she'd tremble. She didn't tremble. She thought she'd feel grief and maybe she did, maybe this was what grief felt like—a total numbness, a brining in nothingness. A cauterized soul.

The three lanes of the highway dropped to two as they crossed into Massachusetts. A car drove up on her right, attempting to cut in front of her as its own lane began to disappear. Signs warning of the lane drop had been posted for the last two miles. The other driver had ignored them until it was convenient for him and inconvenient for her.

He sped up.

She sped up.

He sped up some more. She sped up some more. He pushed the nose of his car toward hers. She held her lane. He sped up again. She accelerated, eyes forward. He beeped his horn. She held her lane. In a hundred yards, his lane ended. He sped up and she gunned it, as much as a Ford Focus could be gunned. He dropped away so fast it was as if his car came equipped with a parachute. It appeared seconds later on her rear.

She noted the Mercedes-Benz symbol on his hood. Made sense. He flipped her the bird and blared his horn. A balding specimen behind expensive wraparounds, cheeks just beginning to turn to jowls, thin nose, nonexistent lips. She watched him rant and rage in her rearview and definitely made out the word *fuck* several times and *cunt* a couple more. She assumed his dashboard was speckled with spit by now. He wanted to jerk his car into the passing lane and race up on her side, then cut her off, she assumed, but the traffic to their left was too heavy, so he just kept his hand on his horn and thrust his middle finger at her and screamed in his car about what a cunt she was, what a fucking cunt.

She tapped her brakes. And not a light tap. Dropped her speed a solid five miles an hour for a moment. His eyebrows shot up over his sunglasses. His mouth froze in a desperate O. He gripped his steering wheel as if it were suddenly electrified. Rachel smiled. Rachel laughed.

"Fuck you," she said to the rearview, "you nothing man." She wasn't sure the words made a bit of sense, but they felt good to say.

A mile more and traffic had spaced itself out enough that the Mercedes driver could swerve into the left lane and come abreast of her. Normally she would have looked straight ahead—normally? There was no normal. Three days ago she never would have gotten behind the wheel of a car—but today she turned her head and looked at him. His glasses were off, his eyes as small and lightless as she would have expected. She looked at him steadily, hurtling down the highway at seventy miles an hour. She looked calmly at this little man until the rage in his eyes became confusion and then guilt and then he went for something approximating disappointment, as if she'd morphed into the teenage daughter who'd stayed out past curfew, came home smelling of schnapps and Scope. He shook his head, an impotent scolding gesture, and turned his eyes to the road. After one last look, Rachel did the same.

Back home, she returned the Focus to the Zipcar lot and took the elevator up to fifteen. Walking toward her door, she felt lonelier than an astronaut. Unmoored. Untouched. Floating past frontiers with no way someone could hook her and bring her back. It didn't help that of the four units on fifteen, her and Brian's was the only one regularly occupied. The other three were owned by foreign investors. Every now and then they'd run across an older Chinese couple or the German financier's wife, three children, nanny, and their shopping bags. She had zero idea who owned the third unit.

The penthouse above was owned by a young man they'd dubbed Trust Fund Baby, a boy so young he'd probably been learning to read about the time Rachel lost her virginity. As far as she knew, he used the place to indulge a penchant for hookers. The rest of the time, Rachel and Brian never heard or saw him.

Most times she preferred this quiet and the privacy it afforded, but walking down the hall right now, she was a castoff, a mark, a fool, something amputated from the herd, an idiotic dreamer who'd been awakened via assault. She heard the cosmos laughing at her.

Didn't you know, silly girl, that love is not for you?

The condo overwhelmed. Every wall, every angle, every view. This had been them, this had been theirs. It was all the places they'd made love, all the spots in which they'd talked or argued or shared meals. It was the art they'd picked out, the rugs, the dining set, the lamp they'd found at the antique store in Sandwich. It was the smell of him on his bath towel, the newspaper with the half-finished cross-word puzzle. It was the curtains and the lightbulbs and the toiletries. Some of these she'd carry into her new life—whatever that new life would be—but almost everything else felt too much *them* to ever comfortably become *hers.*

To give herself a moment away from it, she took the elevator back down to the lobby to retrieve the mail. Dominick sat at his post behind the desk reading a magazine. Probably a tenant's; might even be hers. He looked up and gave her a nod and the kind of bright smile that had absolutely nothing behind it and went back to his magazine. She walked into the mailroom behind him and opened her and Brian's box, pulled out the stack inside. She added the circulars and junk mail to the recycling bin on the floor and was left, in the end, with three bills.

She came out behind Dominick's chair and shot him a "Take care" as she did.

"You too, Rachel." As she reached the elevator bank, he called, "Oh, I got something for you, sorry."

She turned back and he was going through a bin of oversize mail. He handed her a yellow manila envelope. She didn't recognize the sender—Pat's Book Nook & More in Barnum, Pennsylvania—but then remembered the VHS she'd ordered the other night. She hefted the envelope in her palm; that's exactly what was inside.

Back up in the condo, she opened the envelope and pulled out the tape. The box was battered, some of the cardboard missing from the corners. Robert Hays and Vivica A. Fox stared back at her with happy smiles, their heads tilted to the left. She was opening a bottle of pinot noir to accompany her when she realized she didn't have a VCR. Who did anymore? She was about to go online and see if she could buy one when she remembered they had one in storage over in Brookline. She'd have to rent another Zipcar, drive a couple of miles in rush-hour traffic. And for what exactly? A movie that a drunk had told her to watch. She now knew her husband had another wife in another state. What more could she learn from an obscure movie from 2002?

She drank some pinot and flipped the VHS over, confirmed that the description of the film on the back was indeed the same one she'd seen posted on eBay. Above the description were two small photos. One was of Robert and Vivica talking on a sidewalk, giving each other big toothy smiles. The other was of a young man leaning over a young woman in a wheelchair, the young man's lips to her neck, her head thrown back in delight. This must be the two supporting players, she thought, poor Kristy Gale and the guy, what was his name again? She checked the credits—right, Brett Alden.

She put her wineglass on the counter for a moment, closed her eyes.

Alden Minerals Ltd.

That's why it had struck a chord.

She looked closer at the thumbnail photo in the top right corner. Brett Alden's face was half obscured by the angle it took when he leaned into Kristy Gale's neck to kiss it. You could only see his hair (dark, voluminous, and unruly), his forehead, the left side of his face—one eye, one cheekbone, half his nose, half his lips.

But she knew those lips, that nose, that cheekbone, that blue eye. The hair had receded some, the skin near the temple had sprouted wrinkles.

But it was Brian. No question.

21

P380

What if he came *back*?

She'd been lying on the couch with her eyes closed when the thought sat her up.

What if he walked through the front door and he knew she knew? Polygamy was against the law. So was impersonating someone else for financial gain. However little she understood of it, Rachel was witness to a series of crimes. She suspected that men who led double lives didn't react well when exposed.

She went to their walk-in closet and reached up on the high shelf where he kept some of his shoes. And behind the shoes, he kept a gun. A P380 subcompact, slightly larger than a cell phone but a pistol he assured her would put down any home invader not wearing Kevlar.

It wasn't there. She stood on her tiptoes and reached back on the left side of the shelf until her fingers touched the wall.

She heard a click from the front of the apartment. Or did she? Could have been the front door opening, could have been the AC kicking on. Could have been nothing at all.

So the gun was gone. Which meant . . .

Nope. There it was. Her fingertips closed over the black rubber grip and she pulled it out, knocking one of his loafers off the shelf as she did. The safety was on. She dropped the clip out of the gun and into her hand to confirm it was loaded and then slid the clip back until she heard a click. They used to practice at a range on Freeport Street in Dorchester, Brian joking that if there was one place in the city where the locals didn't need help learning how to shoot—or dodge—bullets, it was Dorchester. She enjoyed the range, the *crack crack crack* of rifles in the neighboring bays, the *pop pop pop* of the pistols. She was less enamored of the *brrrrapt* of the assault weapons because it called to mind dead schoolchildren and dead moviegoers. It could feel like a fantasy camp for overly aggressive children in there, most of the shooters well past the point where they needed to practice their shooting; several just wanted to fantasize what it would feel like to actually kill that burglar, that abusive ex-boyfriend, mow down that dark horde of gangbangers. They let her try other guns besides the P380, and she proved a good shot with a pistol, less so with a rifle, but the P380 was a perfect fit for her. Soon she could put all seven bullets—six in the mag, one in the chamber—center mass. After that, she stopped going to the range.

She confirmed with a glance that she'd hooked the chain on the front door, so whatever sound she had heard from the closet, it hadn't been Brian returning. In the kitchen, she opened her laptop and looked up Alden Minerals Ltd. It was a mining company headquartered in Providence, Rhode Island, that owned a single mine in Papua New Guinea. According to the recent assessment of that mine by a consulting firm, Borgeau Engineering, the mine was sitting on resources in excess of 400,000,000 troy ounces. A recent item in the *Wall Street Journal* made reference to a rumor that the dominant mining concern in Papua New Guinea, Houston-based Vitterman Copper & Gold, was contemplating a friendly takeover of Alden Minerals.

Alden Minerals was family-owned and family-run by Brian and Nicole Alden. Rachel found no pictures of them. She didn't need pictures. She knew what they looked like.

She called Glen O'Donnell at the *Globe*. She and Glen had come up together, first at the *Patriot Ledger*, then at the *Globe*. She'd worked in investigative features, he covered business. After five minutes of pleasantries in which she learned he and his partner, Roy, had adopted a daughter from Guatemala and bought a house in Dracut, she asked Glen if he'd research Alden Minerals for her.

"Sure, sure," he said. "I'll get right back to you."

"Oh, you don't have to do—"

"Be my pleasure. I'm not doing shit now anyway. Call you right back."

Another glass of pinot later, she sat in the living room by the picture window and watched night find Arlington, Cambridge, and the river. As the world turned brass and then blue, she considered her life without him. The panic attacks would return, she suspected, as soon as the numbness wore off. All the progress she'd made in the last six months would vanish. Not only would she go back to zero, she feared that this series of shocks—oh, your husband has another wife; oh, your husband has another life; oh, you might not even know your husband's real name—would plunge her into free fall. Already a ball of mild hysteria clotted her windpipe when she imagined interacting with the world again, with people, with strangers, with those who could not rescue her, who would run from her pain the moment they smelled it. (*Thin the herd, thin the herd, thin the herd.*) One day she wouldn't be able to board the elevator again; the next she'd need to have her groceries delivered. She'd wake up a few years from now and realize she couldn't remember the last time she'd left the building. She'd have no more power over herself or her terrors.

And where had that power come from? It had come from herself, yes, of course it had. But it had also come from him. It had come from love. Or what she mistook for love.

An actor. Her Brian was an actor. He'd practically rubbed her face in it during the argument after his "return" from London when he'd made reference to Clark Rockefeller. Which meant not only was Brian not Brian, he wasn't a Delacroix. But how was that possible?

She went back online, searched for "Brian Delacroix." The bio that came up matched what Brian had told her—forty, employee of Delacroix Lumber, a Canadian lumber concern with holdings in twenty-six countries. She clicked "images" and found only four, but there he was, her Brian—same hair, same jawline, same eyes, same . . . not the same nose.

Her Brian had that bump just above the septum at the beginning of the nasal bone. Unnoticeable head-on, but discernible in profile. Even then it could escape notice if you weren't looking for it. But if you were, it wasn't up for argument—he had a bump on the bridge of his nose.

Brian Delacroix did not. Two of the photos were profiles; no bump. She took a longer look at the head-on shots, and the longer she looked into Brian Delacroix's eyes, the more she realized she'd never looked into them before.

Her Brian Delacroix/Brett Alden was an actor. Andrew Gattis, his inconvenient friend from the past, was an actor. Caleb knew both of them quite comfortably. It seemed a rational leap that Caleb might be an actor too.

As the dark settled over the river, she texted him.

Got a moment to swing by?

A minute later, he responded.

NP. What do you need?

Tiny bit of muscle. Rearranging a few things b4 B gets back.

See u in 15.

Thx.

Her cell vibrated. Glen.

"Hey."

"Hey," he said. "What's this company to you, Rachel?"

"Nothing much. Why?"

"It's a rinky-dink operation that owns a rinky-dink mine in Papua New Guinea. However . . ." She heard him click his mouse a couple times. "Turns out the mine might not be so rinky-dink. Rumor has it a consulting firm did an assessment and found out Alden Minerals could be sitting on resources of up to four hundred million troy ounces."

"I came across something about that," she said. "What're troy ounces, by the way?"

"Gold measurement. Sorry. It's literally a gold mine. Won't do them much good, though. The major competition in that region—the only competition they'd have—is Vitterman Copper & Gold and they don't play nice in the sandbox. And Vitterman would *never*, fucking *ever* allow a mine to be sitting in that region on that kind of lode and not have their name on it. So at some point there's going to be a hostile takeover. Which is why Alden has been trying to keep news of the consulting company's findings hush-hush. Unfortunately for them, they needed more cash. They took several meetings with Cotter-McCann."

"Who's that?"

"A venture capital group. Last week Cotter-McCann leased several parcels of land suitable for commercial real estate near Arawa township in Papua New Guinea. What's that tell you?"

Rachel had drunk too much wine for it to tell her anything. "I don't know."

"Well, it tells me Cotter-McCann gave Alden Minerals an infusion of cash probably for a shitload of shares in that mine. When it starts to pay off, they'll push Alden Minerals aside and clean up. It's what they do; they're sharks. Worse than sharks, some say. Even sharks stop eating when they're full."

"So Alden Minerals will probably fail."

"'Fail' is not quite the right word. They'll be subsumed. Either by Vitterman or Cotter-McCann. They went from A ball to the major leagues overnight. I doubt they can handle the pitching."

"Ah." She couldn't put any of it together. "Thanks so much, Glen."

"Of course. Hey, Melissa told me you're making your way back out into the world."

"She did?" Rachel swallowed a scream.

"You've got to come out to the house, meet Amelia. We'd love to see you guys."

A wave of despair hit her. "We'd love that."

"You okay?"

"Oh, yeah. Just got a cold."

For a moment it felt like he might press the issue. But then he said, "Take care, Rachel."

When Caleb rang the bell, she buzzed him up. She'd laid her evidence on the kitchen counter by a scotch glass and a bottle of the bourbon, but he didn't notice it when he first came in. He looked distracted and worn out.

"You got a drink?"

She pointed at the bourbon.

He took a seat at the counter. He poured himself a drink, didn't even notice the other items on the counter. "Hell of a day."

"Oh, you had one too," she said.

He took a long pull on the glass. "Sometimes I think Brian was right."

"About what?"

"Getting married. Having a kid. It's a lot of moving parts, lotta balls in the air." He glanced at the items on the counter and his tone grew distracted. "So what needs lifting?"

"Nothing really."

"So why . . . ?" He narrowed his eyes at one of Brian's plane tickets, the receipt from the shop in Covent Garden, a photo she'd printed up of the selfie Brian had "taken" outside the Covent Garden Hotel, the VHS of *Since I Fell for You*.

Caleb took a pull from his drink and looked across at her.

"You wrote the date wrong." She pointed at the receipt.

He gave her a confused smile.

"You wrote it as month, day, year. In Britain, it would read day, month, year."

He glanced at the receipt, then back over at her. "I have no idea what you're—"

"I followed him."

Caleb took another drink.

"To Providence."

Caleb was very still.

The building was just as still around them. Trust Fund Baby was definitely not home; she would have heard his footsteps. The other tenants on fifteen weren't there either. It was as if they sat atop an aerie in a forest at the far reaches of the earth.

"He has a pregnant wife." She poured herself more wine. "He's an actor. But then you knew that. Because"—she pointed her wine-glass at him—"you're an actor."

"I don't know what you're—"

"Bullshit. Bull*shit*." She downed half her wine. At this rate, she'd be peeling the foil off a second bottle soon. But she didn't care, because it felt good to have focus for her rage. It gave her the illusion of power. And at this point she'd take illusions if they beat back the terror.

"What do you think you know?" he said.

"Don't you fucking speak to me in that tone."

"What tone?"

"The condescending one."

He held up his hands like a man being robbed at gunpoint.

She said, "I saw Brian go to Providence. I saw Brian at Alden Minerals. I saw Brian go to a camera store and buy flowers and go to a bank. And I saw Brian and his preg—"

"What do you mean, he went to the camera store?"

"He went to a camera store."

"The one on Broadway?"

She didn't know how she'd managed to strike a nerve, only that she had. Caleb scowled at his reflection in the marble countertop, scowled at his glass before draining it of bourbon.

"What's in the camera store?" After a minute of silence, she said, "Caleb—"

He held up a finger to silence her and called someone on his cell. As he waited, she could hear the rings on the other end. She was still back to the finger he'd raised to silence her, the contempt in it. It reminded her of Dr. Felix Browner; he'd dismissed her in the same way once.

He pressed "end" on his cell and immediately tried another number. No answer there either. He pressed "end" again and then squeezed the phone so hard she expected it to shatter.

He said to her, "Tell me some—"

She turned her back on him. She retrieved the bottle of wine from the counter beside the oven, kept her back to him as she refilled her glass. It was petty of her, but that didn't make it feel any less sweet. When she turned back to him, the glare on his face vanished a half second after she noted it and he smiled a very Calebesque smile—boyish and sleepy.

"Tell me some more about what you saw in Providence."

"You first." She placed her wine down on the counter across from him.

"There's nothing for me to tell." He shrugged. "I don't know anything."

She nodded. "Then leave."

His sleepy smile turned into a sleepy chuckle. "Why would I do that?"

"If you don't know anything, Caleb, then I don't know anything."

"Ah." He unscrewed the cap on the bourbon and poured himself another two fingers. He put the cap back on, swirled the liquor in his glass. "You're one hundred percent sure you saw Brian enter the camera store."

She nodded.

"How long was he in there?"

"Who's Andrew Gattis?"

He gave that a touché nod as he took a drink. "He's an actor."

"I know that. Tell me something I don't know."

"He went to Trinity Rep in Providence."

"The acting school."

Another nod. "It's where we all met."

"So my husband's an actor."

"Pretty much, yeah. So the camera store. How long was he in there?"

She looked across the counter at him for a bit. "About five minutes, tops."

He gnawed the inside of his mouth. "He come back out with anything?"

"What's Brian's real name?" She couldn't fucking believe the words left her mouth. Who in her life ever expected to ask that about her husband?

"Alden," he said.

"Brett?"

He shook his head. "Brian. Brett was his stage name. My turn."

She shook her head. "No, no, no. You've been withholding information from me since we met. I just started tonight. You get one question for every two of mine."

"What if that isn't good enough?"

She wiggled her fingers at the door behind him. "Then fuck off, my friend."

"You're drunk."

"I'm buzzed," she said. "What's at the offices in Cambridge?"

"Nothing. It's never used. A friend owns it. If we need it—like, say, you're coming over and we have warning—we dress it. Just like a stage."

"So who are the interns?"

"You've already had your two questions."

But in that moment she saw the answer, as if it had descended from the heavens decked out in neon.

"They're actors," she said.

"*Ding!*" Caleb checked an imaginary box in the air before his eyes. "Gold star. Did Brian leave the camera store with anything?"

"Not that I saw."

He checked her eyes. "Did he go to the bank before or after the camera store?"

"That's a second question."

"Be kind."

She laughed so hard she almost threw up. Laughed the way flood victims and earthquake survivors laughed. Laughed not because something was funny but because nothing was.

"Kind?" she said. "Kind?"

Caleb made a steeple of his hands and placed his forehead to their point. A supplicant. A martyr waiting to be sculpted. After no sculptor arrived, he raised his head. His face was ash, his eye sockets dark. He was aging as she watched.

She swirled her wine but didn't drink it. "How'd he fake the selfie from London?"

"I did it." He rotated his glass of bourbon on the countertop a full three-sixty. "He texted me, told me what was up. You were sitting right across from me in Grendel's. It was all just hitting buttons on a phone, snatching an image here, an image there and running it through a photo program. If you'd looked at it in hi-res on a decent computer screen, it probably wouldn't have held up, but for a selfie supposedly taken in low light? It was easy."

"Caleb," she said, the wine definitely hitting her now, "what am I part of?"

"Huh?"

"I woke up this morning, I was someone's wife. Now I'm . . . I'm, what, I'm one of his wives? In one of his lives? What am I?"

"You're you," he said.

"What's that *mean*?"

"You're you," he said. "You're unaltered. Pure. You haven't changed. Your husband's not who you thought he was. Yes. But that doesn't change who you are." He reached across the counter and took her fingers in his hands. "You're you."

She pulled her fingers free of his. He left his hands on the counter. She looked at her own hands, at the two rings there—a round solitaire diamond engagement ring sitting atop a platinum wedding band with five more round diamonds. She once took them to be cleaned at a jeweler's on Water Street (one, she now realized, Brian had recommended), and the old man who owned the place whistled at them.

"A man who would give you such precious stones," the old man said, adjusting his glass. "Whoo. He must love you very much."

Her hands began to shake as she looked at them, at the flesh, at the jewels, and wondered if anything, anything in her life, was real. These last three years had been first a crawl and then a climb toward sanity, toward reclamation of her life and her self, a series of baby steps taken in a tsunami of doubt and terror. A blind woman walking down a series of corridors in an unfamiliar building she could not remember entering.

And who had arrived to guide her? Who had taken her hand and whispered, "Trust me, trust me," until she finally did? Who had walked her toward the sun?

Brian.

Brian had believed in her long after anyone else had gone home. Brian had pulled her out of the hopeless dark.

"All of it was a lie?" She was surprised to hear the words leave her mouth and surprised to see the tears fall on the marble countertop and on her hands and on her rings. They rolled down the sides of her nose and off her cheekbones and into the corners of her mouth; they burned a bit.

She moved to get a Kleenex, but Caleb took her hands again.

"It's okay," he said. "Let it out."

She wanted to tell him it wasn't okay, any of it, and would he please let go of her hands?

She pulled her hands out of his. "Leave."

"What?"

"Just go. I want to be alone."

"You can't be alone."

"No, I'll be fine."

"No," he said, "you know too much."

"I . . . ?" She couldn't repeat the rest of his threat. It was a threat, wasn't it?

"He won't like it if I leave you alone."

Now she repeated it. "Because I know too much."

"You know what I mean."

"No, I don't."

She'd left the gun in the chair over by the picture window.

"Brian and I have been at this for a very long time," he said. "There's a lot of money at stake."

"How much?"

"A lot."

"And you think I might tell someone?"

He smiled and drank some bourbon. "I don't think you necessarily *will*, but I think you *could*."

"Uh-huh." She carried her wineglass with her to the window, but Caleb came right along with her. They stood by the chair and looked out at the lights of Cambridge, and if Caleb looked down, he'd see the gun. "Is that why you married a woman who didn't speak the language?"

He said nothing and she tried not to look down at the chair.

"Who doesn't know anyone in this country?"

He looked out at the night, but moved his hip slightly closer to the chair and kept his eyes on her reflection in the window.

"Is that why Brian married a shut-in?"

Eventually, Caleb said, "This could be so good for everyone." He met her eyes in the dark glass. "So don't make it bad."

"Are you threatening me?" she said softly.

"I think it's you who's been doing the threatening tonight, kid." And he looked at her the way the rapist, Teacher Paul, had in Haiti.

Or at least that's how it felt in the moment.

"Do you know where Brian is?" she asked.

"I know where he might be."

"Can you take me to him?"

"Why would I do that?"

"Because he owes me an explanation."

"Or?"

"Or what?"

"That's what I'm asking. Are you giving us an 'or else'?"

"Caleb," she said, and hated how desperate she sounded, "take me to Brian."

"No."

"*No?*"

"Brian has something I need. Something my family needs. I don't like that he has that and hasn't told me."

She felt herself trying to swim up through the wine again. "Brian has something you . . . ? The camera store?"

Caleb nodded. "The camera store."

"What—?"

"He has something I need. And you're something he needs." He turned to face her, the chair between them. "So I'm not going to take you to him just yet."

She reached down, grabbed the pistol, thumbed off the safety, and pointed at the center of his chest.

"Yes," she said, "you are."

22

THE SNOWBLOWER

Driving them south in his silver Audi, Caleb said, "You can put the gun away."

"No," she said, "I like having it."

She didn't. She didn't like having it at all. It sat in her hand like dead vermin that might spring back to life. Its power to stop a life with the flexing of a finger was suddenly one of the ugliest concepts she'd ever considered. And she'd pointed it at a friend. Was, even now, pointing it generally at him.

"Could you put the safety on?"

"That would add an extra step in case I have to pull the trigger."

"But you're not going to pull the trigger. It's me. And you're you. Do you get how ridiculous this is?"

"I do," she said. "It's ridiculous for sure."

"So now that we've agreed you're not going to shoot me—"

"We haven't agreed on that."

"But I'm driving," he pointed out, his tone falling somewhere between helpful and condescending. "So you're going to shoot me and—what?—sit in the passenger seat as the car goes flying across the expressway?"

"That's what air bags are for."

"I don't believe you."

"If you try to take the gun from me," she said, "the only choice I'll have is to, you know, shoot you."

He jerked the wheel and the car lurched into the next lane. He smiled at her. "Well, that felt unpleasant."

She could feel the power dynamic shifting and she knew from the housing projects and the ride-alongs and the long nights in Haiti that when power shifted it stayed shifted unless you grabbed it back immediately.

His eyes were on the road when she flicked the safety on. It didn't make a sound. She shifted in her seat, leaned forward slightly, and slammed the butt of the pistol down on his kneecap. The car lurched and swerved again. A horn blared.

Caleb hissed. "Holy fuck. What is wrong with you? That fucking—"

She did it again, exactly the same spot.

He jerked the car back out of a third swerve. "*Enough!*"

They'd be lucky if another car on the freeway wasn't calling 911 right now to report a drunk driver, giving the operator Caleb's license plate number.

She flicked the safety off again.

"Enough," he repeated. Riding his vocal cords along with the anger and attempt at authority was a clear timbre of anxiety. He had no idea what she was going to do next, but he was definitely afraid of the possibilities.

So now the power had shifted back.

He exited the freeway in Dorchester, in the southern tip of Neponset. He headed north on Gallivan Boulevard, stayed right at the rotary, and at first she thought they were crossing the bridge to Quincy, but instead he headed for the on-ramp back onto the expressway. At the last moment, he turned right, and drove down a street badly in need of repaving. They bounced along until he turned right and took them into a blocks-long stretch of bent, weather-lashed houses and Quonset-shaped warehouses and dry dockyards filled with boats that ran to the smaller side. At the end of the street, they found the Port Charlotte Marina, something Sebastian had pointed out to her a few times on their sails through Massachusetts Bay their first few summers together. Sebastian, showing her how to steer and navigate at night by the lights in the sky. Sebastian, out on the water with the wind in his Nordic hair, the only time she'd ever known him to be happy.

A restaurant and yacht club sat just past a near-deserted parking lot, both buildings looking freshly painted and hopeful for a marina in which there were no yachts. The biggest boat moored at the dock looked to be a forty-footer. Most of the others looked to be lobster boats, aged and constructed of wood. A few of the newer ones were fiberglass. The nicest of those was about thirty-five feet long, the hull painted blue, the wheelhouse painted white, the deck a honey teak. She paid attention to it because her husband stood on it, bathed in their headlights.

Caleb exited the car fast. He pointed back at her, told Brian his wife was not taking things well. Rachel was happy to note Caleb limped even as he speed-walked to the boat. She, on the other hand, moved slowly, her eyes on Brian. His gaze barely left hers except for the occasional flicks in the direction of Caleb.

If she'd known she'd end up killing him, would she have boarded the boat?

She could turn around and go to the police. My husband is an impostor, she'd say. She imagined some smarmy desk sergeant replying, "Aren't we all, ma'am?" Yes, she was certain, it was a crime to impersonate someone and a crime to keep two wives, but were those serious crimes? In the end, wouldn't Brian just take a plea and it would all go away? She'd be left the laughingstock never-was, the failed print reporter who'd become a pill-addicted broadcast reporter who'd become a punch line and then a shut-in and who would keep the local comics stocked with weeks of fresh material once it was discovered that Meltdown Media Chick had married a con man with another wife and another life.

She followed Caleb up the ramp to the boat. He stepped aboard. When she went to do the same, Brian offered his hand. She stared at it until he dropped it. He noticed the gun she carried. "Should I show you mine? So I feel safer?"

"Be my guest." She stepped aboard. As she did, Brian caught her by the wrist and stripped the gun from her hand in the same motion. He pulled his own gun, a .38 snub-nosed revolver, from under the flaps of his shirt and then laid them both on a table by the stern. "Once we get out into the bay, sweetheart, you let me know if you want to walk five paces and draw. I owe you that."

"You owe me a lot more than that."

He nodded. "And I'm going to make good on it." He unraveled a line from the cleat, and before she'd even realized she could hear the engine, Caleb was under the standing shelter with his hand on the throttle and they were chugging up the Neponset River toward the bay.

Brian sat on the bench on one side of the deck and she sat across from him, the front edge of the table in between them.

"So you own a boat," she said.

He leaned forward, hands clasped between his knees. "Yup."

Port Charlotte receded behind her. "Am I ever going to get back off it?"

He tilted his head to the side. "Of course. Why wouldn't you?"

"Because I can expose your double life for starters."

He sat back, opened his palms to the idea. "And where will that get you?"

"It won't get me anywhere. Get you in jail."

He shrugged.

"You don't think so."

"Look, if you want, we'll turn this boat around right now and take you back. And you can drive to the nearest police station and tell them your story. And if they believe you—and let's face it, Rachel, your credibility is a little shaky in this town—then, sure, they'll send some detective out tomorrow or the next day or a week from Tuesday, whenever they get around to it. But by that point, I'll be smoke. They'll never find me and you'll never find me."

The thought of never seeing him again slid through her intestinal tract like a shiv. Losing Brian—knowing he was out in the world somewhere, yet she would never see him again—would be like losing a kidney. It was a certifiably insane reaction, and yet there it was.

"Why aren't you already gone?"

"I couldn't synchronize every part of my timetable as fast as I wanted."

"What the fuck are you talking about?"

"We don't have much time," Brian said.

"For what?"

"For anything but trust."

She stared across the boat at him. *"Trust?"*

"I'm afraid so."

There were probably a thousand things she could have said to the galactic absurdity of his asking her to trust him, but all she managed to say was "Who is she?"

She hated the words as they left her mouth. He'd stripped her of every foundation she'd built the last three years of her life on, and she was coming off like the jealous shrew.

"Who?" he said.

"The pregnant wife you keep in Providence."

Another smile, bordering on a smirk, as his eyes rose to the starless sky. "She's an associate."

"At your mineral company?"

"Well, tangentially, yes."

She could feel them dropping into the rhythm of all their fights—she typically played offense, he played an evasive defense, which usually made her more and more aggressive, like the dog chasing the rabbit that has no meat under its fur. So before it could deteriorate any further, she asked the real question.

"Who are you?"

"I'm your husband."

"You're not my—"

"I'm the man who loves you."

"You lied to me about everything in our lives. That's not love. That's—"

"Look in my eyes. Tell me whether you see love there or not."

She looked. Sardonically at first, but then with growing fascination. It was there, no question.

But was it? He was, after all, an actor.

"*Your* version of it," she said.

"Well, yeah," he said, "that's the only version I'd know."

Caleb cut the engine. They were about two miles out in the bay, the lights of Quincy off to their right, the lights of Boston back and to their left. In front of them, the ink dark was interrupted by the ridges and crags of Thompson Island to their west. Impossible to tell in this dark if it was two hundred yards away or two thousand. There was some kind of youth facility on Thompson, Outward Bound maybe, but whatever the organization, they'd turned in for the night because the island emitted no light whatsoever. Small waves broke softly against the hull. She'd once piloted herself and Sebastian home on a night like this using only their running lights, the two of them chuckling nervously through most of the journey, but Caleb had cut every light but the small bulbs of uplighting on the deck by their feet.

Out there in the impermeable dark on a moonless night, she

realized Brian and Caleb could quite easily kill her. In fact, all of this could have been orchestrated to get her to think she was supervising the events that led her to this boat and this bay and this callous dark when in fact it was the other way around.

It suddenly seemed important to ask Brian, "What's your real name?"

"Alden," he said to her. "Brian Alden."

"Are you from a lumber family?"

He shook his head. "Nothing so glamorous."

"Are you from Canada?"

He shook his head. "I'm from Grafton, Vermont."

He watched her carefully as he removed a plastic sleeve of peanuts from his pocket, the kind they gave you on planes, and opened it.

"You're Scott Pfeiffer," she said.

He nodded.

"But your name isn't Scott Pfeiffer."

"No. That's just the name of some kid I went to high school with, used to make me laugh in Latin class."

"And your father?"

"Stepfather. Yeah. He was the guy I described. Racist, homophobic, scared the world was run by a large-scale conspiracy to fuck his life up and piss on everything he'd put his faith in. He was also, paradoxically maybe, a nice guy, good neighbor, help you put up a fence or fix a gutter. He keeled over from a heart attack while shoveling a neighbor's walk. Neighbor's name was Roy Carrol. Funny thing? Roy was never even nice to him, but my stepfather shoveled his walk because it was the decent thing to do and Roy was too poor to hire anyone to help and he lived on a corner lot. You know what Roy did the day after my father's funeral?" Brian popped a peanut in his mouth. "Went out and bought himself a three-thousand-dollar snowblower."

He offered her some peanuts and she shook her head, feeling numb to all of it suddenly, feeling as if she'd stepped into a virtual-reality booth and this was the set onto which she found herself projected.

"And your real father?"

"Never really knew him." He shrugged. "Something we have in common."

"How about Brian Delacroix? How'd you come up with that identity?"

"You know, Rachel. You know because I told you."

And she did. "He went to Brown."

Brian nodded.

"And you were the pizza delivery guy."

"Delivered in forty minutes or less or you get it for half price." He smiled. "Now you know why I drive so fast." He shook some more peanuts into his hand.

"Why," she said, "are you sitting there eating peanuts like nothing's changed?"

"Because I'm hungry." He popped another one in his mouth. "It was a long flight."

"There was no *flight*." She clenched, then unclenched her teeth.

He cocked an eyebrow at her and she wanted to tear it off his face. She wished she hadn't drunk so much. She needed to be clearheaded right now and she wasn't even close. She had wanted to have all her questions lined up in perfect sequence.

"There was no flight," she said, "because there's no job and you're not Brian Delacroix, which means our marriage isn't even legal and you've lied to me about . . ." She stopped. She could feel the dark all around her and all inside of her. "Everything."

He slapped the peanut dust off his hands and pocketed the empty plastic sleeve.

"Not everything."

"Really. What's real?"

He waved his fingers between their chests. "This."

She mimicked the gesture. "*This* is bullshit."

He actually had the temerity to look hurt. The balls. "No. It's not, Rachel. It's as real as anything."

Caleb joined them on the deck. "Tell me about the camera shop, Brian."

Brian said, "What is this, bad cop/bad cop suddenly? You're both gonna grill me?"

"Rachel says she followed you to Little Louie's."

A heartless cast found Brian's face. He'd worn the same look when he'd slapped Andrew Gattis, wore it when he'd walked out of the Hancock Tower in the rain, and it had flashed across his face during a fight once, for just a second. "How much did you tell her?"

"I didn't."

"You told her nothing?"

For a second, she thought Brian's voice sounded funny, like he'd bitten his tongue or cut it somehow.

"I told her we were actors."

"Nothing else?" His voice sounded like his own again.

"I'm right here," she said.

Brian looked over at her and his eyes were dead. No, not dead. Dying. The light bled from them. She felt infinitesimal in them. He swept her body with them in a way that was clinical and lustful at the same time, the look of a man watching pornography when he wasn't even sure he was in the mood.

Caleb said, "Why'd you go to the camera store, Brian?"

Brian held up a finger to Caleb, his eyes still moving up and down Rachel, and Caleb's face seized with the dismissiveness of the gesture.

"Don't fucking hold your finger up to me like I'm the help. Are the passports ready?"

Brian's jaw tightened even as he chuckled. "Oh, ho, ho, my man, let's not push me tonight."

Caleb took a step toward Brian. "You said they wouldn't be ready for another twenty-four hours."

"I know what I said."

"Is this about her?" Caleb pointed at Rachel. "Her and her bullshit? People could fucking die because—"

"I know people could die," Brian said.

"My wife could die. My child could—"

"A wife and child you shouldn't have."

"But it's okay for you?" Caleb took two more steps. "Huh? It's okay for *you*."

"She's been in war zones," Brian said. "She's battle-tested."

"She's a shut-in."

Rachel said, "What are you two—?"

Caleb stepped to Brian, pointed a finger in his face. "You lied about the fucking passports. You put us all at risk. We're gonna fucking die because you can't see past your dick."

As violence always did in her experience, the next few things happened very fast.

Brian slapped Caleb's finger out of his face. Caleb whacked the side of Brian's head with a hastily clenched fist. Brian rose half out of his seat as Caleb took another swing at him, half connecting with his neck. Brian buried his fist in Caleb's solar plexus. When Caleb doubled over, Brian punched him in the ear hard enough that she could hear the cartilage crunch.

Caleb stumbled sideways. He dropped to one knee and inhaled desperately for a moment.

She said, "Guys, stop," and the words sounded ridiculous.

Brian rubbed his neck where Caleb had hit him and spit off the side of the boat.

Caleb used the table to push himself to his feet. Then he was holding her gun in his hand. She watched him thumb off the safety, and she couldn't make sense of it at first. It characterized the surreal quality that had marked the entire day. They were Brian, Rachel, and Caleb, regular people, boring even, not the kind of people who brandished firearms. And yet it was she who'd forced Caleb to drive her here using the same gun.

And now he was pointing it in Brian's face. "Hey, tough guy, tell me where the fucking—"

When Brian struck Caleb's gun hand, the gun went off. It wasn't as loud as it sounded on the range, with partitions on either side of her. It sounded like a desk drawer being kicked shut. Judging by the muzzle flash, the bullet passed in her general direction. But she didn't scream. Brian swiped the gun out of Caleb's hand and swept Caleb's legs out from under him with the kind of ease that again suggested he'd had some wrestling experience. Caleb landed on his back, and Brian kicked him in the chest and abdomen, kicked him like he was going to kick him to death.

"Point a gun in *my face*?" Brian screamed. "Fucking kidding me?"

With every sentence Brian delivered a kick.

"Try to fuck me?" Brian kicked him in the stomach. "Talk shit about *my* wife?"

A blood bubble popped from Caleb's mouth.

"Try to fuck my wife?" Brian kicked him in the groin. "You don't think I notice the way you fucking drool over her? Stare at her? *Think about* her?"

When the kicks started, Caleb had begged him to stop. Now he just lay there.

"Brian, stop."

Brian turned toward her, his eyes narrowing at his gun in her hand. She couldn't remember picking it up, but she could feel its weight, so much heavier than hers, which, in Brian's hand, looked like a toy.

"Stop?" he said.

"Stop," she repeated. "You'll kill him."

"And why would you care?"

"Brian, please."

"What in your life would change if he was dead? If I was dead? Or just gone? You'll do the same thing—sit inside and look out at the world. But you won't engage it. You won't affect it. I mean, forget about him. What difference would it make if *you're* in the world or not?"

The words seemed to surprise him as much as her. He blinked several times. He looked at the lightless sky and the black bay. Looked at Caleb. Looked at her again. And she could see a realization take root—if he returned to land with an empty boat, no one would be the wiser.

He raised her gun. At least she thought he raised her gun. No, he did. He raised it. Raised it from his knee in a sweep, bringing it up and toward the center of himself, his right arm half-crossing his chest.

And she shot him.

She shot him as she'd been taught—center mass. Bullet straight to the heart.

She heard herself say, *Brian no Brian no.* She heard herself say, *No no no please.*

Brian stumbled backward and the blood bloomed on his shirt and then fell from his body in drops.

Caleb looked at her with a mix of horror and gratitude.

Brian dropped her gun. He said, "Shit."

She said, "I'm sorry," and it left her mouth like a question.

And there was so much love in his eyes. And so much fear. Words left his mouth accompanied by a spoonful of blood that spilled down his chin. And she couldn't compute what he was saying to her because of the blood and his fear.

He took a half stumble-step backward, his palm to his chest. He fell off the boat.

And she heard clearly now what he'd said to her, what had gotten lost while the words fell from his mouth with the blood. "I love you."

Wait. Wait. Brian, wait.

She could see his blood on the deck and a small splatter of it on the white foam cushion of a bench by the rail.

Wait, she thought again.

We were supposed to grow old together.

III / RACHEL IN THE WORLD

2014

23

DARK

The first thing she removed was her watch. Then her necklace, the same one he'd bought her in the mall three weeks back. Kicked off her shoes. Pulled off her windbreaker, followed by her T-shirt and her jeans. Put everything on the table with the gun she'd used.

She moved past Caleb and went down into the hold. Just to the right of the door, she found a flare gun and a first aid kit but no flashlight. Farther down the counter, though, she found one encased in yellow plastic and black rubber. She tested it. Worked beautifully. She checked the base—solar powered. If she'd had time to look for an oxygen tank, she could have stayed down there forever. She went back out on deck, found Caleb waiting for her by the rail.

"Listen," he said. "He's dead. And if he's not—"

She brushed past him. She stepped up on the rail. Caleb said, "Wait," but she dove into the bay. The cold seized her heart, her throat, and her intestinal tract all at the same time. When it found her head it drilled down through her temples, rolled through her sinuses like acid.

The flashlight beam was even brighter than she could have hoped for, though, and illuminated a lime green world of moss and sea-weed, coral and sand, black boulders the size of primitive gods. She descended through the green and felt alien, very much the unnatu-ral intruder into the natural world. The world before the world, so old it pre-dated language, humanity, conscience.

A school of cod passed within feet of her. When they were gone, she saw him. He sat on the sand about fifteen feet below by a rock as old as the world. She swam down to him and treaded water in front of his corpse. She wept, her shoulders convulsing, and he stared back at her with sightless eyes.

I'm sorry.

A thin rope of blood pirouetted along the rim of the hole in his chest.

I loved you, I hated you, I never knew you.

His body was canted to the right, while his head was cocked to the left.

I hate you. I love you. I'll miss you for the rest of my fucking life.

She stared at him and his corpse stared back until her lungs burned and her eyes burned and she couldn't take it any longer.

Good-bye.

Good-bye.

As she swam up, she saw that Caleb had turned the boat lights on. The hull bobbed on the surface, twenty feet up and about fifteen yards to the south of her. She kicked for the surface and was halfway there when something grazed her thigh just above the knee. She slapped at her leg but nothing was there and all she managed to do was drop the flashlight. It dropped faster than she rose, and the last she saw of it, it had settled on the sandy floor, a bright yellow eye looking up toward the world.

When she broke the surface, she took a great guzzle of oxygen, then swam to the boat. As she climbed aboard, she noticed a tiny island off the starboard side that she hadn't been able to make out in the dark. It was an island for birds and crabs only, barely big enough to plant one butt cheek on, definitely not two. A lone and sickly thin maple pointed up from the bedrock, bent about forty-five degrees by the elements. Several hundred yards away, as she'd guessed, sat Thompson, a bit more clearly defined but just as light-less as before.

On the boat, she took her clothes with her into the cabin, ignoring Caleb, who sat on the deck with his hands between his knees and his head lowered. She found a small bathroom with a sliding door just past the bed. There was a picture of them hanging over the toilet, one she'd never seen before. She remembered when it had been taken, though, because it was the first time Brian met Melissa. They'd had lunch in the North End, then walked over to Charlestown and sat on the grassy hill by the Bunker Hill Monument. Melissa had taken the picture, Rachel and Brian with their backs to each other, the monument rising behind them. They'd been smiling—no news there; people always smiled in photographs—but the smiles were genuine. They were happy, radiant. That night he'd told her he loved her for the first time. She made him wait half an hour before she said it back.

She sat on the toilet seat for a few minutes and whispered his name a dozen times and wept noiselessly until her throat clogged. She wanted to explain that she was sorry because she'd killed him and she wanted to explain that she hated him because he'd played her for a fool, but the truth was she didn't feel either of those things one-tenth as much as she felt the loss of him and the loss of who she'd been with him. So much of her essential wiring had been shorted in Haiti—her empathy, her courage, her compassion, her will, her integrity, her sense of self-worth—and only Brian had believed it would come back. He'd convinced her the shorted wires could be re-fused.

"*Oh, Rachel,*" she heard her mother say, as she'd said more than once, "*isn't it sad that you can only love yourself if someone else gives you permission?*"

She looked in the mirror and was shocked to see how much she resembled her, the famous Elizabeth Childs, the woman whose bitterness everyone always mistook for courage.

"Fuck you, Mother."

She stripped off her bra and underwear and dried herself with a thick towel she found on a shelf. She put her jeans, T-shirt, and windbreaker back on, found a brush and did the best she could with her hair, staring in the mirror again at her mother around the time *The Staircase* had been published, yes, but also at a new version of Rachel. A killer. She had taken a life. The fact that the life had been her husband's didn't make the fact worse or better; the act itself was empirically grave no matter who was killed. She was the agent of removing human life from this planet.

Had he been raising his gun?

She'd thought he had.

But would he have pulled the trigger?

In the moment, she'd been certain he would.

Now? Now she didn't know. Was the man who'd given his coat to a homeless man on a night of drenching rain capable of murder? The same man who'd psychologically nursed her through three years of illness with nary an impatient word or frustrated glance? Could that man commit homicide?

No, that man couldn't. But that man was Brian Delacroix, a falsehood.

Brian Alden, on the other hand, could slap an old friend with imperious calm. He could kick his partner and best friend with enough fury to suggest he'd never stop kicking until that friend was dead. Brian Alden had raised that gun toward her. No, he hadn't pointed it directly at her and no, he hadn't pulled the trigger.

Because she hadn't given him the chance.

She went back out on deck. She felt calm. Too calm. And she recognized it for what it was—shock. She could feel herself in her body but not of it.

She found her gun on the deck where he'd dropped it. She tucked it in her waistband at the small of her back. She lifted Brian's gun off the table. She walked toward Caleb with it and he narrowed his eyes at her, too late to stop her from whatever she planned to do with it.

She flicked her wrist and tossed it past his head into the ocean. She looked down at him.

"Help me wash the blood off the deck."

24

KESSLER

On the drive back, Caleb had trouble taking clean breaths without pain. They both began to suspect Brian had fractured at least one of his ribs. Once they reached the city proper, Caleb bypassed the first exit for Back Bay. At first she thought he meant to take the next one, but when he passed that too, she said, "What're you doing?"

"Driving."

"Where?"

"I have a house that's safe. We need to go there, figure this out."

"I need to go to my apartment."

"No, you don't."

"Yeah, I do."

"There are very pissed-off people who could be after us by now. We have to get out of this city, not into it."

"I need my laptop."

"Fuck your laptop. With the money we'll have you can buy a new one."

"It's not the laptop, it's the book that's on it."

"Download another one."

"Not a book I'm reading, a book I'm writing."

He looked wildly at her as they passed under a series of bright lamps, his face white, slightly ghoulish, and helpless. "You didn't back it up?"

"No."

"Put it in the Cloud?"

"*No.*"

"Why the fuck not?"

"I need my laptop," she repeated as the exit approached. "Don't make me pull the gun again."

"You don't need your book with the money you'll—"

"It's not about money!"

"Everything's about money!"

"Take the exit."

"Fuck!" He screamed it at the ceiling and swerved the car into the exit lane.

They came out of a short tunnel onto the edge of the North End and turned left and headed through Government Center toward Back Bay.

"I didn't know you were writing a book," he said at one point. "Is it, like, a mystery? Science fiction?"

"No. It's nonfiction. It's about Haiti."

"That could be a tough sell." His tone was almost chiding.

She loosed a bitter chuckle. "Check your fucking privilege, my man."

He shot her an apologetic smile. "I'm just telling you the truth."

"Your truth," she said.

Up in the apartment, she went into her bedroom and changed again, back into a dry bra and underwear and swapping out the jeans for black tights, a black T-shirt, and an old gray sweatshirt from her college days at NYU. She opened her laptop and dragged the book files into a folder, something she probably should have been doing all along. She addressed an e-mail to herself and attached the folder and hit send. *Voilà*. Her novel was now accessible to her no matter what computer she used to access it.

She came out of the bedroom with the laptop under her arm to see Caleb had made himself a drink, as she'd known he would. The kicks to the groin, he said, made sitting uncomfortable, so he stood at the kitchen bar and sipped his bourbon and gave her a thousand-yard stare as she entered the kitchen.

She said, "I thought you were in a rush."

"We have an hour's drive ahead."

"By all means then," she said, "imbibe."

"What did you do?" he said with a hoarse whisper. "What did you do?"

"I shot my husband." She opened the fridge but then couldn't remember why and closed it. She brought a glass to the bar and helped herself to some of the bourbon.

"In self-defense?"

"You were there," she said.

"I was on the ground. I'm not even sure I was fully conscious."

The equivocation irritated her. "So you didn't see it happen?"

"No."

No equivocation there. So what would he say from the stand someday? Would he say she acted to save his life and her own? Or would he say he wasn't "fully conscious"?

Who are you, Caleb? she could have asked. *And not in the day-to-day parts of you but in the essential ones?*

She drank some bourbon. "He turned his gun toward me and I could see in his face what was going to happen, so I shot first."

"You're so calm."

"I don't feel calm."

"You sound robotic."

"It's consistent then with how I feel."

"Your husband's dead."

"I know that."

"Brian."

"Yes."

"Dead."

Now she looked across the bar at him. "I know what I did. I just can't feel it."

"Maybe you're in shock."

"That'd be my guess." A horrific realization lurked at the back of her skull, deep in the lizard folds, that for all the grief she could feel swelling in her heart, pushing and scraping at its walls, the rest of her body felt alive in a way it hadn't since Haiti. The grief would consume her when she stopped moving and stopped focusing on the problems immediately at hand, so the trick for now was to not stop moving and not widen her focus.

"Will you go to the police?"

"They'll ask why I shot him."

"Because he was kicking me to death."

"They'll ask why he was doing that."

"And we'll say he freaked out because you discovered his double life."

"And they'll say it wasn't because you were fucking each other?"

"They won't go there."

"It's the first place they'll go. Then they'll want to know what business you were in together and if you had any recent disputes over money. So whatever you and Brian were into, you better hope none of it gives you motive to kill him. Because *then* they'll decide not only were you and I fucking each other, we were fucking over Brian on a business deal. And *then* they'll want to know why I threw the gun in the water."

"Why did you?"

"Because, Jesus Christ, I was fucking confused? In shock? Over-whelmed? I mean, take your pick. And now, once Brian's death comes to light, I can't imagine one scenario in which I don't end up serving some time in prison. Even if it's just three or four years. And I won't go to prison." Now she could feel something, a flutter of fear that bordered on hysteria. "I won't sit in a box with someone else holding the key. I won't fucking do it."

Caleb watched her, his mouth a small oval. "Okay. Okay."

"I will not."

Caleb drank a little more bourbon. "We've got to go."

"Where?"

"A safe place. Haya's already there with the baby."

She took her laptop and keys off the counter and then stopped. "His body will resurface." The realization kicked something loose in the center of her. She felt a little less numb suddenly, a little less calm. "It will, won't it?"

He nodded.

"Then we have to go back."

"Go back and do what?"

"Weigh the body down."

"With what?"

"I don't know. Bricks. A bowling ball."

"Where are we going to get a bowling ball at"—he looked at the clock on the microwave—"eleven o'clock at night?"

"He has barbells in the bedroom. Two of them."

He stared at her.

"For curling. You know the little ones. They're twenty pounds each. Two of those should do the job."

"We're talking about weighing down Brian's corpse."

"Yes, we are."

"It's absurd."

There was nothing absurd about it. Rationally, she knew exactly what she needed to do. And maybe her shock wasn't shock at all but was, instead, her brain divesting itself of all unnecessary data in order to process only that which was vital. She'd felt the same way in the squatters camp in Leógâne, moving from tent to tent, tree to tree. Complete clarity of purpose—move and hide, move and hide, move and hide. There were no larger existential questions in play, no shades of gray. Her sense of smell, sight, and hearing were not employed in pursuit of gratification but in pursuit of survival. Her thoughts didn't wander; they marched in a straight line.

"It's absurd," Caleb said again.

"It's where we find ourselves right now."

She headed for the bedroom to get the barbells but stopped halfway there when the doorbell rang. It wasn't the buzzer, which is what normally rang if someone was outside the building. And it wasn't the intercom on their phone, which is how the doorman announced visitors. No, this was the small doorbell just outside her front door, ten feet away.

She looked through the eyehole and saw a black man with a trim goatee in a brown half-fedora, wearing a leather car coat over a white shirt and black skinny tie. Behind him were two of Boston's finest in uniform, both women.

She kept the security chain on as she opened the door a crack. "Yes?"

The man held up a gold shield and a Providence Police ID card. His name was Trayvon Kessler. "Detective Kessler, Mrs. Delacroix. Is your husband home?"

"No, he's not."

"Do you expect him back tonight?"

She shook her head. "He left today on a business trip."

"To where?"

"Russia."

Kessler had a very soft voice. "Would you mind if we came in and chatted for a few minutes?"

If she hesitated, this would turn adversarial, so she opened the door. "Come in."

He removed his hat as he crossed the threshold and placed it on the seat of the antique chair to his left. His skull was shaven, as she'd somehow known it would be, and gleamed in the dim light of the entryway like polished marble. "This is Officer Mullen," he said, indicating the blond cop with bright friendly eyes and freckles that matched her hair, "and that's Officer Garza." He indicated the dark-haired, heavyset woman with a hungry gaze that was already drinking in the apartment. The gaze fell quickly on Caleb, standing at the kitchen bar with a bottle of bourbon. Rachel noticed she'd left the bottle of wine she'd polished off earlier on the corner of the bar as well, between an empty wineglass and the rocks glass she'd just half filled with bourbon. It looked like they were throwing a party in here.

Caleb came over and shook their hands, introduced himself as Brian's partner. Then in the silence that followed, with the three cops looking at the apartment with cop's eyes, Caleb got nervous.

"First name's Trayvon?" he said to Kessler, and Rachel wanted to shut her eyes in horror.

Kessler took in the bottle of bourbon and the empty wine bottle. "Everyone calls me Tray, though."

"But like that kid in Florida, right?" Caleb said. "The one who got killed by the neighborhood watch guy?"

Kessler said, "Same first name, yeah. What, you never met no one else named Caleb before?"

"Well, sure."

"Then . . ." Kessler raised his eyebrows, waited.

"Trayvon's just a less common name."

"Where *you're* from."

Rachel couldn't stand another fucking second of this. "Detective, why are you looking for my husband?"

"We just want to ask him a couple of questions."

"You're from Rhode Island?"

"Yes, ma'am. Providence PD. These wonderful officers are serving as my liaisons."

"What does my husband have to do with something in Providence?" She was pleasantly surprised with how effortlessly she slipped into the role of the befuddled wife.

"You got a mouse under your eye," Kessler said to Caleb.

"'Scuse me?"

Kessler pointed and now Rachel could see it too, a red welt in the fold of Caleb's right lower eyelid, growing angrier as they watched. "Look at that, Officer Mullen."

The blond cop stooped a bit to get a better look. "How'd you happen to come by that, sir?"

"An umbrella," Caleb said.

"An umbrella?" Officer Garza said. "It jump out and bite you?"

"No, a guy had one on the T when I was coming over here. I work in Cambridge. Anyway, he had it resting on his shoulder and we came to his stop and he turned real quick and it poked me in the eye."

"Ouch," Kessler said.

"Exactly."

"Had to hurt twice as much when you think how little rain there's been this week. I mean, the beginning of the month, sure, that was crazy. But lately? When's the last time it rained?" he asked the room.

"Ten days easy," Officer Mullen said.

"Fuck's this guy doing carrying an umbrella then?" Again Kessler spoke to no one in particular, a bewildered smile on his lean face. "'Scuse the f-bomb," he said to Rachel.

"No problem."

"Crazy world we live in, dudes walking around subway cars with umbrellas when there ain't no rain." He looked at the bottles and glasses on the bar again. "So your husband is in Russia?"

"Yes."

He turned to Caleb, who was clearly hoping he wouldn't. "And you came by to drop something off?"

"Hmm?" Caleb said. "No."

"Business papers or something like that?"

"No," Caleb said.

"So . . . I mean, stop me if I'm being too personal here . . ."

"No, no."

"But why are you here? Man's out of the country, and you just drop by to get your drink on with his wife?"

Officer Mullen cocked an eyebrow at that. Officer Garza wandered around the living room.

Rachel said, "We're all friends, Detective. My husband, Caleb, and me. Whatever antiquated notions you're bringing in here about whether a man and a woman can hang out as good friends while her husband is away, I'd really like it if you parked those notions somewhere outside these walls."

Kessler leaned back a bit, gave her a wide smile. "Well, all right." The words rode a soft chuckle out of his mouth. "All right. I stand corrected. And I apologize for any offense I may have given."

She nodded.

He handed her a photograph. One look, and the blood rushed along her hairline and behind her eyes and barreled through her heart. Brian sat with his arm around the pregnant woman she'd seen this afternoon. She wasn't pregnant in the picture and Brian's hair had less gray in it than it did now. They were sitting on a couch. It had gray cushions and looked to be made of white rattan that blended with the white beadboard wall behind them. It was the kind of wall you found in a beach house or, at the very least, a house in a beach town. Above them hung a reproduction of Monet's *Water Lilies*. Brian appeared very tan. He and the woman sported big white smiles. She wore a blue flower-print summer dress. He wore a red flannel shirt and cargo shorts. Her left hand lay quite casually on his right thigh.

"You don't look well suddenly, ma'am."

She said, "How am I supposed to look, Detective, when you hand me a photograph of my husband and another woman?"

He held out his hand. "Can I have it back?"

She handed it to him.

"Do you know her?"

She shook her head.

"Never seen her before?"

"No."

"How about you?" He handed the photograph to Caleb. "Know this woman?"

"No."

"*No?*"

"No," Caleb said.

"Well, you've missed your chance." Trayvon Kessler returned the photograph to the pocket of his car coat. "She turned up dead about eight hours ago."

Rachel said, "How?"

"Shot once in the heart, once in the head. It probably led the news tonight if you'd been watching." He gave the bar another glance. "But you were engaged in other activities."

"Who was she?" Rachel asked.

"Her name was Nicole Alden. Beyond that, I don't know much. No criminal record, no known enemies, worked in a bank. Knew your husband, though."

"That picture's old," she told him. "Might even pre-date when I met my husband. So what's to say he's still in contact with her?"

"You say he's in Russia?"

"Yeah." She found her phone, opened the last text he'd sent her claiming to be on the runway at Logan. She showed it to Kessler.

Kessler read it and handed the phone back. "He drive himself to the airport or take a cab?"

"He drove himself."

"In the Infiniti?"

"Yes." She stopped. "How do you know—?"

"What he drives?"

"Yes."

"Because an Infiniti FX 45, registered to your husband at this address, was found parked across the street from the victim's home this afternoon. And a witness saw your husband exit the home on or around the time of the murder."

"And, what, he just walked away and left his car behind?"

"Can we all sit down?" He tilted his head at the bar.

All five of them took stools around the bar, Kessler in the middle, like the father at a family meeting.

"Our witness says your husband drove up in the Infiniti, but he drove off again an hour later in a blue Honda. You ever use one of those map programs where you can see the actual street? Either of you?"

They both nodded.

"What the map companies do to get that picture is drive around in a van and film the streets. So you're looking at pictures that could be months old or weeks but not years. So I went on a real estate site and I punched in the victim's address and then I went to street view and I clicked around a bit. And guess what I found?"

"A blue Honda," Caleb said.

"A blue Honda parked halfway down the block on the east side of the street. Got me a license plate, ran that plate, and discovered it was registered to a Brian Alden. Ran Mr. Alden through the DMV, got a driver's license photo that looks identical to your husband."

"Jesus," Rachel said, not having to bring much to the performance to make it convincing. "You're telling me my husband is not my husband."

"I'm telling you your husband may be living a couple of lives, ma'am, and I'd like to talk to him about that." He folded his hands on the bar and smiled at her. "Among other things."

After a minute, she said, "I only know he's in Russia."

Trayvon Kessler shook his head. "He's not in Russia."

"I only know what he tells me."

"And that's looking like it could be a lot of lies, ma'am. He go on business trips a lot?"

"At least once a month."

"Where to?"

"Canada and the Pacific Northwest mostly. But he also goes to India, Brazil, the Czech Republic, the United Kingdom."

"Some cool places there. You ever go with him?"

"No."

"Why not? I'd like to see me some Rio, maybe walk around Prague."

"I have a condition."

"A condition?"

"Or, I mean, I had one until recently."

She could feel them all looking at her, particularly the two female cops, wondering what "condition" could possibly afflict an entitled Back Bay princess like her.

"It kept me from leaving the house," she said. "I couldn't fly, that's for sure."

"So you're afraid of flying?" Kessler's tone was helpful.

"Among other things."

"You agoraphobic?" he said.

She looked in his eyes and they were far too wise.

"I majored in psychology at Penn." Again with the helpful tone of voice.

"It's never been officially diagnosed," she said eventually and thought she heard Officer Mullen sigh. "But I definitely had symptoms that suggested it."

"Had? Past tense?"

"Brian's been working with me on it."

"But not enough to take you on a business trip."

"Not yet, no."

"Would you like protective custody?"

He said it so casually it took her a moment to process the words.

"Why would I want that?"

He turned on his stool. "Officer Garza, you got that other picture?"

Garza handed him a photograph and he turned it faceup on the bar so she and Caleb could see it. The blond woman lay facedown on a kitchen floor, her lower half out of frame. Blood had billowed out from under her chest and pooled above her left shoulder. Her left cheek and part of the refrigerator door were also splattered with blood. But the worst image, the one Rachel suspected she'd be woken up by for the rest of her life, was the black gouge at the top of her head. It didn't look like someone had shot her; it looked like something had taken a bite out of her skull. And the hole left in the wake of that bite had immediately filled with blood that spilled into her hair and turned black.

"If your husband did this and—"

"My husband didn't do that," she said loudly.

"—I'm not saying he did but he's the last person we know of to see her alive. So let's just say, let's just *say*, Mrs. Delacroix, that he did do this?" He turned on his barstool and pointed. "Well, ma'am, he has a key to that door."

He's beyond using it, she thought.

She said, "So you'd like to take me into your custody?"

"Protective custody, ma'am. Protective."

Rachel shook her head.

"Officer Mullen, please make note that Mrs. Delacroix declined our recommendation of PC."

"Got it." Mullen scribbled on a pad.

Kessler tapped a finger on the marble bar top, as if testing it, then looked at her again. "Will you be willing to come down to the precinct and talk about when you last saw your husband?"

"The last time I saw Brian was eight o'clock this morning when he drove himself to the airport."

"He didn't drive himself to the airport."

"So you say. That doesn't mean you're right."

He gave that a small shrug. "But I am."

He exuded equal parts serenity and skepticism. The odd mixture made her feel as if he knew all her answers before they left her mouth, as if not only could he see into her, he could see into the future; he knew how this was going to end. It was all she could do to hold his mildly curious gaze and not fall to her knees and beg for mercy. If she ever went into an interview room with this man, the only way she'd exit would be in handcuffs.

"I'm tired, Detective. I'd like to get into bed and wait for my husband's phone call from Moscow."

He nodded and patted her hand. "Officer Mullen, please make a note that Mrs. Delacroix declined to join us at the precinct to answer further questions." He reached into the inside pocket of his car coat and placed his business card on the bar between them. "My personal cell is on the back."

"Thank you."

He stood. "Mr. Perloff." His voice was suddenly louder and sharper, though he kept his back to Caleb.

"Yes?"

"When's the last time you saw Brian Delacroix?"

"Yesterday afternoon when he left work."

Kessler turned to him. "You're in the lumber business together, correct?"

"Yes."

"And you knew nothing about your business partner's other life?"

"No."

"Care to come to the precinct and speak about that at length?"

"I'm pretty tired too."

Another short glance at the bar, followed by a slightly longer one at Rachel. "Of course you are." Kessler handed Caleb one of his business cards.

"I'll call you," Caleb said.

"Yes, you will, Mr. Perloff. Yes, you will. Because, can I tell you something?"

"Sure."

"If Brian Delacroix-slash-Alden is as dirty as I think he is?" He leaned into Caleb and spoke in a whisper loud enough for all of them to hear. "Then that means you're fucking dirty, my man." He slapped Caleb hard on the shoulder and laughed like they were old friends. "So you stay in plain sight now, hear?"

Officer Mullen jotted in her notepad as they headed for the door. Officer Garza moved her head on a slow swivel, as if everything she saw was transmitted to a central database. Detective Kessler paused at a Rothko reprint Brian had brought with him from his previous apartment. Kessler gave the painting a squint and then a soft smile, looked back at her and raised his eyebrows in approval of her taste. His smile broadened, and, man, she did not like what she saw there.

They let themselves out.

Caleb went straight to the bourbon. "Jesus," he said. "Jesus."

"Calm down."

"We've got to run."

"Are you nuts? You heard what he said."

"All we've got to do is get to the money."

"What money?"

"*The* money." He drained his glass. "So much money these fucking guys, they'll never catch us. Get the money, get to the safe house. Jesus. Shit. Fuck." He opened his mouth to loose another expletive but then closed it. His eyes widened and welled. "Nicole. Not Nicole."

She watched him. He pressed the heel of his hand to each of his lower eyelids and exhaled through pursed lips.

"Not Nicole," he said again.

"So you knew her."

He glared at her. "Of course I did."

"Who was she?"

"She was . . ." Another long exhale. "She was my friend. She was a good person. And now she's . . ." He shot her another heartless glare. "Fucking Brian. I told him not to wait. I told him you'd either catch up or you wouldn't. We'd either send for you when it was safe or he'd forget about you."

"Wait a minute," she said. "Me? What were you waiting for me to—?"

The doorbell rang. She looked at the door and noticed Trayvon Kessler's half-fedora sitting on the chair beside it. She crossed the condo and picked it up. Had it in her hand when she opened the door.

But it wasn't Detective Kessler on the other side of the threshold.

It was two white men who looked like actuaries or mortgage brokers—middle-aged, bland, forgettable.

Except for the guns in their hands.

25

WHAT KEY

Each man held a 9mm Glock in front of his groin, their hands crossed at the wrists, barrels pointed at the ground. If anyone passed in the hall, they'd see only the men, not the guns.

"Mrs. Delacroix?" the one on the left said. "Good to see you. May we come in?" He flicked the gun barrel toward her and she stepped back.

They came into the apartment and shut the door behind them.

Caleb said, "Who the fuck are—?" and then saw the guns.

The shorter of the two, the one who'd spoken, pointed his at Rachel's chest. The taller one pointed his at Caleb's head. He used it to gesture toward the dining room table.

"Let's all have a seat over there," the shorter one said.

Rachel immediately saw the logic—of all the places in the apartment, the dining area was the farthest from any windows.

The only way you could see it from the front door was to enter the apartment, close the door behind you, and then look to your left.

They sat at the table. Rachel placed Detective Kessler's hat on the table in front of her because she had no idea what else to do with it. Her throat closed up. Fire ants scuttled along her bones and crawled over her scalp.

The shorter man had sad eyes and a sadder comb-over. He was about fifty-five and paunchy. Wore a fraying white polo shirt under a sky-blue Members Only jacket, the kind that had been ubiquitous when Rachel was in grade school but which she hadn't seen much of since.

His partner was maybe five years younger. He had a full head of gray hair and fashionable gray stubble on his cheeks and chin. He wore a black T-shirt under a black sport coat that was a size too big for him and looked to be cheaply made. The shoulders spiked at the ends from spending too much time on wire hangers and in between the spikes and the corresponding lapels lay a poppy field of dandruff.

Both men gave off a whiff of curdled dreams and dead ambitions. That's probably how they ended up here, Rachel thought, threatening ordinary citizens with guns. The one in the Members Only jacket, she decided, looked like a Ned. The one with the dandruff she dubbed Lars.

She'd hoped humanizing them would reduce her terror but it actually had the reverse effect, particularly once Ned screwed a silencer onto the muzzle of his Glock and Lars followed suit.

"We," Ned said, "are pressed for time. So I'm going to ask you both to look after your best interests and not go down the 'I don't know what you're talking about' route. Fair enough?"

Rachel and Caleb stared at him.

He pinched the bridge of his nose, closed his eyes for a moment. "I said, 'Fair enough?'"

"Yes," Rachel said.

"Yes," Caleb said.

Ned looked at Lars and Lars looked at Ned and then they both went back to looking at Rachel and Caleb.

"Rachel," Ned said. "It is Rachel, right?"

Rachel could hear the tremor in her voice when she answered. "Yes."

"Rachel," he said. "Stand up for me."

"What?"

"Stand up for me, hon. Really. Just right here in front of me."

She stood and the tremor that had been in her voice found her legs.

Ned's nose, red-veined and pitted, was eye level with her belly. "Good, good. Stay right there now and don't move."

"Okay."

Ned leaned back in his chair so he could get a clear look at Caleb. "You're his partner, right?"

Caleb said, "Whose?"

"Ah ah ah." Ned tapped the butt of the Glock on the table. "What'd we say about that?"

"Oh, Brian," Caleb said quickly. "Brian's partner. Yes."

Ned rolled his eyes at Lars. "'Oh, Brian.'"

"Oh, *that* Brian," Lars said.

Ned gave it a rueful smile. "So, Caleb, where's the key?"

Caleb said, "What key?"

Ned punched Rachel in the stomach. Punched her so hard she could feel the impression of his knuckles as they burrowed under her windpipe and lifted her off her feet. She landed on the floor and lay there, stripped of oxygen, her insides aflame, her mind filled with black gum, unable to process anything. And once she could process, around the time that the air returned to her lungs, the pain intensified. She ground her head into the floor and made it to her hands and knees. She gasped several times. But the pain was nothing compared to the realization that she was going to die tonight. *Not soon.*

Not someday. Probably in the next five minutes. And definitely tonight.

Ned lifted her to her feet. He grasped her shoulders. He seemed worried she might collapse. "You okay?"

She nodded and for a moment was sure she was going to vomit.

"Say it." His eyes searched hers. Ned, the Good Samaritan.

"I'm okay."

"Good."

She went to sit down but he held her upright.

"I'm sorry," he said, "but we may have to go again."

She couldn't stop the tears. She tried, she did, but she was overwhelmed by the memory of his knuckles, of the loss of breath, of pain so acute and immediate it short-circuited her ability to think, and, worst of all, the advance knowledge that it was coming, that this sad-eyed man with the comb-over and the concerned voice would hit her again and keep hitting until he got what he wanted or she was dead, whichever came first.

"Ssshhh," Ned said. "Turn around. I want him to see your face."

He put his hands on her shoulders and turned her so that she was facing Caleb. "My first punch, young man, was to her solar plexus. Hurts like hell but it's not all that harmful to your health. My next punch will blow up her fucking kidneys."

"I don't know anything."

"Sure you do. You're the IT guy. You were part of this from the beginning."

"Brian went rogue."

"He did, huh?"

Caleb's eyes danced. His face was covered in sweat and his lips twitched and he looked for all the world to see like the frightened boy she now realized he'd always been. He glanced at Rachel and at first she mistook the emotion in his eyes for empathy but then realized, to her horror, that it was embarrassment. Shame. Pity. He was ashamed because he knew he'd never have the courage to save her. He pitied her because he knew she was going to die.

He's going to pulverize my kidneys, Caleb. Tell him what you know.

Ned ran the silencer down the side of Rachel's right temple and then along her neckline. "Don't make me do this, young man. I got a daughter. I got sisters."

Caleb said, "Look—"

"There's no *look*, Caleb. There's no 'Hang on a second,' or 'Let me explain, or 'This is just a big misunderstanding.'" Ned inhaled deeply through his nostrils, a man trying to retain his cool. "There's only a question and an answer. That's it."

Rachel felt his penis stiffen against the back of her left hip. He was hard, this father of a daughter, this brother of sisters. Monsters, her mother had told her and she had learned herself over the years, don't dress like monsters; they dress like humans. Even stranger, they rarely know they're the monsters.

"Where's the key?" Ned said.

"What key?" Caleb said, his entire face quivering.

It stopped quivering when Ned fired a bullet into it.

She wasn't sure what had happened at first. She registered the slap of the bullet entering flesh. She heard Caleb make a surprised yelp, the last sound, it turned out, he'd ever make. His head snapped back hard, as if he'd just heard the funniest of jokes. His head snapped forward, except now it was covered in a beaded curtain of blood, and Rachel opened her mouth to scream.

Ned placed the silencer to the side of her neck. It was hot enough to burn if he left it there too long. "If you scream, I have to kill you. I don't want to kill you, Rachel."

But he would.

No, Rachel, he *will*. The moment they're done here. The moment they get whatever it is they want. A key. What fucking key? Brian had so many keys on his key ring that it would take a mathematical savant to notice he'd added one. But if he did have this key they were looking for, that's where it probably was—on his key ring.

Which was on his person.

Which was sitting at the bottom of Massachusetts Bay.

Caleb's corpse slipped sideways in the chair and would have slid all the way to the floor, but his shoulder wedged underneath the arm. For a moment, the only sound came from him dripping.

"So the answer you want to give my next question," Ned said, "is definitely not 'What key?'"

No matter what answer you give, he will kill you.

She nodded.

"Are you nodding because you have my answer or because you agree that saying 'What key?' would be a big mistake?" He took the gun away from her neck. "You can talk. I know you're not going to scream."

"What am I supposed to say?"

On the other side of the table, Lars stood. Clearly bored. Ready to leave. And that was far more unsettling than if he'd tried to be menacing. What was happening here was coming to a close. And the period on the sentence would be another bullet to another face, this time hers.

"So here we go," Ned said. "Only one answer we're looking for and that'd be the right one. Rachel," he said with the utmost delicacy and concern, "where's the key?"

"Brian has it."

"And where's Brian?"

"I don't know," she said and then, rushing, as Ned raised his gun, "but I have an idea."

"An idea?"

"He has a boat. Nobody knows about it."

"What's the name of it, and where is it moored?"

She'd never seen the name. She'd never thought to look. She said, "It's moored—"

The doorbell rang.

They all looked at the door, then at one another, then back at the door.

"Who would that be?" Ned asked.

"I haven't a clue."

"Your husband?"

"He wouldn't ring the bell."

The bell rang again. Followed by a knock on the door. "Mrs. Delacroix, it's Detective Kessler."

"Detective Kessler." Ned tried the words out. "Huh."

"I forgot my hat, ma'am."

Ned and Rachel both looked down at the half-fedora Rachel had placed on the table.

Another knock, insistent, the knock of a man used to knocking on doors whether the people on the other side wanted him to come in or not. "Mrs. Delacroix?"

"Coming!" Rachel called.

Ned shot her a look.

Rachel shot him a look back: *What did you want me to do?*

Ned and Lars looked at each other. Whatever telepathic language they spoke, they arrived at a decision. Ned handed her the hat. He raised his palm in front of her face. "You see the width of my hand?"

"Yes."

"That's how far you open the door. And then you give him his hat and you close it."

She started to step away from him, but he grabbed her arm at the elbow and turned her to face Caleb. The blood curtain on his face was darkening. If this were Haiti, his head would be covered with flies.

"If you deviate from my instructions one iota, I do that to you."

She started to shake and he spun her toward the door.

"Stop shaking," he whispered.

"How?" Her teeth chattered.

He slapped her hard on the ass. She looked back at him and he gave her a small smile because the shakes had stopped. "Now you've learned a new trick."

She took the hat and crossed her apartment. To the left of the door, on a hook, was her bag, a mini shoulder bag, brown leather, a Christmas gift from Brian. She put her hand on the doorknob and decided what she was going to do as she was doing it, not giving herself time to think, not giving them time to think. She opened the door past the recommended two to three inches, opened it so that Detective Trayvon Kessler had a clear angle past her left shoulder, could see the hallway that led to the bedrooms, the half-bathroom door, the kitchen bar. She pulled her bag off the hook, crossed the threshold, and handed him his hat, pretty much all in the same motion.

The bullet entered her back, cut her spine in half, spewed the bone chips into her bloodstream as she collapsed into Detective Kessler. The fall kept him from clearing his own gun. Ned kept firing, shot Kessler in the head and the shoulder and the arm. He fell with Rachel. They landed in a heap on the marble floor, and Ned and Lars straddled their bodies. They looked down on them with nothing in their faces and fired into their bodies until their corpses jumped . . .

"Detective." She closed the door behind her. "I'd been wondering if you'd come back for that. I was about to call your cell."

He fell into step behind her as she walked to the elevators. "Heading out?"

She looked back over her left shoulder at him. Brian, Sebastian, and two ex-boyfriends had all told her it was her sexiest look. She could see it scored with Trayvon Kessler by the way he blinked at it, as if to deflect it from landing. "Just trying to walk off the buzz."

"Isn't sleep for that?"

"Can I come clean on something? A secret?"

"I love secrets. Why I'm a cop."

They reached the elevator bank. She pressed down and risked a glance back up the corridor to her apartment door. What would she do if the door opened? Run for the stairs?

They'd just kill her in the stairwell.

"I'm a closet smoker," she said. "And I ran out."

"Ah." He nodded several times. "I bet he knows."

"Hmm?"

"Your husband. I bet he knows you smoke but he chooses not to let on. Where's Mr. Perloff?"

"Passed out on the living room couch."

"I'm sure your husband's cool with that too, another man sleeping over. He's progressive that way, your husband. Nothing 'antiquated' about ol' Brian."

She looked at the numbers above the left elevator and saw the car was stalled on three. Looked at the numbers on the right elevator and saw nothing was lit up. They'd shut it down for the night. It was probably on a timer to save energy costs.

Fucking timers, she thought, and looked back at her door.

"You expect it to move?" Trayvon Kessler asked.

"What's that?"

"Your door. You keep looking back at it."

If Ned and Lars walked out now, guns drawn, they'd have the drop on Kessler. But if she told him—told him they were in there, told them what they'd done—he'd pull his gun, shield her with his body, and call for the cavalry. And this nightmare would be over.

All she had to do was tell him. And prepare herself for jail.

"Do I? I'm not myself right now."

"Why's that?"

"Learning my husband is living a double life could have affected me a bit."

"There's that." He looked above the elevator. "Should we take the stairs?"

She didn't give it a thought. "Sure."

"No, wait. It's moving."

The elevator car crawled from three to four and then picked up speed and shot from four to five to six to seven to eight to nine.

And stopped.

She looked at Kessler.

He gave her a "Sue me" shrug.

She said, "I'm taking the stairs," and turned toward them.

"It's moving again."

The red light jumped from nine to ten, and then zipped from eleven to fourteen. And stopped again. She could hear laughter from the shaft, the people getting off on fourteen sounding Saturday-night drunk on a Tuesday.

Trayvon Kessler had his back to the corridor when Ned stepped out of her apartment. She thought of screaming. She thought of running for the stairs, the red EXIT sign beckoning like the hand of God. By the time Kessler followed her gaze and turned, Ned had strolled up the corridor to them, his hands free, the gun probably tucked at the small of his back, hidden by the hem of his Members Only jacket.

"Rachel," he said. "Haven't seen you in a while."

"Ned." She watched a quick flare of confusion in his eyes. "Been staying home mostly, ordering in."

Ned turned to Detective Kessler. "Ned Hemple." He stuck out his hand.

"Trayvon Kessler."

"What brings the Providence police to Boston?"

Kessler looked confused for a moment, until he glanced down at his own belt, saw the gold badge clipped there.

"Checking out a few leads."

The elevator dinged as the car arrived and the doors opened. They got in. Kessler pressed L.

26

MOUTHPIECE

"Is everything okay, Rachel?" Ned looked across the car at her, his face the picture of concern.

"Sure. Why?"

"Well, I just . . ." He looked embarrassed as he turned to Trayvon Kessler. "I live next door to Rachel and Brian. Sorry, I should keep my big mouth shut."

Kessler gave that a loose grin. "Should he keep his mouth shut, Rachel?"

"Not on my account."

Kessler held out his hand. "Proceed, Mr. Hemple."

Ned hemmed and hawed and looked at his shoes for a moment. "I heard some, a little, uh, shouting a few minutes ago. I guess you and Brian aren't getting along. Same thing happens with me and Rosemary. No big deal. I just hope everything's okay."

"Shouting?" Kessler's grin grew broader.

"People fight," Ned said.

"Oh, I know people fight," Kessler said. "I'm just surprised Rachel was fighting with Brian. Only a few minutes ago, huh?"

The car stopped at seven and Mr. Cornelius, who owned three nightclubs in the Fenway, got on. He gave them all a polite smile and went back to texting someone on his phone.

Ned had served her up to Kessler on a platter. Even if she managed to get away from both of them when they reached the lobby—and she had no idea how she'd manage that—Kessler would go back to her apartment, this time with a warrant, and find Caleb dead inside. Not passed out. Dead.

She realized they were both looking at her, awaiting a response. "It wasn't Brian, Ned, thank you."

"No?"

"It was his partner. You've met him a few times. Caleb?"

Ned nodded. "Good-looking fella."

"That's him."

Ned said to Kessler, "Like I'm always telling the wife, though, looks fade."

Rachel said, "He wanted to drive home and I didn't want to let him. Too much bourbon."

Kessler said, "But he took the T."

"What?"

"Over from Cambridge, he told us he took the subway."

"But he lives in the Seaport and he didn't want to take the T back there. He wanted to borrow my car. That's what the fight was about."

Jesus, how many fucking details could she keep straight here?
"Ah."

"Makes sense," Ned said in a tone suggesting that it didn't.

"Why wouldn't he just take a cab?" Kessler said.

"Uber," Ned ventured.

"What he said." Kessler jerked his thumb at Ned.

"You'll have to ask him when he sobers up," she said.

Now Mr. Cornelius was watching the three of them, not sure what was going on, but recognizing conflict when it was in front of his face.

They reached the lobby.

The moment they exited the building, Kessler would, she presumed, leave her. Even if she stalled, chatted Kessler up on the sidewalk, Ned would just *act* as if he'd walked away. And the moment Kessler did, in fact, drive off, Ned would reappear. Or just shoot her from across the street.

She placed her hand up to the back of her neck, fingered the clasp of her necklace. If she could twist it a bit and then snap her fingers, she might be able to break the strand. The beads would hit the floor. The men would bend to retrieve them. And she could scoot out through the mail room.

"Got a bite?" Kessler asked.

"What?"

"An itch," he said. "Is your neck itchy?"

Now Ned was looking at her.

She dropped her hand. "Yeah. A little bit."

They walked into the lobby. Mr. Cornelius turned right into the hall for the garage elevators. Ned and Kessler kept moving forward.

Dominick, behind the desk, glanced up at them, seemed mildly baffled by the presence of Kessler and Ned, but he gave Rachel a nod and went back to his magazine.

"No garage?" she asked Ned.

"Hmm?" Ned followed her gaze to the garage door. "No."

"You're parked on the street?" she said.

Ned looked back over his shoulder at her. "Oh, no, I'm just going out for a walk, dear."

"Everyone's going for a walk tonight," Kessler said. He patted his stomach. "Makes me feel like I gotta hit the gym."

He opened the front door, inward, and made an "after you" gesture to them both. Ned went through the door, followed by Rachel.

On the sidewalk, Rachel said to Ned, "Enjoy your walk. Tell Rosemary I said hi."

"Will do." Ned stretched out his hand to Kessler. "Nice to meet you, Detective."

"You too, Mr. Temple."

"Hemple," Ned said, shaking his hand.

"Of course. My bad." Kessler dropped his hand. "Take care, sir."

For an odd few seconds none of them moved. Eventually Ned turned and headed east along the sidewalk, his hands in his pockets. Rachel glanced over at Detective Kessler, who seemed to be waiting on something. When she looked back down the darkened street, Ned was nowhere to be seen.

"So that's Ned."

"That's Ned."

"He and Rosemary been married a long time?"

"Ages."

"No wedding ring, though. He didn't strike me as the bohemian type thinks rings are just symbols of societal oppression from the dominant paradigm."

"Probably just in for a cleaning."

"That could be it," he said. "What's he do, our friend Ned?"

"You know, I'm not sure."

"Why am I not surprised?"

"Some kind of manufacturing, I think."

"Manufacturing?" Kessler said. "We don't make shit in this country anymore."

She shrugged. "You know how it is with neighbors these days."

"Oh, do tell."

"Everyone guards their privacy." She gave him a tight smile.

He opened the passenger door to a dark four-door Ford. "Let me give you a ride to get your cigarettes."

She looked back down the street. Every twenty feet was a pool of light cast by the streetlamps. In between those lights lay the dark.

"Sure." She got in the car.

Kessler got in, put his hat between them on the seat, and pulled away from the curb. "I been on some fucked-up cases, if you'll excuse my language, but this is one of the more fucked-up ones I been on of late. I got a dead blonde in Rhody, a missing guy leading a double life, his lying wife—"

"I'm not lying."

"Oh ho!" He wagged a finger at her. "*Yes yes yes* you are, Mrs. Delacroix. You're telling so many lies I can't even count them. And your neighbor there, the married guy in the Members Only jacket and the JCPenney slacks without the wedding ring? Guys like him don't live in buildings like yours. He didn't even know where the fucking garage was, and the doorman had clearly never seen him before."

"I didn't notice."

"Lucky I'm a cop. They fucking pay us to notice shit like that."

"You say 'fuck' a lot."

"And why not?" he said. "It's a great word. Verb, noun, adverb, adjective. 'Fuck' is fucking utile." He turned left. "My problem with your lying is that I don't know why or what you're lying about. It's still too early in the case. But, man, do I know you're lying."

They stopped at a light and she felt certain Ned was going to appear by Kessler's window and start firing into the car.

The light turned green and Kessler took another left and parked outside the Tedeschi's on Boylston, across the street from the Prudential. He turned in the seat toward her and all the hard mirth left his eyes and what replaced it was something she couldn't identify.

"The late Nicole Alden," he said, "was executed. As professional a hit as I've ever seen, and I've seen a few. So your husband with the double life? There's a good chance he's a pro at, you know, ending

lives. And either him or some of his friends may come a-calling.
And Rachel?" He leaned across the seat, close enough that she could
smell the Altoids. "They will fucking execute you."

He couldn't save her. Even if he was interested, and she doubted
he was. His job was to close the Nicole Alden murder. He'd decided
with a cop's narrow certitude that the best way to do that was to pin
the murder on Brian. But when Brian didn't turn back up, Kessler
would dig deeper. Maybe he'd find out she'd been in Providence just
before the victim was killed. Zipcars, she was fairly certain, had
tracking devices on them so the company always knew where their
cars were. Wouldn't take much to put Rachel on that street outside
Nicole Alden's house. And then the scenario was easy to see—wife
discovers husband has another wife with a baby on the way to boot
and kills her. And if that scenario wasn't damning enough, there
was the dead body of her husband's business partner sitting up in
her apartment. And a coroner's examination would prove said partner was dead prior to Rachel claiming to this very police officer that
he was alive and well and passed out on her couch.

"I don't like being bullied," she told Detective Kessler.

"I'm not bullying you. I'm stating facts."

"You're stating conjecture. In the most threatening manner possible."

"It's not conjecture," he said, "to notice you're terrified right
now."

"I've been terrified before."

He shook his head slowly, this tough cop looking at this entitled
yuppie without a day job. Probably pictured her walk-in closet full
of high-end workout clothes, Louboutin heels, silk business suits she
wore to restaurants no cop could afford.

"You think you have but you haven't. There's darkness in this
world you can't learn about watching TV and reading books."

That night at the camp in Léogâne, the men strode back and
forth through the mud and the heat in the light of the trash can

fires, *serpettes* and bottles of cheap liquor in hand. Around two in the morning Widdy said to her, "If I let them have me now, they may only"—she made a circle with one hand and drove the index finger of the other hand in and out of the circle several times—"but if we make them wait, they may grow angry and"—she drew the same finger across her throat.

Widdy—Widelene Jean-Calixte was her full name—was eleven years old. Rachel had convinced her to stay hidden. But, as Widdy had predicted, all that did was make the men angrier. And a short time after sunup, they had found her. Found them both.

"I know a little bit about the darkness in this world," Rachel told Trayvon Kessler.

"Yeah?" His eyes searched hers.

"Yeah."

"And what have you learned?" he whispered.

"If you wait for it to find you, you're already dead."

She got out of the car. When she came around to the sidewalk, he'd rolled down his window. "You planning on giving me the slip?"

She smiled. "Yes."

"I'm a cop. Kinda good at keeping people in my sights."

"But you're from Providence. And this is Boston."

He acknowledged that with a slight tilt of his head. "Next time you see me, then, Mrs. Delacroix, I'll have a search warrant in my hand."

"Fair enough." She walked up the sidewalk as he pulled away. She didn't even pretend to walk into the store, just watched Kessler turn right at the next corner before she crossed Boylston to the cab stand in front of a hotel. She hopped into the back of the first cab and told the driver to head for the marina at Port Norfolk.

The parking lot at the marina was empty, so she had the driver wait a few minutes to see if anyone had followed her but the entire neighborhood was gone to bed, so quiet you could hear the boats bump against their slips and the old wood buildings creak in the night breeze.

Back on the boat, she went into the galley, turned on the lights, and pulled the keys out of the drawer where she'd left them when they'd tied the boat off. She untied the ropes next and then motored out into the harbor, running lights on full. Twenty minutes later, she could see Thompson Island appear in the starlight, and a minute after that she reached the minuscule island with the one bent tree. She went back into the galley, and this go-around, with the luxury of time, she found the scuba gear: mask, flippers, oxygen tank. She rummaged around a little more and found another flashlight and a wet suit, woman's medium, belonging, she presumed, to the late Nicole Alden. She changed into the suit, donned the oxygen tank, flippers, and mask, and returned with the flashlight to the stern. She took her seat on the gunwale and looked up at the sky. The cloud bank from earlier had moved on and the stars arrayed themselves in clusters, as if seeking the protection of the herd, and she felt them not as celestial things, as gods or the servants of gods, but as castoffs, exiles, lost in the vast ink sky. What appeared as clusters down here were, up there, fields a million miles wide. The closest stars were light-years apart, no closer to one another than she was to a tribeswoman of the Saharan steppe in the fifteenth century.

If we are this alone, she wanted to know, then what is the point?

And she tipped back and fell through the ocean.

She turned on her flashlight and soon discerned the one she'd dropped. It winked up at her from the floor of the bay. As she descended, she saw that it had landed in the sand about twenty yards from the boulder where Brian lay. She trained her light on the top of the boulder and moved the shaft down and down some more until she reached the sand.

There was no body there.

So she'd gotten the boulders mixed up. She turned her beam to

the left and saw another boulder about twenty yards away. She swam
halfway to it but then grew certain it was the wrong shape and color.
She'd left Brian against a tall, conical rock. Just like the one she'd
landed near. She swam back, moving her flashlight continually left
and then right. Then farther left. Then farther right. No boulders
that looked anything like the one where she'd left him. The one in
front of which she now floated.

This was the boulder where she'd left him. She was sure of it. She
could tell by the depth of its craters and the conical shape.

Had he been carried off by the current? Or worse, a shark? She
kicked her way over to exactly where she'd last seen him. She checked
the sand for signs of indentation, an impression of his legs or but-
tocks, but it had been worn smooth by the water.

She caught a glimpse of black that was blacker than the boulder.
It was just a flicker of it, like a flaking of skin along the left edge of
the rock. She kicked to her left and shone her light around the corner and at first she saw nothing.

But then she saw everything.

It was a mouthpiece.

She swam around to the back of the rock. The mouthpiece was
attached to a tube that was attached to an oxygen tank.

She looked back up through the dark water to the hull of the
boat.

You're alive.

She kicked for the surface.

Until I find you.

27

II

She motored out to Thompson Island and found the dock within four hundred yards of where Brian had fallen in. There was no boat there, of course. Whatever boat had been there was long gone.

And he was on it.

She had to wait a long time for the cab. It was four in the morning and the dispatcher didn't know where the Point Norfolk Marina was. She heard him tap his computer keyboard for about half a minute before he grumbled, "Twenty minutes," into the phone and hung up.

She stood in the dark parking lot and imagined all the things that could be going wrong right now. Trayvon Kessler could have gotten his warrant. (*No, Rachel, he'd have to go back to Providence, find a judge, deal with jurisdiction issues. Maybe by sunup, but probably not even then. Breathe. Breathe.*)

Breathe? Brian was alive. Ned had shot Caleb in the face. She could see the older man's face as he did it, lupine somehow, wholly comfortable with predatory dominance. He'd looked at a fellow human being sitting four feet away from him and killed that human being as easily as a hawk would spear a chipmunk with its talons. There was no pleasure to be had in the killing for Ned but no regret either.

Brian was out there, eluding her. Alive. (Had she always known somewhere deep in her lizard brain that he'd never died?) But vengeance on Brian was, at this immediate moment as she stood in an empty parking lot at the witching hour, a luxury.

Ned and Lars were out there, hunting her.

Smartphones could be hacked. Turned quite easily into tracking devices and listening devices for hostile parties or government snoops. If Ned or Lars knew how to hack into hers, they'd know where she was.

Headlights appeared two hundred yards away, at the beginning of the rutted street that led from the edge of Tenean Beach to here. The two lights bounced and canted and glowed brighter as they neared. Could be a cab. Could be Ned. She wrapped her hand around the gun in her bag, the gun her husband had tried to kill her with. Or acted as if he were trying to kill her. She wrapped her finger around the trigger and thumbed off the safety even as it occurred to her that it wouldn't matter. If the car belonged to Ned and Lars, they could just accelerate at the last possible second and run her over. Not a thing she could do about it.

The headlights swept the parking lot and the car turned in an arc to pull in front of her. It was brown and white and had BOSTON CAB painted on the doors. The driver was a middle-aged white woman with a beige afro. Rachel climbed in, and they pulled out of the marina.

She had the cab drop her two blocks south of her apartment and walked up through an alley as a false dawn grayed the lower edges of the sky. She crossed Fairfield and walked down the ramp to the garage grate. She entered her code in the keypad to the right of the grate and the grate rose and she entered the garage. She took the elevator to eleven, got out, and walked up the stairs to fifteen. Soon she stood outside her door.

This was the step she'd agonized over. If either Ned or Lars had remained behind, she was dead as soon as she entered the apartment. But if—no, when—Trayvon Kessler returned with that warrant and broke down this door, she needed to know what he'd find on the other side. The ride back from the bay to the marina, she'd debated if it was worth the risk and decided that Ned and Lars would assume she'd never return. It made no sense. Then again, she mused as she stood outside the door with the key in her hand, maybe they were counting on her to do the stupid thing. She had no experience dealing with people like them, but they had plenty of experience dealing with rubes like her. On the other side of that door was either death or knowledge. Plus a stash of cash Brian kept in a floor safe. Not much, a couple thousand, but enough to run on if Kessler had already taken the step of shutting down her credit cards. She doubted, on one hand, that he had the power to do so, but then, on the other, what did she know about police procedure when dealing with a murder suspect? And by now that's what she could be, a murder suspect. By midmorning, she could be a suspect in two murders.

She looked at the lock. At the key in her hand. She took a breath. Her hand shook when she raised it, so she lowered it again. Took several more breaths.

Brian was alive. Brian had put her in this situation. Somehow, some way, she was going to find him and make him pay.

Or she was going to die in the next thirty seconds.

She inserted the key in the lock. But she didn't turn it. She imagined a fusillade of bullets punching through the door and into her head, neck, and chest. She closed her eyes and tried to will herself to turn the key, turn the key, but once she did, the only step to take would be forward. Into the apartment. And she wasn't ready. She wasn't.

If they were on the other side and if they were close enough to the door to have heard her insert the key, they could simply shoot her through the door. But just because they hadn't didn't mean they weren't in there. They could be waiting patiently on the other side of the door, exchanging glances, maybe even smirks, screwing their silencers onto their pistols, taking careful aim at the doorway, and waiting for the moment when she opened the door.

She'd wait them out. If they were in there, they'd heard the key enter the lock. Sooner or later, if she didn't enter, they'd open the door.

Then again, Rachel, you dumb fuck, they could be watching you through the spyhole right now. She stepped to the right of the door, pulled the pistol from her bag, thumbed off the safety yet again. Waited.

She waited five minutes. Felt like fifty. Checked her watch again. Nope. Five.

In some time continuum, we're all dead as soon as we're born. By that logic, she was long dead somewhere, looking back through the portals of time at this very moment and smiling at all the fuss Corporeal Rachel was putting herself through.

I'm already dead, she assured herself. She turned the key in the lock and threw the door open, the gun pointing straight into the apartment, completely useless if either Lars or Ned was to her right or her left.

They weren't. Caleb still sat at the table, his flesh the white of soap, the blood crusted and black in the center of his face. She closed the door behind her and moved to her right, inching down the wall until she reached the open doorway of the half bath. It appeared empty. She looked in the crack between the open door and the jamb and saw that no one was hiding on the other side.

She moved toward the bedroom. The door was closed. She put her palm on the handle but her flesh was so slick with sweat it slid off. She wiped it on her pants, used her sleeve to wipe the door handle. Grasped it with her left hand, held the gun in her right. Swung the door inward. As she did, she imagined Lars sitting on her bed, waiting for her. A soft pop and she'd be on her back, leaking.

He wasn't there. The room appeared empty. But it reinforced what she'd felt entering the apartment—they were better at this than she was. If they were in here with her, she *was* already dead. She entered the master bathroom and then checked the his and her walk-in closets with a sudden fatalism. She felt closer to death than at any time since Leógâne. She felt it emerge through the floorboards and penetrate her body, conjoin with her blood and pull her back down through the floor into the cellar of the next world.

That's what was waiting, what had always been waiting, the next world. Whether it was above or below, white or black, cold or warm, it was not this world with its comforts and distractions and knowable ills. Maybe it was nothing at all. Maybe it was just absence. Absence of self, absence of sense, absence of soul or memory.

She realized now that in Haiti, even before the camp, as far back as Port-au-Prince and the corpses smoldering in the streets and stacked in the parking lot of the hospital, stacked like old cars in junkyards, beginning to swell and balloon in the heat, as far back as then, the truth of their deaths became the truth of her own: We are not special. We are lit from within by a single candle flame, and when that flame is blown out and all light leaves our eyes, it is the same as if we never existed at all. We don't own our life, we rent it.

She searched the rest of the apartment, but it was clear they weren't there. Her initial instinct had been right—if they'd been waiting to kill her, they would have done so the moment she came through the door. She returned to the bedroom and packed a backpack with hiking boots, several pairs of warm socks, a heavy wool coat. She took a gym bag with her into the kitchen and added one carving knife, one paring knife, a flashlight and batteries, half a dozen power bars, several bottles of water, and the contents of the fruit bowl on the counter. She left the bag and the backpack by the door and returned to the bedroom. She changed into cargo pants, a thermal long-sleeved T-shirt, a black hoodie. She tied her hair back into a ponytail and covered it with a Newbury Comics ball cap. She opened the floor safe in his closet and removed the cash there and took it and the gun into the bathroom and placed them on the counter and looked in the mirror for a long time, and the woman who stared back at her was exhausted and angry. She was also afraid, but not paralyzed with it. She said to herself, with the compassionate authority of an older sister speaking to a younger, "It is not your fault."

What's "it"?

It was Widdy and Esther and the ex-nun, Veronique, and all the dead in Port-au-Prince. *It* was her mother's toxicity and her father's absence and Jeremy James's abandonment. *It* was Sebastian's disappointment in just about everything she did. *It* was the feeling she'd had as long back as she could remember that she was unforgivably inadequate and worth abandoning.

And the voice in her head was primarily correct—most of *it* was not her fault.

Except for Widdy. Widdy was her insurmountable sin. Widdy was four years dead. And Rachel, who'd gotten her killed, was four years older.

She lifted a picture of her and Brian off the dresser. Their unofficial wedding photo. She looked in his lying eyes and his lying smile and she knew she was just as much a liar as he was. From grade school through high school, college, grad school, and out into the working world, she had assembled herself into a character she played every day for most of her life. Once that character failed to connect with the audience any longer, she disassembled it and assembled a new one. And on and on. Until, after Haiti, after Widdy, she couldn't reassemble. All that was left of her was the nub of her hollow, manufactured self and the whole of her sin.

We are liars, Brian. We.

She left the bedroom. In the living room, she realized her laptop wasn't on the bar where she'd left it. She looked around for a few minutes but surmised pretty quickly that Lars and Ned had taken it with them when they left.

Fine. She had a smartphone.

What she didn't have was a car. Even if Kessler hadn't frozen her credit cards, she couldn't rent a car or use Zipcar because then she'd be a cinch to find. She looked around the apartment again, as if it could tell her something, looked everywhere except at the corpse at her dining room table. And then she realized that's exactly where she should be looking.

The key fob was in the right front pocket of Caleb's jeans. She could see the bulge of it when she came around the table to him. She didn't look at his face. She couldn't.

What about Haya? she wondered. What about AB? At the party just four days ago, Caleb had lifted his daughter in front of his face and she'd gripped his upper lip and pulled it toward her like a drawer. He'd let her do it. He'd laughed, even as it was clearly painful, and when Annabelle released his lip, he held her to his chest and pressed his nose to the crown of her head and breathed her in.

Caleb had been an actor. Just like Brian. Just like her. But the acting was just one aspect of the whole. He wasn't acting the father. He wasn't acting his loves. Wasn't pretending what his dreams and desires and hopes for the future were.

He had been, she realized, her friend. She'd always thought of him as Brian's friend, as Brian's partner because those roles (there was that word again) had been firmly entrenched when he'd entered into his association with her. But time and attrition had created a familiarity and comfort with each other that one could only call friendship.

She reached into his pocket. The denim was stiff and his body was stiffer. Rigor mortis had set in, and it took her a solid minute to work the key fob up his thigh and out of the pocket. In that time

it occurred to her that if they'd never returned here so she could
e-mail her book to herself, he might still be alive.

But, no. *No, no, no,* that big sister's voice whispered in her ear.
He stayed behind to drink. He stayed behind to collect his thoughts
before an hour's drive. And if that weren't enough, whatever game
he and Brian were playing, they had set it in motion a long time ago.

She looked at him now. For a full minute.

"You're not my fault." The tears fell and she wiped at them. "But
I'll miss you," she said and walked out of the apartment.

28

PLUNGING

She gassed up Caleb's Audi and then got breakfast at the Paramount on Charles Street once it occurred to her that she hadn't eaten in about twenty-four hours. She didn't feel hungry, but she ate like it. She drove back over into Copley Square and parked at a meter on Stuart Street and walked the small side street that ran between the Copley Plaza Hotel and the Hancock Tower. She passed the loading dock and the rear door where she'd seen Brian exit in the rain and climb into the black Suburban. She walked around the building, walked along St. James, and at one point she saw a dozen Rachels reflected and re-reflected in the panes. They formed a disjointed ribbon, like a chain of Rachel dolls cut from construction paper. When she rounded the corner, they all took flight. And she never saw them again.

It was almost nine and the streets were filled with morning commuters. She reached the entrance to the skyscraper and followed

the stream heading in through the revolving doors. She found the
directory to the right of the security desk. She went through the As
and saw no Alden Minerals. Went through the Bs and saw nothing
she'd consider germane to her quest. But in the Cs, there it was—
Cotter-McCann, the venture capital firm Glen O'Donnell had mentioned. It wasn't a guarantee, but it was certainly a fair assumption
that Brian had come here that day to meet with representatives of
Cotter-McCann and sell off a part of his mining interest.

She exited the building and walked back a block to the central branch of the Boston Public Library. She passed through the
McKim building into the Johnson building where the computers
were and set to researching Cotter-McCann's acquisition of an
interest in Alden Minerals. There wasn't anything on it save one
tiny item in the business digest section of the *Globe*, which must
have been the source of Glen's information because it told her
nothing new.

She clicked off and looked up Baker Lake, worked her way to a
satellite map, click-click-clicked the zoom icon until she could discern the only abodes in the area, eight roofs in the northeast corner
of the lake along the Canadian border, three more she almost missed
peeking out a bit to the west of the eight. She printed several images of the region, zooming out a little bit more each time, until she
was satisfied she had a reasonable representation of the area. She retrieved the pages from the printer tray, quit all applications, cleared
her history, and left the library.

Just before Haiti, Rachel had done a story for Little Six on the tax
breaks the Commonwealth was offering to lure Hollywood film
production to Massachusetts. In order to assess the economic effect
of the tax breaks on the local economy, she'd interviewed Hollywood studio execs and statehouse reps on Ways and Means as well

as local actors, location scouts, and one casting director. Her name was Felicia Ming. She was a jaded gossip, as Rachel recalled. She and Rachel had met for drinks a few times in the months before Rachel left the country for Port-au-Prince. They'd fallen out of touch after that, but Felicia had sent her a few kind e-mails after the meltdown and Rachel still had her contact info in her phone.

She called her standing outside the library and asked her how she'd track down an actor starring in a local production.

"Why are you trying to find him?"

Rachel tried a version not far from the truth. "He got into a drunken tiff with my husband in a bar the other night."

"Oh, do tell."

"I just feel bad. He got the worst of it, and I want to apologize to the guy."

"Was this fight over you, honey?"

Rachel hoped her instinct was right on this one. "It was, I'm afraid, yeah."

"Somebody's making a *comeback*," Felicia Ming said. "You return to this world with us, honey, and you make them crawl to you."

Rachel forced a chuckle. "That's the plan."

"What company is he working with right now?" Felicia asked.

"The Lyric Stage."

"What's his name?"

"Andrew Gattis."

"Give me a sec."

While Rachel waited, a homeless guy walked by with his dog. Rachel recalled the night Brian forfeited his coat to a needier soul in the park. She gave the dog a pat and the homeless guy ten bucks and Felicia came back on the line.

"He's at the Demange. It's corporate housing in Bay Village." She gave Rachel the address. "Want to grab a drink soon? Now that you've rejoined the living?"

Rachel actually felt bad about lying. "I'd love to."

Twenty minutes later, she stood on a sidewalk in Bay Village and rang his doorbell.

When his voice came through the intercom it was groggy. "Yeah?"

"Mr. Gattis, it's Rachel Delacroix."

"Who?"

"Brian's wife." The pause that followed was so lengthy she finally said, "Mr. Gattis, you there?"

"I'd like you to go away."

"I won't." The calm force in her voice surprised her. "I'll wait down here until you have to come out. And if you slip out the back, I'll come to your performance tonight and cause a scene in the middle of it. So, let's—"

The door buzzed and she grabbed the handle and entered the building. It smelled of Lysol and linoleum in the lobby, Indian food as she climbed to the second-floor landing. A woman passed her leading a huffing French bulldog on a leash, the dog reminding Rachel of something you'd get if a pug impregnated a wombat.

Gattis was waiting in the doorway of 24, his stringy gray hair yellowed by nicotine. He tied it back into a bun as he led her into the apartment. It was a simple layout—kitchen and living room to the right, bedroom and bathroom back to the left. The window at the back of the living room opened onto a fire escape.

"Coffee?" he said.

"Sure. Thanks."

She took a seat at a small round table by the window and he brought them each a cup of coffee, put a carton of creamer and a bowl of sugar between them. In the morning light, he looked even worse than the drunk she'd met Saturday night. His skin was scaly and pink and blue veins had erupted along the sides of his nose like electric bolts. His eyes swam.

"I have rehearsal in an hour and I have to shower, so we're going to have to move this along."

She sipped her coffee. "You and Brian were actors together."

"Caleb too." He nodded. "Brian had more raw talent than I've ever seen before or since. We all knew he'd be a star as long as he didn't find a way to fuck it up."

"What happened?"

"Couple things, I guess. He had no patience. And maybe, I dunno, he didn't respect it because it came so easy to him? Who knows? He was angry, I remember that. Charming and angry. Cut quite the romantic figure in that regard. Chicks were fucking crazy about him. No offense."

She shrugged and drank her coffee. Say what you would about Andrew Gattis, he made good coffee. "What was he angry about?"

"Being poor. Brian had to *work*. I mean we were dawn to dusk at school. We had acting classes and improvisation classes and improvisational movement classes. We had dance and playwriting and stagecraft and directing classes. Voice class, speech class, and something called Alexander Technique, which taught command of the body so you could use it as an instrument, you know? Morph it to your will. All that work was no joke. You'd get to six o'clock, your eyes would be shutting and your muscles screaming and your head throbbing. You'd go to bed or you'd go to the bar. Not Brian, though. Brian would go to work until two in the morning. And then right back at it at seven. Most of us were in our mid-twenties so, shit, plenty of energy, but even at that age we wondered how he did it. Then all that work added up to nothing anyway when he got kicked out."

"He was kicked out of Trinity?"

Gattis nodded and took a long chug of coffee. "I look back now and I think he was probably popping a lot of speed or doing blow to keep up his pace. Either way, he was getting edgier and edgier during our second year. We had this one professor, real to-the-manner-born dilettante douchebag named Nigel Rawlins. He was one of those break-you-down-to-build-you-up kind of teachers, but I always suspected he didn't really know about building anyone back up, he just liked to break them down. He was notorious for getting students to drop out. He built his rep on it. One morning he went after the only student there who was poorer than Brian. This kid had Brian's bare pockets but not his talent, not a tenth of it. Anyway, Nigel Rawlins, one morning they're rehearsing a scene set in a men's room, right? And this kid's got a monologue about unclogging a toilet—that's all I remember about it to this day; I think it was a student piece—and the kid, he's just not selling the scene. He's fucking gassing it, to be quite honest. Which is setting Nigel off. He tore into that kid for being a shit actor and a shit human being, an embarrassment as a son and a brother, a source of shame to anyone unlucky enough to have him as a friend. He'd been on the kid for months, but that morning he was the fucking Terminator. Kept coming and coming. The kid pleads for him to stop, but Nigel gets stuck in this rage-loop about how the kid is a log of shit covered in hair that's clogging the drain and it was Nigel's job to plunge him the fuck out of the class before he dragged everyone else into that clogged toilet with him. So Brian, man—I mean, nobody ever even saw him leave the stage—but when he came back he had an *actual* plunger in his hand, not the fucking stage prop, and it was dripping with piss. He flipped Nigel on his back and he fitted that plunger over his mouth and nose and he just started . . . plunging. Once Nigel managed to push his head off the floor, grab at Brian's legs, and Brian punched him so hard in the center of his face, you could hear it in the back row of the theater. And Brian went back to plunging and plunging and fucking *plunging* Nigel's face until Nigel passed out." He sat back and drained his coffee. "They kicked Brian out the next morning. He hung around Providence for a while, delivering pizzas, but I think it grew too embarrassing, ya know, handing over pies and taking sweaty bills from people you used to party with. He lit out one day and I didn't hear from him again for, I dunno, nine years."

She sat with that a bit, wishing she hadn't heard it because it actually made her like the lying prick again, if only for a moment. "What happened to the other student? The one who was being abused?"

"You mean Caleb?"

She chuckled in sadness and surprise and Gattis refilled their coffee cups.

She said, "When's the last time you saw Brian before the other night?"

"Ten years ago, maybe twelve." He looked out the window for a bit. "Can't remember exactly."

"Any idea where he'd go if he didn't want to be found?"

"That cabin he has in Maine."

"Baker Lake."

He nodded.

She showed him one of the satellite photos. He looked at it for a bit and took a Sharpie from a cup on the windowsill. He circled the cluster of three rooftops.

"Those other eight cabins over here? They're part of a hunting camp. These three, though? Brian owns them. We had a Trinity reunion there around 2005. Not too many showed up but it was fun. Don't ask me where he got the money for them because I didn't ask. Brian preferred the middle cabin. It was painted green when I was there, had a red door."

"And that was 2005?"

"Or 2004." He nodded at the bathroom door. "I got to shower."

She returned the satellite photo to her bag and thanked him for his time and the coffee.

"I don't know if this is worth anything," he said as she reached the door, "but he looks at you different than I've ever known him to look at anyone." He shrugged. "Then again, he's a very good actor."

He remained in the bathroom doorway. She held his gaze and saw his eyes change as, she presumed, he watched hers do the same.

"Wait," she said slowly.

Andrew Gattis waited.

"He paid you to crash our party that night, didn't he? He staged the whole fight, everything."

Andrew Gattis stroked the jamb of his bathroom door, a jamb that looked to have been painted so many times over the decades she bet the door never latched correctly. "And if he did?"

"Why are you helping him?"

His shoulders rose and fell in a half shrug. "When we were young, at a crucial time in the development of our selves, Brian and I were great friends. Now he's where he is and I'm where I am"—he looked around the room, which suddenly appeared grim and insignificant—"and I'm not sure who we are anymore. When you spend so much time in the skins of others that you don't even recognize the smell of your own anymore, maybe the only allegiance you owe is to the people who remembered you before the makeup and the stagecraft took over."

"I don't follow," she said.

He gave that another half shrug. "You remember how I told you that at Trinity we studied every discipline, no matter what our focus—dance, acting, writing, what have you?" He gave her a soft, distant grin. "Well, Brian was a hell of an actor, like I said. But you know what his real passion was?"

She shook her head.

"Directing." He disappeared into the bathroom. He closed the door behind him, and she was mildly surprised to hear it latch.

29

ENOUGH

I-95 took her through Massachusetts, New Hampshire, and what she would have previously described as deep into Maine, up all the way to Waterville. But from there, she had to leave the interstate and hop onto Route 201, after which everything grew first rural, then desolate, then slightly ethereal, the air and sky turning the cast of newspaper, the land eventually disappearing in thickets of trees as tall as skyscrapers. Soon the sky was gone, and all she knew of the world was the brown trunks and the dark treetops and the ashen road feeding into the space between her thrumming wheels. It felt as if she moved under heavy cloud cover; soon that gave way to the sensation of driving at night, even though it was three in the afternoon in late May.

She reached a clearing between two forests. Miles of green. Farmland, she presumed, though she couldn't see any houses or silos, just swaths of well-tended fields, spotted with cows and sheep and the occasional horse. Her phone was propped in the cup holder and she looked down at it long enough to confirm it no longer received service out here. When she looked up again, the sheep—or goat, she'd never be sure which—stood six feet from her bumper. She spun the wheel and swerved off the road, bounced into a small ditch hard enough to bang the top of her head off the roof and the bottom of her chin off the steering wheel. All four wheels detached from the earth. She shot back out of the ditch like something strapped to a booster rocket and hit the road on the front quarter of her left bumper. The air bag punched her in the face as it deployed, and she could taste blood after she bit her tongue. The back of the vehicle rose and the front lifted off the pavement again. It flipped twice to the soundtrack of breaking glass, grinding metal, and her screams.

It came to a stop.

She was upright. She shook her head several times and small chunks of glass, dozens of them by the sound of it, flew out. She sat where she was a while longer, chin resting on the air bag like it was a pillow, until she ascertained that she wasn't in any pain, nothing felt broken, she didn't seem to be bleeding anywhere but her tongue. The back of her head throbbed and her neck felt stiff and the muscles closest to her spine had turned to rock, but otherwise it seemed possible she was all in one piece. The console compartment and glove compartment had divested themselves of their contents and they were strewn across the dashboard and passenger seat and foot wells—maps, insurance cards, registration, packets of handkerchiefs, loose change, pens, a key.

She unlocked her seat belt.

She bent over the passenger seat. She pushed aside a pair of cracked sunglasses and lifted the key off the mat. It was small and thin and silver. Not a house key, not a car key. A locker key, or padlock key, or safe deposit box key.

Was this *the* key? Which would mean Caleb had had it, not Brian. Which would mean he'd died rather than give it up.

Or it was just a key.

She pocketed it and got out of the SUV. It sat dead center in the middle of the road. The sheep or goat was long gone. The black crescents of her skid marks snaked from the center of the road, off the edge, and vanished where she'd left the road. A shower of glass—some clear, some red—marked her return and littered the road along with pieces of chrome, hard black plastic, and a detached door handle.

She got back in and tried starting the SUV. The engine turned over followed by a repetitive *ding-ding-ding* to remind her to fasten her seat belt. She used the paring knife she'd packed to cut away the air bag. She popped the hood. She checked under there and couldn't find any obvious danger. Checked the tires and they looked fine. She turned on the lights—that'd be a problem. The right headlight was shattered. The left was cracked but functional. In the rear, it was the reverse—where the driver's-side brake light had been, only a metal cavity remained. The passenger's-side brake light, on the other hand, looked fit for a brochure photo.

She considered the endless stretches of farmland, the forest behind her and the one ahead. It could be hours before any help arrived. Or it could be minutes. No way to tell.

The last time she'd looked at the trip meter she'd been seventy miles away from Baker Lake. And that had been ten minutes before the accident. So sixty-five then. Brian had paid Andrew Gattis to show up that night at their party and leave her a series of clues. He'd wanted her to know about Baker Lake. It's possible his motive had been to draw her up here and kill her. She'd mulled that over a lot. But if he wanted to kill her, he could have done it on the boat. Instead he'd faked his own death at her hand. Every time she'd looked at Baker Lake on the maps, it felt like a door. If you crossed the lake, you reached another country. Was Brian leading her to the door?

Whether he was or he wasn't, she was out of alternative plans that didn't involve a jail cell and eventual prison. At this point, it was find Brian in Maine or game over.

"Here we go," she whispered. She got back in the car and drove away.

Above her, the sun was on the run.

She left 201 at a place called The Forks. Not The Fork, singular. The Forks. It was so named, she suspected, because if you wanted to enter the wilderness by trekking northeast from here, the roads, as faint on her map as veins in an X-ray, splintered off 201 and then off one another and then off one another's progeny until it appeared the only way back would be scent trails or prayer. It was full dark now, the dark of Germanic fairy tales and solar eclipses.

She turned onto Granger Mills Passage and drove along it for several miles—or it could have been just a couple; it was slow going up here—before she realized she must have missed the turnoff for Old Mill Lane. She turned back and drove through the black until an anorexic sliver of road appeared on her left. There was no marker to tell her what the road was or where it went. She turned onto it, drove about four hundred yards, and it ended. She flashed her sole high beam and all she saw beyond her grille was an embankment about four feet tall and a field on the other side of it. The road had never been a road, just the idea of one, soon abandoned.

There was no place to turn around, so she put the battered, creaking SUV in reverse and tried to navigate her way back through the pitch with one shattered brake light. Twice she drove into the shoulder. When she reached Granger Mills Passage, she drove back the way she'd come for about three miles until she found a cutout alongside some farmland. She pulled in there and killed the engine.

She sat in the dark. There'd be no more driving tonight. She sat in the dark and prayed that movement would be just as impossible for him, at least until morning.

She sat in the dark and realized she hadn't slept in over thirty-six hours.

She climbed into the backseat, pulled her coat from her backpack and wrapped it around her, and used the backpack as a pillow.

Lying in the dark now, as opposed to sitting in it. Closing her eyes.

The sun woke her.

She looked at her watch. It was six-thirty in the morning. A low mist hung over the fields, beginning to smoke along the upper edges as the sun burned it away. A cow stood about ten feet away, on the other side of some loose barbwire fencing, staring through her with cow eyes, its tail swishing at a small squall of flies. She sat up and the first thing she wished was that she'd thought to pack a toothbrush. She drank one of the bottles of water, ate a power bar. She stepped out of the car and stretched and saw more cows in the field across the road, more smoking mist. It was cool, even with the sun, and she tightened the coat around her and breathed in the clean air. She peed by the side of the car under the steady, disinterested gaze of the cow, its tail still swishing like the needle of a metronome, and then she got back in the car, U-turned, and headed off.

It was only twenty-five miles to Baker Lake, but it took her three hours. Anything one would call a road gave way to what one could only charitably call trails, and she was forever grateful she'd stopped last night because she would have ended up in a ditch or driving into a pond. Soon she was so deep into the wilderness that the trails lost their names and some that appeared on the map had been reclaimed by the weeds and the brush. She relied on the SUV's compass to continue heading due northeast. The rocky dirt paths crunched under her wheels and the chassis rocked from side to side like a child's carnival ride, exactly the type of motion that often nauseated her, but she gripped the wheel and stared through the window for the next hard curve or sudden rock formation, and she felt fine.

The farmland had given way to tumultuous fields of overgrowth and those eventually gave way to the return of woodlands, the kind of woodlands Brian had always claimed to be part and parcel of his family history and subsequent career. She realized now that Brian had chosen a symbol to represent himself that was the exact opposite of who he actually was. Wood was dependable, sturdy, you could place your faith in it for generations.

Brian, on the other hand, was the biggest liar she'd ever known. And as a reporter, she'd known a lot.

Then how did he manage to deceive you?

Because I let him.

And why would you do that?

Because I wanted to feel safe.

Safety is an illusion we sell to children to help them sleep.

Then I wanted to be a child.

The path ended in a small clearing. There were no other paths beyond it. Just the small oval of weeds and sand and then the next forest. She checked her map, but it wasn't detailed enough to include this. She checked her satellite photos and felt hopeful that she'd reached a pale spot on one of them that, if she were correct, would mean she was about three miles south of the hunting camp. She changed into her hiking boots and checked that the safety on the P380 was on before she slipped it into her waistband at the small of her back. She'd barely walked ten feet before the rise and fall of it back there grew uncomfortable and she moved it to the pocket of her coat.

The trees were gargantuan. Their canopies blotted out the sun. She presumed bears lived in these woods, and she had a moment of panic when she couldn't recall how recent her last period had been. But then she remembered—it had been about ten days ago, so at least her blood wouldn't attract a predator. By the looks of these woods, though, the scent of her flesh might be enough; nothing human had passed along her footpath in a long time. And whatever hunter may have done so in years past, she was fairly certain he'd been quieter than she. She pushed through like the awkward city girl she was, crunching leaves, snapping twigs, breathing audibly.

She heard the lake before she saw it. It wasn't gurgling or lapping against the land. It presented itself as a pocket, a lack of density that removed pressure from her left ear, pressure she hadn't even known was there until it wasn't. Soon small patches of blue winked through the tree trunks. She turned toward them. In fifteen minutes she stood along the water's edge. There was no shore, just the edge of the forest and a six-foot drop to the water. She made her way along it for another half an hour before the light changed ahead of her, the trunks of the trees brightening with it, and she picked up her pace and stepped through the last of them into a clearing.

The first cabin she encountered was missing all its windows and half its roof. One wall was caved in. The one next to it, however, was the one Gattis had described—faded green trim, faded red door, but clearly kept up, no sense of the land reclaiming it, no cracks in the foundation, the steps leading up to it swept clean, the windows dusty but intact.

The boards creaked when she climbed the four steps to the door. She removed the pistol from her jacket and tried the door. The knob turned in her hand. She pushed the door open. It smelled of must inside, but not mold or rot, and it smelled of the forest, of pine and moss and bark. The fireplace was swept clean. It didn't smell as if it had been used in a while. In the tiny kitchen, the counters bore a thin film of dust. The fridge was stocked with waters, three tall cans of Guinness with the plastic ring still holding them together, and some condiments still shy of their use-by dates.

The den, also small—the entire cabin wasn't more than five hundred square feet—sported a cracked brown leather couch and a small bookcase filled with adventure novels and positive-thinking manuals. This was Brian's place, all right. In the bathroom, she found the toothpaste and shampoo brands he preferred. In the bedroom, she found a queen-size brass bed that squeaked when she sat on it. She walked around a bit more but found no evidence anyone had been there recently. She went outside and looked for footprints around the cabin but found none.

She sat on the porch as exhaustion found her bones and her brain. She wiped at a tear with the heel of her hand and then another, but then she sucked hard through her nostrils and stood and shook her head like a dog who'd been caught in the rain. It wasn't just that she would have to trek to the car and drive back toward civilization with not enough daylight to reach it before she'd probably have to pull over with her one working headlight and sleep along the side of the road again. It was that she had nothing to return to. By now they'd have found Caleb and would have ascertained that she'd been in Providence the same time Nicole Alden had been murdered. The circumstantial evidence might not be enough to convict her in a trial, but she would most definitely go to jail until such a time as that trial was held. Could be a year or more. And who's to say that the circumstantial evidence *wouldn't* be enough to convict her? Certainly for Caleb's murder; a policeman would go on record saying she'd lied about the victim being alive in her condo when, at that point, he'd been dead. Once they had you on record lying about anything, they could convince a jury you were lying about everything.

So she had no home. No life waiting for her. She had two thousand dollars in cash. She had a change of clothes in a bag in a car she'd have to abandon in the first city where she could find a bus terminal.

But a bus to where?

And wherever she got, how was she going to survive on two thousand dollars with her picture on every TV screen and every Internet news site in this country?

Trudging back through the woods, she rifled through her options until she came to the grim conclusion that she had only two— turn herself in or take the gun from her pocket right now and use it on herself.

She found a rock and sat. The lake was an hour back. All she had to look at were trees. She took the gun out of her pocket, hefted it in her palm. Brian, by this point, was probably a continent or two away. Whatever scam he'd been running through Alden Minerals and that mine in Papua New Guinea, he'd run it. And run off with the profits.

She'd been played. That was possibly the worst of it. That she'd been used and discarded. To what end, she had no idea, couldn't see what her role had been in all this. She was simply the dupe, the rube, the unforgivably innocent pawn.

How long would her body lie among the trees before it was found? Days? Seasons? Or would animals come to feast on it? Years from now someone would find a bone or two and the state police would arrive to find the rest. And the mystery of the missing reporter suspected in the murders of two people would finally be solved. Parents would tell it as a cautionary tale to wayward teens. See, they'd say, she didn't get away with it. Justice prevails, the status quo is reaffirmed, she got what was coming to her.

Widdy stood about fifty feet away and smiled at her. Her dress was not bloodied, her throat was intact. She didn't open her mouth when she spoke, but Rachel heard her more clearly than the birds.

You tried.

"I didn't try hard enough."

They would have killed you.

"Then I should have died."

And who would tell my story then?

"No one will care about your story."

But I lived.

Rachel wept into the dirt and the dead leaves. "You lived poor. And black. On an island no one gives a shit about."

You gave a shit.

She stared through the trees at the girl. "You died because I convinced you to hide. You were right. If they had found you earlier they would have raped you, but they wouldn't have cut your throat, they wouldn't have, they would have let you live."

What life?

"*A* life!" Rachel screamed.

I wouldn't want that life.

"But I want you to be alive," Rachel begged. "I need you to be alive."

But I'm gone. Let me go, Miss Rachel. Let me go.

Rachel was staring right at her. And then she was staring at a tree. She wiped her eyes and nose on her sleeve. She cleared her throat. She sucked the forest air into her nostrils.

And she heard her mother's voice. Jesus. This had to be dehydration or exhaustion or low blood sugar or maybe she'd already put the gun to her head and fired and she was already dead, but here came Elizabeth Childs and her nicotine vocal cords.

Lie down, her mother said with a distinctly weary benevolence, *and soon we'll be together again. And it'll be like that week you were sick in bed and I never left your side. I'll make all your favorite foods.*

Rachel caught herself shaking her head, as if her mother could see her, as if the trees could, as if she were anything but alone. Was this how people went crazy? Ended up talking to themselves on street corners, sleeping in doorways, skin covered in sores?

Fuck that.

Rachel pocketed the gun and stood. She took in the woods all around her. And she knew she wasn't going to die to make life easier for Brian or Kessler or anyone else who assumed she was too weak for this world.

"I'm not crazy," she told her mother, told the trees. "And I don't want to be with you in the afterlife, Mother." She looked at the sky. "One lifetime of you was fucking plenty."

It was one o'clock by the time she reached the SUV. It would take two hours to get back to 201. Three hours on 201 until she hit a town big enough to have a bus station. She'd have to hope buses ran through that small town after six in the evening. That's if she were lucky enough to get from here to there without being pulled over for driving an SUV that looked like it had been dropped from a crane.

She got behind the wheel and pulled out onto the dirt road. She'd driven for about a mile when the man lying on the backseat said, "Fuck happened to Caleb's car? You look good, by the way."

He sat up, smiled at her in the rearview.

Brian.

30

PRIMAL SELF

She stood on the brakes, slammed the gearshift into park, and un-latched her seat belt. Brian sat up halfway in the backseat as she came through the space between the two front seats and punched him in the side of the face. She had no experience with hitting someone, particularly with a closed fist—it stung her knuckles far worse than she would have expected—but she knew a direct hit when she heard one, and her fist connecting with Brian's face made a sound as sharp and solid as any she'd ever heard. She watched his eyes water and grow disoriented.

So she hit him again. She pinned his shoulders with her knees. She punched his ear and his eye and the side of his face again. He bucked at her with his upper body, but the weight imbalance was all on her side and she knew the only rule at this point was to not stop until something forced her to. She heard his voice asking her to stop, her own voice calling him *motherfucker* over and over, saw his eyes scrunched up against the flurry of her fists. He squirmed his right shoulder free and that turned her awkwardly to her left, and he pushed off the foot well and the seat. She fell back through the space between the two front seats and he loomed up in the backseat, surging toward her.

She kicked him in the face.

If anything, it connected more thoroughly than her first punch. Bone or cartilage cracked, and the back of his head slammed into the window. He opened and closed his mouth several times, as if he were nibbling on the air, and then his eyes rolled back to the whites, and he lost consciousness.

I. Knocked. Someone. Out.

A small laugh popped from her mouth as she watched Brian's eyes flutter under his sagging eyelids. Her right hand was already swelling and was slick with blood. His blood. His face, she realized with both shock and surprising concern, was battered. And she was pretty sure it hadn't been battered five minutes ago.

I did that?

She took the car key and the gun with her and got out of the car and stood on the road. She experienced the worst craving she'd had for a cigarette since she'd quit seven years ago. She inhaled the impossibly fresh forest air instead and she couldn't relate even a little bit to the person she'd been just hours ago, the one who'd contemplated suicide, the one who'd thought of giving up.

Fuck giving up. I'll give up when I die. And it won't be by my hand.

His door creaked open and his palms appeared above the window. The rest of him stayed below the roofline. "You done?"

"With what?"

"Beating the shit out of me."

Her right hand was screaming now, but she wrapped it around the pistol just the same. "Yeah, I guess."

He raised his head above the roofline and she pointed the pistol at him.

"Jesus!" He ducked down again.

She came around the car in three long strides and trained the gun on him. "Blanks?"

He lowered his hands from around his head and straightened from a crouch, resigned to his fate suddenly. "What?"

"Did you put blanks in this gun too?"

He shook his head.

She pointed the gun at his chest.

"No, really!" He raised his hands again. So maybe not so resigned after all. "Those are real fucking bullets in there."

"Yeah?"

His eyes widened because he could see hers suddenly, could see what was in them.

She pulled the trigger.

Brian hit the ground. Well, he bounced off the vehicle first, trying to break to his left to escape the bullet. Bounced off the SUV, landed on the ground, hands still up in the universal, if wholly ineffectual, please-don't-shoot-me gesture.

"Get up," she said.

He stood, looked at the chunk of bark she'd shot out of the thin pine to his right. Blood dripped from his nose, over his lips, and off his chin. He wiped at it with his forearm. He spit red into the green grass by the side of the road.

"That looks like real blood. How'd you fake the blood in your mouth on the boat?"

"Wanna guess?" A small smile found his eyes but not his lips.

She put herself back on the boat, back in their conversation. She could see him sitting there so calmly as she confronted him about his second wife and second life. And he just sat there, eating.

"The peanuts," she said.

He gave her a halfhearted thumbs-up. "Two of them were squibs, yeah." He shot the gun a wary eye. "What are you going to *do* here, Rachel?"

"I haven't decided yet, *Brian*." She lowered the gun for a moment.

He lowered his hands. "If you kill me—and I wouldn't blame you—you're fucked. No money, no way of getting any, wanted for questioning in a murder, and hunted—"

"Two murders."

"Two?"

She nodded.

He processed that and then continued. "You're also being hunted by some very bad fucking guys. If you kill me, you're staring down two, maybe three more days of free air and picking your own clothes to wear. And I know how you like to be stylish, honey."

She raised the gun again. He raised his hands. He cocked an eyebrow at her. She cocked one back at him. And in that moment—what in the hell?—she felt connected to him, felt like she wanted to laugh. All the rage remained, all the sense of betrayal and fury at him for dismantling her trust, her *life* . . . and yet entwined with it, for just a moment, were all the old feelings.

It took every bit of muscle control she could muster not to smile.

"Speaking of stylish," she said, "you're not looking it right now."

He touched his face with his fingers, came back with blood. He looked at his reflection in the window of the SUV. "I think you broke my nose."

"Sounded like it at the time."

He lifted the hem of his T-shirt up his chest and dabbed at his face. "I've got a first aid kit stashed nearby. Could we go back for it?"

"Why should I do you any favors, dear?"

"Because I've also got an SUV back there that doesn't look like someone drove it off a fucking bridge, *dear*."

They drove back to the clearing and then walked into the woods no more than twenty feet and there sat, perfectly camouflaged, a forest green Range Rover, early nineties vintage, some rust in the wheel wells, some dents in the rear quarter panels, but the tires were new and it had the look of something that would run another twenty years. She kept the gun on Brian as he retrieved a first aid kit from a canvas cargo bin in the back. He sat on the bed under the raised hatchback and rummaged around in the bin until he came up with a shaving mirror. He went to work swabbing the cuts clean with rubbing alcohol, wincing occasionally, scrunching his face against the stings.

"Where should I start?" he said.

"Where can you?"

"Oh, it's easy. You came in during the late innings. I put this in motion a long time ago."

"And what is 'this'?"

"In the parlance of my business, it's a salting scam."

"And your business is?"

He looked up at her with mild hurt and dismay, like a fading movie star she'd failed to recognize. "I'm a grifter."

"A con man."

"I prefer grifter. It's got some panache to it. 'Con man' just sounds like, I dunno, some guy could be selling you penny stocks or fucking Amway."

"So you're a grifter."

He nodded and handed her some alcohol swabs for her knuckles. She nodded her thanks, tucked the gun in her waistband, and took a few steps back from him as she cleaned her knuckles.

"About five years ago, I came across a bankrupt mine for sale in Papua New Guinea, so I formed a corporation, and I bought the mine."

"What do you know about mines?"

"Nothing." He worked on the blood in his nose with a Q-tip. "Jesus," he said softly with something akin to admiration, "you fucked me up, girl."

"The mine." She suppressed another smile.

"So we bought the mine. And simultaneously, Caleb created a consulting company, with an entirely fictitious but quite believable deep history in Latin America, generations of it, if you didn't look too closely. Three years later, that company, Borgeau Engineering, undertook an 'independent' study of the mine. Which by that point, we'd salted."

"What's salting?"

"You sprinkle a mine with gold in places that are easier to access—but not too easy—than others. The idea is one of extrapolation—if x percentage of gold is found here, then one can assume the totality of the mine is sitting on y percentage. That's what our independent consultants—"

"Borgeau Engineering."

He tipped an imaginary cap to her. "That's what they ascertained—that we were sitting on resources worth up to four hundred million troy ounces of gold as opposed to four million."

"Which would drive your stock up."

"If we had stock, but we didn't. No, what it would do was make us a potential threat to any competitors in the region."

"Vitterman."

"You *have* been doing your research."

"I did spend ten years as a reporter."

"You did. So what else did you find out?"

"That you probably got a loan from a VC concern called Cotter-McCann."

He nodded. "And why would they loan us money?"

"Ostensibly to help shore the company up against a hostile take-over by Vitterman while you pulled enough gold out of there to make the company impregnable to takeover."

He nodded again.

"But," she said, "word around the campfire is that Cotter-McCann is predatory."

"Very," he confirmed.

"So they were going to eat up your little mine and all its profits anyway."

"Yup."

"But there wouldn't be any profits."

He was watching her carefully now, dabbing at the last of his cuts.

"How much was the loan for?" she asked.

He smiled. "Seventy million."

"In cash?" She had to force herself to keep her voice low.

He nodded. "And another four hundred and fifty million in stock options."

"But the options are worthless."

"*Sí*."

She walked in a small circle, her feet crunching leaves and pine needles, until she got it. "All you've been after from the beginning was the seventy million."

"Yup."

"And you got that seventy million?"

He tossed the last of the bloody swabs into a plastic bag, held the bag out in front of her. "Oh, did I ever. It's sitting in a bank in Grand Cayman, waiting for me to walk in and pick it up."

She dropped her own bloody swabs in the bag. "So what's the hitch in this great plan of yours?"

His face darkened. "The hitch is that the moment we wired the money out of the account in Rhode Island, we were on a clock. That kind of transaction gets noticed quick, particularly by the likes of Cotter-McCann. We made two mistakes—we underestimated just how *fast* they'd notice the wire because we had no way of knowing they had someone on the payroll in Homeland who flagged it for an SAR."

"Which is?"

"Suspicious Activity Report. We *knew* we'd get flagged, but there's normally a delay between the flagging and the payer hearing about it."

"What else didn't you count on?"

"You got an hour?" he said ruefully. "You try something like this, there's about five hundred things that can go wrong and only one that can go right. So we didn't count on them putting a tracker on my car. And they didn't even do it because they were suspicious at that point. They did it because it's their standard operating procedure."

"And they followed you where?"

"Same place you did. Nicole's." Something caught in his voice. Authentic grief, she would have assumed, if she didn't know how good an actor he was. "They probably missed me by ten minutes. But they found her. And they killed her." He exhaled a steady stream of air through pursed lips. He stepped out from under the hatchback abruptly, closed it, and clapped his hands together. "Anything else you really, really need to know right now that can't wait?"

"About a hundred things."

"That *can't* wait," he repeated.

"How'd you look so dead? At the bottom of the harbor? With the blood flowing out of you and the . . ." She waved her hands as she trailed off.

"Stagecraft," he said. "The blood was easy. That's all squibs. The ones in my chest were wired up before you got on the boat. The ones in my mouth came out of the bag of peanuts, as you know. The oxygen tank was waiting for me as long as I could get to that rock in time. You dove in fast, by the way. Shit. I barely had time to get situated."

"The look," she said impatiently. "You looked right at me with dead eyes and a dead face."

"Like this?"

It was as if someone had plunged a needle full of strychnine into the base of his brain. All light bled from his eyes and then from the rest of his face. It wasn't only that his face grew impossibly still, its spirit vacated.

She waved her hand in front of his eyes and they remained fixed on nothing and never blinked.

"How long can you do this?" she asked.

He let out a breath. "I probably could have done another twenty seconds."

"And if I'd stayed down there looking at you?"

"Oh, I had maybe forty more seconds, a minute tops. But you didn't. And that's what a good grift always relies on—that people will act predictably."

"If they're not Cotter-McCann."

"Touché." He clapped his hands together again and the ghoulish aura of death left his face. "Well, we're still on a tight clock, so mind if I download the rest to you while we go?"

"Go where?"

He pointed north. "Canada. Caleb's meeting us there in the morning."

"Caleb?" she said.

"Yeah. Where'd you ditch him, the safe house?"

She stared back at him, no idea what to say.

"Rachel." He stopped with his hand on the driver's-side door. "Please tell me you went to the safe house after the boat."

"We never made it."

His face drained. "Where's Caleb?"

"He's dead, Brian."

He put both hands to his face. He brought them back down and then pressed them flat against the windows of the Range Rover. He lowered his head and didn't seem to breathe for a full minute.

"How'd he die?"

"They shot him in the face."

He came off the car, looked at her.

She nodded.

"Who?"

"I don't know. Two men looking for a key."

He looked helpless. Worse, she realized. Bereft. He gave the woods a wild look, as if he were about to faint again, and then he slid down the side of the Range Rover and sat on the ground. He trembled. Wept.

In three years, she'd never seen this Brian. She'd never seen anything close. Brian didn't cave, Brian didn't break, Brian didn't need *help*. She was witnessing the reduction of him, the essential pieces at the core of him being removed and carted off. She engaged the safety on the pistol and placed it behind her back and sat on the ground across from him. He wiped at his eyes and sucked air in through wet nostrils that still glistened with blood.

His hands shook along with his lips when he said, "You saw him die?"

She nodded. "He was as close to me as you are now. The guy just shot him."

"Who were these guys?" He blew air through his lips in short bursts.

"I don't know. They looked like they sell insurance. And not the high-end kind, the kind you get at strip malls."

"How'd you get away from them?"

She told him, and in the telling, she watched him return a bit to form. The trembling stopped, his eyes cleared.

"He had the key," he said. "It's over. Game fucking over."

"What key?"

"Safe deposit box at a bank."

She fingered the key in her pocket. "Bank in the Caymans?"

He shook his head. "Rhode Island. That last day? I carried around a bad feeling, an ugly hunch, I guess. Either that or I simply panicked like a fucking child. I dropped our passports in the bank. If anyone got to me, I figured Nicole could get to them. But they got to Nicole instead. So I handed the key off to Caleb."

"What passports?"

He nodded. "Mine, Caleb's, Haya's, the baby's, Nicole's, yours."

"I don't have a passport anymore."

He stood wearily and held out his hand. "Yes, you do."

She took the hand and allowed him to pull her to her feet. "I'd know if I had a passport. Mine expired two years ago."

"I got you another one." He still hadn't dropped her hand.

She still hadn't pulled it away. "Where'd you get a picture?"

"The photo booth in the mall that time."

Not bad, she thought. *Not bad*.

She pulled the key out of her pocket. She held it up and watched him come back from the dead for the second time in fifteen minutes. "This key?"

He blinked several times, then nodded.

She put it back in her pocket. "Why did Caleb have it?"

"Caleb was supposed to get the passports. He and I could impersonate each other in our sleep. Shit, his version of my signature looked more like mine than mine." He looked up at the hard sky. "You and I were supposed to slip into Canada, meet the others in a place called Saint-Prosper. From there—*fuck*—from there, we'd all go to Quebec City, fly out of the country."

She looked in his eyes and he looked back and neither of them said a word until she said, "So all six of us were supposed to leave the country together?"

"That was the plan, yeah."

"You, your best friend, his wife and child, and your two wives."

He dropped her hand. "Nicole wasn't my wife."

"Then who was she?"

"My sister."

She stepped back and took a hard look at his face to see if he was telling the truth or not. But then what did she know about that? She'd lived with him for three years and never knew his real name or profession or history. Just two nights ago, he'd convinced her he was dead, stared back at her with sightless eyes from the bottom of the ocean. This was not a man who wore his lies the way normal people wore theirs.

"Was your *sister* pregnant?"

He nodded.

"Who was the father?"

"We don't have time for this."

"Who was the father?"

"Guy named Joel, okay? Worked at the bank with her. Married guy, three kids of his own. It was a fling. But Nicole always wanted a kid, so even after she broke things off with Joel, she went forward with the pregnancy. She didn't need Joel's support; we were going to be sitting on seventy million. You want to meet Joel? I can set it up. You can ask him if his dead ex-mistress was six months' pregnant with his child when someone executed her in her kitchen because her brother"—he was pacing now, agitated—"her *dumb fuck brother* left his car in front of her house while he went back to Boston to shock you back to reality."

Her laugh sounded like a bark. "You *what*? You tried to shock me back to reality?"

He was all earnest innocence. "Well, yeah."

"That's the biggest load of horseshit I've ever heard."

"I needed you ready to run. I didn't expect Cotter-McCann to bite down hard on the hook for, shit, three months. Six? I was hoping for six. But they fucking bit early because they're aggressive and greedy and they want what they want on their timetable, no one else's. I didn't expect them to put the money into our account and hire an independent consulting firm to double-check the mine on the same day. But they did. And I didn't expect them to put a two-man hit squad on me and my crew simultaneously. But, once again, they did. So I had to skip plan A, dump plan B, and go right to plan C, the one where I shock you the fuck awake. And, whattaya know, it worked."

"Nothing worked. Nothing—"

"You afraid to drive anymore?"

"No."

"Afraid to take cabs?"

"No."

"Afraid of wilderness or wide open spaces? How about elevators? Diving into the ocean? Have you had a panic attack, Rachel, since this whole thing started?"

"How could I tell? I've been in a state of panic ever since I saw you walk out of the back of a building in Boston when you said you were in London."

"Right." He nodded. "And you've overcome that panic, every minute of every day since, to do what needed to be done. Including killing me, by the way."

"But you didn't die."

"Yeah, well, my apologies." He put his hands on her shoulders. "You're not afraid anymore because you stopped listening to anyone but your own primal self. You had all the 'evidence' you needed to crawl back into your life and stay there. I didn't paint the clues in neon; I made you work for them. You could have trusted your eyes— the visa stamps looked real enough, to give you just one example— but you trusted your instinct, babe. You acted from what you knew there"—he pointed at her chest—"not here." He pointed at her head.

She stared at him for a long time. "Don't call me 'babe.'"

"Why not?"

"Because I hate you."

He took that into consideration. Shrugged. "That's how we usually feel about the things that wake us up."

SAFE HOUSE

They left Caleb's smashed-up SUV in the woods and drove the Range Rover three hundred miles south to Woonsocket, Rhode Island, just south of the Massachusetts border and about fifteen miles north of Providence. They'd had a lot of time to talk on the drive but hadn't really, except about the essentials. They'd listened to the radio long enough to hear they were both considered "persons of interest" in the deaths of two people in two different states. Police in Providence and Boston were tight-lipped as to why they believed the murder of a small-town bank employee in Providence was connected to the murder of a businessman in Boston, but they were determined to meet with Brian Alden, the brother of the Providence victim and business partner of the Boston victim, and with Brian Alden's wife, Rachel Childs-Delacroix. Handguns registered to both "persons of interest" had not been recovered at their Back Bay home, so they were to be considered armed.

"Basically my life is ruined," Rachel said somewhere near Lewiston, Maine. "Even if I could clear my name."

"Big if," Brian said.

"I'd fuck myself financially to do it."

"Spend a lot of time in jail while that was happening."

She shot him a dirty look he didn't see because his eyes were on the road. "And they could still bury me deep on ancillary charges."

He nodded. "Obstruction of justice comes to mind. Cops tend to get a bit miffed when you forget to tell them there's a corpse sitting at your dining room table. Leaving the scene of a crime, unlawful flight, reckless driving, I'm sure I'll think of a few more."

"This isn't funny," she said.

He looked over at her. "When did I give the impression it was?"

"Right now. You're being sarcastic, snarky."

"I get that way when I'm terrified."

"You're terrified? You."

He raised his eyebrows. "Beyond terrified. *If* no one's found the safe house and we can do what we need to do there and *if* we can slip into Providence without being made, and *if* we can get into the bank and get to the safe deposit box where I stashed the passports and the running money, *if* we can still get back out of that bank and out of Providence and grab Haya and the baby and find an airport where no one's looking for us and our faces aren't plastered over everyone's home screen and the nine TVs tuned to CNN in the airport bar, and *if* they don't have someone waiting for us in Amsterdam, then, yes, we could possibly survive the year. But I'd put our odds at successfully navigating all those obstacles at, oh, I dunno, grim to none."

"Amsterdam," she said. "I thought the bank was in the Caymans."

"It is, but they'll definitely be waiting for us there. If we get to Amsterdam, we can wire it all to Switzerland."

"But why stop in Amsterdam?"

He shrugged. "I've always liked Amsterdam. You'd like it too. The old canals are pretty. Lotta bikes, though."

"You talk like you're taking me sightseeing."

"Well, that's the plan, isn't it?"

"We're not together," she said.

"No?"

"No, you lying sack of shit. This is a business arrangement from here on out."

He rolled down his window for a moment, took a blast on his face to wake himself up. Rolled the window back up.

"Okay," he said, "you play the business tip. But I'm in love with you."

"You don't know the first thing about love."

"Guess we'll have to agree to disagree on that one."

"Did you ever search for my father?"

"What?"

"When I met you, you were a private investigator."

"That was a scam. My first one, actually."

"So you were never an actual private investigator?"

He shook his head. "I set up that front to do background checks for all the employees of a tech start-up that was setting up shop in the area."

"Why would you set up a front just to do background checks?"

"There were sixty-four employees of that company, if memory serves. Sixty-four DOBs, sixty-four SSNs, sixty-four histories."

"You stole sixty-four identities."

He nodded. It was a quick nod but full of pride. "One of them's on your passport."

"But when I came through your office door?"

"I tried to talk you out of hiring me."

"But when I came back a few months later, you just took my money and—"

"I looked for your father, Rachel. I busted my ass on it. I wish I'd been smart enough to consider that James was his last name, but I wasn't. But I ID'd every professor with the first name James who'd taught in that region over the previous twenty years, just like I said I did. The only honest work I ever did as a private eye, I did for you."

"Why?"

"Because you're good."

"I'm *what*?"

"You're good. You're one of the only good people I've ever met. And you're worth fighting for and fighting with. You're worth everything."

"You're such a liar. You're running a fucking con right now. On me."

He thought about that. Eventually he said, "When I met you in the bar that night, Caleb and Nicole kept telling me to get rid of you. Grifters can't have love lives, they said, just sex lives. This from my sister who would end up getting knocked up by a married guy. She's giving me advice on love. And Caleb, who would marry a woman who couldn't speak English. Those are my Dear Abbys." He shook his head. "'Don't fall in love.' Well, that worked out fucking great for all of us."

She willed herself not to look over at him but instead out the window.

"I fell for you because that's what you do when you meet the woman whose face you want to be looking into when you die. You fall. And keep falling. And if you're really lucky, she falls with you and you never get back up again to where you were because if that was so great, you wouldn't have needed to fall in the first place. But when I fell, I fell all the way. I had just started this con. I met you the night I closed papers on the mine. Caleb was supposed to meet me at the bar to celebrate, but I saw you and I texted him and told him I'd eaten bad tuna at lunch, and he went out to dinner somewhere by himself. And I looked across the bar and I thought, 'That's Rachel Childs. I tried to find her father once. I used to watch her on the news.' I used to wonder who was lucky enough to go home to you. And then that drunk fucked with you and I got to come to your rescue and the irony is, you thought it might be a con. I always loved that. Made me believe in God for a minute. And you left and I ran out onto the streets looking for you." He looked across at her. "I found you. And then we had the walk and the blackout and found our amazing bar."

"What was playing when we entered?"

"Tom Waits."

"What song?"

"'Long Way Home.'"

"Should have been '16 Shells from a Thirty-Ought-Six.'"

"Be nice." He shifted in his seat, resettled his wrist against the top of the wheel. "You might not like my methods, Rachel, and it may be unwelcome news to learn I make my living running long cons. So you can fall out of love with me, but I can't fall out of love with you. I wouldn't know how."

She almost bought it, if only for a second, but then she remembered who this man was—an actor, a con man, a grifter, a professional liar.

"People who love each other," she said, "don't wreck each other's lives."

He chuckled softly. "Sure they do. That's what love is—where once there was one, now there's two, and that's so much less convenient and less orderly and less safe. You want me to apologize for blowing your life up? Okay. I'm sorry. But what did I blow up? Your mother's dead, you never knew your father, your friends are transitory at best, and you never leave the apartment. What life did I take, Rachel?"

What life indeed, she wondered, as they entered Woonsocket at sundown.

It was a faded, cauterized mill town with hopeful pockets of gentrification that couldn't compensate for the air of abandonment. The main street was peppered with vacant storefronts. Some mills rose up behind those buildings, their windows broken or nonexistent, the brick edifices festooned with graffiti, the land reclaiming the lower floors and punching cracks through the foundations. It had happened before she was born, this wholesale discarding of American industry, this switch from a culture that made things of value to a culture that consumed things of dubious merit. She'd grown up in the absence, in other people's memory of a dream so fragile it had probably been doomed from the moment of conception. If there had ever been a social contract between the country and its citizens, it was long gone now, save the Hobbesian agreement that had been in play since our ancestors had first stumbled from caves in search of food: Once I get mine, you're on your own.

Brian drove over a series of dark hilly streets and then down to a quartet of long, four-story buildings that comprised a failed mill sitting along the river with nothing else around it for blocks. Each brick building had at least a hundred windows fronting the street and the same amount again on the river side. The high window frames in the center of the buildings were twice as large as the others. Brian drove around the complex to reveal a pair of covered passageways between the fourth floors connecting the buildings, so that the complex, if seen from the air, would look like a double H.

"This is your safe house?" she said.

"No, this is an abandoned mill."

"So where's the safe house?"

"Nearby."

They rolled past broken windows and weeds the height of the Range Rover. Gravel and rocks and pebbles of broken glass crunched under his tires.

He took out his phone and fired off a text to someone. A few seconds later it vibrated with the return text. He put the phone back in his jacket. He drove around the mill twice more. At the tip of the property, he killed the headlights and rolled up a small knoll, just upriver from a dam by the sound of it. At the top of the knoll, partially obscured by a stand of half-dead trees, stood a small brick two-story house with a black mansard roof. He put the Rover in park but left the engine running and they sat and watched the house.

"Used to be the night watchman's. City's owned all this land ever since the mill went tits-up in the seventies. Most of the land is probably poisoned and no one has the money to test it, so they sold us this house for pennies on the dollar." He shifted in his seat. "It's got good bones, actually, and clear sight lines. Impossible to approach without being seen."

"Who'd you text?" she asked.

"Haya." He nodded at the house. "She's inside with Annabelle. Wanted her to know I was coming."

"So why aren't we going in?"

"We will."

"What're we waiting for?"

"For my sense of terror to be overridden by my impatience." He looked up at the house. A light came from somewhere deep in the back of it. "If all was clear, Haya was supposed to text 'I am OK. Come in.'"

"And?"

"She only texted the first half."

"Well, it's not her native tongue. And she's scared."

He chewed on the inside of his mouth for a moment. "We can't tell her about Caleb."

"We have to."

"If she thinks he's just held up and will meet us in Amsterdam in a couple days, she'll keep her shit together. But if she doesn't?" He turned in the seat, touched her hand. She pulled it back. "We can't tell her. Rachel, Rachel."

"What?"

"If this goes south, they will kill us all. The baby too."

She stared through the dark Range Rover at him.

"We can't give her any reason to be any more unpredictable than she's liable to be already. We tell her in Amsterdam."

She nodded.

"I need to hear you say it."

"We tell her in Amsterdam."

Brian looked at her for a long time before he said, "You still got your gun?"

"Yup."

He reached under the seat and came back with a 9mm Glock, put it behind his back.

"You've had a gun the whole time," she said.

"Shit, Rachel," he said with a distracted sigh, "I've got three."

They walked around the outside of the house twice in the dark before Brian led them up the sagging back steps to a door that had lost most of its paint over the years. The floorboards squeaked underfoot and the house itself creaked in an unseasonably cool wind, more early autumn than early summer.

He moved along the porch, checked all the windows and the front door before they returned to the back. He unlocked the door and they entered.

An alarm beeped to their left and Brian punched in her birthdate on the keypad and the beeping stopped.

The central hallway ran straight from the back door, past an oak staircase to the front door. The house smelled clean but dusty, maybe a light foundational odor of mildew that a thousand house-cleanings could probably never remove. He produced two penlights from his jacket, handed her one, and turned on his own.

Haya sat below the mail slot in the front door, junk mail off to her right, a gun clasped in her hands.

Brian gave her a wave and a warm smile and came down the hall to her. She lowered her gun and he hugged her awkwardly and then they stood in front of her.

"Baby is asleep." She pointed at the ceiling.

"You need sleep," Brian said. "You look exhausted."

"Where is Caleb?"

"The bad men, Haya, they may be following him. He didn't want to lead them here. To you and Annabelle. You understand?"

Her breath was coming too fast. She bit her upper lip so hard Rachel feared it would spout blood. "He is . . . alive?"

Jesus.

"He is," Brian said. "He's going to go out through Maine. Remember how we talked about it? He's going to cross into Canada and fly out of Toronto. No one will be able to track him in Maine. We know that terrain. You understand 'terrain'?"

She nodded twice. "He will be . . . okay?"

"He will be," Brian said with a firmness Rachel despised.

"He does not answer his . . . mobile phone."

"We explained that. They can track a phone, Haya. If any of us thinks they're being followed, they stay off the phone." Brian took her hands in his. "It's going to be okay. We'll all be out of here in the morning."

Haya looked at Rachel, woman to woman, a look that transcended any language barrier: *Can I trust this man?*

Rachel blinked an affirmative. "Get some sleep. You'll need the rest."

Haya climbed the dark stairs and Rachel resisted the urge to run to her and tell her everything they'd said was a lie. Her husband was dead. The father of her child was dead. She and her infant were about to go on the run with a pair of two-faced strangers who lied to her and would continue to lie to her until she couldn't fuck up their escape.

Haya turned right at the top of the stairs and Rachel lost sight of her.

Brian read her mind. "What do you want to tell her?"

"That her husband is dead," she whispered.

"Fine. Be my guest." He waved his arm at the staircase with a flourish.

"Don't be cruel," she said after a moment.

"Don't be judgmental," he said, "unless you're willing to walk the walk."

They checked the downstairs together, room by room, and it was empty.

Only then did he turn on the lights.

"Sure that's wise?" she asked.

"If they knew about the place," he said, "they'd have been out in the mill or inside with her. They aren't, which means this safe house is still safe. Nicole didn't give it up. Probably because they didn't know to ask her."

"Haya's got the bedroom up top on the right." His body sagged with exhaustion all at once and she realized how wiped she was as well. He used his gun hand to point vaguely back up the stairs. "There's a linen closet outside the bathroom. The first bedroom on the left has a dresser with a bunch of clothes in your size. Let's each take a shower, I'll put on some coffee, and we'll get back to work."

"What do we have to work at?"

"I gotta teach you a little forgery."

32

CONFESSION

Hair still wet, coffee in a mug, wearing a T-shirt, hoodie, and sweats that were, as promised, in her size, she sat at the table with her husband—*was he still that?*—as he placed a pad of blank paper in front of her with a pen. He then laid down several documents with his sister's signature on them.

"I'm going to be Nicole?"

"For the five minutes it should take to get in and out of that bank, you're going to be Nicole's last alias." He dug around in a gym bag until he came back with a small stack of IDs and credit cards wrapped in a rubber band. He extracted a Rhode Island driver's license. It was in the name of Nicole Rosovitch. As he placed it on the table in front of her, Brian shook his head tightly. She got the feeling he didn't know he was doing it.

"I don't look anything like her," she said.

"Similar bone structure," he argued.

"Eyes are different."

"That's why I keep a set of color contacts."

"They're shaped differently." She pointed. "And hers were bigger. Her lips are thinner."

"But your nose is close and so's your chin."

"Anyone will be able to tell I'm not her."

"A straight, almost-middle-aged guy with the two-point-two kids, the world's most boring job, and I'll assume the corresponding world's most boring wife? He's gonna remember one thing about the hot blonde in his office three months ago—that she was a hot blonde. So let's make you a blonde. The hot part's already covered."

She ignored the appeal to her vanity. "You've got the right hair dye in this place?"

"I got wigs. Same one she wore."

"Banks have face recognition software these days, you know."

"Not at this bank," he said. "That's why I picked it. When in doubt, go mom and pop. This bank has been in Johnston for three generations. They only got an ATM four years ago and only after their customers filed a petition. The owner, that's who you'll be meeting, is also the bank manager and handles all safe deposit transactions. His name is Manfred Thorp."

"Get the fuck out of here," she said.

He straddled the chair beside her. "No, really. He told me the name Manfred goes back in the family a thousand years. Says every generation has to name one kid 'Manfred' and he, as he put it, drew the short straw."

"How well do you know him?"

"Just met him once."

"But you know all that about him."

He shrugged. "People like talking to me. My father was the same."

"Who *was* your father?" She turned her chair toward him. "Your real father."

"Jamie Alden," he said brightly. "People called him Lefty."

"Because he was left-handed?"

He shook his head. "Because he never met a place or a person he wouldn't leave. Left the army without telling them, left about twenty jobs, left three wives before my mother and two more after her. He'd pop back in and out of my life until he stuck up the wrong jeweler in Philadelphia. Guy was armed to the teeth and Lefty wasn't a shooter anyway. Guy killed my dad." He shrugged. "Live by the sword, die by the sword, I guess."

"When did this happen?"

He looked up at the ceiling as he searched his memory. "While I was at Trinity."

"When you got kicked out?"

He acknowledged her scoop of that little fact with a head cock and a small smile. Stayed that way for a moment, staring across the table, and eventually nodded. "Day after I found out he was dead, yeah, I kicked the shit out of Professor Nigel Rawlins."

"With a plunger."

"It was on hand." He chuckled suddenly at the memory.

"What?"

"That," he said, "was a good day."

She shook her head at him. "You got thrown out of acting school for assault."

He nodded. "And battery."

"How's that a good day?"

"I acted on my instinct. I knew what he was doing to Caleb was wrong, and I knew what I had to do was right. Nigel kept his job, might still be teaching second-rate method-acting tips to students right now, for all I know. But I'd bet my share of the seventy million, he'll never treat another student like he treated Caleb or the victims

who came before Caleb. Because he's got it in the back of his head
that one of the other students in his class might go all Psycho Brian
Alden on him and face-fuck him with a plunger. What I did that day
was exactly what I needed to do."

"And me?" she said after a bit.

"What about you?"

"I don't act on my instincts. I don't engage the world."

"Sure you do. You just fell out of practice. But now you're back,
babe."

"Don't call me babe."

"Okay."

"You've been running this mining scam for, what, four years?"

He thought about it, did some math in his head. "About that,
yeah."

"But how long have you pretended to be Brian Delacroix?"

Something akin to shame found his face. "On and off for almost
twenty years."

"Why?"

He was quiet for a long time, turning the question over as if no
one had ever thought to ask him before. "Back in Providence, I was
at work one night at the pizza place when a coworker said, 'Your double's in the bar across the street.' So I went over and, sure enough,
there was Brian Delacroix with several guys like him, looked like
they came from money, and a bunch of hot girls. Long story short,
I hung around the bar long enough to figure out which coat was his
and I stole it. It was a beautiful coat—black cashmere with blood-
red lining. Every time I put it on, I felt . . ."—he searched for the
word—". . . substantial." His gaze was that of a little boy lost in a
shopping mall. "I couldn't wear the coat much, not in Providence,
too many chances I'd run across him, but once I got bounced from
Trinity, I went to New York, and I started wearing that coat everywhere. If I needed to talk myself into a job, I wore it, and the job was
mine. Saw a woman I liked, I put it on, and *abracadabra*, she ended

up in my bed. I realized pretty quick that it wasn't the coat per se. It was what I covered with it."

She narrowed her eyes at him.

"The coat," he explained, "hid my old man bailing on me and my drunk old lady, hid the Section 8 unit we lived in that always smelled a little bit of the dude who OD'd in it just before we moved in, hid all the shitty Christmases and the birthdays we never celebrated and the WIC checks and the power getting shut off and the drunk assholes who hung around my mother and how I'd probably just become one of those drunk assholes someday in the life of a woman just like my mother. I'd have the same nothing jobs and the same barroom stories and put some kids into the world I'd neglect until they grew up to hate me. But none of that was in my future when I put on that coat. I put that coat on and I wasn't Brian Alden, I was Brian Delacroix. And being Brian Delacroix on his worst day always trumped being Brian Alden on his best."

The confession seemed to exhaust him and embarrass him in equal measure. After looking at the wainscoting along the wall for a bit, he sighed and glanced over at the papers his sister had signed. He turned one of them upside down on the table. "The trick to forging a signature is to see it as a shape, not a signature. Try to duplicate the shape."

"But then it'll be upside down."

"Oh, right, I wouldn't have thought of that. We might as well quit then."

She elbowed him. "Shut up."

"Ooof." He rubbed his rib cage. "I'll teach you how to do it right side up, once you master upside down. Fair enough?"

"Fair enough." She put her pen to the page.

In the spare bedroom, she could hear him on the other side of the wall, first as he turned back and forth in the bed, and then as he began to snore. So she knew he was on his back then, which is when he snored, never when he was on his side. It also meant his mouth would be open. Typically, she'd nudge him—gently, it never took much—and he would turn on his side. She pictured herself doing so now but that would mean climbing in bed with him, and she didn't trust herself to do that and stay clothed.

On one hand, this was the definition of insanity—her life could end tomorrow or even tonight *because* of this man. No other reason. He'd unleashed demons from their basement cages who would not stop until she was dead or in prison. So to feel a sexual pull toward him was batshit.

But, looked upon another way, her life could end tomorrow or even tonight, and that knowledge opened up every pore and receptor she had. It transformed and sharpened everything she saw, smelled, felt. She could hear the ping of water moving through the pipes and smell metal in the river and hear rodents scuttle along the foundation. Her flesh felt as if it had been freshly slathered over her body this morning. She bet if she tried to guess the thread count of these sheets she'd come close, and her blood raced through her veins like a train moving across a desert at night. She closed her eyes and imagined waking as she had once, in the first months of their relationship, to find his head buried between her thighs and his tongue and lips moving softly, ever so softly, along her folds, which were already as wet as the bath she'd been taking in her dream. When she'd come that morning she kicked her left heel into his hip so hard she left a bruise. He grasped the fresh injury, still working the kinks out of his jaw, looking so silly but so sexy at the same time, and she was giggling and still trembling from the orgasm, still, in fact, receiving small electric aftershocks as she apologized. She didn't even wipe herself off his mouth before she kissed him, and once she started kissing him, she couldn't stop until she had to take a gulp of air, a big ravenous gasp of it. He'd refer to that kiss over the years, say it was the best he'd ever had, that she climbed so far into him with that kiss he could feel her swimming in the darkness of himself. And after she'd brought him to climax and they lay in the wreckage of the bed with stupid grins and sweaty brows, she wondered aloud if sex was its own mini life cycle.

"How so?" he asked.

"Well, it starts with a thought or a tingle but something small and then it grows."

He looked down at himself. "Or shrinks."

"Well, yeah, after. But for the sake of my argument, it grows and grows and builds in power and then there's the explosion and after that a kind of death or dying, a diminishing of expectation, and usually you close your eyes and lose consciousness."

She opened her eyes now in the strange bed and assumed the reason she was contemplating sex with a man she currently hated was because of her proximity to death. And even though her rage at him was as close to the surface as her top layer of skin, she had to tamp down the urge to slide out of this bed, pad barefoot around the corner into his room, and wake him the way he'd woken her that morning.

Then she realized it wasn't sex she wanted. Not at all. It wasn't even touch.

She walked down the hall and let herself into his room. His breathing changed as she closed the door softly behind her. She knew he'd woken and was trying to adjust his eyes to the darkness as she removed her T-shirt and underwear and left them at the door. She climbed onto the bed, but did so in the opposite direction, her back to the footboard, her feet up by his elbow.

"Can you see me?" she said.

"Mostly." He placed a hand on the top of her foot but otherwise didn't move.

"I need you to see me. That's all I want, nothing else right now."

"Okay."

She took a minute to compose herself. She didn't have a firm grasp on what she was doing here, only that it was mandatory in some way. Essential. "I told you about Widdy."

"The girl in Haiti, yeah."

"The one I got killed."

"You didn't—"

"I got her killed. I didn't kill her myself," Rachel said, "but she was right—if I'd let them take her four, even two hours, earlier, they wouldn't have been as crazed. They might have let her live."

"What kind of life, though?"

"That's what she said."

"What?"

"Never mind." She took a deep breath, felt the warmth of his hand as he stroked her foot. "Don't do that."

"What?"

"Caress me."

He stopped. But he kept his hand there as she'd hoped he might.

"I told you that she wanted to go to them and I talked her out of it but later they found her."

"Yeah," he said.

"And where was I during that?"

He opened his mouth to speak, but no words came out for a bit. "You never told me," he said eventually. "I always assumed you two got separated somehow."

"We were never separated. Not until the end anyway. I was right by her side when they found her."

"So . . . ?" He sat up slightly.

She cleared her throat. "The leader of the . . . pack, no other word for them, was Josué Dacelus. He's actually quite the crime kingpin there these days, or so I've heard, but back then he was just a young thug." She looked across the bed at her husband as the night rattled the window casings in the old house. "They found us just before sunup. They pulled Widdy from me. I fought, but they pushed me to the ground and spit on me. They stomped on my back and punched me in the head several times. And Widdy wasn't screaming, she was just crying, the way a girl that age would cry over a dead pet, you know? A hamster, say. I remember thinking that's what a girl *should be* crying over at eleven. And I tried to stop them again, but, man, it just infuriated them. I might have been a white woman with press credentials and that made raping and killing me a far riskier proposition than raping and killing Haitian girls and Haitian ex-nuns, but they were ready to throw that caution to the wind if I kept it up. I'm looking at Widdy as they're pulling her away. And Josué Dacelus slides the barrel of his filthy .45 into my mouth and he moves it back and forth and in and out over my tongue and my teeth like a cock and he says, 'Would you like to be good? Or would you like to live?'"

For a moment, she couldn't go on. She just sat there with the tears falling on her body.

"Jesus," Brian whispered. "You know you couldn't have—"

"He made me say it."

"What?"

She nodded. "He pulled the gun from my mouth and he made me look at her as the men dragged her off and he made me say the words." She wiped her cheeks and pushed the hair out of her face in the same motion. "I. Would. Like. To. Live." She lowered her head, let the hair fall back in her face. "And I said them out loud."

When she raised her head a minute or two later, Brian hadn't moved.

"I wanted to tell you that for some reason," she said. "Some reason I haven't figured out yet."

She slid her foot out of his hand and got off the bed. He watched her put her underwear and T-shirt back on. The last thing she heard as she left the room was his voice as he whispered, "Thank you."

33

THE BANK

The baby's crying woke her.

It was just after sunup. She went down the hall as the cries lessened and found Haya removing Annabelle's diaper on a changing table beside a crib. Brian or Caleb had even thought to hang a mobile above the crib and paint the walls pink. Haya wore a Green Day concert T-shirt Rachel recognized as Caleb's over a pair of plaid men's boxer shorts. Judging by the dishevelment of the bedsheets, Haya had tossed and turned through the night. She dropped the soiled diaper and wipes into a plastic bag at her feet and pulled a fresh diaper from a shelf below the table.

Rachel retrieved the bag. "I'll throw it away."

Haya gave no indication she'd heard her as she placed the fresh diaper on Annabelle.

Annabelle looked at her mother and then over at Rachel and kept looking at her with her warm dark eyes.

Haya said, "Do women in America keep . . . secrets from their husbands?"

"Some do," Rachel said. "Do women in Japan?"

"I do not know," she said with her usual stop-and-start cadence. And then, quite smoothly: "Probably because I've never been to Japan."

A wholly transformed Haya stared back at Rachel suddenly, a Haya marinated in cunning and curdled wisdom.

"You're not Japanese?"

"I'm from fucking San Pedro," Haya whispered, eyes on the doorway behind Rachel.

Rachel went to the door and closed it. "Then why are you . . . ?"

Haya exhaled so hard her lips flapped. "Caleb was a mark. I knew he was a con man the day I met him. So I was always stunned he never picked up on my bullshit."

"How did you meet? We all suspected like a mail-order bride thing."

She shook her head. "I was a hooker. He was my john. The woman who ran the escort service would always tell someone who'd never been with me that I'd only been in the country three weeks, I was very new at the business, etc." Haya shrugged. She lifted Annabelle off the changing table and gave the baby her left breast. "Drove the price up. So Caleb shows up and right away it doesn't make sense—he was too good looking to pay for it. Unless he was into violence or severe kink and he wasn't. Not even close. Straight missionary style, very tender. Second time he came around, he talked after about how I was the perfect girl for him—knew my place, knew my role, didn't speak the language." She smiled ruefully. "He said, 'Haya, you can't understand me, but I could fall in love with you.' I looked at his watch, his suit, and I said, 'Love?' Gave him a real searching, lost-child look, pointed between me and him, and said, 'I love.'" She stroked her baby's head and watched her suckle. "He bought it. Two months later he paid the owner of the service a hundred grand to steal me away. I've been watching and listening as him and Brian put this scam together ever since."

"Why are you telling me?"

"Because I want my end."

"I don't have anything to—"

"Is Caleb dead?"

"No," Rachel said with the emphasis of someone who was almost offended by the absurdity of the question.

"Well, I don't believe you," Haya said. "So, here's the thing—if you two run on me, I will drop a dime on you before you can ever get near an airport. And I won't just tell the cops. I'll reach out to Cotter-McCann. And they will find you and they will fist-fuck you in the ass until you die."

Rachel believed her. "Again, why tell me?"

"Because Brian would take his chances if he knew. He rolls dice. You, though, you're not that suicidal."

No? Rachel thought. *You shoulda seen me yesterday.*

"I'm telling you because you'll make sure he comes back for me." She indicated the baby. "For us."

Haya was back in character when she asked Brian if Caleb was alive or not as Brian went over the game plan for what to do if anyone came calling while they were out.

Brian lied to her as Rachel had. "No. He's fine." Then he asked Haya, "Which shade do you pull?"

"The orange," she said. "In . . ." She pointed.

"The pantry," Brian said.

"The pantry," she repeated.

"And when do you pull it down?"

"When you . . . text."

Brian nodded. He reached his hand across the kitchen table. "Haya? It's gonna be all right."

Haya stared back at him. She said nothing.

Cumberland Savings and Loan was, as advertised, a family-owned business with a history in Providence County, Rhode Island. The strip mall that abutted it had been, until the late 1980s, farmland. Most every bit of land in Johnston, Rhode Island, had once been farmland, and that's who the Thorp family had originally gone into the banking business to serve—the farmers. Now the strip malls were overtaking the farms, Panera had replaced the produce stands, and the farmers' sons had long since declined a seat on the tractor in favor of a cubicle in an industrial park and a split-level ranch with travertine countertops.

The Panera was doing a bang-up business, judging by the number of cars out front. The bank, on the other hand, had fewer cars when she pulled into its lot at nine-thirty in the morning. She counted eleven cars in the lot. Two were close to the front door in designated spots—a black Tesla in the "Bank President" spot, a white Toyota Avalon in the "Cumberland S&L Employee of the Month" spot. The Tesla gave her pause—when Brian had described Manfred Thorp she'd pictured a doughy suburban yokel in a butterscotch sport coat and a cornflower tie, maybe with man boobs and a double chin. But the Tesla didn't fit that image. She scratched her nose to obscure her lips from anyone who could be watching. "Manfred drives a Tesla?"

Brian, lying on the backseat under a painter's tarp, said, "So?"

"Just trying to picture him."

"Dark hair, young guy, works out."

"You said he was middle age." She scratched her nose again and spoke into her palm and felt ridiculous.

"I said almost middle age. He's, like, mid-thirties. What do you see in the lot? Pretend you're talking on your cell."

Ah. He had mentioned that.

She lifted her cell to her ear, spoke into it. "The two cars by the front door. Four other cars in the center of the lot. Five employee cars against the slope at the far end of the lot."

"How do you know they're employee cars?"

"They're all grouped together at the edge of the lot when there are plenty of closer spaces. That usually means the section is for employees."

"But Manfred's car is by the doors?"

"Yup. Beside the employee of the month's."

"Seven employee cars? That's too many for a bank this small. You see any heads in any of those cars?"

She looked. The knoll backed up to a great red maple that had probably been there when the first Puritans arrived. Its branches were long, its leaves abundant, and the five cars sitting underneath it could have been sitting under a bridge for all the sunlight that reached them. If there was a suspicious car among them, she would say it was the center car. The driver had backed into the spot. The other four cars were parked nose-in. The grille emblem told her it was a Chevy. By the length of it, she'd guess a four-door, but the interior was impossible to discern under the cover of that shade.

"Hard to tell," she said to Brian. "They're in the shade." She reached for the gearshift. "Should I drive over?"

"No, no. You're already parked. It'll look weird. You sure you can't see into the cars?"

"Pretty much. And if I stare too long and there is somebody in one of those cars, won't it look suspicious?"

"Good point."

She let out a long, steady breath. Her blood slithered through her veins; the tom-tom beat of her heart echoed in her ear canals. She felt like screaming.

"I guess there's nothing to do but gut it out at this point," he said.

"Great," she said into the phone. "Great, great, fucking great."

"There could also be someone inside the bank. Someone just sitting around leafing through brochures or something. They could have flashed a fake badge, told the bank they were staking it out because of blah-blah-blah. That's what I'd do anyway."

"Will the person inside be smart enough to spot a wig?"

"I don't know."

"Will they be smart enough to recognize me under a disguise?"

"I. Don't. Know."

"Is that all you got? A Hail Mary and I-don't-knows?"

"That's what most cons are made up of. Welcome to the club. Dues payable at the end of every month and don't park on the lawn."

"Fuck you." She got out of the car.

"Wait."

She reached back in for her bag. "What?"

"Love ya bunches," he said.

"You're an asshole." She slung her bag over her shoulder and shut the door.

As she walked toward the bank, she resisted the urge to look across the parking lot where the five cars sat under the shade of the maple. By the position of the sun, she guessed she might catch the light right just as she reached the door, but she couldn't conceive of a casual way to turn her head that far left. She caught her reflection in the front door—honey blond hair that fell to her shoulders and looked completely unnatural to her, though Brian assured her this was only because she wasn't used to it yet; bright blue, alien eyes; dark blue skirt, peach silk blouse, black flats, the uniform of a supervisor at a medium-size software development company, which is what Nicole Rosovich claimed paid her bills. Her bra matched the color of the blouse; they'd decided on a push-up bra with just a hint of cleavage, not so much to be obvious, but not so little Manfred Thorp would refrain from stealing a glance every now and then. If it helped keep him from looking too closely at the rest of her, she would have agreed to waltz in there naked.

Ten steps from the front door now and all she wanted to do was turn and run. The recent history of panic attacks had at least prepared her for a body awash in hysteria—the Saharan tongue, the spastic heart, the electrified blood, every sight too sharp, every sound too loud—but she'd never had to function normally with a panic attack. But now if she didn't fake calm at an Oscar-caliber level, she would die or be arrested. Wasn't really a Door Number Three that she could see.

She entered the bank.

The history of the bank was documented on a plaque just inside the front door and in a series of photographs within the bank itself. Most of the photographs were tinted sepia even though the bank had been established in 1948 as opposed to 1918. There it was as two men in ill-fitting suits and too short, too florid ties cut a ribbon. There it was surrounded by miles of farmland. There it was surrounded by tractors and other farm machinery on what looked to be some kind of holiday.

The door to Manfred Thorp's office was as old as the first photo. Its wood was thick and painted a reddish brown. The office's glass walls gave way to wooden or faux-wooden blinds that were closed. No way to tell if Manfred was even in there.

The bank had no customer service station. She had to stand in line behind an elderly woman who sighed a lot until the two tellers dispatched both their previous customers at roughly the same time. The male teller, dark skinny tie over a red plaid shirt, nodded to the elderly woman. The female teller said, "Help you, miss?"

She shot Rachel a vague smile as she approached and emitted the air of someone who was rarely present in a conversation but who'd learned her lines enough to imitate someone who was. She was about thirty, in a sleeveless top, the better to show off well-toned arms and a spray-on tan. She had straight brown hair that fell to her shoulders, a rock the size of a Prius on her left ring finger, and she might have been pretty if the skin weren't stretched so tight against her face it gave her the unfortunate look of someone who'd been struck by lightning during an orgasm. She flashed eyes as bright as they were dead and said, "What can we do for you today?"

Her name tag identified her as Ashley.

Rachel said, "I need access to my safe deposit box."

Ashley crinkled her nose at the counter. "Do you have ID?"

"Yes, yes." Rachel produced the Nicole Rosovich license and dropped it into the tray beneath the glass partition.

Ashley pushed it back out with two fingers. "I don't need it. You'll need it for Mr. Thorp, when he's available."

"And when will that be?"

Ashley gave her that nothing smile again. "I'm sorry?"

"When will Mr. Thorp be available?"

"You're not the first customer of the day, ma'am."

"I never claimed to be. I'm just wondering when Mr. Thorp will be available."

"Mmmm." Ashley gave her another smile, this one tight with waning patience. She crinkled her nose again. "Shortly."

Rachel said, "Is that ten minutes? Fifteen? How would you define it?"

"Please take a seat in the waiting area, ma'am. I'll let him know you're here." She dismissed her by looking past Rachel's shoulder and saying, "Help you, sir?"

Rachel's spot was overtaken by a guy with snow-white hair and a shy, apologetic gaze that he dropped as soon as she stepped away from the counter.

She sat in the waiting area with a twentysomething woman with a blue-black dye job, a few New Age neck and wrist tattoos, and sapphire eyes. She wore high-end biker boots and high-end wrecked jeans and a black tank top over a white one, both under a white cotton shirt that was perfectly pressed but two sizes too big. She leafed through a local real estate magazine. After a few glances, Rachel ascertained that she was quite pretty under the dye job and had the kind of posture one associated with supermodels and finishing-school grads.

Not the kind of person one would assume worked for Cotter-McCann and spent her days staking out a bank. In fact, she'd barely looked at Rachel, her eyes locked on the pages of the real estate magazine.

But it was a suburban real estate magazine, the homes on the cover of the small Cape, starter home variety, and this girl didn't give off that vibe at all. She was downtown loft space all the way. Then again, Rachel herself had leafed through plenty of literature that she'd normally never pick up in a variety of waiting rooms over the years; once, while waiting for her car to be serviced, she'd read an entire article on the best after-market chrome accents for your Harley, fascinated by the similarities between that article and one she'd read in a hair salon a few weeks prior on the best ways to accessorize your spring wardrobe.

Even so, the way this girl read the real estate magazine, her brow furrowed, her eyes studiously—conspicuously?—glued to the pages made Rachel wonder why she could be sitting there. The accounts manager, Jessie Schwartz-Stone, sat in a typical glass-enclosed office, tapping on her desktop keypad with the eraser of a pencil, and both tellers were currently unburdened of customers. The office of Vice-President Corey Mazzetti, also glass-enclosed, was empty.

She's waiting for the same guy you are, Rachel told herself. Maybe she has a safe deposit box as well. Not something you usually see in the possession of a twentysomething at a hick bank twenty miles from a medium-size city, but the box could have been passed down through generations.

Who passes a safe deposit box down through generations, Rachel?

She glanced at the girl again only to find her staring directly back at her. She shot Rachel a smile—of confirmation? of triumph?

of simple acknowledgment?—and went back to her ridiculous magazine.

The brown door opened and Manfred Thorp stood in the doorway in a light pinstripe shirt, red skinny tie, dark suit pants. As Brian had said, he looked quite fit. He had dark hair and dark eyes she didn't like—they seemed hooded, although that could be because his eye sockets were slightly large for his face. He looked at the two women in his waiting area and said, "Miss . . ." He looked down at a scrap of paper. "Miss Rosovich?"

Rachel stood and smoothed the back of her skirt, thinking, Okay, so who the fuck *is* she waiting for?

She shook Manfred Thorp's hand as he ushered her into the office. He shut the door behind her and she imagined the girl in the waiting room diving into her bag, grabbing her cell phone, and texting Ned or Lars: *She's in the bank.*

Ned and Lars, if they were watching the parking lot from one of the cars under the great sugar maple, would now search the parking lot. They'd find Brian easily enough—lying on the backseat of a car under a tarp was hardly foolproof. One of them would open the door, place the muzzle of that silencer to his forehead, and—*pop!*— lather the backseat with his brain matter. Then all that would be left to do would be to wait for her to exit the bank.

No, no, Rachel. They'd need Brian alive to get the money wired back into their account. So they wouldn't kill Brian.

But what did they need her for?

"Now how can I help you?"

Manfred was looking at her funny, waiting for her to speak.

"I need to access my safe deposit box."

He opened a drawer. "Of course. Can I see your driver's license, please?"

She opened her bag, fumbled inside for her wallet. She retrieved it. Opened it. Pulled out the fake license and handed it across the desk to him.

He didn't look at it. He was too busy staring at her. She hadn't been wrong about his eyes—they were, if not cruel, callous and entitled. He'd never formed an opinion about himself and his place in the world that wasn't flattering.

"Have we met?" he said.

"I'm pretty sure," she said. "My husband and I rented this box about six months ago."

He tapped a few keys, looked at his computer screen. "It was five months ago."

Like I said, she thought, about *six months ago, dick*.

"And you have all-access privileges." Another click on the keyboard. "So if all's in order, we can take you down there." He held her license up to the screen—comparing signatures, she assumed—and his eyes narrowed. He sat back in his chair, pushed the chair an inch or two back on its wheels. He flicked his eyes at her and then back at the screen and then down at the license in his hand.

Her throat closed.

Followed by her nasal passages.

No oxygen coming in, no oxygen going out.

The office was unreasonably hot, as if it sat on a thin ledge of shale over the mouth of an active volcano.

He dropped her license to the floor.

He leaned sideways in his chair and picked it back up, tapped it off his knee. He reached for the phone and she thought of pulling the gun from her bag, pointing it across the desk at him, and telling him to take her to the fucking safe deposit box right fucking now.

She couldn't imagine a world in which that scenario ended well.

"Nicole," he said, the phone in his hand.

She heard herself say, "Uh-huh?"

"Nicole Rosovich."

She realized she'd sucked her lower lip so deeply into her mouth it probably looked like she'd vacuumed up her chin in the process. She opened her mouth and looked across the desk at him, waiting.

He shrugged. "Cool name. It's got a good hard sound to it." He pressed a button on the phone. "You work out?"

She smiled. "Pilates."

"It shows." He said into the phone, "Bring the keys over to the office, Ash." He hung up. He handed her license back to her. "Should be just a minute."

The relief flooded her body like a broken fever until he reached into a drawer and said, "Just a quick signature."

He slid a signature card across the desk to her.

"You still use these things?" she said lightly.

"As long as the old man is still with us." He looked up at the ceiling. "And thank God he is, as I say every day."

"Well, he built all this."

"He didn't build it. My grandfather did. He just . . ." His voice trailed off. "Whatever." He unclipped a Montblanc from his shirt pocket and handed it across the desk to her. "If you'd do the honors."

Thankfully she hadn't returned her license to her wallet. It was on the desk by her elbow. She'd learned last night through two hours of practice that even when the signature was right side up—*particularly* when it was right side up—the only way to duplicate it was by seeing it as a shape. Last night, she'd also done best when she'd taken it all in with one quick glance and then plunged straight into duplicating it without pause. But that had been last night, at the kitchen table in Woonsocket, without any stakes.

I am enough.

She looked at the license, drank in the signature, and put the tip of the Montblanc to the signature card. She was halfway through the signature when the door flew open behind her.

She didn't look back. She finished writing.

Ashley came around to Manfred's side of the desk and handed him a key ring. She remained by his side and stared down at Rachel as if she knew her name wasn't Nicole, as if she could see the clips that held her wig in place.

Manfred went through the key ring until he found the one he liked. He noticed Ashley beside him.

"Are you on break?"

"Sorry, Manny?"

"Thank you for the keys, but we have a bank to run."

Ashley smiled at him in such a way that Rachel knew he'd pay for it later, and just like that Rachel knew they were fucking, which may or may not be news to the blank-faced wife in the pictures, but probably would be to the two hopeful, pudgy boys in the same photos. As Ashley left, Rachel decided Manny cheated on the wife because of her blankness, but he cheated on his sons because they were fat. And you don't even know it, do you, you son of a bitch? Because you have no integrity. So vows—the ones you made in a church or the ones you should have made to yourself—mean nothing.

He didn't even glance at the signature card before he came out from behind the desk. "Let's go then, shall we?"

When they exited the office, the girl had left the waiting area. Had she been waiting on a boyfriend or girlfriend, perhaps? They'd agreed to meet here because her lover had some banking to do before they could pop over to the Chili's across the road. She wasn't in the bank any longer, at least not the parts Rachel could see. So that was it—boyfriend or girlfriend came to meet her and they were now ordering the Tequila Lime Chicken across the road.

Or scenario number two: She'd ID'd Rachel, texted Ned, Lars, or men like them, and now she was driving home with plausible deniability in her pocket should the police ever question her about the woman in the blond wig who'd been assassinated in the parking lot around 10:15 that morning.

Manny stopped before an eight-foot-high vault door. He stepped in close to a keypad and punched some numbers onto it. He took one step to his left and pressed his thumb to another pad. The vault door clicked open. He pulled it back. Now they faced a gate. He unlocked that with one of the keys on his ring and then led her into the vault.

They stood there, surrounded by safe deposit boxes, and she realized she'd never asked Brian for the number.

And he'd never told her.

How do you spend hours teaching someone how to fake a signature, weeks, if not months, prepping for this worst-case scenario, make fake IDs, fake passports, pick the perfect bank . . . and still not tell your wife the actual fucking number of the actual safe deposit box?

Men.

". . . in case you want privacy."

Manny had been talking to her. She followed his gaze to a black door on her left.

"Did you use the privacy room last time you were here?"

"No," she heard herself say. "I didn't."

"Will you need it today?"

"Yes." There had to be six hundred boxes in here. For a small, former farming community? What were people putting in here—recipes for peach cobbler? Daddy's Timex?

"Well," Manny said.

"Well."

He led her to the middle wall. She reached into her bag for the key. Held it between her index and thumb, felt the numbers there. She dropped it into her palm—865—as Manny inserted his own key into the box marked 865. She placed her key in the other lock and they turned them together. He withdrew the box, rested it along his left forearm.

"You said you would be needing privacy?"

"Yes."

He indicated the door with a jut of his chin and she opened it. The room beyond was tiny, nothing in there but four steel walls, a table, two chairs, and thin white shafts of recessed lighting.

Manny placed the box on the table. He looked directly at her with their bodies only inches apart and she realized the asshole was actually hoping for a "moment," as if his charms were so universal and magnetic, women had no choice but to act like porn stars in his presence.

"I'll be out in a few minutes." She moved around to the other side of the table and slipped her bag off her shoulder.

"Of course, of course. See you out there."

She didn't even indicate she heard him and only looked back up again once he'd closed the door behind him.

She opened the box.

Inside, as promised, was the messenger bag she'd seen Brian enter the bank with four days ago. Had it only been that long? It felt like a thousand years in her rearview.

She wrenched the bag out of the tight space and held it by the handles as it unfurled. The cash was on top, as he'd said it would be, stacks of hundred- and, in one case, thousand-dollar bills, neatly rubber-banded together. She transferred them to her bag. All that was left were the six passports.

She reached in and pulled them out and a small bit of bile and vomit reached her mouth when she saw that there were only five of them.

No.

No, no, no, no.

She beseeched the recessed lighting and the cold steel walls: Please, no. Don't do this to me. Not now. Not after I've come this far. Please.

Hold it together, Rachel. Look at the passports before you lose all hope.

She opened the first one—Brian's face stared back at her. His latest alias was there as well: "Hewitt, Timothy."

She opened the next one—Caleb's. His alias had been "Branch, Seth."

Her hands shook when she reached for the third passport. Shook so bad she had to stop for a moment and clench them into fists and then press the fists together and breathe, breathe, breathe.

She opened the third passport, saw the name first—"Carmichael, Lindsay."

And then the photograph:

Nicole Alden.

She opened the fourth passport: "Branch, Kiyoko." Haya stared back at her. She opened the fifth and final one—the baby's.

She didn't scream or throw anything or kick over a chair. She sat on the floor and placed her hands over her eyes and stared into the darkness of herself.

I've watched my life away, she thought. *I've failed to act at every step of the way, and I've justified that by claiming I was here to bear witness. But in reality I was just choosing not to act.*

Until now.

And look what that's gotten me. I am alone. And then I die. All else is window dressing. Wrapping paper. Sales and marketing.

She found a pack of Kleenex at the bottom of her bag, past the stacks of money, and used a couple of tissues on her face. She found herself staring back in the bag, the money taking up the left side, and on the right, her keys, her wallet, the gun.

And as long as she stared at it, and it could have been ten minutes or one, she had no idea, she knew in the end she could never point a gun at him and pull the trigger a second time. She didn't have it in her.

She was going to let him go.

Without his passport—fuck him, that was staying here—and without his money, because she was walking off with that.

But she couldn't kill him.

And why?

Because, God help her, she loved him. Or at least the illusion of him. At least that. The illusion of how he'd made her feel. And not just during the false happiness of their marriage, but even in these last few days. She would rather have known the lie that was Brian than the truth of anything else in her life.

She dropped the pack of tissues back into her bag and pushed the stack of money in over it and that's when she saw the flash of dark blue vinyl. It slipped out between two stacks of bills like a card used to cut the deck.

She pulled it out of the bag. It was a United States passport.

She opened it.

Her own face stared back at her—one of the photos taken that rainy Saturday in the Galleria Mall three weeks ago. The face of a woman who was trying hard to look strong but hadn't gotten all the way there yet.

But she was trying.

She put all six passports into her bag with the money and left the room.

34

THE DANCE

Leaving the bank, she again looked for the woman with the neck tats and the perfect posture but, if she was in the building, she wasn't anywhere Rachel could see her. She turned right past the waiting area and saw Manny behind the teller's window, speaking to Ashley with his chin tilted toward her shoulder. They both looked up as she turned left at the door, Manny's mouth opening as if he were about to call after her, but she went through the front door and into the parking lot.

Now she had the perfect angle on the cars under the tree, and the sun was cooperating too. Of the four cars that remained, only one was clearly occupied. It was the Chevy that had backed into its spot, and a man sat behind the wheel. It was still too shady to see his features, but it was definitely a man's head—squared off at the top and at the jaw, ears the size of change purses. No way to tell if he was there to kill her or survey her or if he was simply a middle manager ducking out on his work, a john getting a blow job, or an out-of-town salesman who'd arrived early for an appointment to beat the traffic that clogged I-95 in Providence between eight and ten.

She looked straight ahead as she passed between the Employee of the Month's car and a van parked in the handicap spot. It too had backed in, the sliding door by her left shoulder now, and she imagined the sound it would make as it was pulled open and hands reached out and yanked her inside.

She passed the van and a long black SUV approached from her right. She watched with a strangely detached fascination as the driver's tinted window slid down and the driver thrust his arm through the opening even before the window had completed its journey down into the door slot. He wore a dark suit with a white shirt cuff peeking out at the wrist. She hadn't thought to reach into her bag for the gun or at least try to run back behind the van for cover before his arm reached full extension, a cigarette nestled between the index and middle fingers as he exhaled a grateful plume of smoke, his head pressed against the headrest. He shot her a lazy grin as he passed, as if to say, *It's all about the little pleasures, ain't it?*

After he rolled past, she put her hand in her bag, thumbed the safety off the P380, and kept her hand there as she reached the Range Rover. She opened the door with her left hand and climbed inside. Put the bag on the front passenger seat and the gun on the console beside her, finger still on the trigger, safety off. She said, "You still there?"

"Had a few birthdays while you were gone," he said mildly. "Fucking took you so long?"

"Really?" She removed her finger from the trigger, thumbed the safety back on, and put the gun in the space between her seat and the console. "That's my greeting?"

"Gosh, hon, you look beautiful. Is that a new something? You look like you dropped a few pounds too. Not that you ever needed to."

"Fuck you," she said, surprised to hear a chuckle trail the words.

He laughed. "My bad. How'd everything go? Should probably start the engine, by the way, and do the phone trick if we're going to keep talking."

She turned the car on. "Couldn't they assume I'm going hands-free on the cell?"

"You're not wearing a headset and you're driving a car from 1992."

She put the phone to her ear. "Touché."

"Was there a plant in the bank?"

She pulled out of the slot, turned toward the exit. "Hard to tell. There was a girl in the waiting area I'm still unsure about."

"How about the parking lot?"

"One guy in a car in the employee section. Couldn't tell if he was watching us or not."

She reached the road.

"Turn right," Brian said.

They drove up a mild incline and then passed a cluster of clapboard houses—most red, a few blue, the rest faded to the brown-gray of old baseballs. Once they passed the houses, they hit a straightaway between two pastures that unfurled for miles. The sky that rose before her was a blue she'd seen only in dreams and old Technicolor movies. A bank of white clouds formed in the southeast corner but cast no shadow on the fields. She could see why Brian had chosen this road—there were no crossroads for miles. What was left of Johnston's farming community, it appeared, was right here.

"Well," Brian said after about two miles.

"Well what?" She laughed for some reason.

"You see anyone in the rearview?"

She glanced up. The road behind her was a gunmetal ribbon with nothing on it. "No."

"How far back can you see?"

"I'd guess about two miles."

After another minute, he said, "Now?"

She looked again. "Nothing. Nobody."

"Rachel."

"Brian."

"Rachel," he said again.

"Brian . . ."

He sat up in the backseat and the smile that broke across his face was almost too big for the car.

"How do you feel about yourself today?" he asked. "Right now? Pretty fucking bad or pretty fucking good?"

She caught his eyes in the rearview and presumed hers were as adrenalized as his. "I feel . . ."

"Speak it."

"Pretty fucking good."

He clapped his hands together and whooped.

She stepped on the gas and punched the roof and let out a howl.

In another ten minutes, they reached another small strip mall. She'd clocked it on the way in; it contained a post office, a sub shop, a liquor store, a Marshalls, and a Laundromat.

"What're we doing here?" Brian peered at the low-slung buildings, all gray except for the Marshalls, which was white fading to eggshell.

"I need to run a quick errand."

"Now?"

She nodded.

"Rachel," he said, and failed to keep a whiff of condescension out of his voice, "we don't have time to—"

"Argue?" she said. "I agree. Be right back."

She left the key in the ignition and the bag she'd carried out of the bank at his feet. It took her ten minutes in Marshalls to change out of her Nicole Rosovich outfit and into a pair of jeans, cranberry V-neck tee, and black cashmere cardigan. She handed the tags to the cashier, transferred her previous outfit to a plastic store bag, paid up, and left.

Brian watched her exit and started to sit up, but then his face darkened as she gave him a quick four-finger wave and entered the post office.

She came back out five minutes later. Brian looked a lot paler when she got behind the wheel. Smaller, too, and a little sickly. Her bag still sat at his feet, but he'd clearly gone through it—a stack of bills peeked through the opening.

"You went through my bag," she said. "So much for trust."

"Trust?" It came out sharp and high like a hiccup. "My passport isn't in there. Neither is yours."

"No."

"So where are they?"

"I have mine," she assured him.

"That's wonderful."

"I think so."

"Rachel."

"Brian."

His voice was nearly a whisper. "Where's my fucking passport?"

She reached into the Marshalls bag and retrieved a shipping label, handed it to him.

He smoothed it on his thigh and stared at it for some time. "What's this?"

"It's a shipping label. Global Express. Guaranteed from the United States Postal Service. That's your tracking number right there in the upper right corner."

"I can see that," he said. "I can also see you addressed it to yourself as a guest of the Intercontinental Hotel in Amsterdam."

She nodded. "Is that a good hotel? Have you ever stayed there? It looked good on the website, so I went with it."

He looked at her like he was thinking about hitting something. Her, perhaps. Or himself. The dashboard possibly.

Probably her, though.

"What did you mail to the Intercontinental Hotel in Amsterdam, Rachel?"

"Your passport." She started the Range Rover and pulled out of the parking lot.

"What do you mean, my passport?" His voice was, if possible, even quieter. It was how he got in an argument just before he exploded.

"I mean," she said with the slowness one reserved for very young children, "I mailed your passport to Amsterdam. Which is where I plan to be by tomorrow night. You, on the other hand, will still be here in the States."

"You can't do this," he said.

She looked over at him. "I kinda already did."

"You can't do this!" he repeated, but this time he shouted it. And then he punched the ceiling.

She waited to see if he'd hit anything else. After a mile or so, she said, "Brian, you lied to me through our entire marriage and for the year leading up to it. Did you actually think I was going to overlook that? Say, 'Gosh, you big lug, ya, thanks for looking out for me?'" She turned left at a sign for 95, still ten miles away from the on-ramp.

"Turn the fucking car around," he said.

"To do what?"

"Get the passport back."

"You can't get mail back once you've handed it over. Something to do with interfering with a civil servant on his appointed rounds or something."

"Turn the car around."

"What're you going to do?" She was surprised to hear a chuckle trail the words. "Go back and stick up a post office? I'm going to guess they have cameras, Brian. You may get the passport, but by then you'll have Cotter-McCann, the local police, the state police, and—since this would surely be a federal crime—the FB fucking I on your ass. Is that really the option you most want to explore right now?"

He glowered at her from the other side of the Range Rover.

"You hate me right now," she said.

He continued to glower.

"Well," she said, "we always hate the things that wake us up."

He punched the ceiling again. "Fuck you."

"Aw, sweetness," she said, "would you like me to elucidate your remaining options?"

He popped the glove compartment with the side of his fist and pulled out a pack of cigarettes and a lighter. He lit the cigarette and cracked the window.

"You *smoke*?" she said.

"You mentioned options."

She held out her hand. "Give me one."

He handed her his and lit another one and they drove the empty road and smoked and she felt a hundred feet tall for a moment.

"You can kill me," she said.

"I'm not a killer," he said with a weary indignation that fell somewhere between charming and offensive.

"But if you do, you'll never get your passport. With all the heat on you, even if you could get someone to make you another one, they'd probably charge you a king's ransom and sell you out to Cotter-McCann anyway."

She looked in his eyes and saw that she'd scored a direct hit.

"You've got no one left to trust, do you?"

He flicked his ash out the crack in the window. "That's what you're offering? Trust?"

She shook her head. "That's what I'm demanding."

After a while, he asked, "And what's that look like?"

"It looks like you scurrying around for a few days like a rat with everyone chasing you while me, Haya, and AB wander the canals of Amsterdam."

"You like that image," he said.

"And at the appointed time and place, you retrieve the passport I'll have sent back stateside."

He sucked so hard on the cigarette the tobacco crackled as it burned. "You can't do this to me."

She flicked her own cigarette out the window. "But I already have, dear."

"I rescued you," he said.

"You *what*?"

"From a prison you built for yourself. I spent fucking *years* getting you ready for this. If that's not love, then what—"

"You want me to believe you love me?" She pulled to the side of the road and slammed the shift into park. "Then get me out of this country, give me access to the money, and *trust* I'll send you the passport." She stabbed the air between them with her finger, surprised at the swift appearance and infinite depth of her rage. "Because, Brian? There is no other fucking deal on the table."

He dropped his gaze and looked out at the gray road and blue sky and the fields yellow with the promise of summer.

Now, she thought, comes the moment when he threatens you.

"Okay," he said.

"Okay, what?"

"I'll give you what you want."

"And what's that?"

"Apparently," he said, "everything."

"No," she said, "just faith."

He gave his own reflection a rueful smile. "Like I said . . ."

Brian texted Haya from the interstate. For the second time in twenty-four hours, he didn't like her response.

As agreed upon, he wrote,

How's everything?

If everything was all right, she was supposed to write back,

Perfect.

If anything had gone wrong, she was supposed to respond,

Everything's fine.

After fifteen minutes, she sent a text back:

All OK.

In Woonsocket, he directed her up the main hill and then south several blocks. They turned onto a dusty scar of a street that dead-ended at a mound of landfill, crumbled Sheetrock, and bent rebar. From there they had a perfect view of the river and the mill and the night watchman's house. He pulled a pair of binoculars from the glove box and adjusted the focus as he looked down at the house.

"The pantry shade is still up," he said.

The sparrow flapped twice in her chest.

He handed the binoculars to her and she saw for herself. "Maybe she forgot."

"Maybe," he said.

"But you were pretty clear with your instructions."

"But I was pretty clear with my instructions," he agreed.

They sat and watched the house for a while, passing the binoculars back and forth, looking for movement of any kind. Once Rachel thought she saw the shade of the far left window on the second floor move, but she couldn't swear to it.

Still, they knew.

They knew.

Her stomach eddied and for a moment the Earth's atmosphere felt too thin.

After a little more watching, Brian took the wheel and they drove back down through the neighborhood and he drove a bit beyond where he had last night and approached the mill from a few blocks farther north. They entered the grounds from an old trucking route that ran parallel to the railroad tracks, and in daylight the skeleton of the mill was both more pathetic and more resplendent, like the sun-bleached bones of a slaughtered god king and his once-majestic retinue.

They found the pickup truck parked a few yards into the shell of the building closest to the river. There was no northern wall left and most of the second floor was gone. The truck was a beast of a machine, a black full-size Sierra, all hard form and function, its wheels and sides splattered with dried mud.

Brian put his hand on the hood. "It's not hot but it's a little warm. They haven't been here too long."

"How many?"

He looked in the cab. "Hard to tell. Seats five. But I doubt they'd bring five."

"Why?"

He shrugged. "Manpower's expensive."

"So's losing seventy million," she said.

He looked around the mill for a bit and she knew him well enough to know this was how he processed, his eyes clocking his surroundings without actually seeing them.

"You want to confront them?" she said.

"I don't *want* to." He widened his eyes. "But I don't see a choice."

"We could skip returning to the house and just run from here."

He nodded. "You're willing to leave Haya and the baby behind?"

"We could call the police. Haya doesn't know anything. She can easily claim ignorance."

"If the police show up, what's to stop the guys inside from shooting Haya and the baby? Or shooting the cops? Or entering into a standoff with hostages?"

"Nothing," she admitted.

"So do you still want to hit the road? Leave them behind?"

"Do you?"

"Asked you first." He shot her the tiniest of smiles. "What's it that asshole said to you in Haiti?"

"'Would you like to be good? Or would you like to live?'"

Brian nodded.

"Can you get us out of here?" she asked.

"I can get you out of here. Can't get *myself* out of here the way you've fixed it, but I can get you out, honey bunch."

She ignored the dig. "Right this second?"

He nodded. "Right this second."

"What're our chances?"

"*Our* chances?"

"My chances," she said.

"About fifty-fifty. Every hour, they drop five percent in Cotter-McCann's favor. We add a terrified woman and a baby—that's if we can extricate them from guys who know how to use firearms a lot better than we do—your odds of success drop even further."

"So right now the odds are about even. But if we go up to that house"—she pointed at the other end of the mill—"it's more likely we die."

His eyes widened a little more and he nodded repeatedly. "Way more likely, yeah."

"And if I say I want to run, you'll just take me out of here now?"

"I didn't say that. I said it was an option."

She looked up through the blackened rafters and the shredded roof at the blue sky. "There's no option."

He waited.

"All four of us go." She took several quick breaths and it made her light-headed. "Or none of us do."

"Okay," he whispered and she could see he was as terrified as she was. "Okay."

She dropped the hammer. "Haya speaks perfect English."

He squinted at her.

"She grew up in California. She was gaming Caleb."

He let loose a high chuckle of disbelief. "Why?"

"So he'd rescue her from a shitty life, it sounds like."

Brian shook his head so many times he resembled a dog after a bath. Then he smiled. The old Brian smile—surprised to be surprised by the turns of the world and somehow tickled at the same time.

"Well, shit," he said, "I finally like her." He nodded once. "She told you?"

Rachel nodded.

"Why?"

"So we'd know not to abandon her."

"I'm not above leaving her behind," he said simply. "Never was. But I wouldn't leave Caleb's kid up there to die. Not even for seventy million."

He lifted the cover over the tire jack compartment in the Rover and came back with a short ugly shotgun with a pistol grip.

"How many guns do you need?" she asked.

He looked off in the direction of the house as he loaded shells into the gun. "You've seen me shoot—I suck. A shotgun levels the playing field a bit." He shut the hatchback.

Whatever he'd just claimed about being unable to leave Caleb's daughter behind, it didn't alter the fact that he could kill her right

now with that ugly weapon. It wouldn't be the rational choice necessarily, but at this point rational choice was a luxury in the rearview mirror.

It didn't seem to be the first thing on his mind, though, so she
opened the driver's door of the truck. The floor mat was caked with
dried mud. She craned her head over the seat and saw the floor mat
on the passenger seat was crusted with the same. Wherever they'd
been searching for her or Brian lately, they'd walked through some
dirt to do it. She opened the rear driver's-side door—the mats back
there were pristine. She could still smell the showroom in the rubber.

She showed it to Brian. "There are only two of them."

"Unless the other car's parked somewhere else."

She hadn't considered that. "I thought you were Mr. Positive
Thinking."

"We'll call this an off fucking day then."

"I mean—" She started but couldn't finish the thought. Her hand
dropped back to her side. She felt closer to vomiting than she had in
a while. She mentioned this to Brian.

"Where's a Scientologist when you need one, uh?" He pointed
the shotgun down the end of the building, past mounds of dirt and
trash and all the pieces of wall that had been torn out when the scav-
engers came for the copper wire. "Right at the end there's a set of
stairs. You go down them and you find a really small tunnel."

"A tunnel?"

He nodded. "Caleb and me dug it over the last couple months.
When you thought I was out of the country."

"Lovely."

"Figured if we were ever in that house and we had time to see
the opposition coming for us, we'd scoot out, get over here, and
make a run for it pretty much from where we're standing now. You
can go down—"

"*I* can?"

"We can, yeah. We'll crawl over there and—"

"How tight is this tunnel?"

"Oh, it's bad," he said. "It's more like a trough. If I ate a pizza right now, I'd probably get stuck in there."

"I'm not doing that," she said.

"You'd rather die?" He waved the shotgun like it was an extension of his arm.

"I'd rather die above ground than below it, yes."

"You got a better idea?" It came out sharply.

"I haven't even heard yours. All I've heard is the word 'tunnel.' And point that fucking thing at the ground, would you?"

He considered the shotgun. He shrugged an apology and pointed it at the ground.

"My plan," he said calmly, "is that we take the tunnel under the house. We come up in the back bedroom on the first floor. We come out into the house, while they're peeking out the windows for us."

"And what's to stop them from shooting us then?"

"We'll have the drop on them?"

"The drop?" she said.

"Yes."

"They're professionals. A good man with a gun can't defeat a bad man with a gun if the bad man is at ease in violent confrontation and the good man is not."

"Fine," he said, "your turn."

"What?"

"Your turn," he repeated. "Give me a better idea."

She took a minute. It was hard to think over the terror. Hard for any word to find space in her brain besides *Run*.

She told him her idea.

When she finished, he chewed his lower lip and then the inside of his mouth and then his upper lip. "It's good."

"You think?"

He stared at her, as if judging how honest he could afford to be. "No," he eventually admitted, "it's not. But it's better than mine."

She stepped up close to him. "There's one big problem with it."

"Which is?"

"If you don't do your part, I'm dead within a minute."

He said, "Maybe even less."

She took a step back and flipped him the bird. "So how do I know you'll hold up your end?"

He pulled the pack of cigarettes from his jacket pocket and offered her one. She waved it off. He put one between his lips, lit it, and returned the pack to his pocket.

"Be seeing you, Rachel." He gave her a small shrug and walked off through the mill toward the night watchman's house and never looked back.

35

FAMILY PHOTO

She drove the Range Rover along the train tracks that ran between the mills and the river. She left the tracks just past the last redbrick building and bounced over cinder block and boulders, and hoped that none of the things scraping the underside of the vehicle was strong enough or angled in such a way that it could puncture the gas tank. She bounced along until she found the little road Brian had described and then she was clinging to the backside of the hill that led up to the night watchman's house.

Near the top, she stood on the gas and lurched up and over the ridge, the Rover tilting hard to the left, so hard she feared she'd tip over, so she went against her natural instincts and pressed down even harder on the gas, and the vehicle slammed back down on all four wheels and shot up into the clearing behind the house.

Both Ned and Lars came out on the back porch. They were armed. Ned cocked his head at her in surprise but also triumph, a look in his small eyes that she'd seen plenty of times in her life, a look that never failed to make her feel tiny and yet outraged at the same time:

Stupid girl.

She put the Rover in park and stepped out of it, keeping it between her and the porch.

"Don't run," Ned said. "We'll just have to chase you. And the story will end the same way but with us just a bit more fucking perturbed."

Ned had the Glock he'd killed Caleb with in his hand, the silencer already attached. The soundtrack of her death, she feared, would be a soft *pffft*. Then again, Lars cradled a large hunting rifle, the kind she imagined could take down a bear, so maybe her death would come with a bang.

They both walked off the porch at the same time.

She pointed her pistol across the hood at them and said, "Stay there."

Ned held up his hands, looked over at Lars. "I think she's got us."

Was Brian somewhere safe, watching the scene play out with a smile on his face?

Lars kept walking toward the Rover. But he did so on a diagonal line. And so did Ned. But in the opposite direction. So that each step they took brought them closer to her yet farther from each other.

"Fucking *stop*."

Lars sauntered a few more steps before he did.

It was quite possible Brian kept a backup passport. He could just let her die and go spend all the money.

"What's this?" Ned said. "Red Light, Green Light?"

He took two steps toward her.

Brian, she wanted to scream. *Brian!*

She extended her arm across the hood. "I said stop."

"You didn't say red light." He took another step.

"Stop!" Her voice bounced off the house and echoed down the hill.

Ned's voice stayed level and smooth. "Rachel, you've seen some movies, I'm sure, where little girls with guns hold off big bad guys with guns. But, honey, it doesn't work that way in real life. You let us come off that porch. And then you let us get meaningful separation from each other. Which means that now, in this real life of ours, you can't shoot both of us before one of us shoots you. Instead, I'll shoot you or he will and it's not gonna be real hard to pull off."

Brian, Jesus. Where the fuck are you? Did you abandon me?

Her hand shook enough that she placed her elbow to the hood of the Rover to steady it. She pointed the gun at Ned, but that left her unable to cover Lars.

Ned cocked an eyebrow at her elbow vibrating off the hood. "See what I'm talking about?"

Oh shit. Shit. Shit. Did you forsake me?

Out of the corner of her eye, she saw Lars take two more steps.

"Please," she said. "Just don't move."

Ned smiled at that. Checkmate.

From upstairs, the baby cried.

Lars looked up at the sound. Ned kept his eyes on Rachel.

And Brian stepped out on the porch, leveled the shotgun, and pulled the trigger.

The blast entered Lars's back. It exited his front while the rifle was still in his arms. Pieces of buckshot and pieces of Lars hit the passenger side of the Rover and the rifle left his arms and landed on the hood. Lars went to his knees, and she shot Ned.

She couldn't actually remember squeezing the trigger but she must have because he shouted as if he were shouting at a ref making a bad call at a sporting event, a dismayed and disgusted "Ahhhhhhhh," and then he toppled back against the porch steps and she could see the gun was no longer in his hand.

She came around the Rover, kept the gun pointed at him. He watched her come, watched Brian come too, pointing that shotgun at him. Brian's arm shook—hers, to her surprise, did not anymore—but it didn't much matter when you were talking about a shotgun.

Lars made a soft thud when his face planted in the dirt.

She picked up Ned's gun. She held on to it and put her own in the waistband of her jeans. Then they were both standing in front of him, wondering what they were going to do.

The hole she'd put in Ned was in his shoulder. His left arm drooped, as if there were nothing to hold it up anymore, so she presumed her bullet had shattered his collarbone.

He looked at her, breathing shallowly through his mouth. He looked forlorn and lost, a salesman at the end of a bad week. The blood spread down his off-white shirt and soaked the left side of his jacket, one of those plaid, fleece-lined shirt-jackets a lot of construction workers wear.

"Where's your cell phone?" Brian said.

Ned grimaced as he reached into the right pocket of his corduroy pants. He handed Brian a flip phone.

Brian opened it, scrolled through the call log and then the texts.

"When did you arrive?" he asked.

"'Bout nine," Ned said.

Brian opened one of his texts. "You told someone 'We got C.' What's that mean?"

"Perloff's wife was Objective C. You're Objective A." He gave Rachel a weary flick of the head. "She's B."

The baby wailed again, muffled by glass and distance.

"Where's Haya?" Rachel said.

"Tied up upstairs," Ned said. "Same room as the baby. Baby's in the crib, and she's not climbing-out age yet. They're not going anywhere."

Brian rechecked the call log and then the texts again. He pocketed the phone. "No texts or calls since nine-thirty. Why?"

"Nothing to report. We were waiting on you, Brian. Didn't think you'd show."

"What's your name?" Rachel asked.

"What difference does it make?" Ned said.

Rachel couldn't argue the point one way or the other.

Brian said, "How'd you find this place?"

Ned blinked a few times, hissed at the pain as he adjusted his position on the steps. "Dummy corp's docs on your partner's laptop. Same company that rented the mining probes out of Jakarta two years ago bought this place."

"Where else are you looking?"

"Sorry," Ned said. "Even if I could help you—and I'd probably serve up everything I know for a bottle of water right now—I'm only looped in on what applies to my project and my department, no one else's."

Rachel retrieved a bottle of water from the Rover, went to hand it to Ned, but he was struggling one-handed with his wallet, thumbing out a photograph. He dropped the wallet to the porch. Now, if she really wanted to know, she could pick it up and look at his license to learn his name. She left it there.

He handed her the photograph as he took the bottle of water.

It was of a blond girl, maybe eleven or twelve, with a wide chin, big eyes, and an uncertain smile, her arm slung around a brown-haired boy, a couple years younger, with Ned's small lips and wide nose, the boy's smile bigger and more confident than his sister's.

"Those are my kids."

Brian looked over. "Put that fucking thing away."

Ned held Rachel's eyes, went on like Brian hadn't spoken. "Caylee, that's my girl, she's real smart, you know? She's founded the Big Buddies program in her school. That's where—"

"Stop," Rachel said.

"—where the older kids, like her, they mentor the first and second graders, you know, buddy up with them so they're not scared. It was Caylee's idea. She's got a huge heart."

"Stop," Rachel said again.

Ned gulped some water. "And, uh, Jacob, that's my boy, he—"

Brian pointed the shotgun at Ned. "Shut the *fuck* up!"

"Okay!" Ned spilled a bunch of water on his lap. He'd thought Brian was going to pull the trigger. "Okay, okay."

She watched him tremble as he drank more water and she tried willing her heart to calcify and shrivel but she failed.

Ned drank a bit more water and licked his lips several times. "Thank you, Rachel."

Suddenly she didn't want to meet his eyes.

"My name," he said to her, "is—"

"Don't you do it," she whispered. "Don't."

Now she met his eyes and he met hers and he looked at her a long time, long enough for her to see both the little boy and the terrible man inside him. Then he flicked his eyelids in acquiescence.

Brian walked to the edge of the hill, cocked his arm, and threw Ned's cell phone in a high arc that ended when it splashed into the river. He spoke with his back to them. "What're we going to do with you, man?"

"I've been thinking about that."

Brian turned. "I bet you have."

"You're not killers."

Brian tilted his head toward Lars. "Your road dog there might debate that point."

"He had a gun on your wife. He was an immediate threat. You did what you had to do. That's different than executing someone. So, so different."

"What would you do if you were us?" Rachel asked.

"Oh, you'd already be dead," Ned said. "But I forked over my soul a long time ago, Rachel. You still have yours." Ned adjusted himself on the stairs again. "Whether you kill me or you tie me up, it'll add up to the same thing. The company's going to send a second team, if they haven't already. They don't give a shit about me. I'm just a fucking coolie. If they find me alive or they find me dead, the story is still the same—they continue to hunt you. They might get me to a doctor or not, but they will continue pursuit of you. My point is, you leave me alive, the end result is the same as it would be if you kill me. Except if you kill me in cold blood, you've got to look in the mirror every night."

Brian and Rachel considered that, considered each other.

Ned stood slowly, using the column to the right of the broken railing to do so.

"Hey," Brian said.

"If I'm going to die, I'd rather be standing."

Brian looked wildly at Rachel and she looked wildly back. Ned was right—shooting him and Lars had been easy when there'd been no time to think about it. But now . . .

Upstairs the baby howled. It was shriller this time, more frenzied.

Brian said, "That doesn't sound right. You want to check on her?"

Rachel didn't know shit about checking on a baby. She'd never even babysat. And the thought of being up there, trapped, if something went wrong down here was more terrifying than standing guard.

"I'll stay with him."

Brian nodded. "He moves, you fucking shoot him."

Easy for you to say.

"You bet," she said.

Brian went up the steps and put the shotgun barrel under Ned's chin. "Don't fuck with her."

Ned said nothing, just kept his eyes on something in the general vicinity of the blown-out mills.

Brian entered the house.

The moment he was gone she felt half as strong and twice as weak.

Ned wavered in place against the post. He dropped the water bottle and looked about to keel over but kept his balance by slapping his wrist into it at the last second.

"You're losing too much blood," Rachel said.

"I'm losing too much blood," Ned agreed. "Could I ask you for the water?"

She went to pick up the water but stopped. She caught him watching her, and for the briefest of seconds, he looked far less helpless. He looked hungry and ready to pounce.

"The water," he said.

"Get it yourself."

He let out a groan and reached for the bottle, his fingers pawing at the wood riser just above it.

A window opened above them, and several things happened in the same two- or three-second span:

Brian called, "They killed Haya!"

Ned surged off the porch and rammed the top of his head into her chest.

Ned reached for her gun.

Rachel jerked her gun hand free.

Ned drove his good shoulder into Rachel's chin.

Brian called, "Shoot him!"

Rachel pulled the trigger and fell to the ground.

Ned came off her body and she heard him grunt and she fired the pistol again. The first time she fired at nothing—it was purely defense. The next shot, as she rolled, she aimed in the direction of Ned's legs as they scrabbled away from her. She fired the final shot as she came to her knees, fired in the direction of his ass as he reached the top of the incline.

He dove over the hill and she may or may not have heard him make a sound when she'd fired that third shot, a yelp possibly. Or she'd imagined it.

She got to her feet and ran to the edge of the hill and she saw him down at the bottom on his knees. She jumped into the brush and the high grass and the weeds and the bottles and old burger wrappers and came down the hill with the gun held high by her right ear.

Ned was on his feet now, staggering toward the first brick building. By the time she reached the bottom of the hill he was holding a hand to his belly and lurching as he walked and he made it to an old office chair with rusted legs and a rusted metal frame. Someone had slashed a horizontal line across the seat and the foam that spilled out was brown. Ned sat in it and watched her come.

Her phone vibrated. She put it to her ear.

"You okay?" Brian asked.

"Yeah."

She looked back up the hill at him standing on the back porch, the baby to his shoulder, the shotgun in his other hand.

"You need me?"

"No," she said. "I got this."

"They shot her in the head." Brian's voice was thick. "In the room with the baby."

"Okay," she said. "It'll be okay, Brian. I'll be right back."

"Hurry," he said.

"Why'd you have to kill her?" she asked Ned when she reached him.

He pressed a hand to the exit wound. One of her bullets—she had no idea which one—had entered his body somewhere in the back and come out by his right hip.

"Performance bonus," he said.

What came out of her mouth sounded like a laugh. "What did you say?"

He nodded. "Our hourly rate is for shit. We're incentive-based." His head lolled as he looked around at the husk of the mill. "My old man worked in a place like this up in Lowell."

"Cotter-McCann could turn this into an apartment complex or a mall," she said. "A casino, for Christ's sake. Make their seventy million back in a year."

He gave that a weary raise of the eyebrows. "Land is probably poisoned."

"What do they care?" She was hoping if she kept talking he would just fucking bleed out in front of her. "By the time people start getting sick they'll have pulled their money back out and be long gone."

He gave that some thought and half nodded, half shrugged.

"She didn't know anything. She barely spoke English."

"Police have translators," he said. "And she spoke English just fine in her last few minutes. Believe it." He was turning gray, but the hand he pressed to the wound still looked firm and strong. He gave her puppy-dog eyes full of apology. "I don't make the rules, Rachel. I don't control anything. I just do a job to put food on my family's table and I sit up some nights just like every other parent hoping my kids' lives will be better than mine was. That they'll have more options than I did."

She followed his gaze around the mill. "You think they will?"

"No." He shook his head. He looked down at the blood soaking into his lap and his voice cracked. "I think those days are over."

"Funny," Rachel said. "I'm starting to wonder if they ever existed at all."

Ned heard something in her voice that made him look up. The last thing he said was "Hold on."

She aimed at his chest from three feet away, but her arm was shaking so badly when she pulled the trigger that the bullet entered his neck. He went rigid against the back of the chair for a moment and panted like a parched dog and blinked at the sky. His lips moved but no sound came out; the blood pooled in the hollow of his throat and dripped into the crevices between the chair frame and the cushions.

He stopped blinking. His lips stopped moving.

Rachel walked back up the hill.

Brian stood with Annabelle to his shoulder. Her eyes were closed, her lips slightly parted. She was sleeping.

"You want to have kids?" she asked him.

"What?"

"Simple question."

"Yes," Brian said to her, "I want to have kids."

"Beyond this one?" she said. "Because I think she's ours now, Brian."

"Ours?"

"Yes."

"I don't have a passport."

"No, you don't. But you have our kid. Do you want another?"

"If I live?"

"If you live," she conceded.

"Yes," he said.

"Do you want to have kids with me?" Rachel asked.

"Well, who else?" Brian said.

"Say the words."

"I want to have kids with you," Brian said. "No one else."

"Why no one else?"

"Because I don't love anyone else, Rachel. Never have."

"Oh."

"I want a few actually." Brian nodded. "Kids."

"A few?"

"A few."

"You going to birth them?"

"Already playing the violin for herself," he said to the child on his shoulder. "Get a load of her."

She looked at the house. "I'm going to say good-bye to Haya."

"You don't have to go in there."

"Yes, I do. I have to pay my respects."

"They blew her head off, Rachel."

She winced. Haya had pursued a desire to be anyone but what the world had fated her to be with such fierce resolve that Rachel, having only met the "real" Haya a few hours before, didn't want to see her with half her face turned to pulp, lying in a gout of black blood. But if she didn't look, then Haya was just another of the disappeared in Rachel's rearview. Soon it would grow too easy to pretend she'd never been real.

If it's ever within your power to do so, she considered saying aloud to Brian (but didn't), you have to bear witness to your dead. You simply have to. You have to step into the energy field of whatever remains of their spirit, their soul, their essence and let it pass through your body. And in the passing, maybe a wisp of it adheres to you, grafts itself to your cells. And in this communion, the dead continue to live. Or strive to.

Instead, what she said to Brian was "Just because it's unpleasant doesn't mean I get to avoid it."

He didn't like it but all he said was "And then we gotta go."

"How?"

He gestured toward the river. "I got a boat down there."

"A boat?"

"Big boat. Get us to Halifax. You two will be out of the country in two days."

"What'll you do?"

"Hide in plain sight." He placed his palm to the crown of the baby's head and kissed the top of her ear. "You might have noticed I've got a knack for it."

She nodded. "Maybe too much of one."

He gave that a sad tilt of his head and said nothing.

"If we don't make good time on the water?" she asked. "Or if one of us gets injured, breaks an ankle or something?"

"There's a backup plan for that."

"How many backup plans do you have?"

He thought about it. "Quite a few."

"What about me?"

"Hmm?"

"You got a backup plan for me?"

He stood across from her with the baby asleep on his shoulder and he let the shotgun fall to the ground and he touched a strand of her hair with his thumb and index finger. "There's no backup plan for you."

Eventually she looked at the house behind him. "I'm gonna go pay my respects."

"I'll be waiting."

She left him and walked into the house. With all but one shade drawn, it was cool and dark in there. She paused at the base of the stairs. She pictured Haya's corpse and her resolve wavered. She almost turned back. But then she pictured the Haya she'd seen in the bedroom this morning, the true person staring back at her for the first time through eyes as rich and black as the first night or the last. She marveled at her will—the resolve, the *balls* it took to become someone else so completely that the battle for dominance between the captive self and the captor self couldn't become anything but unwinnable. Each would surely subsume the other in a forever war. And, no matter how it ended up, neither could ever return home.

So it had been with Brian Alden, she realized, since the moment he'd donned the purloined coat of Brian Delacroix. And so it had been with Elizabeth Childs and Jeremy James and even Lee Grayson. At times in their lives they'd been one version and then they'd been other versions and some of those versions had brushed up against Rachel and altered Rachel's life or even given life to her. But then they'd gone on to be still other versions. And other people beyond that. Then Elizabeth and Lee had gone even further, into the place where Haya now found herself. Transformed yet again.

And what of Rachel herself? What was she, if not forever in transit? Forever en route. As adaptable as any of them to a journey, but never to an end.

She climbed the stairs. As she did, she could feel his passport tucked behind her own in the front pocket of her jeans. And she felt the dark deepen around her.

I don't know how this ends, she told the dark. *I don't know my true place in it.*

Yet the only response she got from the dark was a deepening of it as she climbed the stairs.

But there might be some light upstairs and there would certainly be light when she went back outside.

And if by some twist of fate there wasn't, if all that remained of the world was night and no way to climb out of it?

Then she'd make a friend of the night.

ACKNOWLEDGMENTS

Thanks to . . .

Dan Halpern and Zachary Wagman for the edits and the patience.

Ann Rittenberg and Amy Schiffman for the added guidance (and the patience).

My early readers—Alix Douglas, Michael Koryta, Angie Lehane, Gerry Lehane, and David Robichaud—who filled in all the blanks when it came to the broadcast news biz.

A special shout-out to Mackenzie Marotta for keeping the balls in the air and the trains running on time.